THE TRIAL OF
ROOKER FLYNN

LOCKE INSTITUTE TRILOGY

BOOK 2

A. R. WITHAM

Nepenthe House

ISBN 979-8-9874072-5-7

Book Cover Design by Alejandro Colucci

Map by Erin Shales from sketch by Sara Ferrari

Minor Illustrations by A. R. Witham

Published by Nepenthe House

arwitham.com

For Brian Snyder,
Who Laughs.

TABLE OF CONTENTS

Fargil's Map
(Annotated by Jack Swift)

Lake

Clearing

Butte

Buzzard

Vulture

Swamp

Paradise Road

Hyena

Jackal

Once Upon a Time...

....there were two friends.

Rooker Flynn & Jack Swift planned to escape the Locke Institute together, but Headmistress Gerba Whipmarples made Rooker an offer he couldn't refuse. If the pirate could trick his friend into summoning the remaining pieces of his majik staff Nepenthe, she would return Rooker to his beloved ship, the *Venture Brigand*.

Bound together, Rooker & Jack attempted to escape with the help of a group of outlaws: Patch Picaroon, Boss West, Ransom Adare, and Barney Bialik. However, the tunnels they'd hoped to use were crawling with shiq spiders. Their dwarf digger, Barney Bialik, was eaten in the dark. The rest of the escapees were captured and forced to play human targets as sport for the rich.

Chained to a gravely injured Jack, Rooker managed to escape. With nowhere to run, they were trapped on a lone cliff at sunset, surrounded by spiders. Jack fell, suspended only by the link that bound the two men together.

Gerba Whipmarples offered Rooker the means to sever his bond with Jack.

Rooker Flynn cut the cord.

The Locke Institute
Known Criminals

Jackal

~~Boss Mamba~~
Rooker Flynn
~~Jack Swift~~
Patch Picaroon
Copper Dave
Billy Pilgrim

Hyena

~~Boss West~~
Ransom Adare

Vulture

Boss Eightfingers
~~Barney Bialik~~
Yenrab Bialik

Buzzard

Boss Hook
~~Fancy Nan~~

BATTLE OF THE
BARREL
STRAIT

*Love is but the discovery of ourselves in others,
and the delight in the recognition.*

Alexander Smith

N O SONGS WERE EVER sung of the Battle of the Barrel Strait. Only one survivor lived to tell the tale, and he never spoke of it until the day of his execution.

It was the Winter of the Snake, a dismal year for merchants and pirates alike. Unrelenting hailstorms and lightning strikes at sea made for dangerous sailing, and commerce ground to a halt. Only one cargo vessel, the Patience Mann, was desperate enough to brave the Barrel, and only one pirate ship, the Seagle, was mad enough to go after her. The pirates attacked from the north, masked by the frozen Waste, and cut off the Patience Mann and her shore-hugging route. The Seagle harried her for fourteen hours, picking off crew and punching holes in her keel with ballistae, catapults, and harpoons. The captain of the Patience Mann displayed true courage and repelled boarders six times before his ship foundered, his stalwart crew outmatched, outplayed, and outmanned.

All hands were put to the sword.

In relieving the doomed ship of her treasures, the pirates tarried too long and became trapped in the ice. The world heaved beneath the Seagle as storms reshaped the sea. Lightning struck the mast. Shifting icebergs tore the ship apart like grinding rocks, the hull splintered. In the end, both ships struck headfirst into the rocky bottom of the Barrel along with the treasures each crew had fought so hard to possess. Forty frightened pirates entered the freezing water and desperately swam for shore as sharks picked them apart.

Only one slave boy made it out of the water alive.

Pip woke to the stench of corpses.

One eye had swollen shut; the other blinked at the frozen beach. Littered along the white sand were the bodies of his former crew, strewn like mannequins frozen solid in the surf. Crowsman Bondi lay face up, his head rocking back and forth as waves washed over his open eyes. A pack of gulls worked on Kite, picking at the guts spilling out of his shirt. Grace had made it a few feet up the shore before she'd bled out. Horseshoe crabs crawled over the shark bite of her missing arm.

I'm alone.

Pip looked up the shoreline. Corpses littered the beach like driftwood. None moved.

Alone.

Pip's teeth chattered as he stared at the frozen waste around him. "Hello? Hello!"

Nothing. Just the sounds of the waves.

They're gone. They're all gone.

Pip limped across the snow-covered beach. Wrapped around a barrel, fishnets tangled around him, lay his captain.

Roper Jon's hands were blue and puffy, his face frozen in a rictus grin. The gold chain around his bloated neck *tinked* against the barrel. One boot was gone and his exposed toes looked like fat, sodden mushrooms.

Gone.

Pip picked up a hunk of wood and prodded the corpse.

A sigh of trapped gas escaped the dead pirate's smile, a last foul breath.

Pip hit him with the stick. Again. His blows intensified, striking over and over at the body. Pip didn't realize he was screaming until the stick broke. Roper Jon's corpse still smiled at him. Pip kicked his teeth.

"Yes!" the boy shouted at the top of his lungs, grinning like a wolf. "Gone! *Ha!*"

Shivering, Pip drew in a long breath. He was trapped at the edge of the world, surrounded by the dead, and freezing to death.

He had never felt so free.

Alone.

He had no tinder or flint to make a fire, but Roper Jon had shown him, drunk over cards, how to create flame with the snap of his fingers. It had been a knack of the captain, a cheap bit of majik, but Pip had never learned the trick.

Timber and flotsam from both ships littered the shore. Pip gathered it into a pile, stealing coats and shirts from the dead crew, covering himself in layers of wet wool. As he did, he stared at the wood, focusing. *I can do this.*

He knelt next to the pile of timber and snapped his fingers. Nothing. He closed his one good eye and drew on the *wikk* of the world. He snapped again, but the majik eluded him. He glared at Roper Jon's corpse. *Couldn't teach me one good trick before you died, couldja?*

For an hour, Pip hunched in the howling wind, snapping numb fingers, trying to summon the spark. The last embers of the sun faded as lightning split a frost-cracked horizon. Night fell, as did the temperature, and the cold threatened to reunite Pip with his crew.

Lord of Sea and Sky, help me.

One last snap and the fire blossomed at his fingertips. The orange glow reflected in his eyes, the only bit of warmth in an empty world.

Fire.

By the time the moons came up over the Irridin, the bonfire was big enough for twenty men. Pip picked up scraps of his old ship piece by piece and tossed them in. He collected a net, four empty barrels, a pair of oars, six lengths of rope, eight sheets of canvas, and nine wineskins and built a lean-to that protected it all.

Pip popped open the barrel Roper Jon had been clutching. Inside were two twenty-pound hams packed in salt. He grinned.

Alone and rich.

He chucked another piece of the *Seagle* into the flames and danced.

O, I got a gal who's always rotten
Stuffs her shirt with a bale of cotton
Six foot tall, eight feet of hair
Poked holes in a barrel for her underwear.
Don't know Liza, don't know me
We got a ticket to the jamboree!
A mule kicked her, she kicked right back
Made her bed out of an old haystack
Sung last weekend in a bass quartet
You ain't seen nothin' like her yet.
Don't know Liza, don't know me
We got a ticket to the jamboree!

When he woke, the hams were gone.

The barrel was open, salt scattered on the ground. The melting snow was scarred with the jagged claw marks of some lupine animal Pip didn't recognize. All that remained of the food was one pinky-sized gobbet of pink pig.

Dammit!

Pip eyed the tracks. Furious, he snatched up an oar and followed them, swearing vengeance on the thief.

Sleet raked across his face as he tromped to the tree line, entered the windbreak, and took a breath. The ghostly pines were sheeted in white icing, making Pip think of old Wint's strawberry cakes. His stomach rumbled.

A shadow loped through the trees, dark on white. It went on all fours, furry and rangy. *Wolf.* Hesitating, Pip watched the creature drop something in the snow and savage it with a carnivorous growl.

My ham.

Enraged, Pip ran at it, rearing his oar. Branches smacked his face, snow exploded everywhere. The beast pelted off, running faster than the boy, and disappeared into the icy wind. Pip gave pursuit, falling farther and farther behind, his heart hammering as the snow pulled at his feet, trying to drag him down.

Mine.

Pip broke through the trees to find a windblown lake, frozen beneath a sheet of black ice. Snow gusted across the surface in little whirlwinds, revealing the beast. It stood on the ice, quaking. A high keening sound escaped its ham-rimmed mouth.

It was not a wolf. Tan fur lined its small body, decorated with a white blaze on its chest. An akita dog, triangle-eared with a curled furry tail. It stared at him with mismatched eyes, one brown, one blue. On its flank it wore the brand of the *Patience Mann.*

A ship dog.

Pip strode forward, fear gone.

"You rooked my ham, you bit—"

His foot went through the ice.

Stumbling, Pip's hands skidded on the surface as the chill water bit his feet. He scrambled backward to shore and watched a dark wet crack cut through the ice toward the dog. It whined and turned to flee, but the ice splintered and the dog went through. It yelped and swam for the surface, paws raking furiously at the ice, trapped in a black crack within a world of white.

The akita flailed at the ice and more pieces broke away. Pip watched it struggle and splash, but it refused to let the ham go. Soon it became clear the dog would not survive.

I don't need to see this. Pip turned toward the forest. He heard the dog whine, terrified. Frowning, Pip stopped and gritted his teeth.

He stepped into the water, extended his oar, and broke the ice. The akita tried to paddle away from him and only succeeded in making a bigger hole. Pip stepped further out into the water and felt the cold tighten his gut, then his chest, then his neck. He extended the oar as far as he could, breaking the ice between him and the dog. It paddled for the oar, clawing at it. Pip drew it back to shore.

Fangs bit into the webbing of his thumb. The dog gnashed at him and Pip stumbled onto shore, bleeding. The akita snapped the ham out of the water and raced up the bank.

Well, that was stupid.

Pip cradled his bitten hand and watched the dog escape. It turned and stared at him triumphantly, then fled into the woods.

The boy lurched through the trees back to his camp, freezing. He threw more ship timber into the coals and built a fire with shaking hands. Within minutes, the wreck of the *Seagle* was burning once again.

Pip threw himself down near the fire, shivering. As he warmed, he rolled over and saw the akita standing in the snow only a few feet away, a tan ghost with a ham in its mouth.

Pip scowled. "No! You rooked my ham, you can't rook my fire!" Pip threw sand at it. "No! *Bad dog!*"

The akita whimpered.

"No!" yelled Pip.

The dog hunkered down on its forelegs and belly-crawled toward the fire. It kept coming, paw by paw, mismatched eyes pleading.

Pip snatched the ham. The dog snarled but only kept half. Covered in dog slobber and sand, pink meat hung limp in Pip's hand. "Ha!" He shoved the gobbet into the fire and let the meat cook.

The akita cowered on its belly and raised a paw to him, whimpering. Pip saw its frozen fur, the icicles around its nostrils, heard its pleading whine.

He's as lonely as I am.

Pip shrugged. "Fine. You can come, rooker."

It joined him. The dog walked nervously around the blaze thrice before it finally picked a warm spot on the far side and lay down.

Pip smiled. "Okay."

He plucked the ham from the fire, brushed away the sand, and took a bite. He eyed the dog, its tan coat glowing orange in the firelight. As the wind howled, Pip stared at the animal, thinking of Bondi. Of Kite. Of Roper Jon.

All things considered, the thieving dog was better company.

Pip watched the sunset and felt the night air go crisp and brittle. Snow fell, big white puffs that drifted from the sea and settled on his knees. He scooted closer to the fire and tucked the rest of the ham into the salt barrel, making sure to seal it tight.

When he woke, the akita was nuzzled against his chest, sleeping like a baby.

Despite the cold and sleet, the next few days were the best of Pip Winegrad's life.

Together, the boy and his dog explored the vast white wilderness. Mysteries awaited beyond each shadow, every one a peril to be faced together. Every day an adventure, every hunt a victory, every meal a feast. The world was theirs.

Fishing was easy; Pip's lines trapped four or five fish a day. They ate grayling and salmon for the first tenday until they discovered a species of ptarmigan that roamed the island. The little birds' wings were no more useful than a chicken's, and they made for easy prey.

Pip ran into a covey of birds, waving his arms and hollering. Ptarmigan scattered, waddling away from him and squawking. As they fled, Pip hollered, "Get 'em!"

The akita darted from his hiding place and snapped sharp teeth around a ptarmigan's neck. The covey fled into the woods and left their brother to his fate.

Smiling, Pip walked toward the dog, hand out. The akita growled, hanging on to the bird.

"Rooker!" Pip yelled. "Gimme that snow chicken!"

The dog backed away, snarling. *Mine.*

Pip threw up his hands and headed back toward camp. "Fine. *You* carry it."

They raced each other down the beach. After eating the bird, they tussled in the sand, hollering and barking. When the moons came out, they howled at them together, a triumphant duet in the winter night.

Within the month, the bodies began to stink. Even frozen corpses decay, and more arrived each day, washed ashore with the wreckage of the *Patience Mann.*

Exploring the coast, they found a towering cone-shaped outcrop that jutted from the sea like a thumb. The boy eyed the peak, three hundred feet high. *Good place for a signal fire.* Throwing a stick for the dog to fetch, he investigated the little mountain and considered the pooling eddies below. *Good fishing spot too.*

"What do you think, boy? Is this our new home?"

Rooker barked, annoyed that he wasn't throwing the stick. Pip obliged him.

When they returned to camp, several bodies were missing.

They had been dragged into the trees by large animals. Pip couldn't read sign well, but he saw the tracks. *Two or three of them. Long claws. Dragging tails.*

Hell's bells.

"Alright, boy." He dusted snow off his pants. "Let's get to work."

Rooker was no help. The akita barked and ran in circles around Pip while he hauled the remains of the *Seagle* and the *Patience Mann* to their new camp, piece by piece. Pip christened the big rock Thimble Tower and set his fishing lines. Pine boughs jammed between rocks made good poles and his lines were sturdy, their hooks baited with ptarmigan guts.

After a long day, Pip slumped on his backside, exhausted. "Yer gonna hafta carry yer weight, Rooker. Toughen up." The akita barked, agreeing. Pip assessed his new camp near Thimble Tower. He'd made more than a dozen trips, but he still didn't have half the gear. *Got to go back for more.*

That night was their last at the site of the wreck.

Pip was plucking a ptarmigan when Rooker snarled and dashed off into the dark, barking. The boy snatched his oar and stared into the blackness, hollering for the dog. Rooker returned after a few minutes, his muzzle wet with blood.

Pip patted him, thumping Rooker's side as the dog growled into the dark.

In the morning, the rest of the bodies were gone.

More tracks peppered the sand, the same as before. *A dozen of them now. Damn.*

Not for the first time, Pip wished for a bow and arrow. Or even a sword. He gripped his oar. "Okay, Rooker. Time to go."

The akita barked and spun in a circle, excited.

Plenty of firewood surrounded Thimble Tower, but there was no way to get it to the top; the rocks were too steep. Pip knew he would only get one opportunity to signal a passing ship, so he dragged piles of firewood to both port and starboard sides of the little mountain. It took hours of hauling timber, but his wood was stacked, his tinder was dry, and flint and steel stood at the ready, just in case.

Now all we need is a ship. And a kiss from Lady Luck.

Cold and shivering, Pip rubbed Rooker's chin. "Who's my lucky penny? You are." Rooker barked, tongue hanging out the side of his mouth. "Yes, you are."

That night, Pip got his first look at an ice weasel.

Low and long, as big as the dog, it slunk into the firelight as Pip ate dinner. Rooker was too distracted by his meal to notice until Pip shouted. The dog leapt to his feet and barked.

The weasel fled into the dark. Rooker tried to chase after it, but Pip grabbed his rope collar. Outside the firelight, he spotted several pairs of hungry eyes staring back at him. Rooker barked until they disappeared, and long after.

They followed us.

In the morning, Pip suspended a hammock from the trees nearest Thimble Tower and hoisted all his food into the air. He added sharpened pongee sticks around the camp for protection, piled the campfire high, and stacked his wood deep. As the sun set, Rooker refused to get in the hammock until Pip picked him up and settled the dog on his chest. He patted the akita's head and felt the dog's warmth against his body.

Pip knew he would be dead without the dog. It wasn't just hunting game or guarding him while he slept; the akita gave him something more. The dog gave him a reason to get up every morning when he woke to a frostbitten wilderness. Every night, he had a friend to keep loneliness at bay.

For the first time since Jasper had sold him for four bags of grain, Pip Winegrad wasn't alone.

Together, he and the dog had survived twenty-eight nights on the frozen coast, better than most full-grown men could have done. Pip stared at the fire, feeling his eyelids grow heavy. *But we can't hold out forever.*

He flashed awake when something bit his finger. He yelled and kicked the weasel out of his hammock. It plopped to the ground, scattering the dying fire, and skittered off to join a hundred hungry eyes that prowled the firelight.

Rooker barked long into the night. Pip stroked his fur and watched the monsters in the shadows.

Sooner or later, they're going to win.

The next morning, Pip searched Thimble Tower, looking for a place to hide. The pack of weasels had lost its fear. Pip knew neither he nor the dog would survive another night. He explored the Tower for crevices, but all were too damp to call home. Desperate, Pip climbed, hunting for any crack that might offer even scant protection, a hole they could defend. "Come on, Rooker."

The dog was no good at climbing and decided to lend his support by barking at Pip from below. Pip scoured the rock but found nothing useful.

They're going to tear us apart.

Soon, the dog's barking grew urgent. Giving up, Pip climbed down, worried the weasels were coming by daylight and the dog was trapped alone. He rounded the final corner to discover Rooker was only yapping at a rock.

Stupid dog.

The akita pawed at the base of the tower, head tilted to the side, barking. He looked like a puzzled child, and Pip couldn't help but laugh. "Yeah? What is it boy? A crab?"

Rooker whined, his mismatched eyes locked on the stone. Pip pulled the dog away and spotted an opening under the rock. He got on his belly and peered up into a narrow tunnel lined with orange and purple starfish.

A cave. Pip smiled. *A cave we can block.*

He patted Rooker on the head and rubbed his neck. "Who's my lucky penny?"

Rooker barked, happy to help.

Pip crawled through squishy starfish into the jagged tunnel, careful to avoid the sea anemones in the pools, not knowing if their spines were poisonous.

He came around a bend and saw a low flicker of green light. Pip stopped. *Some kind of... glowy seaweed maybe?* The light moved, dancing, calling to him. Then it came around a corner toward him. *A pixie.*

Pip had only glimpsed a few pixies, tiny green lanterns dancing through the late-night forest, will-o-wisps drifting in the air. There had been no pixies during his year at sea. Now, one was just a few feet away. Glowing dragonfly wings fluttered faster than he could see, creating a green halo around it. He saw its feminine figure, legs, torso, arms, all in miniature. The pixie paused long enough for Pip to see her face, her big eyes, her little smile. And then she was gone.

Pip dragged himself through the tunnel after her. "Come on, boy!"

Whining, Rooker crawled after him, his fur wet, eyes frightened.

The tunnel grew wider and somewhere in the dark Pip heard the undulation of waves. The sound echoed against the rock, an orchestra of drum brushes, hissing, rolling, never-ending, the sea trapped within a stone concert hall.

Pip rounded the last corner to find Thimble Tower was hollow. The cavern was a hundred feet tall and twice as wide, a vast pool of water, the air thick with pixies.

It was as if the aurora borealis had taken up residence inside the little mountain, living and glowing and moving inside it, a nest of a billion fireflies. It glowed, pulsing as swarms of pixies riffled the air in waves, spinning in lazy cyclones that filled the sea cave in twisting bands of light so thick he couldn't see through them.

Pip laughed, watching them fly. Rooker barked, spinning in circles, mouth open in a big doggy smile.

The boy stepped into the water and walked toward the lights, holding out his hands. Pixies danced before his eyes, slipping toward him and away again. They alighted on his fingers then took off, giggling. As Pip walked, he saw their green reflections on the tranquil water. He laughed and splashed water at them.

The pixies parted and drew back like a curtain to reveal the strangest ship he had ever seen.

It's standing on the water.

The catamaran was massive, three times the size of the *Seagle*, constructed in the shape of a λ. Its feet were gigantic outriggers twice as tall as a man, each attached to curved legs that supported the bulk of the ship above the cove like an enormous water strider. The thing nearly filled the sea cave, towering above the gentle waves like a mythic queen of legend.

His mouth open, Pip stared at the ship and knew, for the first time, what true love was.

He dove into the cove and swam toward the ship. As he approached, he saw the wood was unlike anything he'd ever seen, embellished with dragons and griffins, snakes and hawks. He reached the massive outrigger and brushed the wood with his hand. A warm glow spread through his fingers as gooseflesh rippled up his arm.

His first touch of the *wikk* was like a kiss from a long-lost lover.

She's beautiful.

Pip found a series of pegs on the side of the outrigger, a hidden ladder. Barking, Rooker splashed after him into the water. "Come on, boy! Let's get a look at her." He grabbed Rooker around the chest and climbed. Mounting the outrigger, the boy and his dog stared up at the underside of the hull.

Pip grinned. "I bet we can get up there."

He slung the akita over his shoulders and climbed one of the ship's legs. Rooker whimpered, nervous, but Pip's balance was steady. He climbed the arch like a curved ladder until the footholds ended. The last stretch of the arc was flatter, but there was nothing to hold on to, so Pip gripped the wood with his thighs and shimmied up inch by inch until he reached the deckrail.

Lit by pixielight, the ship was covered in a layer of unbroken dust. If anyone had once trod her boards, it had been a long time ago. She was abandoned.

Even so, Pip swore he felt something alive, almost like a heartbeat within the wood.

"Hello?" he shouted, waiting to be attacked by some horror within. None came.

It's just us. Alone.

Pip slid a leg over the rail and planted his feet on the deck. The ship rocked slightly, creaking, and seemed to come alive beneath him.

"Ha!" he shouted, sending a flock of pixies to flight. "She's ours!"

Pip laughed and danced around the deck, shouting at the top of his lungs. Rooker barked, trying to figure out what was happening as pixies raced around the furled sails above, driven to a joyous frenzy.

Pip bent down and held Rooker's face, kissing him. "Ya really are my lucky penny, ain't ya, boy?"

Yeah! barked the dog. *Yeah! Yeah!*

Thrilled, Pip ran to the deckwheel, where the captain piloted the ship. The wheel was bigger than he was, studded with smooth pins waiting for a pair of hands.

Taking a breath, he took hold of the wheel.

Captain Pip.

The ship sighed around him, a wooden moan of pleasure.

Pip giggled. He couldn't help himself. Laughter rolled out of him, shaking off the cold, the hunger, the worry; it all unclasped from his mind, falling away in hysterics. He laughed like only a ten-year-old boy could, loud and long and free.

He wrapped his arms around the deckwheel. *O, I love you.*

Ting-ting.

Something fell onto the deck with a metallic sound.

Pip looked down. At his feet, two brass rings gleamed in the dust. He glanced around, not understanding where they had come from. *Maybe they rolled off when I grabbed the wheel?*

He bent down and picked them up. The rings were warm to the touch and trembled with the *wikk*. He slipped the rings on his middle finger and they fit perfectly, as if by majik. He held his hand up, watching the light of the pixies shimmer over the twin brass circles.

Like a pair of wedding rings.

The ship shifted, sighing. *Yes.*

He heard her voice. He could swear it. The ship spoke to him, wanted him, longed for him. And he knew, in that moment, that he longed for her too.

Pip nodded. *Yes.*

On a peg nearby rested a big purple hat with a dusty peacock feather. A captain's hat. He plopped it on his head.

"We're captains now, Rooker!" The dog spun in circles, barking happily as the ship sighed. "The world better watch out for *us!*" Pip hollered, his voice loud and powerful, echoing against the stone cavern, pixies darting through the air above his ship, his dog, his world.

"You and me, boy!" Pip grinned like a madman, his eyes bright and sharp. "You and me."

PART 1

TURNCOAT

CAST= =AWAY

If a clod be washed away by the sea,
Europe is the less.
As well as if a promontory were.
As well as if a manor of thy friend's
Or of thine own were.

John Donne

Y OU AND ME.

Rooker Flynn rode on dragonback, his heart empty.

He could feel the beast's power. Muscles longer than a warship flexed and strained, carrying the great wyrm aloft on membranous wings stretched between eight monstrous legs. Rooker felt the spiky hairs that covered the dragon's skin, saw the cracks between the enormous scales where webs crisscrossed each other as if they held the beast together with sinew made of gossamer. Xeusia's wings beat again, lifting him higher into the sky.

Rooker was aware of none of it. He heard the rush of air like the moan of a freshly dead ghost, but it meant nothing. He smelled the sour sweat slathering his body, tasted coppery blood in his mouth, but he was numb to it. All he could feel was the emptiness of his hand that had been warm just a moment ago.

Dangling from his wrist, the remains of the lightchain hung limp, severed forever.

It joined him to nothing but empty air.

He stared blankly, straight down the cliff that fell away beneath him. The rock precipice upon which he had stood moments ago boiled with shiq, a million giant yellow spiders seeking prey. But he did not see the cliff, did not see the shiq. He only saw what lay beneath, the jungle that had swallowed Jack Swift whole.

(you cut him loose)

Jasper's voice whispered in his mind, so much like his own. Rooker ignored the specter of his dead brother, refusing to let Jasper claim him. Somewhere in the night, he heard a dog howl at Keymark's mismatched moons, a lonely cry that peeled across the sky like an infant's wail.

But no, of course, there was no dog. Not on Huánghūn.

And yet the howling continued, an unbroken moan of despair.

Rooker Flynn had not cried since the day his father had chained him to a tree and commanded he chop it down before the floods took him. He did not cry now. Crying was for the weak, and his weakness had died on that tree. Weakness would never touch him again.

I killed him.

Somewhere in the blackness, the wailing keen of the impossible dog continued. Rooker felt the vibrations come from his own throat and stopped listening. Far below, where Jack had disappeared, the dark palm trees brushed against each other, whispering his shame.

Rooker felt his soul twist, shrink, and draw away from him. A chill filled the vacuum it left, a shard of ice that told him he would never be warm again. He felt Jasper there, occupying that emptiness. His dead brother smiled, his voice cold.

(you see now, pip, now you see)

Rooker felt his flesh tremble as he recognized what he had become.

"Hold on to me, dearie." Gerba Whipmarples folded his arm around her waist. "We would not want you to fall." The headmistress touched the brooch at her breast and the dragon arched toward the cliffs. It flew along the rock wall and skimmed over swarms of shiq.

Out of the blackness, Rooker saw a thick jet of webbing strike the dragon's tail. Iktomi, Gerba's enormous spider mount, emerged from the blackness of the cliffs, clinging to the line. The dragon turned and leapt into the sky, Iktomi dangling behind it by its silken thread. As Xeusia ascended, Iktomi scurried up the line and attached itself to the dragon's belly like a child come home to its mother.

Rooker held tight to Gerba Whipmarples, staring as the world disappeared below.

They flew together, higher and higher. Skybound, Rooker felt his eyes grow dry and bloodshot from the wind, but still he did not blink. His breath was gone, his chest empty, his soul silent.

There are precious few in Keymark who can claim to have seen it by air. Rooker had wondered, as every child had, what the world would look like through the eyes of a gull, a hawk, a dragon. Now he saw. Huánghūn spread out beneath him as a moonlit tapestry: the swarmed hunting cabin, the swamp he and Jack had crossed on horseback, the killing field where nobles had shot convicts down for sport. Soon he saw the four gigantic yingcao palms littered with the nests of raiptar birds that hunted spiders at night. Around the trees, he saw the prison camps: Jackal, Buzzard, Hyena, Vulture. From up here, the raised huts that housed hundreds of outlaws looked like children's toys. And there, in the background, the monolithic eight-mile wall of the Locke Institute. The tapestry of the world was magnificent and covered in yellow spiders. Now that the hateful sun was gone, they covered every inch of Huánghūn. The night was theirs.

High in the sky, Rooker felt small. He was nothing, an insect hovering over a map. Miniscule. Insignificant. With every beat of Xeusia's wings, the land fell further away, diminishing him just a little bit more. And still the great wyrm beat its colossal wings, soaring ever higher.

It was impossible, riding a dragon. A notion for children who did not understand how cruel the world was. The great wyrms would rend asunder any fool mad enough to try. And yet here he was, watching the headmistress of the Locke Institute control Xeusia and its offspring Iktomi as easily as a conductor directed a symphony.

"I began my life as an animal trainer, did you know that?" Gerba Whipmarples did not shout over the wind. Her majik delivered her lilting voice directly to Rooker's ear. "With a little gypsy circus, our travelling band of troupers. A hundred years ago, when I was just a girl, before my family left the Jutts. Before I learned majik." She leaned and Xeusia banked starboard, following her lead. "I started with horses, then bears, wyverns, kitsune... all sorts of animals. I had a knack for it, knew how to control them, manipulate them, and draw them in." She turned toward him, her long horn silhouetted against the orange moon, her sea-green eyes twinkling in the dark. "Do you know what the difference is between animals and men, Mister Flynn?" She flashed a thin smile. "Absolutely nothing."

Rooker stared at the empty night sky, his mind numb. He considered what it would feel like to simply roll to one side and disappear into the dark.

"It is a rewarding profession, a true calling." Gerba held on to her saddle's pommel. "The proud creatures refuse to bend at first. Lions were like that. Headstrong. Proud. Some trainers would whip them, but whipping only broke the animal. It did nothing to make it useful. But. A *true* genius trains a beast to see itself in its trainer's eyes. Subservient. Supplicant. A tool in its master's hand." Her leathery hand gestured to the spider-dragon. "Even Xeusia ul-Styx Hakáti. An ancient great wyrm of the Old World, the last of its kind. And yet it serves me. *Everything* on Huánghūn serves me: the shiq, the attercops, the acolytes, the students. All of them understand who is in control." She lowered her head. "All of them... except you."

Rooker closed his eyes and refused to look at her. He listened to the wind rush past him and imagined himself aboard a ship at sea. The air streamed around him exactly as it might aboard the *Venture Brigand*. The air was his servant, sails replaced with dragon's wings.

Gerba's voice fractured his illusion. "During all my years as a trainer, there was only one animal I could not break. Not a tiger or a wyvern, but a little dog. A terrier named Pepper. He would bark, run, and bite, but he would not obey. I like to think any animal can be broken with the right tool, but not Pepper. He recognized no master but himself." Gerba sighed. "So, at long last, I was forced to confess the truth. I had failed. That night, Pepper found himself in a burlap sack. And that sack found itself in a river."

Keeping his eyes jammed shut, Rooker felt a chill ripple over his skin.

"And I must confess, I am beginning to ask myself..." Gerba's voice grew soft. "Is it time to do the same with you?"

The cyclone of air around him cut off, abrupt as a closing door. Xeusia's body ceased to move. Rooker's eyes flashed open to discover the world was nothing but grey. He was inside a cloud, and the dragon was utterly still. As tendrils of mist drifted past him, Rooker saw Xeusia's gargantuan black wings flung wide and rigid. It rode an air current above the island, carried by the wind.

As the cloud parted to reveal a crystal clear sky littered with diamond stars, he spied the long pier of the Institute that stretched into the Irridin Sea like a pointing finger. In the far distance, he glimpsed the tiny shape of a single ship, a silhouette he knew better than his own face.

The *Venture Brigand.*

Gerba swung her legs around as easily as if she were sitting on a park bench and turned to face him. The gold jewelry that adorned her largest horn tinkled softly in the whispering silence. The headmistress held her body primly as ever, thick fingers steepled together. "I offered you everything you want, Mister Flynn. I offered you freedom. I offered your old life back. I offered you the position of pilot aboard *Venture Brigand*. All you had to do... was deliver Nepenthe." She cocked her head. "And still you would not obey."

Rooker did not look at her. He only had eyes for the *Brigand.* He was nothing, an insect, helpless, and he knew deep in his broken soul he would never set foot on the *Brigand*'s deck again.

And he only had himself to blame.

(she's right)

Shut up, Jasper.

(you made a deal, nepenthe for the brigand, *she guaranteed it under the geas curse)*

Shut your filthy gob.

(you would be aboard right now if you hadn't been so soft. da was right about you)

His numb chest rumbled with an anger hot as lava. Furious, he felt self-hatred boil him from inside. *Idiot!* Jack was gone, dead, and Rooker's only chance of getting home had gone with him. He'd let his feelings for the kid get in the way of the only thing he'd ever cared about. Those feelings had cost him the *Brigand.*

I let him off the hook. He gritted his teeth. *And for what?*

(for a dead man)

Gerba watched him like a hawk watches a mouse. "Perhaps it is time we parted ways, Mister Flynn." She cocked her head to the side. "Some animals cannot be taught."

I'm no animal. Rooker's hatred boiled from his chest, down his arms, and into his fingertips. He gripped the broken lightchain hanging from his wrist, squeezing it tight in a white-knuckled fist. At long last he finally glared the headmistress in the eye. "What d'ya *want*, Gerba?"

"O, Mister Flynn." She flicked a leathery finger under Rooker's chin. He flinched away from her touch. "If only you could learn to see yourself through the eyes of your betters. What would you want if you were *me?*"

"A painful death."

"*Ha.*" Gerba raised a hand to cover her laugh. "I can arrange that." She uttered one syllable and her brooch glowed bright crimson. Instantly, the dragon ducked one set of wings and spiraled downward. Rooker tried to grab hold of its thick scales, but his fingers slipped, and he fell into open air.

Nothing waited between him and death. Heart in his mouth, Rooker watched the ground spin toward him like a cyclone made of jungle.

Gerba's hand flashed out and snatched his. They plummeted through the night sky together, twisting, a lightheaded laugh rippling from the headmistress' throat.

Xeusia pulled up. The dragon righted itself and floated in the Huánghūn breeze, calm as a kite. Trapped in Gerba's hand, Rooker watched the dragon's eight-eyed head turn toward him on a powerful snakelike neck. Mandibles the size of horse legs flexed as it hissed breath that reeked of flame and sulfur. The great wyrm's mouth edged closer to Rooker, ichor dripping from its fangs.

Another man might have quailed, fawned, cowered in the face of the dragon's mouth, but Rooker Flynn only leaned in. He had nothing left to lose. *"Do it!"* he shouted at the top of his lungs. *"Kill me!"* Heart triphammering in his chest, furious at his impotence, he spewed every bit of rage he had at the headmistress. "Ya took the *Brigand*, Jack is dead, so do it! Kill me and be done with it, ya damned wasteka harridan!"

Gerba's reaction was the last thing he'd expected. A laugh rolled from deep within her belly, bubbling from her chest to her lips. "Dead?" She chuckled, waving her hand. "O, you are such a simple creature, Mister Flynn. No, no. We do not waste resources here at the Institute."

Rooker didn't see Iktomi until the giant spider walked over him. One of the baby dragon's gigantic legs brushed his face. Rooker flinched away from the thing as the spider crawled up from Xeusia's belly without a sound. Gerba patted Iktomi's fur as it formed a windbreak, protecting her. As she stroked the beast, Rooker saw a large bundle of webbing attached to Iktomi's side.

He blinked. The giant wad of webs was covered in sticks, dirt, and broken palm leaves. But there, sticking out between two of the fronds—

A bare foot, broken at the ankle.

Jack.

Rooker froze.

No.

A slow smile spread over Gerba's face.

Rooker stared at Iktomi. *It was waiting at the bottom of the cliff, waiting for the kid to fall. And it spun a web to catch him.*

Rooker swallowed. "Is he alive?"

"For now." Gerba patted Jack's body. "The arrow struck deeper than I intended, and I think today took a toll on the poor little fellow. I should get him back to the Great Bell before he passes on."

She touched her brooch and Xeusia's great wings beat once, twice, thrice. It rose toward the mismatched moons, Gamilat and Anika, shining bright in the midnight sky. Gerba stared at them, her eyes reflecting orange and white.

"All things feed each other." The headmistress' voice seemed far away, musing, pensive. "The *wikk* flows between us. We reflect it to each other, magnifying it. You and I are doing it right now, Mister Flynn. And Xeusia. And Iktomi. We make each other stronger, just by being together. That's why an animal in a pack will always resist. They are not alone. Even the wild stallion and the alpha wolf will succumb once the pack abandons them. Isolation breaks the bond." She sighed. "I forgot that lesson when I bound the two of you together." Gerba turned to Rooker. Her cold eyes considered him. "That is what gave the young doktar his stubborn streak. You."

Rooker heard Jack's quiet voice in his head. *You and me.*

Gerba nodded. "He thought you were part of his pack. It didn't matter that it was a lie, he *believed* it. And that belief kept him fighting. I had no choice but to give you the lightknife." She leaned in. "So he could see who you really are."

Her accusation struck like a fist to his gut. Rooker's stomach twisted like a nest of blackened snakes.

(she's right)

He was no friend to Jack Swift.

He was no friend to anyone.

"He saw you cut the cord. He watched you let him die." Gerba revealed a tiny key in her massive hands and unlocked the severed lightchain from Rooker's wrist. "And *that* cut, my dear boy, will never mend."

Rooker dropped his head, listening to the emptiness around him.

Gerba pulled away the empty manacle and considered it. "Now your lies are cut away. Now he understands the truth. He is... utterly alone."

She tossed the lightchain into the darkness.

Rooker watched it tumble into the black and felt some part of himself go with it.

"So." The headmistress brushed her hands. "You have played your part, Mister Flynn, and your time on the stage has come to an end. There are only roles for sheep, and you are nothing but a mad dog." She cocked her head. "Time for that burlap bag."

She touched the brooch at her chest. Rooker felt the great wyrm begin to roll. And he knew, this time, Gerba would not stop his fall.

Toughen up.

Panic galvanized cruel clarity and he barked the words out sharp and hard. "It's the summer solstice today!"

Gerba curled an eyebrow and leveled the dragon out, frowning. "I beg your pardon?"

"The summer solstice." Rooker steadied his voice. "It's not over."

Gerba hmphed. "Technically, no. Not until sunrise."

"Then our deal is still on." Rooker leveled a finger at her nose. "I get you Nepenthe before sunrise and you put me on the *Brigand*."

"Mister Flynn." Gerba sighed. "You had your opportunity. And failed."

"Give me one more shot."

"Why would I?"

Rooker's voice grew cold. "Because I can break him."

Gerba raised an eyebrow. Rooker leaned closer, knowing his life was on the line. A few minutes ago, he wouldn't have cared, but now... now he had something to live for. The *Brigand*. He spun the brass rings on his middle finger. "I know Jack better than anyone. I can break him. Tonight."

From Xeusia's saddle, Gerba Whipmarples studied him like an insect. "If you claim such power over him, why did you not use it before?"

"Because now it's him or me." Rooker stared her down. "And I'll choose me every time."

Gerba's dark eyes shone in the moonlight. "So." A grin curled her lips. "Even a mad dog can learn." The headmistress straightened in her saddle and spoke with the command of a woman who had tamed dragons. "You are my creature. You do my bidding. You obey me. Say it."

Rooker glanced at the silhouette of the *Venture Brigand* on the horizon. He lowered his eyes. "I'm yer creature, I do yer bidding, I..." He swallowed. "I obey *you*." Rooker Flynn thrust out his jaw. "Headmistress."

She tilted her head, pleased. "You understand you only have a few hours until dawn."

"Then stop wasting my time."

Gerba Whipmarples allowed herself a satisfied smile and steered Xeusia's head in the direction of the Locke Institute. As they flew, she pulled up a blanket of webbing around her hips, wrapping herself tight. She extended the webbing to Rooker, and he felt her arm close around his waist, holding him close.

Bound by her great worm, Rooker Flynn glanced over his shoulder at the Irridin, his mother. She rippled in dual moonlight, on and on, forever and ever. Even from up here, even from so high, the sea was infinite, endless, eternal.

And upon her rested the *Venture Brigand*.

Three masts waited to unfurl sails. An anchor craved weighing. A deckwheel begged for his hand. Balanced on her magnificent legs, the catamaran leaned toward him, yearning for him, eager to run.

He felt her in his heart, filling, aching, warming. He couldn't hear her voice, not from so far, but he felt her call, the prayer of true love.

I'm comin', girl.

She rocked in the surf, pleading for his touch.

I'm comin' home.

Chapter

2

COMING HOME

The basic law of capitalism is you or I,
not both you and I.
Karl Liebknecht

D AD COOKED DINNER AT 6:00.

Since returning from Keymark, Dr. Alex Swift had endeavored to perfect the braised salmon with brown sugar glaze that Wellam the Cook had made on Falikos when he'd first arrived. It was impossible to reproduce. There was no Toshan equivalent of herrykin, the spice that completed the mélange of flavors that gave the final sweetness to the dish, but all things considered, Dad had done pretty darn well.

Jack took the pot of edamame off the Viking range and moved around Dad. He laid a silicone mitt on the lid and pulled the top, letting steam escape into the vent hood. He spooned the edamame onto their plates, his mother's china they used every night.

"I'm going to plate the fish." Dad turned. "Can you handle the rice?"

Jack used his scythe to cut away seed from the stalk. "I'm sick of rice."

"Chem 509 was weird today," said Rajiv Banerjee, pouring pepper onto his plate.

"What happened in Chem 509?" asked Dad as he brought the salmon to the table.

"Our new teacher," said Jack.

"You should have seen her face," laughed Rajiv.

"Her nose is like... *this* long." Jack spread his hands as far as he could. As Raj laughed, Jack looked down to see the fish on his plate was still alive, suffocating in the oxygen. "This fish isn't tough enough."

"You boys need to be careful," said Dad. "The Locke Institute isn't Northwestern or UChicago or Notre Dame. Their medical program is rotten." He ate the salmon, his fork held by a hand with three fingers and two bloody stumps.

Now they were on the patio, which was strange because the Swift home didn't *have* a patio. Even if it did, it wouldn't be thirty stories above Michigan Avenue like this one.

Jack looked down, not understanding where the floor had gone.

"Long way to go," said Rajiv.

"Forgive me if you can," murmured Dad. "I don't like you being so far away."

Jack turned to reply, but Dad was dead.

His eyes were white, his skin grey, his mouth open. A spider crawled out.

"I wouldn't worry." Jack turned to see Rajiv using a steak knife to saw at the brown twine holding the table together. "Ya probably won't see him again."

Jack turned back to his father, but the chair was empty.

He stared at the Chicago skyline. Mountains made of mirrors stared back at him. He saw his face reflected in a thousand windows. "I don't know how to get out."

"Ya *can't* get out," came a man's voice.

Jack turned to find Rajiv was gone. In his place sat Rooker Flynn. "But I'll cut ya loose."

The pirate cut the twine. As the string around the table snapped, the balcony fell off the building.

Rooker's grinning face fell away. Up, up, and up, into the sky until there was nothing left of him.

Wind whistled through Jack's hair as he fell, Chicago skyscrapers hissing past him.

Alone.

GONG.

Jack's eyes opened, blinking blue. He stared up at the inside of the Agrat-ban-Haifa. The big bell was suspended over him like a trumpet over a cockroach.

Wikk cascaded over him, pure and bright, flowing from the bell's throat. It wasn't loud, but it filled him: his ears, his nose, his eyes, his mouth, his skin. It touched every part of him, restoring him, refilling him, making his body whole.

Jack felt the arrow hole in his side knit itself closed. The shiq's fang marks wept poison, leaking as they puckered shut. His ankle unbroke. He watched it twist back into position. It should have hurt, it should have made him scream, but he only felt a tickle beneath his skin and heard the snap and crackle like logs on a campfire as his shattered bones were made whole again.

All this and still, he was terrified.

Despair flooded him, cold and empty. He stared up at the inside of the bell, his mind repeating one thought over and over: *Alone. Alone. Alone.*

The interior surface of the Agrat-ban-Haifa was smooth save for one thin crack that ran beneath a raised rune attached to the inner wall. The rest of the bell was ancient bronze, but the gold of the rune shone new. Jack stared at the inscription, his mind absently drifting through the Keymark symbols he knew.

Eight... something. I don't know. He spied the noose hanging from the bellpull. *That's where they hang them.* He remembered the first man he'd seen hang here, Shifty Haan. More than a dozen had followed. He could see their faces perfectly: Jim Six. Feather Lee. Daisuke Book... fourteen executions. A hundred and fifty days since Jack had drawn a free breath.

They died here. Alone.

Jack curled up on his side, not wanting to look at the noose anymore. Turning, he saw smaller bells, each the size of a bowling ball, hanging from chains all around the rim of the Great Bell, each ringing in gentle harmony with the Agrat-Ban-Haifa, resonating as one unified chord.

The lightchain broke for the hundredth time in Jack's mind. He heard the snap, the sudden emptiness. Felt himself falling, flailing. He saw the knife in Rooker Flynn's hand.

Jack's mind shattered into pieces for the hundredth time. In the last few days, he had been shot, bitten, broken, and tortured, and he knew he would never be himself again. Part of him was gone forever. The Great Bell could heal his body, but it couldn't touch the part of him that was dead. The Bell could not heal madness.

"Wakey-wakey," came Gerba's voice. She stood beside the bell, leaning toward him. "You are good as new!"

Jack ignored her, staring at the hanging bells.

"Can you hear me, dearie?" came Gerba's voice. "You look a bit... off."

Jack felt his neck twitch as his voice came from a million miles away. "The chains should be longer."

Gerba's face scrunched into a puzzle. "Beg pardon?"

"The chains. For the bells." Jack's face was blank, his eyes glazed over. "They need to be as long as your arm."

She turned to the acolytes. "I do not understand what is wrong with him. He should be fine."

Hands pulled him from beneath the bell. Jack wobbled, his legs unattached to his brain. Gerba's long horn came into view. "Doktar? Are you well?"

Jack stared at nothing, his insides as hollow as the Great Bell. All he could see was the knife in Rooker's hand.

He killed me.

Gerba snapped her fingers at the acolytes. "Escort the doktar down to my office."

The acolytes dropped him into a wooden seat at a long table in Gerba's office. The room was unlit save for a dull glow from the fireplace. Jack could barely make out the shapes within Gerba's library. Her giant mahogany desk, the hideous stone chair. Jack's fingers absently brushed the brand on his arm, feeling the cold metal embedded in his flesh.

As the acolytes moved away, Jack's eyes adjusted and he spied a figure sitting in the dark at the other end of the table.

A snap, and a tiny flame glowed. It touched a candle. The wick caught, and the flame illuminated a face.

Rooker.

Jack inhaled sharply. He felt the tendons in his neck flinch, a sudden weightlessness in his stomach, as if he were falling again. The acolytes left the room and closed the door behind them with a *thunk*.

Rooker leaned back and put his feet up on the table. He wore a new jacket of dark leather. As he regarded Jack, a slow smile curled his lips. "Hey."

Jack heard a sound escape his own throat, an empty noise. "Hey."

Silence hung between them, heavy and dark.

"So." Rooker spread his fingers. "Yer alive. That's lucky."

Jack said nothing, his mind unable to fathom the emotions crashing through it.

"Hey. Jack." Rooker leaned in. Jack watched candlelight illuminate the pirate's olive-toned skin. "Yer lookin' a little green around the gills. Ya all right, boychick?"

Jack stared at him, the cold gripping his gut. "You cut me loose."

Rooker shrugged. "And here ya sit, pink as a pig." A counterfeit smile crossed his face. "I saw that big spider down there, waitin' with his web. I figured out her game." He tapped his temple. "Outsmarted her." Jack's mouth couldn't move. Rooker mistook it for hesitation. "Hey, when have I ever steered ya wrong? I rescued ya out of Hyena, remember? I got ya galt. I got ya Thunderbuck, I got the pickaxes. Ya remember all that?"

"I remember everything, Rooker." A tremor flit across Jack's heart. "I remember the look in your eye when you let me go."

Rooker got to his feet and walked along the table toward Jack. "Listen. I watched yer back ever since we got here. I saved yer neck a dozen times over. If there's anyone on this island ya can trust, it's me."

Jack flinched when the pirate thumped him on the shoulder. Rooker leaned in close, whispering, "That harridan headmistress trusts me now. Thinks I'm on her side. But you and me, we're gonna swindle her, boychick. We're breakin' out tonight. All ya gotta do"—he reached inside his new jacket and revealed a single rod of pale bamboo that made Jack's heart catch in his throat when he saw the familiar etchings within the wood—"is summon this."

Nepenthe.

Jack's heart quickened in his chest. His fingers flexed, wanting it, craving the power of it. He felt part of his mind sharpen, thinking.

Rooker offered the rod balanced on two fingers, his voice pure temptation. "It'll be just like old times, Jack. Once ya got the whompin' stick in yer hands, nobody's gonna stop us. We fight our way out. We make it to the *Brigand*, ya remember the *Venture Brigand*, yeah? And we just sail away. I'll take ya anywhere ya wanna go, and if ya want, ya never gotta see my pretty mug again." He took another step closer, almost nose to nose. "One last adventure."

Jack met Rooker's eye, unblinking. *I remember who you are.*

"You and me, right, Rooker?" Jack lied.

"You and me, Jack." Rooker lied right back.

Jack felt something inside harden like a stone. He plucked Nepenthe from Rooker's hands. The pirate tensed ever so slightly, and Jack turned the stick in his fingers. "What's the next part of Gerba's plan?"

Rooker scowled, puzzled. "What?"

"Last time, she had archers. Before that, the dragon was waiting." Jack pointed to the empty library above. "No archers now though." Jack lowered his head. "So what's the plan?"

"Jack, what're ya talki—"

He cut Rooker off, eyeing the room. "There are new designs carved in the walls since last time. Lots of curls. Lots of shadows." Jack got to his feet. He stepped to the wall and stuck his finger into one of the deeper designs. "If I'm running a prison, some of those designs have peepholes. If I'm Gerba Whipmarples, some of them have arrow ports. Maybe a blowgun." Jack felt his skin prickle, resentment stabbing at him. "I summon Nepenthe and they shoot me full of poisoned darts like Cant Naysayer used. Am I close?"

Rooker said nothing, but his tan skin blanched.

Finally shut your mouth, didn't I, Rooker? Jack circled toward his friend, his own icy smile curled across his face. *Two can play this game.*

"But if I'm Gerba, that's not enough. That's just the back-up plan. Someone might miss a shot, maybe I get free with the whomping stick." Jack stepped in to Rooker. "So I rely on something simple. Something close."

Sweat beaded on the pirate's brow. "Yer paranoid, Jack."

Jack lifted Rooker's new jacket. Strapped to the pirate's chest was a stiletto, its edge sharp.

Jack stared at the blade. Guessing the truth was one thing. Seeing it was another.

He felt his mind crack again, and part of his soul went with it. *Alone.*

Rooker jerked away from him, his face twisted in anger.

Jack felt the hopeless void waiting to swallow him. His voice was quiet. "What's the matter, Rooker? You already killed me once. It's probably easier the second time."

Rooker slowly pulled the knife from its harness. "Let's find out."

The hatred in Rooker's eyes came from a different man, one Jack had never met. He gripped the bamboo rod and stepped back.

A smooth snarl crossed Rooker's face and he showed his canines. "I never thought I'd meet a better liar than me, but I gotta admit, boychick, ya got me beat. Every word outta you's a lie. Who ya are. Where yer from. What ya want. And I believed you. Ya hoodwinked me good, Jack." He raised the knife. "But now I see ya for who ya are. The man standing between me and the *Brigand*."

Jack backed away. "So that's the deal. Nepenthe for the *Brigand*."

Rooker closed the distance between them. "Summon the stick." He lifted the blade. "Now."

The hard shine in Rooker's eyes was vicious. Animal. A creature of pure survival. *He'll kill me.* Jack squared his shoulders. *Maybe I can—*

"Ya can't beat me. Not without Nepenthe." The blade gleamed in Rooker's hand. "Ya want a chance? Summon the stick."

Alone.

Staring into Rooker's eyes, he felt his own anger turn sour, curdling to despair.

You were my friend. You were my only *friend.*

Rooker glanced out the library window. Night was fading, the sun threatening to rise over the Irridin. He gripped Jack's shirt in his fist and yanked him close enough to smell his breath. "The only reason ya haven't summoned it is because yer a *coward*." Rooker leaned in close. "Because without Nepenthe, you. Are. *Nothing*."

Nothing.

Not a hero. Not a legend. Just a scared kid clinging to a lie, a mask Rooker Flynn had invented. Once Gerba took Nepenthe away, Black Jack would be gone. And without that...

(nothing, that's all you are)

Rooker shook Jack, rattling his teeth. *"Summon it!"*

He could feel the power in his hands, feel Nepenthe begging to come together in a violent *tak-a-tak-a-tak* of radiant blue majik.

One last time.

Alone.

Jack let out a breath. He had lost too much. He couldn't let go of the last piece of himself.

"No."

Rooker released him. Jack fell back. His hand touched his throat, feeling the impressions of Rooker's fingers there. *God help me. Please.*

"Arright," growled Rooker. "Fine." He glanced at the predawn sun. A new day was dawning. A desperation sounded in Rooker's voice. "Ya won't listen to me. Ya won't listen to anyone in Keymark." Rooker's voice came low. "But I know someone ya *will* listen to."

Jack froze as he saw Rooker's eyes filled with pure hate.

"Summon it," he said, his voice cold as ice. "Or I swear by the Lord of Sea and Sky, I will help her track down yer *dad*."

As the word left the pirate's lips, one thought split Jack's skull. There was no hesitation, no uncertainty, just one thought.

I'll kill you.

"Nepenthe."

A thunderclap split the room with a flash of blue lightning. Jangling, sizzling *wikk* surged up Jack's arm, the bamboo in his hand electric, purring raw majik, ready to strike, ready to kill, ready to serve him. Nepenthe's azure flame blazed brightly.

Rooker retreated a step, his eyes wide and frightened.

Nepenthe sung like a furious choir roaring majik. The room distorted and bent inward toward Jack's hand as if Gerba's office was a neutron star collapsing upon itself. Nepenthe's shriek grew louder, screaming, deafening.

The bent room broke like a bubble as a single dart of blue light came like a comet, arriving from nowhere. The lightning collided with the stick in Jack's hand with a sharp *tak!* The electricity in his fist doubled, a shocked vibration that thrummed through his body, making him feel as if he were aflame.

Then it ended.

The star went out, the choir fell silent. The flood of energy disappeared like a snap, gone like fairy dust.

In despair, Jack looked at the thing in his hands. He clutched nothing but a bamboo baton. Two joints of wood shorter than his arm, a truncated version of his seven-piece stave.

No.

Spider webs hit Jack's fist and pasted it to his chest.

No. Nepenthe—

Blue sticks ripped out of Jack's right hand, tearing through the webs. Their path bent in the air, seeking Jack's left. He caught the first and the other joined it with a sharp *tak-tak!*

I can—

More webs hit him, binding his left arm. Attercops descended from the cupola above, half a dozen of them, spraying him with jets of silk.

Jack felt something stab into his thigh. An instant numbness passed through his leg, bringing him to one knee. More webs hit him, lashing him to the floor.

Jack saw two streaks of molten metal leap up from the fireplace and hurtle toward him. They hit Nepenthe, knocking it loose.

The sticks clattered to the floor, coated in white-hot metal. Jack stretched out his hand and called Nepenthe to him, but the sticks didn't budge. Neither piece could move, trapped.

"Cold iron." Gerba Whipmarples descend the library stairs. "I thought that might do the trick."

Jack struggled, but it was no good. The iron was already cooling around Nepenthe, binding the bamboo to the Institute, the same iron that inscribed his arm.

"Just one piece?" Gerba Whipmarples stood over him. "Where is the rest of it?"

Jack was paralyzed from the poison, helpless, his mind screaming.

Nepenthe is hers.

And I gave it to her.

Whatever was left of Jack Swift disintegrated. There was no more Jack Swift. There was nothing. Paralyzed from the waist down, beaten, betrayed, a sound that wasn't human escaped his lips, just the crazed snarl of an animal.

"Interesting." Gerba Whipmarples considered the sticks. "Well, let us look at the silver lining, shall we? Two down, five to go." She took a deep breath. "I am afraid the sun is up, Mister Flynn. Our agreement is forfeit."

Out of the corner of his eye, Jack watched Rooker's face drop. "I did what ya said!" A satisfying whine infused the pirate's voice. "He summoned it! I made him do it!"

"Our bargain was for you to deliver the entire staff, not a single piece of it." Gerba spread her hands with an unctuous smile. "A subtle distinction, but I believe in adhering to the letter of the law."

Unbidden, a sharp laugh split Jack's mouth. He felt a crazed boil gurgle up his throat at the dumbfounded look on Rooker's face. He laughed, high and wild. "Nothing!"

Rooker pleaded with the headmistress. "I thought... I thought if—"

Jack howled, then screamed, *"Nothing!"*

Gerba gestured and attercops descended upon Jack. "The doktar is hysterical. Get him out of here. Down to the coven." As the attercops seized Jack and lifted him into the air, she turned to one of the arriving acolytes armed with blowguns. "And take Mister Flynn back to Jackal camp."

Jack's hysterical laugh continued, high and shrill, as the attercops dragged him out of the room. His eyes never left the pirate.

"You stabbed me in the back, Rooker!" Jack screamed. "You sold me out! And for *what?* Nothing!"

The last thing Jack saw was Rooker staring at him, face white as a ghost. Then the webbing hit Jack's eyes and he was blind.

Jack laughed, screaming.

"Nothing!"

Chapter

3

SHADOW
OF
DEATH

I give the fight up: let there be an end,
a privacy, an obscure nook for me.
I want to be forgotten even by God.

Robert Browning

D OWN THEY PLUNGED, INTO the caves. Jack listened as his own lunatic laughter echoed against the rock like a spectral creature, the maniacal ghost of a dead man. His eyes watered as he plummeted into blackness with a giant spider wrapped around his back, screaming a howling bray that would never end.

"He's freaking me out," an attercop grumbled.

"Shaddup," snapped Winston. "We're almost there."

Jack's stomach heaved as rapid deceleration made him want to vomit. Slowing to a halt above the bottom, he found himself giggling as the spiders descended the last few yards to the tunnel floor.

"Okay, enough with this guy," Winston barked. "Clam him up."

Webbing slapped Jack's mouth shut. His lips were pasted together, his nose clogged with glue. Winston's eight eyes peered at him. "Can he still breathe?"

"Does it matter?"

"She said take him to the coven, so... alive... until they eat him."

"Let's get this over with. I hate the pit."

Legs scuffled along the rock as the attercops hauled him down the third fork—the one where no prisoners went willingly—and descended into the dark.

Jack felt like he was still falling. He had started falling the day he'd come to Huánghūn and he had been falling ever since. Jack had lost part of himself in the oubliette, another on the killing fields, another when Rooker had cut the cord. Too many pieces had broken away, too many to reassemble into the person he'd once been. Somewhere in the back of his head, the logical part of his brain counted the attercops' steps, soothing itself with numbers and reason, hiding in the corner of his mind like a frightened child.

Sunlight struck him as the rock opened to a massive lookout over the bay, and he realized he could see through a bit of the webbing. The dawn sun illuminated the pier beyond. Boats littered the golden harbor like bobbing toys just a few hundred yards away. In the distance, he saw the triple masts of the *Venture Brigand.*

Hysteria bubbled up inside him and he felt another blister of crazy escape his mind. *Never getting out now, are you, Rooker?*

(neither are you)

Jack heard a familiar voice in his head, a dark twin that prowled within.

(never getting out)

The vista disappeared and all light was lost, gone with the sea. For several minutes, Jack could not see a thing. Fresh air became stale as the moisture disappeared, replaced with the curdling stink of rotten eggs. Jack gagged into the web; the spiders seemed unaffected by the stench, speeding their descent.

A reddish-orange light blossomed ahead, joined by the low rumbling of something large. The rational part of Jack's mind continued counting and tried to figure out what the sound was. It felt like the cave was trembling slightly, the slow grind of rock all around him, a continuous earthquake. Curious, the logical piece of his mind wondered where the light was coming from. *Torches?*

They rounded a corner.

No.

Lava.

A trickle of boiling magma bubbled down the wall of the cavern and joined a slow stream that crept downhill into the dark. The heat hit Jack all at once, bone dry air hotter than a Death Valley summer. Sweat broke out on his flesh and trickled into the webbing around his nose.

Something cold looped around Jack's wrist. A lightchain. The attercops clipped the other end to a metal ring in the ceiling. "All right," breathed Winston, relieved. "Let's get back up top." And the attercops were gone.

Alone in the dark, illuminated only by the red of the chain and the orange of the lava, Jack stood, waiting. As the swelter of the cavern settled upon him, Jack felt his nostrils and his throat go dry. Sweat trickled down his face and neck. The webbing around his mouth dried out and drew tighter, then disintegrated from the heat. Panting, he choked on the sulfuric fumes.

His mind wasn't right. The objective part of him recognized the truth, but there was nothing it could do to stop it. He felt dizzy, elated, depressed, angry, everything all at once, unable to filter his mind into distinct emotions. Time seemed out of joint, slipping sideways. He wasn't even sure he was conscious, convinced he kept passing out and not knowing it. If there had been someone to talk to, someone to ask—

But no. There was no one. He was alone in the dark.

Alone.

(alone)

The chill echoed in his mind. The hair on his arms stood on end and something frigid spidered up his spine.

I know what you are. Jack's eyes searched the darkness.

(i know what you are)

The voice was an icicle in his brain, slick and jagged. Jack watched a shadow emerge from the cave wall, towering over him. The gigantic apparition of a wolf.

(i know you so well)

The shadow paced on four long legs. Jack heard the slow click of sharp claws circle him. He turned to find nothing but darkness. *It's just fear, just fear.*

The shadow grew larger.

(i am the only thing that remains)

Its hungry voice whispered behind him. Jack glanced over his shoulder and saw... nothing.

(all alone)

Jack swallowed.

(just like)

He turned.

(you've always)

He spun.

(been)

Fangs snapped at his face.

Jack lurched backward and held up a hand to defend himself. There was nothing there but the fading echo of a wolf's snarl. Nothing but a lupine shadow cast large upon the wall.

Jack sucked in a breath. The shadow loomed over him. No part of Jack, neither the hysterical lunatic nor the analytical scientist, wanted to laugh now. His heart pounded in his throat.

(he never loved you)

Jack heard the wolf's bitter words somewhere behind him. He spun, knowing he would see nothing.

(you were just an unlucky penny)

Jack swallowed. "You're not real!"

(no)

Rooker Flynn lunged at him, snarling, holding the knife. Jack stumbled back and felt the chain yank tight, suspending him by his wrists, helpless. Rooker growled and disappeared into the dark.

(not real)

As Jack gathered his feet beneath him, he heard footsteps approaching. He put up his hands to defend himself, expecting something to strike from the dark.

Two shadowy figures came into view, dragging something between them. Jack eyed them as they approached, not sure if they were real or not.

"Help me, help me, help me."

(no one will help you)

As the figures drew closer, Jack realized they were acolytes, their robes black as soot.

The thing they were dragging was a corpse.

Thin and emaciated, the cadaver looked as if it had been sucked dry, shriveled as a slab of jerky. As Jack's eyes adjusted, he saw the crocodilian tail drag behind it. The llystra's scaly flesh was pocked with bite marks and Jack realized he knew the corpse's face.

(another old friend)

Axie. One of Mamba's underbosses. Jack barely recognized him; the corpse was so desiccated it was nearly mummified. Part of Jack, the lunatic part, wanted to laugh at seeing the murderer dead; the other part was repulsed by how disfigured the body was.

(why so dry)

Arriving at their destination, the acolytes lit a lantern. As its light blossomed, Jack saw a black cage large enough for half a dozen men. At the back of the cage, embedded within the rock wall, was a round brass door that flickered in the lantern light.

The acolytes dragged Axie's body inside the cage and dumped it on the ground. They exited quickly, locking the door behind them with a swing-bar.

Jack narrowed his eyes. *What are they afraid of?*

(what are you *afraid of?)*

Grunting, the men turned a crank and slowly rolled open the big brass door. Beyond lay nothing but darkness.

Churr.

A yellow leg reached out of the black. A single shiq emerged into the lantern light and skittered toward Axie's body. Another darted in behind it, beating it to the prize. A third tackled the second, fangs lashing into its body. More shiq arrived, killing each other to get to the corpse. Axie was lifted into the air by a forest of legs, then pulled into the swarm and torn in half, quarters, eighths. Fighting each other for the meal, the swarm dragged the body out of the cage, back into the darkness. As the shiq fled with their meal, the acolytes rolled the round brass door shut.

Nothing was left inside the cage.

(that is where they will dispose of your corpse)

Jack's mind screamed at itself. *Help me, help me, help me, O God help me.*

(God will not help you)
Stop.
(only I can help you)
Jack felt the soft pelt of a wolf brush his leg.
(if you let me in)
Jack shot a breath from his nose. Shadow's fur brushed against him, stroking his skin, soft, seductive.
No.
(then be alone, boy)
Jack looked and the wolf was gone. Breathing through his nose, he waited for it to return, but the silence lingered. The wolf, the shiq, and the acolytes were all gone. Jack hung by his chain in silence, joined by no sound but the shifting rock that surrounded him.

He had no idea how long he waited there, hanging from the chain. It could have been a few hours or a week. Trapped with his arms over his head, his shoulders burned like fire. Jack's mind drifted, afraid to close his eyes, afraid to keep them open. He felt the fumes addling his head, and his mind drifted, senseless. After a while, he found himself wanting the wolf to come back, if only to have someone to talk to.

The jingling of glass woke him. Tuneless music clattered from a wheelbarrow pushed by a cream-robed acolyte. Jack blinked and saw two more acolytes walk a hooded llystra past him, escorting the croc along the stream of lava.

"Praise RākŞhasa, it's about time." A black-robed acolyte emerged from the area below, his voice irritated. "I was starting to worry you forgot about us."

"Have we ever missed a day?"

The black-robed acolyte jerked his chin at Jack. "What's the story with him?"

"Him too."

Jack's lightchain was released from the ring and the acolytes escorted him down the lava stream. As he passed the wheelbarrow, Jack saw the source of the jingling sound, a hundred little glass cups, each sealed with a cap, each filled with thick crimson liquid.

Those are the cups they use to take our blood.

At the bottom of Huánghūn lay the lava pits. Boiling pools of magma bubbled at the terminus of the cave, a lake of fire. The heat was so intense the air shimmered. Through the haze, Jack saw a silhouette blocking the magma, a gigantic floor-to-ceiling iron lattice wall that separated the cave from the lava pits, the largest cage on the island.

"Come on," muttered an acolyte. "They're getting hungry."

As he was forced toward the lava pit, Jack started. *Did something just... move?*

At the center of the blazing pool of molten rock, Jack watched a shimmering shadow shift. In the heat haze, he saw the thing take a step. Then another. A pale figure took shape and emerged from the smoke, walking through the lava.

That's impossible.

Jack's lightchain was clipped to the lattice. The acolytes opened a small portcullis in the wall and shoved the llystra through, ripping off his hood as they did. Jack recognized the assassin known as the Leech, another Mamba underboss.

"Hey... guys..." Leech sounded nervous. "I didn't—"

One of the acolytes grabbed a soot-blackened sword and shoved it through the bars at the assassin. "Defend yourself."

Jack watched the pale creature step from the lava and walk purposefully toward Leech, dripping magma.

My God.

The thing was horrific. It walked upright on two legs but was nothing close to human. Dark smoke steamed from its powerful body, its skin paper-white and strapped with lean muscle. Unnaturally long arms hung from narrow shoulders, its fingers like black knives.

Jack could smell the thing, a stench he had breathed before. He felt the claw marks that permanently scarred his back prickle fire. *A dæmon.*

Panicked, Leech screamed at the guards, "Let me out! Let me—"

The dæmon tilted its head and hissed. Black smoke escaped its lips, wispy tendrils wreathed its head, and all Jack could see were its red eyes. It darted for the prisoner, faster than a cat. Leech buried his sword deep into the thing's chest as it came. The dæmon never broke stride. It slammed the assassin into the iron lattice and wrapped its mouth around the man's neck. The rumbling of the cave was split by the dæmon's horrific roar that drove fear to the center of Jack, the terrible cry of a predator as it made a kill. Leech flailed and kicked as the dæmon feasted on his jugular, each movement weaker than the last, until he finally hung limp. The dæmon gorged on his neck, a nauseating sucking sound issuing from its needle mouth.

Jack watched the pale vampire suck the life out of Leech.

The acolytes dumped the barrow of blood vials through the iron lattice. Some bounced, some shattered on the stone. As they rolled to a stop, Jack watched a second pale dæmon emerge from the lava, followed by another. They came to the lattice and tore open the glass cups, pouring the blood down their throats. When no cups remained, the dæmons crouched and licked the floor.

Jack stared, his breath quiet as a fieldmouse trying to avoid the attention of a wolf.

(now you see what all men fear)

The wolf's fur brushed against the back of his leg.

(now you see your death)

Jack couldn't take his eyes off the dæmons.

(the strigoi can smell you now)

One of the pale figures raised its head to stare at Jack with coal-red eyes. Black smoke issued from between needle teeth.

(how long until they feast upon you?)

Jack collapsed and turned away from the monster, only to find himself staring into the red eyes of the feral wolf. Its fangs snapped at his face. Jerking back, Jack jammed his eyes shut, but the lupine visage of the wolf was there in the blackness with him.

(you cannot hide from me)

Gasping, Jack smelled the wolf's reeking breath as it opened its mouth to a slavering grin of white teeth. He cowered from it, trembling.

What do you want?

(I want to take you away from this)

Jack swallowed. He glanced at the bloody dæmons, then stared into the wolf's eyes.

(confess you are mine and the strigoi will not touch you)

Jack's mouth moved but nothing came out.

(surrender to me)

Go to hell.

(look around, boy. you are already here)

The wolf leaned in, its eyes hungry and feral.

Leave me alone.

(you are alone)

Jack hung his head. I'm so tired. So tired.

(everyone has abandoned you)

Rooker. Rooker was gone. His only friend in the world had killed him.

(alone)

No. Dad. Dad is—

(gone)

A million miles away, locked in another universe.

Jack thought of Rajiv Banerjee, of Patch Picaroon, but they were no help. He reached deeper, further back into his memory, searching for someone, anyone, to lend him strength, anyone who would not abandon him.

He tried to imagine the face of Valerian Tsai. The Border Knight had rescued him countless times during his first visit to Keymark, the strongest and most noble man Jack had ever met. But the knight's kindly face simply would not come, hidden and silent behind his steel helm.

(the grey man cannot help you now)

Memphis Kubiak. The big brown trol had been almost like an uncle to Jack, a wizard, a protector. When Memphis had been with him, Jack had known he'd had nothing to fear. He tried to picture Memphis' face, his acorn-brown eyes, his loving smile, but the only trol he could picture bore the long, bejeweled horn of Gerba Whipmarples.

(accept the truth)

Jack sagged in his chains, his head hung low. No one was coming for him. No knights or wizards, not Dad, not Rooker. He was cut off from the world.

(only i will never leave you)

So tired.

(come to me and rest)

Temptation closed its grip. Giving in to fear would be so easy. He had been terrified from the moment Chem 509 had turned into a madhouse. Every day, Jack had been afraid. Every night, he'd lain in his hammock and visualized the shiq breaking into the clique, flooding over him in a tangle of legs.

(alone)

Soft fur brushed against Jack's neck, against his cheek, as the wolf's head crept over his shoulder.

(surrender)

Jack reached up and stroked the wolf's neck, feeling its warm coat between his fingers.

Why not? Why not give up? Let it swallow him down and disappear inside.

(yes)

So tired.

(yes)

I can't keep going.

(no)

I can't. I can't.

"You can, doktar. And you will."

He heard her voice like the melody of a flute. Jack saw her face clearly as if she were standing right in front of him. Her red hair was cropped short, a cunning smile on her lips. Jack's heart beat faster as her green eyes shone.

Leah Archer.

The only woman he had ever loved.

She was a Keymark girl, Valerian Tsai's daughter, and part of Jack had loved her from the moment they'd met. Leah had been an impossible aspiration for the boy he'd once been, too beautiful, too perfect, so far above him as to be unreachable. And yet, in Chicago, he had daydreamed of her constantly, replaying their every conversation with perfect clarity. He had confessed the truth to Rooker once, that during his nights on Huánghūn, Jack kept Leah Archer's memory close to his chest, a tiny ember of hope, a fantasy that she would somehow save him. It was a secret dream, a child's dream, one he was barely able to admit to himself.

Leah.

For love, he could go on.

"Yes." She stared into his eyes. "You can."

(no)

Her pretty face distorted, twisting, her gentle brow curling into a cruel scowl. Her voice became harsh. "No one will save you." Her flesh stretched and grew black fur, hideous, and the wolf emerged from beneath Leah's skin, grinning sharp teeth.

(she will never even know you were here)

Jack's eyes flashed open and he faced the wolf.

(no one will save you)

No one will save me.

Jack Swift felt like he had been falling into a bottomless pit since he'd arrived on Huánghūn. Here, in the bowels of the island, he finally hit rock bottom.

Here, with nothing left to lose, his heart turned to stone.

No one will save me.

"Only me." Jack planted one foot on the rock.

(no)

He stood. "Only me."

(no)

Jack straightened in his chains. "I don't need you."

(surrender)

"I don't need anyone."

(stop it, boy)

"The boy is dead." Jack's voice came hard as flint. "All that's left is me."

The wolf snarled at him.

Jack snarled back.

The wolf drew away, retreating into the dark, becoming nothing more than a shadow on the wall again. It twisted, diminishing, growing weaker. It growled, but it was the sound of a dog, not a wolf.

(you will beg for me in the end)

It raised its mouth at the sky and howled. Then it was gone.

Despite the exhaustion, despite the heat, despite the dæmons in the lake of fire, Jack Swift stood.

Alone.

Gerba Whipmarples stood alone.

She remained still for a long, long time, her hands behind her back, eyes toward the ground. In her hand was a red leather book with a clever little lock on the outside cover, open to one of the passages she had memorized years ago.

And the mighty Kos
trapped RākŞhasa
in the blood of the earth,
and at the center lies its heart.

Between Gerba's tremendous feet lay two rods of bamboo, lashed to the floor with molten iron. Blue light crawled within Nepenthe's etchings, reflected in her sea-green eyes.

Such marvelous potential.

"Headmistress?"

Gerba turned, masking the Book of Kos behind her hand. "Yes, Portia?"

"We are ready to return Mister Flynn to camp."

"And Boss Mamba's sycophants?"

"Removed, headmistress."

Gerba nodded. Rooker Flynn would make an excellent new informant for Jackal. He was slipperier than an eel, but Gerba Whipmarples had never met a greedier man, and the pirate understood who buttered his bread. *My creature. My slave.* "Very good, Portia. You may go."

"Headmistress?"

Gerba let irritation enter her voice. "Yes?"

"What do you want done with Black Jack?"

Gerba held her tongue. She had been rash to send him to the pits, she knew it, but she had acted out of the hatred she bore the little doktar. At every turn he had acted like a child, refusing to share what was his. Impudent. Unmannerly. Insolent. Nepenthe, once whole, would lead her to the Heart of Huánghūn, and Gerba Whipmarples would have gladly killed him to get it.

But now, it seemed, she had little choice but to keep Black Jack alive, at least until Nepenthe was whole. She couldn't leave him with the coven forever. *Still.* "We will keep him in the pits for a while longer." She folded her hands behind her back. "Just to make sure he has his mind right."

"Yes, headmistress." As Portia turned to go, Niko, the hammerdwarf crew boss, approached, his hat in his hand.

"You wanted me?" Niko squinted at her. "If this is about the construction on Bounty, everything is going to plan. I've got—"

"Niko." Gerba smiled. "My darling." She spread her hand at the two sections of Nepenthe welded to the floor. "I would like to bolt these pieces of wood to the wall near my desk. Like a hunter's trophy." She gestured to the empty wall. "Each piece stacked atop the other. Each hinged and locked in cold iron."

"Bolted lock clasps?" Niko scratched his beard. "Shouldn't take long to build two of 'em."

"Seven."

She watched as one of the pieces of Nepenthe glowed, vibrating against the molten iron.

"Seven?" Niko raised an eyebrow. "Forgive me headmistress, but I only see two."

Gerba looked at the cupola. At the center of the dome, she saw the faint shimmer of majik. Barely discernable, the air there vibrated, matching the hum of Nepenthe's *wikk*. And ever so slightly, rimmed in vapor blue, the edges of the universe bent.

The portal was small. It was slow. But like a pregnant animal, it pulsed with life, waiting to bring forth something new.

Gerba Whipmarples smiled. "Who knows what tomorrow will bring?"

Chapter

4

KING RAT

_Better to reign in Hell
than serve in Heaven._
John Milton

R UMORS OF BOSS MAMBA'S murder ran through Jackal camp like wildfire. Black Jack was presumed dead, as was every other convict who hadn't returned from the nobles' thrill kill. With no obvious heir at the top of the food chain, the power vacuum was filled by warring outlaws who all claimed prime position. In the morning hours, no fewer than a dozen outlaws fought over who would ultimately succeed Boss Mamba upon the throne of Jackal camp.

According to Rooker Flynn, the answer was obvious: Rooker Flynn.

Attercops dumped him halfway up the dirt path to the camp and turned their backs, returning to the Institute without a word. Rooker had had no sleep since the killing fields. He was exhausted and reeked of dragon. But worst of all was the cold truth that kept hitting him like a punch to the gut: He'd taken his shot at the *Venture Brigand*... and missed. Nothing! Rooker could still hear Jack screaming at him as the attercops dragged him into the pits; the sound clanged in his brain like an alarm bell. *Nothing!*

Damn kid. Rooker dusted off his bloody denims. *Damn, damn kid.*

Nothing!

We'll see about that.

He took a circuitous route through the jungle and snuck into the far end of Jackal camp without being seen. He clambered up the back porch rail of his clique and snatched all his hidden treasures from his secret stash in the roofline. As he stuffed his pockets, he peeked out at the camp. Near the water tower, convicts shouted at each other, shoving and arguing, each trying to show they were the strongest Jackal of the bunch. Most of the camp just watched, enjoying the show. *Good.*

Rooker glanced up at the boss clique, Mamba's old digs on top of the hill. Only Copper Dave, the cartel legbreaker, stood outside, watching the commotion. *He's not bright enough to shine a shoe. Even better.*

Sneaking back into the jungle, he hooked around to the back side of the boss clique and shimmied up the deck strut. At the top, he felt the world tilt as his head swam. His body felt like wet clay, his brain was oatmeal, and his exhaustion was beginning to show. He crouched in the shadows for a moment and caught his breath. It was only yesterday he had outrun the nobles, outfoxed the shiq...

(and killed your only friend)

Rooker jammed his eyes shut. *Toughen up.*

When he came around the corner, he was smiling and relaxed, like he owned the joint. "Heya Copper Dave, how's tricks?"

The big croc took a step backward, surprised. "Rooker? I thought—"

"Don't try thinkin', Dave, it's not yer strong suit. I got somethin' for ya." He opened his hands, revealing a dozen slices of galt and a buck knife from his stash. Dave's eyes widened and reached for it. "Not here, they'll see. Inside."

Curious, Copper Dave followed Rooker inside the clique. *Empty. Good.*

Dave grabbed the galt and shoved a few pieces in his mouth, fingering the ridiculous macaroni heart necklace he wore that looked like it had been slapped together by a child. "They say you dead. Nobles kill. Hunting game."

Rooker ignored him, digging around the edges of Mamba's mattress. "I'm going to make you a rich man, Dave."

"Rich?" The big llystra folded his arms over his chest. "For do what?"

Rooker found the treasures hidden deep in Mamba's mattress. He palmed the gold necklace and the pouch of coins, then held up the jeweled snuff box. "All ya gotta do is nothin'."

He tossed the box to Dave, who caught it and looked at it as if it was a dead fish. "What I do with snuff box? Is for fancy people."

"Trade it. Sell it. Never know what yer gonna find next." Rooker kicked up a floorboard, revealing another secret cache of loot. In the next few minutes, Copper Dave watched wide-eyed as Rooker ferreted out all of Mamba's hidden hoards. He discovered treasures in the water barrel, in the rafters, under the rug, and sealed within a hollowed-out beam. Three machetes, ten knives, twenty pounds of galt, four flasks of alcohol, a dozen cigars, and the map of Mamba's hidden khef farms.

Keep movin'. This ain't gonna last long. Everyone's gonna want a piece of me. He tossed a cigar to Copper Dave. "Go get Patch."

"I spotted you the moment you snuck into camp." Patch Picaroon lounged in the doorway, her slinky feline figure silhouetted against the sun.

Rooker snorted. *Always in the right place.*

He jerked his thumb at Copper Dave. "Go get Jape. Keep it quiet and don't mention my name." As the big llystra exited, Rooker turned on Patch. The jinx-cat was manicured as ever, her coat silky and groomed. "What do they know?"

The nobles had dismissed Patch from the thrill kill before it had begun, but she had seen everything from the prison wagon, and the story had made her a celebrity in camp. Rooker was surprised to learn Billy Pilgrim had also survived the thrill kill, but the troubadour was crazy and mute, which left Patch in the enviable position of being the only outlaw in Jackal camp who could tell the tale. She kept the bones of the story. Mamba and Bocephus, both camp bosses, were dead. So were Fancy Nan and several others.

Beyond that, Patch's version of the truth took on some fanciful embellishments.

In her version of the thrill kill, the nobles were cast as sneering popinjays, the outlaws as bold renegades who wouldn't back down. They laughed in the face of death, too clever to die, and hurled insults at the ass-sniffing nobles as they escaped into the jungle, laughing. According to Patch, Rooker Flynn had dropped his pants and mooned the nobles from the edge of the killing field. One dandy pursued on a stallion, but Black Jack stole the horse and disappeared into the jungle. The popinjay had come back to the pavilion with a broken arm, crying into his silk shirt.

Jackal camp couldn't get enough of Patch's version of the story. With each new telling, it grew more elaborate. And expensive.

"Mooned 'em, huh?" Rooker grinned. "I like that."

"I always thought you'd go out showing your ass." Patch grinned. "By the way, Baronet Ket was crowned King of the Hunt. He seemed proud of himself."

"Are those pukes gone?"

"The nobles? Sailed off yesterday before sunset. They weren't sticking around for the shiq." Patch folded her arms and eyed him suspiciously. "Everybody thought you were dead. Especially me."

"Disappointed?"

"How did you survive a night in the jungle?" The jinx-cat leaned in. "And where's Jack?"

Same answer to both questions: I killed him.

Rooker held no illusions that the kid might still be alive. When Jack failed to summon Nepenthe, Rooker had seen the killing rage in Gerba Whipmarples' eyes. He'd witnessed fury like that a few times in his life, and every time it had ended with a corpse.

"Go get the rest of the Big Six. When ya get back, I'll tell ya how things are gonna be."

"I'm first mate," stated Patch. "*That's* how things are going to be."

The two pirates eyed each other like dogs about to bite.

Rooker set his jaw. Patch was too cunning and too dangerous. If she wasn't with him, she'd be against him, and letting her go with another crew would mean murder. Rooker would get the upper hand on the jinx sooner or later, but Patch Picaroon would cost him.

Still. A woman first mate? "I've got Copper Dave and Jape already."

"Don't insult me. Neither of them can do what I can do and you know it." Patch leaned in. "You've got five big mobs in camp: the llystra, the Shavers, the Rimmy's Cull cartel, Kubla Klan, and the women. Everyone wants the throne for themselves and the only reason they haven't taken it yet is because nobody's sure who's strongest. Plus, all of Mamba's underbosses have gone missing. Almost as if the Locke Institute was clearing the path for the next boss."

Rooker kept his face carefully blank. Patch tilted her head, her eyes too smart for her own good. One eyebrow lifted in a question. "If Black Jack is gone…"

She waited. Rooker didn't say a word, staring her down. *Even if I wanted to, I couldn't say the words.*

"…then I'm the closest thing you've got to a brain." Patch relaxed, sat in a chair, and put her boots up. "If you want to take all comers with just Copper Dave and Jape, feel free. We'll see how long you last."

"I'll get Keeper and Sykes." Rooker was almost certain he could bribe the cartel bruisers into compliance. Almost.

Patch's eyes narrowed. "If you want killers, you need Murpy and Frost."

"And Oleg from the Shavers…"

"Plus Needles. He's crap in a fight but intimidating as hell."

Rooker nodded. *She knows what she's doing. And my old mate is dead.* He shot air through his nose. "Get 'em all here in five minutes and ya got the job."

Patch spat in her palm and extended her paw. "Spit on it."

"You and me, Patch." Rooker spat and shook her hand. "You and me."

By the time the pretenders to the throne realized what was going on, Rooker Flynn was barricaded inside the boss clique, defended by eight bloody assassins. Each killer had been paid handsomely from Mamba's treasure trove and knew that as long they protected Rooker's claim, they were the new Jackal underbosses.

Patch stood on the balcony, telling everyone to calm down. Rooker would see them one at a time and assign their new position. As an extra bit of fun, she told them to choose amongst themselves who should go first, which resulted in a half-hour fistfight between the would-be chiefs. In the end, one of the Shavers took the honor of approaching the throne first and stormed inside the boss clique.

For the next fifteen minutes, the Shaver captain railed at Rooker, insulting him, pacing up and down the rug and shouting. He enumerated the reasons he should be boss and illustrated the injuries that would happen to Rooker if he tried to stand in his way. During the entire harangue, Rooker barely looked at him, trying to achieve the perfect alchemy of mango juice and moonshine.

When the Shaver was done, Rooker sipped his drink. "Do ya know the song about the lady and the walrus?"

"What?" The Shaver glared at him. "No."

"Ya sure?"

"No, I don't know it!"

"Damn. I keep tryin' to remember a line outta that song. It's on the tip of my tongue." Rooker shrugged. "Well. Yer no use to me. Copper Dave?"

The big llystra hefted a club. The Shaver's eyes went wide.

Moments later, he hurtled backward through the door onto the deck. His shirt was torn, his face was bloody, and his mouth was missing a few teeth. Rooker emerged after him, rolling up his sleeves. He kicked the Shaver in the jaw and sent him tumbling down the stairs, ass over teakettle. The man landed unconscious in the dirt. "Next."

Bluster and bravado had always served Rooker Flynn well. When it came to getting your way, the loudest man usually won. And there was nothing quite so loud as good old-fashioned violence.

He glared at the wannabe chiefs, challenging them to send up another victim.

"Hey, Flynn!" yelled a cartel pirate. "How did ya survive the jungle?"

"Where's Black Jack?" hollered a llystra bandit.

For once, Rooker kept his mouth shut. All he had to do was let their speculation grow unanswered, unfettered, and uncorrected. By morning, he'd be prison famous. And that, more than anything, would cement his position as top dog.

Better to have a good story than tell the truth.

The truth was no good at all.

Before the sun set, Rooker Flynn was the new Jackal boss. It was easier than being captain of a ship; all he had to do was stay out of sight and say no. The underbosses, led by Copper Dave, enforced his edicts, making it unnecessary for Rooker to make an appearance. Patch became the sole liaison between him and the rest of the camp and quickly developed a reputation as being the only reasonable person at the top and the only underboss who could get a yes from the new chief.

That night, Rooker Flynn slept alone for the first time in half a year.

Mamba's bed was big enough for four. Stuffed with goose down, it was soft as a pillow, like floating on a cloud. All around him within easy reach lay food, booze, weapons, and various treasures, piled up like a dragon's hoard.

And still he could not sleep.

He watched the shadows of the shiq crawl over his roof, churring, looking for a way in.

(see?)

Beside him in bed, Jasper blew a feather into the air, grinning.

(this is what you get when you do it my way)

Rooker ignored his dead brother and stared at the ceiling.

(everything you wanted, pip. all yours)

In his head, Rooker heard another, more freshly dead ghost laugh at him.

(nothing!)

Rooker twisted his rings around his middle finger and stared at the yingcao walls.

This is what I get.

He rolled over and Jasper was gone. Rooker stared at the expanse of the big clique, hollow and barren, a shadow that required no light, for there was nothing to see. He had the place all to himself, a luxurious emptiness.

He had never felt so lonely.

By the next morning, things had already fallen into a predictable pattern. Rooker took on Mamba's role as boss and made a brief appearance just after sunrise, then retreated to his clique while the rest of Jackal camp trudged off to their work assignments. With no one in camp but the sick and injured waiting for the next healing, Rooker rummaged about the boss clique, rearranging the furniture. He was bored out of his mind by the time the attercops came to fetch him.

Gerba Whipmarples waited for him inside the Institute on a quiet balcony thirty feet up the wall. Rooker winced as her knife cut his arm, but he had learned to ignore the initial pain of the bloodletting. He watched the glass cup fill with red and take another little piece of him. As he did, Gerba went through a list of questions about what had happened in Jackal. Who seemed most unhappy at the change? Who was the most well-positioned to make a move against him? How many galt were stored in Jackal? By the way she talked, the headmistress had more than one mole in every camp.

Rooker wondered who she had spying on him.

After what seemed like an endless string of questions, Rooker decided it was time to ask a few of his own. "How about the other camps? Is the distillery still running? Has Boss West been replaced?" *How did you kill Jack?*

"You bring me information, Mister Flynn," Gerba said, popping the cup from his arm and capping it. "Not the other way around. How many weapons are available in Jackal? And remember, I have figures from your predecessor. If I find you are lying to me, you can easily be replaced. I know it is difficult for you to tell the truth, but you must admit, working with the Institute has its privileges." She lifted the lid off a tray, revealing a plate of poached salmon and peas with a side of candied peaches.

Rooker told her everything he knew through a mouth stuffed with food.

He ate as much as he could but still felt empty. Jasper sat across the table from him, picking at the hunks of pineapple.

(this is the life, ain't it, brother?)

A prison snitch. Sure.

Rooker swallowed another bite, trying to fill the hole within.

By the end of their conversation, Rooker realized he'd traded more words with the headmistress than anyone in Jackal camp. As he got up to leave, Gerba placed one leathery finger, thick as a woman's arm, upon his chest.

"One last thing, Mister Flynn." Gerba dabbed her lips with a napkin. "We should discuss the *Venture Brigand*."

Rooker froze. His eyes flashed and, for a moment, his heart rose from its crypt. "Ya want me to pilot her."

"No, that ship has sailed, so to speak." She tittered at her own rotten joke. "But Cant Naysayer still believes you hold the key to making the *Brigand* sail as it should. If he is correct, I would consider meeting your price for such a key."

"Don't know what yer talkin' about." Rooker fingered the twin brass rings on his finger, spinning them. He would never hand the *Brigand* over, to Gerba Whipmarples, Cant Naysayer, or anyone else. *She's mine.* Rooker straightened, feeling, for once, like he had some control over Gerba. *At least I've still got that much pride left.*

Jasper grinned at him from the other side of the table.

(give it time)

Twenty days after his rule of Jackal had begun, Rooker played cards with Patch on the porch of the big clique overlooking the camp. The summer sun was high and hot, the mosquitoes were biting, and it looked like rain. Rooker had sweated through his second shirt of the morning and was ready for a third. He stripped it off, slung it over the rail, and let the breeze cool his sweat. It was an off-day, a lazy day. Not that the threats ever stopped on Huánghūn.

"How about the Shavers?" Rooker shuffled the cards and dealt.

"Working on ways to kill you." Patch sipped her chicory. "They're talking about punching a hole in your clique before sunset."

Rooker had a backup plan for that: There were four yingcao flytraps within fifty paces that would protect him from the shiq in a pinch. "And the llystra?"

"Them too." Patch raised him five galt. "You're not popular."

Rooker called the bet, wondering how Patch planned to come at him. He had never met a mate that didn't want the captain's chair. *Being closer just gives her the edge.* "And the Femme clique?"

Patch shrugged, too casual. "Still considering options. All we know is that Jackal would be better run by women."

Rooker scowled at the Institute, then the jinx. "Patch, this place *is* run by a woman."

"Point taken." She drew three, but Rooker saw her palm one from the crib deck in her sleeve. *Stay sloppy, Patch.* "We're gonna need to poison that Shaver boss." Rooker watched her deposit the extra card under her hip. "I'm thinking acullio in his food."

"That might not kill him."

"Don't have to kill him. Just make him look weak."

"We should infect him with something nasty. Maybe ringslug slime."

Rooker chuckled. Yesterday, some idiot in the lumber camp had gotten so desperate for food he'd swallowed one of the tree-eating ringslugs. His face had broken out in seeping yellow boils before he'd run out of oxygen from the pressure around his neck. "It would look good on him."

Jackal camp was a hive of two-faces waiting for an advantage, an opening, a moment of weakness. As top man, Rooker had the biggest bullseye on his back. More outlaws arrived every tenday, all of them still strong, still healthy.

Jasper eyed him, his feet propped up on the table.

(how long until you're the one with a knife in your eye, pip?)

Rooker palmed five cards and replaced his hand with a full boat. *I'll last longer than most.*

"Boss Flynn?" Copper Dave ran up the steps, out of breath. "Boss!"

Rooker snapped over his shoulder. "I told you, Dave, everything goes through Patch. Take it—"

"You want to see this." Something in the legbreaker's voice made Rooker turn. The llystra's face was pale green, his eyes wide.

"What..." Rooker eyed Patch. "What is it?"

"Frosh inbound."

"Frosh?" New cons never came straight to camp, they went through selection. *Always.* "Get yer head fixed, Dave, there's nobody..." He slipped off his rings, lined them up like a spyglass, and scoped the camp.

Way up toward the entrance, a crowd gathered on the path into Jackal. Shouts rang out, excited. Prisoners started running, curious to see what the commotion was. By the time the crowd rounded the last copse of palms, it had become a throng.

Rooker couldn't see the outlaw at the center of the mob. The figure was masked by a hundred bodies that blocked them from view. Nearly the entire camp joined the commotion. Their voices formed an excited babble as they jostled for position around the mysterious figure.

Who the hell is th—

Rooker caught a glimpse of a tall bamboo staff moving through the crowd, all black.

He shot to his feet, staring.

It can't be.

Upon his return from the thrill kill, Billy Pilgrim had taken up residence atop the roof of the water tower, where he spent his days constructing an ersatz banjo. His head *buh-buh*-banging days were over, but he still hadn't spoken a single word since the moment he'd arrived on Huánghūn. As the throng moved toward the water tower, Pilgrim screamed, a high cackle that almost sounded like laughter. Smiling, the mud-caked musician slung his banjo into position and belted out a lightning-fast strum in a major chord. Then, impossibly, Billy Pilgrim sang:

Ol' Black Jack, the man with the knack
Stole the people their money back
One quick flick of his walking stick
He fed the poor and healed the sick.
Black devils fear his cunning spear
He'll cut them down and disappear
So play us fair or just beware:
There's nothing ol' Jack wouldn't dare.

The crowd parted and Rooker saw the face of a ghost.

Jack Swift stood in the center of Jackal camp. The cloth draped over his shoulder was blackened with soot. His denims were black, his boots were black, his skin was black. His blackened staff was clutched in bloody knuckles. He drank from the tower pipe and splashed his face. Water carved clean lines through the filth, creating a mask, something otherworldly, a tribal shaman. His eyes were blue. His face was red with blood.

Rooker stagged backward and knocked his drink to the floor, where it shattered. *Impossible.*

"Is that him?" Rooker heard Patch's amazed voice behind him.

Copper Dave laughed. "He come back from dead!"

Rooker stared, unsure what to do. Mouth open, he descended the steps of the clique, drawn toward the water tower like a magnet to a lodestone.

He watched Jack's lips move and someone yelled, "We can't hear you!" "Speak up!" Billy Pilgrim reached down from the ladder. Jack extended his hand and climbed the water tower. The mute minstrel stared up at him like a hero. Most of the camp did the same, waiting. Rooker waited for the kid to duck his head or pull on his lip like he always did when he was thinking, but Jack stood arrow straight, his eyes fierce, sharp, and hard.

Rooker did not recognize the man who spoke.

"The Locke Institute tells us there are three rules!" Jack's voice struck like a whip. Rooker took an involuntary step back. "Obey your betters! Assemble at sunrise! Inside by sundown!" His blackened body was lean and hard, his movements like a coiled panther, burning with a predatory flame. "But on Huánghūn, there is only *one* rule: Every. Man. For. Himself." Jack pointed down at the crowd. "You steal galt from him, she steals a knife from you, and on it goes. We fight for scraps and all the while, Gerba Whipmarples sits up there and *laughs*."

Something shifted in the crowd. It started slow but grew momentum. Jeers and hisses and boos became shouts, hollers, and obscenities. Rooker watched the change ripple through the crowd and in that moment, Jackal camp was united in hatred. Jack's words came again, driving a needle into an ocean of untapped rage. "She gives us nothing! Nothing but sweat and blood and death! She says work will make us free, but the only freedom she offers is at the end of a rope!"

More shouts, more yells. Billy Pilgrim increased the tempo of his chords, lending Jack's voice a tremulous thunder. "As long as we stick to her rules, as long as we keep fighting each other, as long as it's every man for himself, the headmistress doesn't have to lift a *finger* to keep us down!" The crowd erupted into angry, swearing agreement. "Every time we steal from each other, it's a gift to her! We destroy each other and she wins! She's got us so far under her fat thumb, we've forgotten who the real enemy is." Jack stabbed one finger at the Locke Institute. *"Her."*

Jack's words drove the outlaws feral. Rooker couldn't believe his eyes. Three hundred convicts went ape, hollering at the top of his lungs. Rooker glanced around the crowd. The Shavers, the Cartel, the Femmes, the Red Tigers, Copper Dave, and Patch formed a more perfect union with every word.

The dark figure on top of the water shouted over them all. "Are you sick of playing by her rules?" Murderous cheers. "Are you done being manipulated?" More cheers. "Are you ready to fight back?" The response could be heard at the Institute itself.

Black Jack straightened to his full height. "Then we start with the bastards who *play her game!*" His voice was thunder. "The turncoats who will betray any one of us!" He lifted balled fists over the crowd as they hung on his every word. "There's only one name for someone like that!" Jack's cold eyes landed on Rooker Flynn. "A *rat.*"

Rooker froze. *O bloody hell.* Every inmate knows that there's only one thing convicts hate more than the warden, and that's a rat. *They'll tear me apart.*

Anger boiled over the Jackals. The blackened figure on top of the water tower looked every inch a legend, shouting at the top of his lungs. "We'll rip them out of Hyena! We'll tear them out of Buzzard! We'll whip them out of Vulture!" Jack threw up his fist. "Let's go hunt some rats!"

A thunderous roar exploded from the mob, the furious bellow of outlaws bent on murder.

Rooker stumbled backward toward the boss clique.

Black Jack swung down the ladder, landed on the ground, and unslung his staff. He strode across camp followed by a gang of three hundred killers, Copper Dave and half of Rooker's underbosses among them. They grabbed stone knives and clubs, driven to a frenzy, shouting for blood.

Jack stormed straight at Rooker.

So this is it. Never thought I'd get torn apart by a mob. Rooker steeled himself and balled his fists. There was no way he could make it back to the boss clique, and even if he did, the horde would tear it down to get at him. If he had to die, he wasn't going to run first.

He stared Jack down. The kid's eyes were like blue stilettos stabbing through his skull. Rooker slipped the knife from his belt, gripped the handle, and bared his teeth. *Well, if we're going, let's go.*

Jack marched straight up the hill at Rooker... and passed him without a second glance.

Tensed, ready to fight and die, Rooker blinked, dumbfounded.

Jack strode by him, over the rise, and into the jungle. Outlaws poured into the jungle, following their new leader.

Rooker stared ahead as the throng passed him like a wave around a rock. He felt his chest hitch and a wash of unused adrenaline shivered through his system, sour and prickly. He felt his knuckles sweating and realized he still held his playing cards, crushed in one fist.

He didn't even look at me.

Like I wasn't even here.

(because you're dead to him)

"Where are we going?" yelled one of the convicts.

"I don't know," said another as she moved past Rooker. "But I'm going with him!"

Rooker felt a shadow blot out the sun. He turned to find Copper Dave looming over him. "You come, boss." Rooker felt Dave's reptilian hand close around his shoulder. "Black Jack say make sure you come."

Rooker felt himself dragged into the current of the prison mob. "Come on, Rooker." Patch jumped excitedly. "We're going to kill a rat."

Chapter

5

KANGAROO COURT

*No man can put a chain about the ankle
of his fellow man without at last finding
the other end fastened about his own neck.*

Frederick Douglass

R OOKER WALKED LIKE A man approaching the gallows.

Convicts swarmed the jungle like a pack of shiq, a criminal horde out for blood. Copper Dave stuck close by, ensuring Rooker couldn't run off. Patch had a spring in her step and was as keen as she'd ever been, eyes flashing, claws bared. She looked like the old Patch Picaroon, the one who'd tried to outrun the *Venture Brigand*. The one Rooker had locked swords with so long ago. Her excitement was infectious; every outlaw brimmed with dark enthusiasm, eager for the kill.

And Jack's going to point 'em all right at me.

Rooker walked alone in the crowd, hoping his execution would be quick.

Jack called over Fargil Fleet, the dirty runner with the rabbit legs. "Get to Buzzard and Vulture camps, fast!" He had to shout over the crowd. "Get the bosses! Hook. Eightfingers. Let them know Black Jack called a meeting of all the chiefs. Tell them if they're not at Hyena by sunset, we'll be at war."

What the hell is he doing?

"War?" Fargil held up his hands. "Hey, look, I don't want to get involved in—"

"On your way back, pick up Farah."

Fargil blinked. "Who?"

"Fancy Nan's assistant," Jack shot back. "Black woman, young, bone thin. I want her here before sunset, get me?"

The runner blinked, realizing everyone was looking at him. "Yeah. Okay." Fargil took off into the jungle at a sprint.

"Billy." Jack gestured to the mute singer. Pilgrim bounded forward, eager, announcing his enthusiasm with a major chord. "You and Yenrab were chained together on the killing field. Did he say anything to you? Anything about the attercops? Or his brother?"

Rooker eyed Pilgrim. A month ago, the filthy scarecrow had been nothing but a babbling half-mad idiot incapable of stringing two syllables together. But today, for the first time, Billy Pilgrim had sung in full voice, and he'd sung Black Jack's tune. With so much enthusiastic adoration, Rooker half expected Pilgrim to speak.

It didn't happen. Billy stammered a few times, *buh-buh*-but didn't get anything out. He settled for shaking his head *no* but did it with a clown-sized grin on his face.

Jack smiled back. "I like your new banjo." Caked in mud, the troubadour blushed and cradled his ugly instrument like an infant. Jack moved ahead and Rooker watched Pilgrim stare after him, his expression identical to a schoolgirl in love. *He's got 'em eatin' out of his hand.*

Jack got ahead of the throng and, without breaking stride, broke through the trees into Hyena camp. Several prisoners milled about the yard, but few paid attention; only one convict took immediate notice.

"Jack!" Ransom, the blond con who had taken Jack under his wing during his early days in Hyena, broke into a delighted smile. "You're alive! I thought they got you! How did y—"

Ransom pulled up short as three hundred Jackals emerged from the tree line. Ignoring the crowd, Jack slung one arm around the man. "Good to see you too, Ransom."

"Yeah, I'm..." Ransom's face was white. "Wh-what's going on?"

"Where's Yenrab?"

"Um... he's..." Ransom pointed. "Over there."

Jack glanced in the direction Ransom indicated and addressed the Jackal mob. "Spread out. If any Hyenas try to leave, stop them." He gestured. "Ransom, Patch, Copper Dave, you're with me."

Copper Dave urged Rooker ahead; he had no choice but to follow.

Yenrab Bialik sat under a clique on a low rattan stool. A matching stool sat next to it, empty. The Red Dwarf stared into space, fingering a short length of chain, which rattled a low *clink-clink-clink*. His face was blank, made of stone. *Clink-clink-clink*. Jack arrived and stood beside him, waiting. Yenrab didn't seem to notice. *Clink-clink-clink*.

Jack broke the silence. "Yenrab, I need you to come with me."

Bloodshot eyes turned to Jack; a scowl crossed the dwarf's gapped teeth. "I ain't got nothin' to say to you, Freckle."

"Copper Dave." In a flash, the croc grabbed Yenrab, twisted his arm behind his back, and hauled him to his feet. "We're going to talk." The dwarf hurled curses at Jack, but Copper Dave jerked his arm and Yenrab shut up. As they followed Jack toward Boss West's old clique, Rooker saw Hyenas and Jackals squaring off. The Hyenas were shocked to find so many enemies in camp and were too startled to start anything, but the détente wouldn't last long.

Jack tromped up the steps into Boss West's old clique, followed by his crew. It was dark inside, almost black. "Dave, wait outside," Jack commanded. "If anybody tries to enter or leave this clique, break their legs."

"Whatever you say, boss."

Rooker eyes adjusted, and he was surprised to find the clique unlooted. Not a single convict had set foot in Major Bocephus West's clique since he'd died. The place was a shrine. In life, the old major had kept up his military standards; every inch of his clique was ship-shape and squared away.

Jack lit a candle, let the flame kindle, and faced them. "One of us is a rat."

Rooker swallowed. *So. He's gonna have* them *do me in.*

As the others reacted, Jack spoke again. "We're the only ones still alive who knew about the escape tunnel. We were all there when Barney died and the attercops captured us." Jack lit another candle. "But the 'cops *never* come to camp. They're lazy. Stupid. They can't even remember our names or which camp we're in." Jack shook out the match. "In six months, they've only been to camp two times: the day we found the tunnel and the day we delivered Thunderbuck. So why did they come on *those two days?*" Jack's eyes landed on Rooker. "Someone told them what we were up to. And they're sitting right here."

Rooker listened as stunned silence sucked the air out of the room. Each criminal glanced at the other, suspicious. Rooker scowled, shifting. *I didn't sell out to the 'cops. He's trying to pin this on me?*

Jack raised a finger. "It wasn't Boss West. He was furious the 'cops were in his camp. And it wasn't poor dead Barney. He wanted that tunnel more than any of us." Jack shifted his gaze. "Which brings us to Patch."

The jinx edged away from him, eyes narrowing.

"You were at the sinkhole," he said. "And you weren't invited."

Patch scowled. "If you think—"

"I don't." Jack spread his hands. "We kept you out of the Thunderbuck deal on purpose. You didn't even know about it until it was over. Which eliminates you."

Patch breathed a sigh of relief. "Then why am I—"

"Because you're the only one who knows about the tunnel that I can trust. *That's* why you're here." He turned. "To help me with these three."

Rooker swallowed. He glanced at Yenrab and Ransom. *He's gonna put me on the hook for something I didn't do.*

"Yenrab."

The dwarf snarled at him. "Y'all think I flipped on my own twin, Freckle? You got some sand."

"You were there for Thunderbuck, and you got away without getting caught. But at the tunnel, you were missing." Jack took a step closer. "Barney said you were too drunk to dig. Maybe that's true. Or maybe you were talking with the 'cops."

Yenrab scowled. "You don't know what in tarnation you're yap-pin' about!"

Jack stuck a finger in Yenrab's face. "You threatened to turn us in to the 'cops when we first met, and you *always* thought tunneling was a bad idea."

"It was too risky! I told him!" Yenrab threw his muscled arms in the air. "Too exposed, too easy to find. You and your stupid plans! If it hadn't been for you, Black *Jack*, my brother would still be alive!" Rooker watched Yenrab deflate, sinking into himself. "I shoulda been there. I woulda saved him." The dwarf shook his head. "I shoulda been there."

Jack's voice was a sharp whisper. "Then why weren't you?"
Damn, that's cold.

Yenrab snarled at Jack. "I was *drunk!* Okay!? We had a big fight the night before. I *told* him not to tell you 'bout the tunnel, just bury it and forget it. But he wouldn't listen. So I started drinkin' white lightnin', gettin' pissed. When I woke up..." Yenrab's voice cracked. "He was gone."

Jack turned. "Patch. That day at the sinkhole, the 'cops brought Yenrab with them. Did he look drunk to you?"

"Three sheets to the wind." The jinx nodded. "He was messed up. Hair matted, eyes bloodshot. Smelled like he does now, all rotgut. And he cried like a baby." Yenrab shot her a nasty look. "I believe him."

Jack turned his eyes to Ransom. "Which brings us to you."

The blond man smiled and nodded. "Yeah, and I'm in the clear." He turned to Rooker, his eyes accusing. "Which means it's you."

Rooker scowled at him. *I'll rip yer face off, ya third-rate chum-bag.*

"You're right, Ransom. I trust you." Jack nodded. "From my first day here, you were the only person who was kind to me. You offered me advice, friendship, and food."

"That's right." Ransom smiled. "We were pals from the first day."

"Why *was* that?"

Ransom blinked. "What?"

Jack's words came clipped. "Why were you kind to me?"

"I don't... Why would you ask that? I'm just... That's who I am."

"In a prison full of starving murderers, assassins, thieves, pirates, liars, and cheats, you were the only friendly person, Ransom. A good guy."

"We're *both* good guys. That's just how we are, Jack."

"Just like me." Jack nodded. "You even look a little like me. Blond hair. Blue eyes. Almost like looking in a mirror. Maybe you were always *meant* to be a friendly face. A trusted face."

Ransom eyed Jack. "You're not thinking straight—"

"My first day, I came down with nine frosh. Some of them were big guys. Muscular. Athletic. But you convinced Boss West to pick me first." His eyes sharpened. "Why would you pick a skinny teenager when you could have someone useful?" Jack stepped closer and leveled a finger at Ransom. "Because the headmistress *wanted* someone close to me. A *friend*. Someone I trusted, someone I would talk to, someone who could get some leverage against me. But *he* ruined that."

Rooker looked up to realize Jack was pointing at him.

"Rooker pulled me out of Hyena camp, which made you useless to her. And when one of Gerba's pets doesn't have anything to offer, it gets no more special treatment. So when I approached you and Boss West about the Thunderbuck plan, you finally had a way to get back in her good graces."

Ransom edged away, spreading his hands. "Jack. Buddy. Come on. You're being paranoid."

"When we found the cave, you said you were going to get rope. First off, rope's hard to come by, but you just happened to know where some was. Second, you showed up just in time to get pinched by the 'cops with us. That's the only cover that would work. It would be too obvious otherwise. And third, when we got to the killing field, the headmistress whispered to the viscounte ss... right before she dismissed you off the chopping block." He straightened. "Gerba pulled you out."

How the hell did he work that all out? Rooker watched Patch turn on Ransom, her golden eyes narrowed. Yenrab leaned forward, his mouth soured to a drunken scowl.

Ransom's eyes were panicked. "It wasn't me, Jack! It was *him!*" He stabbed his finger at Rooker.

"Rooker Flynn is a cheat and a thief and a backstabbing liar." Jack nodded. Rooker swallowed. "But he didn't do this."

"What?" Ransom almost screeched. "How do you *know?*"

Jack stared him down. "Because I was chained to him the whole time."

Ransom took a breath and broke for the door.

He made it two steps before Patch was all over him. Ransom drew a knife and stabbed at her. Yenrab grabbed his wrist, yanked it back, and pried loose the blade.

"You killed Bocephus, you son of a bitch!" Patch raked his face with her claws.

Ransom howled agony, his face covered in blood, screaming. "No! *No!*"

Rooker watched Jack stand. His voice was ice. "Time you got what's coming to you."

Rooker watched something terrible in Jack's eyes. He'd seen the many faces of Jack Swift. The fresh-faced boy, the determined fighter, the careful doktar, even the half-mad lunatic. But Rooker had only seen this face once before: When he had threatened to help kill Jack's father. It was the face of unchecked fury, the face of murder, and Rooker knew in his heart that face had nothing to do with Ransom.

That face was for him.

Roaring, Black Jack seized Ransom by his shirt, dragged him to his feet, and hurled him through the front door.

Sunlight cut through the opening, blinding Rooker for a moment. He watched Ransom hit the rail and lose his balance. His body bounced down the stairs and hit every step on the way down. At the base of the clique, he landed in the dirt like a sack of garbage.

Six hundred convicts had gathered outside the clique, Hyenas and Jackals. Some of them exclaimed as Ransom hit the dirt, others laughed, jeering. Rooker saw Boss Hook and Boss Eightfingers arrive from the jungle, watching. Fargil emerged behind them with Farah. All of them watched intently as Ransom struggled to his feet, holding up one hand.

"No... no..."

Jack unslung the bamboo stave from his back and belted Ransom across the face. "Rat!" Jack bellowed at the top of his lungs. Rooker winced as Jack struck him again. "Rat!" He jammed his staff into Ransom's gut. *"Rat!"*

Jackals grinned fierce smiles, cheering every blow. Infected by the murderous fury, Hyenas began shouting as well. Someone began chanting and the sound echoed through the camp. *Rat-Rat-Rat!*

"This is what we do to rats!" Jack thundered. "In Jackal! In Hyena! In Vulture and Buzzard! From now on, any turncoat we find gets the same thing!"

"Please," Ransom pleaded through bloody lips. "Don't kill me."

Jack straightened, his black cloak rippling in the breeze. "I'm not an executioner. But you won't have protection from the shiq in Hyena. And you won't have protection from the shiq in Jackal." Jack spun to face Boss Hook. "Does Buzzard protect rats?"

Hook stiffened, all eyes on him. He stammered before answering. "No."

"And Vulture?"

Boss Eightfingers' response was quicker. "Never!"

"You've got nowhere left to go, Ransom. You're an outcast. Enjoy your last sunset."

"Jack, please!" Ransom begged. "We're friends..."

Jack walked away. "Get rid of him."

Rooker watched a score of Jackals rush Ransom. He made it a few limping strides before they caught him and forced him to the ground. In short order, he was lashed to a pole, bound like a roast pig. As they dragged him into the jungle, one of them took a knife and carved a kanji into Ransom's arm directly over his Locke Institute brand.

For the rest of his short life, Ransom Adare would be marked for what he was: a traitor.

Jack strode up the boss clique steps and called over his shoulder. "Eightfingers. Hook. I've got a proposal for you. More food, more security, less work." Jack pointed to a nearby hut. "If you're interested, I'll meet you in that clique." He turned and raised his voice. "Jackals! Hyenas!" He had the attention of everyone in camp. "We'll be here until sunset while I talk to the bosses. Anyone kills anybody, they answer to me."

Jack disappeared into the clique.

Rooker looked at the others, not sure what to do. Patch couldn't keep the grin off her face. Yenrab and Copper Dave nodded, smiling. Their eyes bore the same adoration that Billy Pilgrim's had.

Rooker was ushered inside the clique, certain his turn was next. As they entered the hut, he saw Jack lean over the desk, facing away from them, a shadow in the dark.

"Yenrab, I'm sorry for the loss of your brother." The kid's voice came with its first hint of warmth. "If I could have saved him, I would have. He was a good man. He deserved the truth and so do you." He turned to the group and rolled up his sleeve, revealing the sigil of Black Jack etched into his arm. "Yes, I'm Black Jack. The one who fought at the Paladine Arch." He held up the staff. "No, this isn't the whomping stick." He spread his hands. "And no, I don't age backwards." He took a breath. "We're a clique. Get your things. You're bunking with me now."

The jinx-cat, the llystra, and the dwarf glanced at each other, grinning. "Hot *damn!*" Patch shouted and bounded through the door. Yenrab nodded and walked out, followed by Copper Dave grinning crocodile teeth. Rooker turned to follow.

"Not you."

Rooker Flynn froze mid-step.

Black Jack took a step closer. "You and I have unfinished business."

Rooker eyed Jack and stepped away. Boss West's clique was lit for a cat, shadowed and dim, but the military cleanliness offered no place to hide.

Jack closed the door behind him and the two men faced each other as strangers.

He's almost as big as me now.

Rooker circled one of the posts, trying to get something solid between them.

Nowhere to go. He stopped. Forcing his muscles to uncoil, he leaned back against the pole. Slowly, he cocked a leg up against the wood and lowered his chin, letting his hair cover his eyes. *That's it. Cool and casual. Don't move until he gets close.*

Jack's boots clocked across the floorboards, coming toward him. Rooker's fingers plucked one of Mamba's cigars from his denims. He snapped his fingers and brought his little flame to life. Jack didn't break stride. Rooker puffed the cigar, warming the tip, and snapped the flame out. "Ya made yer point."

The bootsteps didn't stop and suddenly he stood nose to nose with the man. Black Jack didn't blink. "What is my point?"

Don't flinch. "Ya want me dead, I'm dead." Rooker shrugged. "I get ya."

"You told me to toughen up." Jack leaned in. "Well here I am."

Rooker stared at Jack through the smoke-hazed air between them. *I made him into this.* "Here we are."

A slow grin spread over Jack's face, that lunatic grin he'd had when he had been dragged away screaming *Nothing!* He pulled something from his cloak, a sharp hawkbill knife. He offered it to Rooker. "You want to kill me again? Third time's the charm."

Rooker puffed his cigar. "Doesn't seem to do much good."

Jack chuckled, dark and dry. Rooker swallowed and set his feet. Jack gripped the knife, picked up a dried mango from a table, and cut off a piece. "What's Gerba giving you to rat on Jackal?" He thumbed a slice into his mouth. "Dog food and a longer leash?"

On reflex, Rooker felt denial stir in his mouth, but he stopped himself. *It doesn't matter. He says one word and I'm run out on a rail with 'rat' carved in my arm. He doesn't need proof.*

Jack bit the dried mango and shook his head. "I don't blame you, Rooker. It's the scorpion and the frog. It's in your nature. You played the only hand you had." His blue eyes drove a hole through Rooker's skull. "And you lost." Jack gestured with the knife. "Probably not the song you wanted sung about you. But it's the song you earned."

Rooker bit his lip, trying to keep his voice casual. "There's time for other songs."

"Not for us."

Now he flinched. Just a little, under one eye. He felt the finality of the words as if Jack had driven the knife through his heart.

"I don't want to kill you." Jack turned and walked away, examining an open book on the desk. "But I can't have you reporting back to Gerba either."

Rooker didn't blink, didn't swallow, didn't move. As he eyed Jack, he thought he saw something move in the darkness behind the kid. Something lupine and hungry. A wolf made of shadows.

"I've had plenty of time to think about how this goes." Jack riffled his short hair. "If I let you live, you're going to tell her anything she wants. But it won't be about me." He closed the book. "You're going back to Jackal."

Rooker frowned, confused. *He's letting me go?*

"Take over for Boss Mamba. Live like a king, inform on them all you want. But I'm taking my pick of the outlaws. I'm taking Patch. And I'm taking Hyena." Jack leaned in. "I run my camp. You run yours. And if I ever see you here again, I'll tell every convict on Huánghūn exactly what you are." Jack leaned in. "We're done."

Rooker look a long draw on the cigar and eyed Jack through the smoke.

It felt like being inside a slowly shattering mirror, falling apart in pieces.

Jack walked for the exit. He turned in the doorway, a silhouette. "And the mountains made of mirrors? They're called skyscrapers. We make them with cranes and concrete and U.S. Steel. They're marvels of science, something more impressive than you will ever understand." He took a breath, and in that moment, Rooker couldn't see his face. "I'm sorry I lied to you, Rooker. I should have told you the truth about where I was from. And I should have

done it before Gerba Whipmarples did. I owed you that much."
He turned for the door. "Forgive me if you can."

And he was gone.

Rooker leaned against the post, staring at nothing. He let out
a long breath and felt a tremor go through his flesh as his nerves
assaulted him all at once. His hand shook violently, uncontrollably.
The palmed knife inside his fist dropped to the floor. His heart
raced, his body was weak, his head numb.

He slumped against the post, trying to get his breath under
control.

Forgive me if you can.

6

House of the Rising Sun

*We must all hang together,
or assuredly we shall all hang separately.*
Benjamin Franklin

S UMMER TOOK HOLD OF Huánghūn like a slowly closing fist. Little by little, the rains died, leaving Hyena camp parched and steaming. Most convicts adopted wide-brimmed hats woven from palm fronds for protection from the sun, but it did little to cool their bodies. As the days grew hotter, men abandoned their shirts altogether. The women were more creative, devising colorful wraps that left their shoulders and midriffs bare. The old timers called this kind of heat 'earthquake weather,' and they were right. There had always been little quakes on Huánghūn, but now they grew more frequent and more powerful. One of the Hyena cliques collapsed during a quake and its residents were forced to occupy the yingcao flytraps for shelter. At night, convicts lucky enough to have a clique abandoned their bunks for hammocks and fanned themselves with palms, trying to get some air moving inside the sweltering huts. Every prisoner in Hyena was up before dawn, waiting for the shiq to disappear with the sun so they could break out of their sweltering cages and catch a breath of fresh air.

It made good weather for plotting secrets in the dark.

Night after night, the escape team huddled in Boss West's old clique, perfecting Jack's plan. Their secret endeavor would take months of work even if everything went as planned. Patch, Yenrab, and Copper Dave each had a particular task that must be executed perfectly if they were to succeed, and figuring out the details was a matter of life or death. Night after night, the outlaws came at the puzzle from a hundred different angles, streamlining the plot and whittling it down to the bare necessities.

In the end, the plan was as simple as they could make it, and each prisoner knew the role they must play.

It all began with Copper Dave... and a well-placed bribe.

Attercops typically have a lifespan of thirty years or so. Most of them try to spend it enjoying as many vices as possible. From the addictive, heady buzz of khef to the bloody thrill of good old-fashioned violence, attercops pursue their dark thrills with predatory fervor. Half the reason the big spiders enjoyed their position at the Locke Institute was the endless supply of trapped victims to abuse. They were masters of corruption, greed, lust, gluttony, and sloth. Every day, they gathered on the wall to partake in the feast-or-famine thrill of gambling on the dinner dash, the daily battle for food that was one of the oldest traditions at the Institute.

But not anymore.

These days, the big spiders didn't bother to climb the wall after they hauled the galt into the yard; they just hung out near the pallets, bored, as thirty-two prisoners walked toward the crates.

Copper Dave arrived with the rest of the prisoners and started laying out galt in four neat rows, divvying up the food equally between the camps. As he did, the big croc eyed the yawning attercops, waiting for the right moment to act.

One of the attercops lit a khef cigar and took a puff, hacking. His partner turned eight eyes toward the smoke. "Hey Jamedi, give me some of that."

"Get your own, idiot." Jamedi turned his anger on the prisoners. "Come on, you wasteka convicts! It was more fun when you fought for food!"

"It was hilarious," agreed the other attercop. "Come on, where's the hitting? Where's the running? It's boring."

"Is truce." Copper Dave straightened. He'd been told by Patch to let the 'cops talk first. Now it was his turn. He ambled toward the spiders, nervous. "Truce is good."

"Truces are stupid," growled Jamedi.

Copper Dave watched cons walk the line of galt, making sure the shares were equal. "Much nicer, yes? Civilized." He tried a smile. "Like headmistress wants."

"I guess," said Jeeves, clearly disappointed.

Copper Dave knew he was not smart. He excelled at taking orders, but no one had made the mistake of asking him to think during his career as a legbreaker for the Rimmy's Cull cartel. Being an enforcer was a simple job, and he liked things simple. However, his part in Jack's plan required some subtlety. He would have been more comfortable if it had just involved breaking a leg or two.

He fingered the necklace around his neck. Made of hollow macaroni shells, it had been woven into the shape of a heart and painted pink by a little girl's hands. His little girl.

Nina.

She had sent it to him a year ago, the only package Copper Dave had ever received. On the back of the heart, Nina had written, in colored chalk, the words "Lov U Dady." Those pink markings were long since gone, rubbed away by a year of Huánghūn sweat, but the necklace survived.

Copper Dave didn't understand Jack's plan or how it was supposed to work. It was too complicated, too much thinking. All he understood was that, for whatever reason, he had a chance to get off this island and back to his little girl.

He didn't need to know anything else.

As the convicts collected the galt and made for camp, Copper Dave lingered behind with the attercops. "Is beautiful day. Heat is good. You like heat?"

"It sucks," grumbled Jamedi.

"I have friend like you." Dave nodded. "He not like heat. No sun. Likes dark. Likes cool."

"That's a great story." The attercop headed up the wall. "Let's go."

"My friend." Copper Dave took a step closer. "He hate heat. Maybe you help make him cool. Maybe... you make him work in mines tomorrow."

Jamedi made a nasty noise. "I don't care about your friend, you stupid lizard."

"I am sorry. My brain not so good." Copper Dave fingered his shell necklace. "You not care about friend. *I* care about friend. That is what make friend, yes?" He idled closer. "You make friend happy, you make me happy, I make you happy." He produced a fat khef cigar from his back pocket. "All good friend."

Sixteen eyes stared at the cigar like a pack of hungry dogs. "Yeah?" said Jeeves. "What's your friend look like?"

"Little Red Dwarf." Dave lowered his hand, indicating how small his friend was. "No trouble. Good digger. You like."

Jeeves eyed his partner. "How are we supposed to split a cigar?"

Copper Dave tried widening his smile. "I mean one *each*." He revealed another cigar and sniffed it, pulling it slowly across his crocodilian nose. "Nice cigars. You like."

The attercops drooled, saliva dripping from their fangs. "I don't know..."

"I give you these now." Dave extended his hand. "Plus two more tomorrow, when friend goes to mines."

"You've got yourself a deal, dummy." Jamedi snatched the cigars from his hand. "Now get back to camp."

Copper Dave turned back toward Hyena and released a sigh of relief. As he heard the attercops argue over the cigars, all he could think was that he had moved one step closer to Nina...

...if the old drunk pulled off *his* part of the plan.

Yenrab Bialik sat alone in the dark, drinking from a flask.

Beneath the earth, beneath the Institute, he felt at home. The rhythmic symphony of pickaxes, the ashy scent of poorly ventilated lamp smoke, walls black as pitch and covered in soot. It was comfortable as a feather bed.

But without his brother, it was no fun.

Fifteen days spent down in the mines, spreading the word, letting the convicts know what he needed to fulfill his part of the plan. And each day, he found himself unwilling to leave the caves. Without his brother, all that was waiting for him back at the camp was an empty hammock. Copper Dave was too dumb to talk to, and Patch just liked to argue with everyone. If it hadn't been for Black Jack, Yenrab would have given himself over to the moonshine. But the little freckle had a point: If he kept drinking, his chances of getting revenge for his brother's death were zero.

He stoppered the flask.

"Hello?" A young convict appeared at the entrance to Yenrab's hidden cave, peering inside. "Hello?" The Red Dwarf sighed. He knew most jaelin couldn't see well in the dark, but the idiot was only a yard away. Yenrab was covered in fifteen days of soot, the same color as the walls, and he knew only the white of his one eye was visible in the darkness.

He materialized in front of the prisoner. "Boo."

The man shrieked and stumbled backward. "Damn wasteka dwarf!"

"Simmer down, dingleberry." Yenrab scowled. "Y'all got somethin' for me?"

"You're the guy, right? The one looking for this?" The kid held up the sledgehammer chained to his wrist, its handle broken in two.

Every prisoner in the mines was chained to a tool: pickaxes, shovels, sledgehammers, and wheelbarrows. The tools were unlocked and collected one by one at the end of every day, counted and numbered by the acolytes. Any convict caught breaking a tool on purpose got thirty days in the hole, so Yenrab had to wait for it to happen naturally. "Finally." The Red Dwarf breathed a sigh of relief. "Gerba's goons *saw* it break? They wrote it down?"

"N⁰· 48." The convict pointed to the number on the sledge. "Registered as broken."

"All right, swap chains with me."

"What?"

"Bucko, I can't walk out past the cotton-pickin' guards with *two* sledgehammers chained to my wrist, can I?"

"But we can't swap chains." The kid blinked. "It's... a *chain*."

"Y'all are about as sharp as a bag of soup, ain'tcha?" Yenrab slid one link of his chain over the sharp end of a pickaxe, rapped it smartly with a hammer, and popped the weld open. He did the same to the convict's chain, swapped tools, and rapped the chains closed once again. "See? Easy as skinnin' possums."

Barney had taught him that trick back when they'd been slaves. The Bialik twins had never met a chain they couldn't break.

Yenrab jammed a pouch of galt into the man's hand. "Y'all never heard of me. Understand?"

The man disappeared into the dark. Yenrab made sure he was gone, then with one well-positioned strike he separated the iron hammerhead from the handle. It hit the ground with a metallic thud.

The Red Dwarf reached into the darkness and revealed the second hammerhead someone had brought him three days before. "Matching set." He stared at the identical tools, thinking of Barney. "Okay, Barn. How do we smuggle out forty pounds of sledge iron?"

At the end of the work day, miners stood in a grimy line, waiting to be released into the open air. One by one, their tools were unchained, counted, and placed in a numbered rack along the wall. When his chain was unlocked, Yenrab trudged to the metal bin of broken tools, where a bored acolyte kept the list. "Busted sledge. N̲o̲ 48." Yenrab dumped the broken handle in the bin along with the good-sized rock he'd palmed in the other hand. It hit the bottom of the metal bin with a sharp clang, sounding much like a hammerhead. Checking the list, the acolyte nodded and waved him on.

Clumping toward daylight, Yenrab made sure to hunch, limping a bit. The great stone door was majik on the inside, made translucent to watch out for ambushes from the assembly yard. As Barney headed for the light at the end of the tunnel, an attercop grabbed him. "Hey! You're that drunk redneck that likes to mouth off, aren't you? Strip the cloak. And the shirt."

Yenrab relented, removed his layers, and exposed red skin beneath black soot. "Sure, young feller. I ain't makin' no trouble." The attercop pawed through his blackened clothing, finding nothing. As the hairy legs checked his shirt and pants, Yenrab grinned. "You want me to strip off my britches as well?"

The attercop scowled. "Get moving, tiny."

"Whatever you say, boss."

Yenrab clumped through the great stone door and into the light.

No one noticed that he stood a few inches taller as he shuffled out of the mines with two sledgehammer heads strapped to the bottom of his boots.

Each heavy step took him closer to his revenge...

...if the pussycat pulled off the impossible.

Patch Picaroon enjoyed speaking to groups; it gave her an excuse to shout. "All right, ladies!" She raised her hands, calling for silence. "Let's chat."

Sixty pairs of eyes turned her way, some lined in mascara made from coal dust. Sixty women outlaws, every felonious femme on the island, had come to hear what she had to say. Judging by those darkened eyes, the prevailing mood was skeptical at best.

Patch took a breath, knowing that if this didn't work, the plan would fall apart, and it would be her fault.

"It's time we got what's coming to us!" Patch raised her voice. "A united female camp!"

That got their attention. Surprised murmurs rippled through the crowd, most of them snorts and jeers. Patch was prepared for that. She knew there were only six women on the island (seven before Fancy Nan had died) who made any real decisions, and she had been canny enough to bribe them in advance. "Shut up, dolts!" yelled Yolanda, the first palm she had greased. "Listen!"

"Hyena will take all of us! Every woman on Huánghūn!" Patch let that sink in. No faction in Hyena had sixty members; a union would give them a staggering amount of power. If all the women came together, Hyena would, in effect, belong to them. "But!" Patch raised her paws, took a breath, and asked the impossible. "We only get the deal if we build four cliques... in a month."

Protests and groans from the girls. "Give me a break!" "We'll never finish that in time."

"Sure we will. There's sixty of us." Patch hefted Yenrab's sledgehammers. "And two of these." She tossed a twenty-pound hammer to Yolanda, who caught it and grinned. "I'd say we've got a fighting chance."

Knowing she couldn't lose momentum, Patch rolled out a large map of Hyena with a flourish. "Here, here, here, and here. There's a lot of us, and we're going to need new homes."

Patch held her breath as curiosity drew the girls like a magnet. They clucked over the map, pointing and debating. As more approached, Patch unveiled Jack's new architectural designs. One of the Buzzards leaned in and investigated the drawings. "What is this? It isn't a clique."

"New and improved design." Patch gestured. "We wrap the lower level with yingcao palms so we get..."

"...a two-story clique." Another convict nodded. "That's smart."

As the prisoners remarked on the plans, Fancy Nan's old assistant, Farah, did not seem interested in the drawings, only the map. "This doesn't make sense." Farah pointed at one of the proposed build sites. "This one is too far in the back. Why would you put it there?"

Damn, girl's too smart for her own good. "Do you want to ask stupid questions or do you want a new home?" Patch turned to the crowd. "It took me a month of hard bargaining to make this deal happen, ladies. I want to be comfy in a new clique next month. How 'bout you?" Her ringers weren't even necessary. The enthusiasm was organic. "The boys don't think we can pull it off. We're gonna prove them wrong, right?"

That got a cheer.

Patch let a smile curl over her teeth. She had her builders. "O, and speaking of the boys, if you see any of them taking a leak anywhere other than the big jars, throw a rock at 'em. Camp rule. We'll get the stink out of here yet." A few women chuckled. "Now, let's go to work."

As the women departed for the build sites, Patch snatched Farah's arm. "Not you."

The dark girl's eyes narrowed. "What—"

"You helped Fancy Nan with Thunderbuck, right?"

"Well, yes, I... um..." Patch almost felt sorry for the girl. She didn't know where to look and retreated inside herself like a turtle, making herself small. Finally, her quiet voice murmured, "Yes."

"Then start cooking that moonshine, hon. This is going to be thirsty work."

It took twenty-eight days for Patch's crew to build four cliques. The sledgehammers never stopped pounding new caissons into the ground, driving their foundations down to the bedrock. They tore down the broken cliques for lumber and harvested the rest from the jungle. Bamboo scaffolds dressed the skyline as scores of women built the supports, the stairs, the decking, the walls. Some clever lass got the idea to feed blood to the yingcao flytraps and encourage them to release their outer layers faster. Little by little, the new cliques took shape, one layer at a time.

When it was done, the women of the Locke Institute lounged on their new decks, enjoying a rare victory. They were proud of what they had built together, and the two-story cliques made excellent additions to Hyena camp. No one wanted to claim the strange out-of-the-way clique, but there was plenty of room in the others, so Patch offered to take it for herself and a few close friends.

Walking inside the empty clique, Patch Picaroon dropped her guard for the first time in a month. She sagged against a support beam and sighed. Her muscles ached, her feet hurt, her joints were swollen and thick, but she'd pulled off her part of the plan.

Only one puzzle piece remained. A very loud distraction...

...from a man who couldn't speak.

Billy Pilgrim mounted the stairs to the water tower, cradling his homemade banjo.

Before Huánghūn, his voice had been the finest instrument in the world, a voice he had trained to speak and joke and sing in taverns, concert halls, and theaters all over Keymark. The Locke Institute had taken that instrument away when it had kidnapped him, enslaved him, and seared him with a piece of molten metal that branded him a *rebel*. In truth, Billy did not remember much of the last year, nothing but a symphony of starvation and violence more terrible than his worst nightmares. Only his creativity had saved him. An escape hatch had blossomed inside his head, and he had fled inside it, a world of notes and tremolos and a steady, dependable rhythm.

His new world had only cost him his voice... and his mind.

But Black Jack had changed all that.

The audio player from Walter Payton High had survived seven hours before the battery had died, but in those seven hours Billy Pilgrim had been resurrected. A choir of angels had sung inside his head, an otherworldly symphony of music, a concert by God for an audience of one. The voices had been legendary: Sam Cooke, Lady Gaga, the Beatles, the Beastie Boys, Elvis Presley, Aerosmith, Beyonce, and Stevie Wonder. Billy Pilgrim had listened in awe, a wide-eyed virgin hearing another universe's song for the first time.

His mind was still broken as a crushed sparrow. He still could not speak, and part of him knew his speaking voice might never return. But for the first time in a year, Billy Pilgrim could sing.

By *God,* he could sing.

He mounted the water tower and looked out over his new home. The Huánghūn truce had remained unbroken for two months. All the camps had recognized they were in the same boat, and so the greed that came so easily to criminals had been replaced by a burgeoning collaboration. Open trade existed between them now, and a black market had sprung up on Paradise Road, a central point between all the camps out of sight of the Institute. The hatchet had been buried for two moons, an important anniversary in Keymark, and most of the camp bosses had agreed that a celebration was in order.

Drum circles thundered in Hyena from the early hours, calling out to the other camps. Convicts arrived in groups of ten or twenty from Vulture and Buzzard. There were even a few hopeful Jackals. All were handed a cup of Thunderbuck moonshine. Kites danced overhead with yellow and green runners, filling the sky with color. A shiq piñata hung from the yingcao tree and was promptly beaten to death with glee. Nearly a hundred convicts played turtleball, racing each other all over the yard. It was a festival like the Lock Institute had never seen.

Now it was his turn.

Few outlaws recognized Billy Pilgrim as he mounted the water tower roof. Before his resurrection, his empty shell had been covered in filth, banging its head and babbling, but the *buh-buh*-bum was gone. The man who stepped on stage was scoured clean, dressed in a long purple jacket cobbled together from mismatched scraps of cloth and dyed with lingberry oil. His thick orange hair stood straight up in the imitation of a fire. In his hands was the new banjo he had crafted with painstaking love over the last month. The frame was covered in dried raiptar skin stretched tight over a round drum. The strings were spun from dried plant fibers, tightened into tune with bamboo pegs. The neck was yingcao wood, carved into a curved shape that met his hand like a lover.

He did not understand the words the angels had sung to him. They had been in a strange celestial language he could not comprehend, but the majik of music surpassed language, bypassing simple syllables for an ocean of emotion that washed over him in wave after wave. He carried the dead music player strapped around his neck, a talisman that granted him entry to another world, a reminder that the music lived within. No one in Keymark would ever hear those songs again unless he was the one to sing them.

One song, above all others, had driven itself into his heart. It was a lonely song, a painful song, a prisoner's song. Black Jack had translated it for him, teaching him the words and the name of the strange city, just for this moment.

Billy Pilgrim began playing softly, so quietly almost no one could hear him. But little by little, his song grew stronger and the prisoners started to listen. He stood, summoning a lonesome howl from his instrument that wailed over the crowd. His voice joined alongside, crying a wordless counterpoint to his strings. Then he sang.

> *There is a house in New Orleans*
> *They call the Rising Sun*
> *And it's been the ruin of many a poor boy,*
> *And me, oh God, I'm one.*
>
> *If I'd listened what my mama said,*
> *I'd be at home today.*
> *But bein' young and foolish, Lord,*
> *The game lead me astray.*
>
> *Now the only thing an outlaw needs*
> *Is a suitcase and a trunk.*
> *And the only time he's satisfied,*
> *Lord, is when he's on the drunk.*
>
> *Somebody tell my sister;*
> *Not to do what I have done.*
> *But shun that house in New Orleans*
> *They call the Rising Sun.*
>
> *Well, I'm goin' back to New Orleans;*
> *My race is almost run.*
> *Gonna spend the rest of my wicked life*
> *Beneath the Rising Sun.*

Billy finished the last chord and opened his eyes. The crowd stood in silence. Somewhere in the back, someone clapped. They were joined by another, then another and another, until the entire throng applauded, a rolling wave of percussion that flowed over him, its own kind of music. "Hot *damn!*" yelled an outlaw. "Give that boy a holler and a swaller!" Convicts climbed the water tower, bringing him drinks and begging for more songs. "Do One-Eyed Rosie!" "Maiden and the Walrus!" "Tripping Light, do Tripping Light!"

Billy Pilgrim smiled. Every eye in camp was on him, cheering for more...

...just as Black Jack had asked.

"Farah."

She spun at the sound of her name and almost knocked over one of the moonshine jugs.

Farah Ibis never considered attending the festival, and no one expected her to go. She was a mousy girl, quiet, and people made her nervous. She preferred spending time in the company of numbers and figures, perfecting the elegant alchemy of transforming galt into moonshine. She had always been amazed how much a thing could transform, given the right conditions and a little time.

Patch stood in the doorway. "I've got a job for you." The jinx slung her arm around Farah's shoulder and led her out of the distillery. Farah glanced over her shoulder, nervous at leaving Thunderbuck unattended. "Where are we going?"

Patch shrugged. "You don't mind getting your hands dirty, right?"

Farah shrugged back. "Every job on this island is dirty."

Even with everyone watching Billy Pilgrim's performance, Patch took great pains to smuggle Farah out of camp unseen. The pirate led her on a circuitous route, and she soon realized the jinx was making sure they weren't followed. Patch led her to a hollow hidden by a deadfall that blocked the entrance. At the back of the hollow, virtually undetectable behind the branches, was a small cave.

Patch gestured her inside, where she was overwhelmed by darkness.

"Farah."

She spun, startled. A dark figure stood a few feet away.

Black Jack.

His legend had only grown since his coup of Hyena and his truce with the other bosses. No one saw him, no one heard from him, he was all but invisible. She was face to face with a ghost.

"Sir!" Farah stammered. "I mean boss. I mean... sir." She started to kneel, then got caught between standing and bowing, not sure what to do with her body.

"Just Jack." His voice was kind as he helped her up. "There's a question that's been bothering me, but nobody knows the answer. Even Patch couldn't find out."

Farah glanced at the jinx. "And... you think I know?"

Jack smiled. "It's *about* you."

"Me?"

Jack tilted his head. "What crime did you commit to get sent here?"

Farah glanced at Patch. Her mouth moved up and down. Then she finally rolled up the sleeve she always kept buttoned, revealing her brand. "Forgery." She cleared her throat. "I faked letters and decrees from noble houses, copied signets, got the right kind of parchment, used the right nibs. The ink is the hard part. You've got to get the exact mix for the correct viscosity, but I was good at it. I got caught forging documents to get someone out of prison." She rubbed her hands together. "I'm aware of the irony."

"That's meticulous work." Jack nodded. "Methodical. Careful. So is running the distillery. Just the kind of person I need." As Jack took Farah's hand, she felt a thrill run up her skin. "Can you keep a secret? My secret?"

She gulped. "Yes, sir."

Jack pulled back a curtain to reveal two long clay jars sitting on a low fire. Farah recognized them as the urinal pots Jack had brought to Hyena. As he removed the lid, Farah caught a whiff of ammonia. "Uh... you're boiling urine?"

Patch shrugged. "I told you it was a dirty job."

"It's a formula," said Jack. "Like distilling alcohol or crafting ink. Now watch." Inside the jar, most of the liquid had burned off, leaving a wad of sticky goo. Jack used a pair of wooden paddles to move the wad into a clay pan. "You harvest the syrup and heat it in the pan." He did so, and Farah watched a bright red oil bubble to the top. "Remove the oil and let it cool." He took a lump that had already hardened and used the wooden paddle to scrape crystals off the flattened side. "Scrape off the grains, mix the oil back in, and heat it for about sixteen hours." He gestured to a lump that was cooking over a cone of palm leaves that collected the steam into a hollow gourd. "Funnel the steam into one of the gourds and cap it off tight." Jack turned. "Make sense?"

"Syrup, heat, oil, scrape, mix, heat, funnel." Farah nodded. "It's a simple recipe."

"Seven steps." Jack nodded. "Just like the scientific method."

Farah cocked her head. "I don't know what that is."

"We'll fix that." Jack put his hand on her shoulder. "Right now, we're going to test a hypothesis. Follow me."

Jack led her on a hidden route through the jungle. They came to the strange out-of-the-way clique far removed from the party in Hyena. The new two-story clique smelled of fresh timber and the tangy scent of fresh yingcao leaves. Inside, Farah followed Jack and Patch down a ladder to the lower level, where a rock floor twisted around itself like a nest of snakes.

As her eyes adjusted to the dark, Farah Ibis realized they weren't alone. Yenrab the one-eyed dwarf was there, and the big llystra called Copper Dave. And one more person...

A corpse.

Farah froze on the ladder.

Black Jack moved to Copper Dave. "Where'd you find him?"

Copper Dave picked his teeth. "Was in vendetta. He lose."

"Y'all comin' or goin'?" Yenrab's crusty voice startled Farah. As she descended, the dwarf took hold of a large rock and rolled it out of the way, revealing a black hole in the stone floor.

Farah blinked, realizing she stood over a cave.

"Okay, let's lower it." Jack started to wrap a long vine around the corpse.

"*Lower* it?" Patch tilted her head. "Why?"

Jack scowled. "It's respectfu—"

Patch kicked the corpse into the hole. Farah put a hand over her mouth, squelching a scream.

"Here they come!" warned Yenrab.

Then Farah heard it. The same sound she heard every night, the skittering of needle legs, the *churr* of the shiq. She lunged for the ladder, climbing as fast as she could.

"Relax." Patch placed a paw on her arm. "We're not stupid."

Holding on to the ladder, Farah winced as she heard shiq devouring the corpse in the dark, heard the sick echo of flesh rent by fangs.

"Okay." Jack held up the little gourd from his strange jungle laboratory. "Let's find out if all this was worth it."

He let go.

Farah watched the gourd fall. It hit the bottom of the cave and a blinding flash of light seared her eyes. She jerked her head away, momentarily blinded.

A brilliant white light filled the tunnel, brighter than a thousand torches, brighter than the sun. She could see every crack, every stalagmite, every shiq fleeing into the darkness. She saw the body of the dead man, half eaten.

Not one shiq would come near it.

She turned to see light blaze across Jack's triumphant face.

"It worked!" Yenrab thumped Jack on the back. "It *worked!*"

Patch grinned. "Ol' Black Jack, the man with the knack."

Copper Dave's head bobbed up and down, grinning scissor teeth.

Farah blinked. "That's why you make everyone use the urinals. So you can make *this.*"

"Number fifteen on the periodic table. The devil's element." Jack's eyes sparkled in the light. "Phosphorus."

He turned to Farah, silhouetted in the white light. "There's a tunnel system down there. If we can make enough of this stuff, we can map it, find a way out, and escape." He stepped toward her. "But I can't make it all by myself. I need someone to help me. Someone methodical, someone meticulous, someone careful. You're the last piece of the puzzle, Farah." Black Jack cocked his head. "Are you in?"

He held her eyes, waiting.

Farah's smile broke like a wave. "You bet your ass I am."

=TEAM OF ENEMIES=

Beware of no man more than of yourself;
we carry our worst enemies within us.

Charles Spurgeon

U PON THE ROOFTOP OF the Locke Institute, the tan akita pup who had been shipwrecked at the Battle of the Barrel Strait snarled and bit an acolyte's cloak.

As the pup shook its head savagely, a spray of ice flew from its fur and glistened in the brutal Huánghūn sun. When the acolyte did nothing to defend himself, the akita clamped needle teeth onto his silken robe and tore a gigantic rent down the back. When *that* failed to garner a response, the dog bit the acolyte right in the ass.

"Good boy," Rooker muttered.

Portia snapped her fingers at him, commanding him to be silent during Gerba's morning announcements.

The akita pup savaged Portia's ankle. She didn't notice, of course, but it was satisfying just the same. *Good boy.*

Rooker Flynn knew the akita was crazy. Maybe not Billy *Pilgrim* crazy, but crazy enough. The dog didn't exist. Not the mismatched eyes or the wagging tail or the way his tongue lolled out one side of his mouth. Rooker had just conjured the memory of the little pup to keep him company now that he had no one left to talk to.

Except you, right, buddy?

Patch was gone. She'd abandoned him faster than a greased pig. Picaroon had taken the Femme clique with her, including Yolanda, who was a useful enforcer. Rooker missed none of the women. The camp was more peaceful with them gone. He didn't miss Copper Dave, either. The big croc had never come back to Jackal after that first day, and good riddance. Jape was dead, as were all the Red Tigers, killed when their clique had collapsed during a quake one night.

Even crazy Billy Pilgrim had jilted him. From Jackal, Rooker had heard the faint melody of the troubadour's voice during the two-moon concert yesterday. If he regretted anything, it was missing that song.

Worst of all, the *Venture Brigand* was gone, departed on some Naysayer hunt. Rooker couldn't even gaze out longingly at her silhouette. He had been forsaken by all.

The only friends Rooker Flynn had left were imaginary or dead. Given the choice between Jasper and the akita, Rooker chose the dog.

The truth was, either one of them was better than being alone.

Little Rooker trotted past Gerba Whipmarples, who continued to deliver her standard morning propaganda. The pup left dirty paw prints on the hem of her dress and circled to the base of the Agrat-ban-Haifa, where yet another snitch had found himself at the end of his rope. An acolyte pulled the scaffold pin, and the squealer rang the bell with his neck.

Hanging rats had become Gerba's new pastime. Two months ago, Ransom Adare had set the precedent by throwing himself on the mercy of the Institute. That mercy had been on full display when Ransom danced the hangman's jig. Gerba made an example of him, a warning to her other moles scurrying below: If you are discovered, you will find no shelter here.

But the warning didn't work. Six rats had been exposed since then, and all of them had preferred being hanged to being eaten.

Rooker enjoyed watching the wasteka bastards hang, full well knowing he deserved to be next.

The pup scurried away from the twitching snitch, frightened. *It's all right, boy. Just a dead rat.* He watched the dog regain his courage and circle back to Rooker's table, where he sat with the two biggest rats in camp.

Boss Hook and Boss Eightfingers eyed the last kicks of the snitch and shifted in their chairs. It was different watching from this close, and Gerba had made certain they had good seats.

Rooker always assumed the other camp bosses were on the take, but this was the first time they'd all been together, forced to admit what they were. Hook and Eightfingers looked nervous, uncomfortable, exposed. The akita circled Hook, the dumber of the pair, and sniffed his pants. *What d'ya think, boy? Has he wet himself yet?*

"Don't worry so much, Hook." Rooker lounged in his seat. "We're workin' for the house. Remember..." He timed his words to match Gerba's as she concluded her speech. "Work will make ya free. Rehabilitation leads to graduation. Now get out there and have a great day."

Hook slung a rock at him. It struck Rooker's ear, and he felt a trickle of blood roll down his cheek, but he didn't react, refusing to give Hook the satisfaction. He chuckled, snapped his fingers, and lit a cigar. *See, boy? They're not tough enough.*

Little Rooker barked at him, agreeing.

"Gentlemen." Gerba's massive shadow fell over them. "If, perchance, you are wondering why I have called you together today, I am unhappy with your performance."

Ever since the nobles had started visiting more regularly, the headmistress had doubled down on her wardrobe, appearing in more and more fanciful frocks. Today's was an expansive mermaid gown glistening with orange sequins that made her look like she was on fire. It matched her mood.

"I spent an *inordinate* amount of time and effort developing my resources inside the camps." Rooker savored the stress in Gerba's voice as she gestured to the dead rat hanging from the bell. "I will not lose any more informants. You will *stop* this mole hunt."

"Whadaya want us to do about it?" Boss Hook was a bitter old jaelin, a bandit chief in his former life. Rooker hated everything about him. "Hyena's got everybody so riled up they're seeing spies in the rice paddies. They're even starting to look at *me* sideways." Rooker grinned; he enjoyed the idea of Hook ridden out of Buzzard on a rail.

"If it continues, the hunt will lead to the three of you." Gerba lowered an eyebrow. "Paint a target on someone's back, find a patsy, do whatever it is criminals do and make. It. *Stop.*" She tapped her parasol with every syllable.

Rooker opened his mouth to speak but was cut off.

"It'll cool down before long." Eightfingers had a sandwich in each hand. Despite the rampant starvation on Huánghūn, the pinkyless pirate had leveraged his position as Vulture boss to grow even fatter. "Everything will go back to norma—"

"Normal?" Gerba cut him off. "The monkeys are running the asylum! Every day I assign work, and every day I see students break off and go with the wrong group. Explain that."

"Another Black Jack idea." Eightfingers shrugged. "Play to our strengths. Dwarves and razorbacks work the mines. Llystra brutes do lumber. Burglars and pickpockets do fabrication. Everyone else does rice. We work less and still hit quota."

Rooker couldn't help but smile as Gerba Whipmarples realized she had been outmanaged by her own inmates. "*Hmph.* Fine. The attercops will crack down on it to keep up appearances, then let it resume. The students will think they won a battle."

"Right." Hook slapped his hands together as if everything was settled. "Everyone works a little harder with a victory under their belt."

Gerba stared at Hook like she might throw him off the cliff. "Quite."

Hook failed to notice, chomping on a mango. "I'll give you another good idea, Whipmarples. Stop putting two camps in the mines at the same time. We've got nearly six hundred cons down there. It's too tight."

"The mines will operate at full capacity." Gerba's voice cracked like a whip. "The mines will continue to grow until we can fit all four camps down there. The *mines* are the reason the Locke Institute exists!" It was rare for the big trol to raise her voice, and it was terrifying. "If you care to offer more of your *stunning* insight to that particular project, Mister Hook, I can ensure you become an *expert* at mining and spend the rest of your days digging in the dark."

Hook quaked in his seat, regretting he'd ever spoken.

Rooker ignored them both. He glanced over the edge of the cliff and saw a few familiar faces headed to the work camps. There was Copper Dave, fondling that stupid heart necklace he always wore. Patch moved among the jinx, trafficking galt for swag. And there was Billy Pilgrim with his new banjo. The pup moved to the edge of the cliff and barked at them, but they didn't hear.

"At least the food-sharing thing works." Eightfingers stuffed another sandwich into his fat mouth. "No more fights over galt." Rooker snorted, knowing the bandit chief didn't see the big picture. Bounty hunters from all across Keymark delivered more wanted men every day; the bay was thick with mercenary boats and the camps were full to swelling. As far as Rooker was concerned, the new batch of frosh weren't even proper criminals, just a cluster of intellectuals, artists, and political troublemakers. But no matter how many new cons arrived, there was never more galt. Eightfingers bit into his sandwich. "Equal shares for everybody."

Gerba Whipmarples plucked the sandwich from Eightfingers' hand and flicked it into the sea. "Mister Chiba." She brushed crumbs from her glove. "Let me be *crystal* clear. The Locke Institute is not a commune. Competition is healthy. Struggle breeds success. Challenges yield strength. This is the beauty of the galt. It provides victors and losers." She straightened to her full height. "As bosses, your only job is to ensure the camps do *not* work together. Buzzard, Jackal, Vulture, and Hyena must fight for food. Otherwise, they will have too much time to *think*, and we can all agree..." She indicated the hanged rat. "We do not want that."

Rooker puffed his cigar, wishing Whipmarples would arrive at the point.

"Tomorrow"—the headmistress steepled her fingers—"when the galt is handed out, there will be a tragic incident. One member of each camp will be killed by a rival. There will be outrage, mistrust. And the dinner dash will resume as it should. You will see to it personally, gentlemen." She loomed over them. "That is... if you wish to *retain* your positions of privilege."

Hook and Eightfingers glanced at each other. Rooker snorted. *So. We're back at war.*

"Headmistress?" An acolyte appeared behind the trol.

Gerba could not keep the irritation from her voice. "What *is* it, Winnifred?"

"Excuse me, headmistress. The foreman on Bounty is requesting more workers. Also..." Winnifred revealed a sheaf of letters. "You have received the first responses to your invitation."

Rooker watched as Gerba's face transformed at the sight of the silk-ribboned envelopes and she squealed like a little girl. "O, that *is* good news, Winnifred." She took the letters and rifled through them. "Lordling Lund has accepted, Daimyo Singh, Viceroy Chen, all of them." She raised her horn. "Tell Niko he can have his workers. We need to complete construction on Bounty as soon as possible if we are to be ready for the trial."

Bounty. Rooker chewed on his cigar. *What is that? A city? A boat?*

"This discussion is concluded." The headmistress addressed the three bosses. "You have been granted certain privileges because of your ability to control your camps. If you cannot *enforce* that control, rest assured new potential bosses arrive at the Institute every day."

Toe the line or hang with the rest of the rats.

"Dismissed."

Hook and Eightfingers got to their feet and fought over the remaining food, stuffing it into their pockets as they descended the steps. Rooker did not join them. He lounged in the chair, thinking.

Not one of them traded a single word with me.

Just orders and rocks.

Rooker had not been in solitary confinement for a long time, but his current predicament felt much the same. He might as well be invisible.

He stood and looked over the cliff to watch the outlaws disappear into the jungle, every back turned to him.

Rooker sighed, empty. He turned to see his only remaining friend, the little akita pup, prance over to Gerba, lift his leg, and piddle on her dress.

Good boy.

He descended the wrong set of stairs to discover himself in the headmistress' office. Her study was littered in pineapples. The hammerdwarves were in the process of painting hundreds of the spikey fruits on the lilac walls. The clash of purple, yellow, and green was garish, ugly, and larger than life, much like its owner.

The pup romped through the office and sniffed the headmistress' giant stone chair. As Rooker strolled past the ugly thing, a gust of wind blew from her balcony and billowed the new red curtain on the wall behind Gerba's desk. The fabric pulled aside slightly, revealing what lay beneath.

Nepenthe.

She was pinned to the wall. Bolted to the stone in padlocked metal clasps, the bamboo was mounted like a huntsman's trophy, pale wooden fingers trapped in fresh-rolled iron. The piece Jack had brought with him from the Tosh was bound to the top, followed by the one he had summoned when Rooker had threatened to kill his da.

A new piece was bolted below.

Three.

Rooker glanced up at the cupola where a warbling thin spot in the universe hung in midair, pulsing a slow rhythm of majik. A hole between worlds.

It's coming through, piece by piece. Rooker considered the locks on the wall. *Three down, four to go.*

"You're not supposed to be in here, pretty boy." Rooker knew that voice well. Winston was one of the few creatures on the island who still spoke to him, if only to torture him. "Time to go in the hole."

Winston loved throwing students down the big shaft that ran through the center of the Institute, the attercops' vertical highway, but Rooker had enough of feeling like he was in a free fall.

Winston reached for Rooker, who slapped away the attercop's hairy leg. "Same team, clown. I'll take the stairs."

Come on, boy. He resisted the urge to ruffle the dog's head, knowing his fingers would touch nothing but air. *Let's go home.*

On the way back to camp, Rooker stopped at the stream and checked his appearance. His hair had filled in since his days as a bald frosh. Long curls cascaded like black oil from his head, wending over his ears and the top of his neck, sleek and shiny. His pants were clean, his brown leather boots were polished, and his shirt was tucked in tight, a bloody red.

Jackal camp was unique on Huánghūn in that every inmate was required to look their best. Rooker demanded his crew's appearance was buttoned up, scrubbed down, and ship-shape. All hair, facial and otherwise, was groomed and combed, free of nits and lice. If Rooker Flynn was going to be boss of a prison gang, you could bet your last penny they were going to look good.

It did nothing to improve his popularity.

He'd thwarted three assassination attempts and six insurrections, but they hadn't gotten him yet. Rooker checked to make sure his hidden knife was secure and turned the corner into Jackal.

A few dozen men had bribed their way out of work duty, all of them malingering parasites. "Tuck in that shirt, damn you!" Rooker shouted, getting in some nameless outlaw's face. "You want to dress like a bum, go join Vulture!" Several outlaws scowled as he passed. They hated the dress code, but they knew the penalty for disobeying him. Rooker ran a tight ship.

"Hey, Boss Flynn?"

Rooker glanced at the convict, trying to remember his name. *Malium? Malvolo?* "*Captain* Flynn."

Mal wrung his hands, gesturing to the baldheaded frosh behind him. "I got him."

Rooker scowled, confused. *Got who?* But that wasn't a question a boss could ask; it would make him look weak or stupid. He growled instead. "So?"

Mal stammered. "You... you said you'd pay three galt for a mage."

Rooker's eyes snapped to the frosh. He was a thin razorback, nebbish and pale. "That's no wizard."

"I'm not," said the piggy frosh, his eyes nervous. "They kill all the outlaws who know majik. My master is dead. I'm more of a wizard's... librarian."

Rooker glared at Mal. "Librarians are worth three slices." He slapped the galt into Mal's hand. "Get out of here."

"Yes, sir, thank you, captain, sir." As Mal retreated, Rooker hooked his arm over the razorback's shoulder and led him to a secluded spot. The pig looked scared; Rooker realized his reputation preceded him. *Good.* "All right, magician's librarian..."

"Walter, sir."

"I don't care. I need ya to tell me what this is." Rooker grabbed a stick and drew a symbol in the dirt. *If I can remember it right. It was on Gerba's brooch. The night Jack... fell.*

"It's a rune," stated the razorback. "Technically a glyph. Like... a majik spell in writing."

"I know it's a rune," growled Rooker, although he'd known nothing of the sort. "What does it *mean?*"

"That's the Caged Eight."

Rooker smacked the pig in the face. "If ya make me ask one more time—"

"The Caged Eight! Command majik!" the librarian stammered. "Like hypnosis for spiders."

So that's how she controls them. Rooker nodded, eager. "Keep goin'."

"It's not common, not very useful. I think wealthy homes use it to ward off spiders. But I guess it would work on anything with eight legs."

Like attercops or razorsquid... or a giant spider dragon. Rooker's heart quickened. "So we could put this rune around the camp. Keep the shiq out."

"No," the librarian shook his head. "It's little majik, garden majik. It might work on a grass spider or an orbweaver, but it wouldn't do anything against something as big as a shiq. Not unless you found a way to infuse it with a ton of raw *wikk*. I mean like Elven Fremest-level majik."

Rooker frowned. He was no wizard, but it was impossible to power a rune with that much maji—

The Agrat-ban-Haifa.

Rooker straightened. There was no more powerful majik in Keymark than the Great Bells, but they were meant only for healing. Changing a majik's purpose, perverting it, was nearly impossible. Altering the healing majik into something else would require dark majik, blood majik.

A sacrifice.

Rooker stared at the shadow of the Agrat-ban-Haifa atop the Institute.

An execution.

Rooker took a step back as the cold truth sent a shiver up his spine.

Every time she executes a prisoner, she gains control over every spider on the island. She's feeding us to the Caged Eight.

Rooker scraped his boot through the rune in the dirt and grabbed the librarian by his shirt. "Tell anyone about this and yer gonna spend a night chained outside, ya get me?"

The librarian's eyes went wide. "Yes! I mean no, I won't—"

Rooker shoved him away and walked, frowning.

The captives of the Locke Institute weren't students. They weren't prisoners. They were fodder. Live bodies to feed Gerba Whipmarples' control over Huánghūn. Fuel for the fire.

"Cap'n."

A convict waited for him at the entrance to the boss clique, one of the old Shaver gang. Rooker couldn't remember his name either. "What?"

"You know anyone who has a field glass?"

Rooker scowled, thinking about the Caged Eight. "What?"

"A field glass. A spyglass? Or maybe a... whaddayacallem... lorgnette?"

"Why?"

"Hyena is offering a reward for one. Ten pounds."

Rooker lowered an eyebrow. "*Who* in Hyena?"

"I heard it was Black Jack."

Rooker thumbed the brass rings on his finger. *I might know just the man.*

He looked down, imagining the little akita pup staring up at him with its mismatched eyes, a hopeful smile on its face.

Okay, boy. Maybe it's time for two old enemies to have a little talk.

Chapter

8

TREEHOUSE

*A man sees in the world
what he carries in his heart.*
Johann Wolfgang von Goethe

C HANGES WERE AFOOT IN Black Jack's Hyena. The camp boasted a much-improved water tower, well-fed yingcao flytraps, and a designated field for turtleball. Of all the changes, however, Rooker was struck most by the new two-story cliques. Many of the older huts were being retrofitted to the new design. *I bet he came up with that.* He eyed the lower levels. *So what? They made a cellar. When the rains come, that bottom layer's going to get torn apart.* He considered it. *Still. Doubles the space.*

Quit stalling.

Rooker walked into Hyena camp like he owned the joint. Copper Dave noticed him first, but Patch caught wind of him shortly after.

"Rooker. What are you doing here?"

He tossed a package wrapped in linen into the air, forcing her to catch it. "Have a cookie." He slid onto the bench beside her. "Jackal got our hands on some flour and oats." Rooker cocked one leg up on the rail. "Added some figs. You'll like it."

Patch looked at the thing in her hands. "I don't want a cookie."

Rooker flashed a grin. "Who doesn't want a cookie?"

"Rooker." Copper Dave cast a threatening shadow over him. "You not come here."

"Guys, it's almost like yer not happy to see me."

Patch's eyes narrowed. "Jack said you wouldn't be back to Hyena. Ever."

"Did he tell you why?"

Patch eyed Copper Dave but neither responded. *So. He hasn't finked on me yet.* "Word is yer lookin' for a spyglass." He leaned back, pretending to relax. "Yer never gonna guess who has one."

"Fine," said Patch. "We'll pay ten galt."

"Not for sale." Rooker picked his teeth. "I do rentals, though."

"Fine. Two galt to rent it. Hand it over."

"Can't do that either. Where it goes, I go." Patch scowled. Before she could protest, Rooker cut in. "Patch, no offense, but I'm talkin' to the wrong person here. Let's go see the boss and see if we can cut a deal."

Rooker could not figure out why Jack didn't live in the boss clique. Boss West's old hut had been taken over by the Femmes. Instead, Rooker followed Copper Dave to the back of the camp where somebody had made the mistake of building a clique in a uniquely inconvenient spot. *He's keeping himself out of sight. The invisible man.*

Copper Dave ushered him through the door, and suddenly he was face to face with Jack Swift for the first time in two months.

The kid looked good, healthy. His hair had grown out and his eyes were sharp. He stood with Patch, who had run ahead. Both of them stared at him like something they'd scraped off the bottom of their shoe. Rooker leaned against the doorframe. "Heya, Chicken Legs. Remember me?"

"Patch." Jack scowled. "Would you give us a moment?" Picaroon glanced at them, then pulled Copper Dave out the door and pulled it shut. The two men stood alone for a moment without speaking, then Jack broke the silence. "I thought I was clear." His eyes narrowed. "If you ever set foot in Hye—"

"There's something ya need and I'm the only one who's got it." Rooker spread his hands. "Even if we're not friends, we can do business. Call it professional courtesy."

Jack looked him up and down. "I don't see a spyglass."

Rooker grinned. "Funny thing is, ya do."

He pulled the brass rings off his finger. He'd given the speech about how they worked a hundred times since the *Venture Brigand* had dropped them at his feet. As Rooker went through the monologue, he watched Jack's eyes. The kid wouldn't remember this conversation in a few minutes, so Rooker took advantage of the time to feel him out. He was hard to read, like he'd built a wall of rock between them. But more than that, Rooker was struck by the cold calculation playing out behind his eyes. As he talked, Rooker glanced down and saw parchment and a quill on a nearby table. *Let's build some trust.*

Jack sneezed, a sign the forgetting majik had completed its work. He got that dumb-dog look on his face that everybody got, and for a moment, Rooker saw him soften. "Sorry." Jack wiped his nose. "I lost track of what you were saying."

Rooker grinned. "I said ya were gonna forget."

"Forget what?"

"Look, I get ya don't trust me. And yer not wrong." Rooker grinned. "But at least trust yerself."

Jack sighed, frustrated. "What the hell is that supposed to mean?"

"It's right there in black and white." Rooker pointed at the slip of paper sticking out of Jack's pocket. Puzzled, Jack unfolded it and saw the marks in fresh ink. Rooker couldn't read it, but Jack could.

Rooker's rings
are a
spyglass.

Jack blinked. "I didn't write that."

"It's yer handwriting, isn't it?" Rooker spread his hands. "Besides, I'm pretty sure no one here but you writes Toshan."

Jack blinked at the page, confused. *Good. He's off balance. Keep it that way.* Rooker slapped his hands together. "So. Let's get a gander at whatever yer ganderin' before ya ask me another dumb question."

Thirty yards up the big yingcao tree in the center of Hyena camp, Rooker was no longer smiling.

He didn't mind heights; he'd spent a year in the crow's nest under Captain Singh. But a ship's mast had rope ladders. This was climbing bareback. He wedged his foot into another crack in the bark and grabbed hold of the limb. Above, Jack scampered through the tree like a monkey. *Wonder how many times he's been up here.* Struggling to keep up, Rooker moved around the side, looking for a better handhold. A sleeping raiptar burst from the branches and took off in a shower of feathers. Rooker almost lost his grip, scrabbling for a handhold. As the bird flew away toward Vulture camp, he blew out a breath and continued climbing. *Ever heard of a rope?*

Jack waited for him in a man-made bird's nest. Planks of wood made an uneven walkway between the branches where two empty hammock chairs were strung up alongside a supply crate and a jug of water. *Got your own little tree fort, don't ya, kid?* He glanced down. A hundred feet below, Hyena camp went about its business, unaware of the two men above. "There are easier ways to kill me."

"Dropping you from a height is first on my list," Jack said. "Spyglass."

Rooker made the mistake of slapping his rings into Jack's hand. He regretted it instantly. Jack flinched away from his touch like he was a leper. Rooker felt the distaste in the kid's eyes and turned away. "Don't drop 'em."

Jack's expression turned from disgust to puzzlement as he stared at the rings. "*Why* do I keep forgetting these?"

"Maybe yer not as smart as ya think. Now get to work." Rooker slid into a hammock chair and let himself swing free over the hundred-foot drop. Jack fiddled with the rings, lined them up, and gazed at the Locke Institute wall. Rooker recognized the look on the kid's face, the one he got when that brain was cooking. *He's got a plan.*

Hopeful, Rooker dropped his first bread crumb. "So. What are we lookin' for?"

Jack shot air through his nose. "You think I'm going to tell you?"

Rooker managed to keep his mouth shut. *Let it simmer.*

They sat in silence for a long time. Rooker watched a ringslug munch happily on the yingcao bark nearby. As the sun descended to afternoon, a colony of pillbugs skittered down the tree, making their long journey to the ground. A flock of raiptars arched across the sky and came to rest in the branches a hundred feet above him. A warm ocean breeze picked up and flickered within the palms, making them dance. A tropical paradise.

Rooker was bored out of his mind. He had thought the silence would lead to conversation, but the kid was a clam. *Get him talking.* "Hey?"

"Hey." Jack didn't even look at him, scanning the Institute.

Rooker grabbed a vine. "What's it like there? In the Tosh? In Chegago?"

Jack stared through the rings. "Fewer giant spiders."

"Tell me about those skyscratchers."

"Skyscrapers. And no."

"C'mon, bubba." Rooker swung his hammock closer to Jack. "Say *something*. I don't even care if it's true."

"Bubba?"

"Ya don't like boychick or Chicken Legs so yeah... bubba."

"Fine." Jack refused to stop staring through the rings. "You're a sailor... so... here. Toshan boats don't need sails. They're powered by propellers. There you go."

Rooker scowled. "What's a propelpeller?"

"It's like a big screw. Or, no, think of it like a fan. Pushes the boat through the water."

"Like a mermaid's tail?"

"Kinda. But, like, in a spinning circle. Really fast."

"How fast?"

"Fast enough to pull a man on skis."

More made-up words. "What's a skis?"

Finally, Jack looked at him. "You don't have skis here? Even snow skis?" Rooker shrugged. "You strap flat wooden boards to your feet and you go so fast you stand on the water. Like the *Venture Brigand*."

Rooker chortled. "A man on skis? That wouldn't work." *He thinks I'll believe anything.*

For the first time, Jack made a noise that sounded something like a laugh. "It works. We make boats faster than the *Brigand*."

Rooker snorted, insulted. "I doubt that."

"Some boats are gigantic. Bigger than a town. All made of metal."

Rooker laughed. "Now I *know* yer lyin', bubba. Metal *sinks*."

"No, it's all about water displacement and air density—" Jack broke off. "Forget it. You wanted me to tell you something. I told you something."

Rooker felt the end of the conversation like a man watching a rope slip away. He scrambled for a way to keep it going, but, surprisingly, the kid did it for him. "Quid pro quo. I tell you something, you tell me something." Jack refused to take the rings from his eye, staring away from Rooker. "Do you know anything about the strîgoi?"

Rooker blinked. "Strîgoi? They're an old wives' tale. Dæmons. Boogeymen." Off Jack's blank look, Rooker got it. *Right. They don't have strîgoi in Chegago.* He slapped his hands, eager for a good ghost story, even if he already knew the end. "The Highway of the Nomads. It's a stretch of road between Rimmy's Cull and the Deuce, used to be called the Lake Line. Way back when, the Lake Line was a trade route, but then pilgrims started disappearing off the road. Single travelers at first, then wagons, then whole caravans. The old witcher-women blamed it on a coven of strîgoi. Dæmons that drain the blood of the living like a leech. Pale as milk. Black breath like smoke. Some stories said they could slip inside the strongest men and walk in their skin, take their body over like a puppet. Now, nobody believed the stories, of course; not until it was too late. Whole towns went missing. By the time winter came, there wasn't one village left on the road. Thousands of men, women, and children, gone in the night. The only ones left to tell the tale were a few scattered vagrants fleeing north. The strîgoi took the rest. And that's how it came to be called the Highway of the Nomads."

Rooker nodded, satisfied with the telling. Jack, however, looked vaguely ill. "How did it end?"

He leaned back, scratching his scalp. "Can't remember. One of the kings beat 'em back into the ground. Esau, I think."

At long last, Jack finally lowered the rings and looked at Rooker. "How?"

Rooker shrugged. "Only three things work against dæmons, kid: a silver blade, an iron cage, or a ring of salt."

Jack nodded, staring at nothing. "That explains some of it."

"Some of what?"

"Huh?" Jack snapped back to reality. He turned away, resuming his lookout. "Just a story Billy was singing. I didn't understand it."

"Uh-huh." Rooker nodded. *So we're back to lies again. Why would he care about dæmons nobody's seen in two hundred years?*

Rooker caught something out of the corner of his eye then, a shape in the tree behind Jack. It was impossible to tell if the thing was really there, just a yellow glow of two eyes, a wolfish mouth. Part of Rooker's brain recognized it looked like Jack's old dog, Shadow. Then it was gone, a figment of his imagination. And by that time, the opportunity for conversation had passed him by.

Another long silence amassed between them, the gulf widening moment by moment. For once, Rooker didn't know what to say. He wanted to extend an olive branch, figure out a way to make peace, but he didn't know how. He crossed his arms and retreated back in his chair, wondering why he'd bothered to come. There was no way to earn the kid's trust, no way to mend this fence. Whatever friendship they'd had was over and done with. There was no going back to the way things had been.

"You remember Leah?" Jack's voice was soft, his words hesitant. Rooker blinked. "Leah?" He sat straighter. "Archer. That redhead you carried a torch for, way back when?" He nodded, remembering Leah's pretty face from a lifetime ago. Another time, another land. "Spectacular nose."

Jack stared at nothing, his voice soft as a breeze. "I've been thinking about her. A lot."

"Well, sure, ya probably—"

"I dream about her every night, Rooker. Every single night. Like… She comes and rescues me or just makes me free. We fly away together. I don't know why it's her. It should be Valerian or Memphis or Dad, but it's always her. Just… spiriting me away."

Rooker stared at nothing, thinking of the past. Of long-gone freedoms. He nodded, dreaming with Jack. "That would be a sight to see."

The two men locked eyes. Jack surrendered a half-smile. "Guess I'm stuck on the way things used to be."

"We could fix that." Rooker eased toward him, trying to keep hope out of his voice. "Ya can team up with me again, just like old times."

"Rooker." Jack leveled his eyes at him. "You tried to kill me. Twice."

"I didn't try very hard."

Jack laughed, one of those surprised snorts that tackled you before you saw it coming. He tried to hide it and just wound up with spit all over his arm. Smiling, Rooker knew his moment when he saw it. *Now or never.* "Yer summoning worked. She has Nepenthe."

Jack's head snapped to him. *Now I've got yer attention.*

"Three pieces." Rooker leaned in. "Pinned to the wall of her office in cold iron. And as far as I can tell, the rest is on the way from Chegago."

Rooker watched a thousand questions flicker through Jack's head, but the kid had been in prison long enough that cynicism earned first position. "Why are you telling me about this?" Jack eyed him narrowly. "You're working for her."

"Maybe ol' Gerba's got nothing left to offer me." Rooker shrugged, sly as a cat. "Maybe you do."

Jack blinked. "You sold me out to her. Now you're selling her out to me?" He laughed again, but this time there was no joy in it. "Whatever side gives you what you want, that's the side you're on, Rooker. You don't know what loyalty *is.*"

"Listen to me, Jack. I'm going to say this one time. I'm the most trustworthy person yer ever gonna meet, because ya know for a *fact* I do what's best for *me.*" He stuck a finger in Jack's face. "All I want, the only thing I want, is the *Venture Brigand.* Right now, the person that gives me the best shot at her is you." He tilted his head. "I know ya schemed up some kind of escape plan, and whatever it is"—he set his jaw, trying not to sound like a beggar—"I want in."

Jack shut his mouth. A pure poker face.

Rooker scowled. "When the *Brigand* gets back, I steal Nepenthe, and we fight our way on board. From there, I can take us the rest of the way. I can outrun any ship Gerba puts after us. And from there... yer free." Jack's face remained blank. Rooker decided to push a little harder. "Without me, yer never gonna make it out of the harbor. If you want to run, the *Brigand* is the only solution." Rooker searched Jack's eyes. "Ya don't like me right now, I get it. We aren't partners, we aren't teammates, and we aren't friends. We're just two guys with the same problem." He leaned in. "And after this is over, you'll never see me again. Hate me all ya want, Jack. But do it in Chegago."

He had him. He knew it. The hook was set. All Rooker had to do was reel in the line. "I got the key to set ya free, bubba. And you got mine." He set his jaw. "The only way we get off this island is together."

Jack pulled his bottom lip, considering. "How do I know you won't go running straight to Gerba and tell her what we're planning?"

"The same way I know yer not gonna tell anyone I'm a rat." Rooker showed his teeth. "No profit in it."

Jack chuckled at that.

Rooker got close. "C'mon, bubba. Level with me. Why do you need a spyglass? Why are we hiding in a tree, staring at a wall?"

Jack took a breath, thinking. Finally, he nodded. "You remember the night I tried to get Fancy Nan's journal?"

Finally. "Yeah?"

"When the sun set, the shiq came up the wall, but something stopped them, something that protected the Institute. Little lights along the wall, glowing red, like... stoplights."

Rooker blinked. "What's a stoplight?"

Jack's brow furrowed. "It's like a... um..." Jack's mouth moved up and down, searching for an example, then gave up. "Keymark doesn't have anything like a stoplight. It's a sign that has three lights on it. The bottom one is green and it's *go* and the middle one is yellow and that's *slow down* and the one on the top is red to make you *stop*."

"Yer world has some stupid stuff." He crooked an eyebrow. "But yeah, I get it. A spider stoplight." He felt the realization hit, remembering his conversation with the librarian. *The rune. That's how Gerba is protecting the Institute at night. A barrier of runes in the wall.* For a shining moment, Rooker's chest swelled, savoring the experience of, just once, being smarter than Jack Swift. He cocked a satisfied grin. "And I know how it works."

Jack cocked his head. "You know about the Caged Eight?"

Wait, what? Rooker blinked. "*You* know about the Caged Eight?"

"Yeah. I saw it welded inside the bell. In gold. Controls anything with eight legs. Farah knew all about it."

Rooker scowled. "Who the hell is *Farah*?"

"Fancy Nan's assistant. Every time Gerba hangs one of us..."

"...she gets more control over the spiders. Blood for majik."

Jack frowned. "That's not all she's using our blood for."

Rooker cocked his head. "What does *that* mean?"

"Nothing." Jack turned his head. "How did *you* know about the Caged Eight?"

Eager for answers, Rooker spoke quickly. "Gerba used it that night on the cliff, right before..." He cut himself off, realizing he'd walked right into a trap of his own design. For a moment, he felt like a puppy, ashamed and guilty for what he'd done. "Right before you... fell."

At that moment, he might have asked for forgiveness.

Jack had done it.

Forgive me if you can.

But Rooker Flynn was not a puppy. Begging for mercy would only make him look weak, an unforgivable surrender. He would never lower himself to that level. That choice had been beaten out of him long ago.

Ice blue eyes stared at him. Cold. Calculating. A long and barren moment passed between them. When Jack spoke, his voice had the same tone as when they'd first ascended the tree, flat and hard. "Sun's getting low. We should head back."

"Jack, c'mon..."

The kid handed Rooker's brass rings back to him and descended the yingcao palm without saying a word.

Rooker sat in the tree, alone, cursing himself. For a moment, it had seemed he'd almost had his friend back. Almost.

They descended in silence, Jack leading the way.

As he clambered down the yingcao tree, Rooker watched the kid, trying to come up with some way to recapture that moment they'd shared, something he could say, something he could do to make it like old times. But the rift between them was wider than ever, and he had only himself to blame.

That thought kicked him in the gut all the way down.

Rooker's feet hit dirt, a cloud of dry dust around his boots. He eyed the new water tower, the two-story cliques. He saw how clean the camp was, how many familiar faces there were, and how many of them were smiling. Even the old drunk Yenrab was grinning, chatting up a lady dwarf.

The camp felt more like home than Jackal ever had.

He glanced at Jack. "So, ya want me to bunk over? Little pow-wow between camp bosses? We could talk some more. Come up with a plan."

Jack brushed invisible dirt from his pants. "I don't think so, Rooker."

Rooker nodded. "Once I leave, there's no guarantee I'll come back."

"See you at assembly, Boss Flynn."

Rooker turned and walked back toward Jackal, spinning the rings on his finger.

It didn't work.

He doesn't trust me.

But it's a start.

PART 2

TRIAL

Chapter

=BOUNTY=

No matter how hard the past,
you can always begin again.
Buddha

P IKACHEEPS ARE A RARITY in Keymark. Their eggs are fragile, thin as tissue paper. Few survive the incubation process, easy prey for infection, mold, and the egg-eating iguanas that populate their homeland. When they finally hatch, they are the size of a walnut, covered in pink and yellow feathers. Nesting in large groups of twenty to thirty, the flightless birds spend their lives pecking for food, running from predators, and forming tight family bonds.

Little by little, the hatchling worked her beak through her eggshell, struggling toward daylight. After several hours, she emerged, peeping quietly. She nearly fell over on wobbly legs smaller than toothpicks. On her head was a little piece of shell she wore like a tiny hat. She cheeped, then hopped forward, looking for her mother.

"O, isn't that darling!" Massive brown hands collected the baby bird and held it with utmost care. Gerba Whipmarples gazed lovingly at the tiny thing. "So, so precious."

"Headmistress?"

"Yes, Winnifred?"

The acolyte simpered to Gerba's desk, holding a stack of packages, excited. "Responses from Baronet Ket, Thakur Kroll, and Viscountess Jimenez. Even one from the Sheikh of Baaza." The girl was practically bouncing on her toes. "They have responded to your invitation, headmistress."

"Isn't that wonderful?" Gerba cooed at the pikacheep. "They're all coming! Yes, they are! Yes, they are, my little birdie-wirdie!" She snuggled the pikacheep with her horn.

The responses from the nobles had been exceptionally good indeed. The first test at the killing field had gone swimmingly, and word was starting to spread. The nobles had, of course, complained about plenty. The carriage ride had been too long, Lordling Lund had been embarrassed at having his poor archery skills on display in front of his peers, and of course, none of them had liked the shiq. But Headmistress Whipmarples had ironed out all those details, smoothing the path for her fragile new friends.

Despite their complaints, it was clear they had developed an appetite.

"We will begin the transfer to Bounty today, Winnifred. Please see to it."

"Yes, headmistress. Right away."

"Yes, she will." Gerba Whipmarples snuggled the darling little pikacheep with her face. "Yes, she *will!* We are going on a little *trip,* aren't we?"

She flicked the bird into her mouth and bit down, savoring the flavor.

Scrumptious, she thought. *Just delightful.*

"I don't think that's going to fill your belly." Cant Naysayer descended the library steps on cat's feet, his eyes hidden beneath the brim of his hat.

"A delicacy from Chult, a gift from the sheikh's second son. Very rare. Very expensive." Gerba dabbed her mouth with a silk napkin and slid the tiny pikacheep nest toward him. "Would you care for one?"

Cant Naysayer took his accustomed place before her desk, standing just out of easy reach. His expressionless black mask betrayed no emotion. "I had breakfast."

"New bounties." Gerba slid him the broadsheets. "Contracts on sixteen outlaws, all high-profile, all guaranteed. Captain Ito, Lobo Gris, and this new one they call the Rooster. Shouldn't take you a month to fetch them all." She leaned back in her chair. "Have you considered my offer on the *Venture Brigand*? I happen to be flush with coin at the moment, and I am feeling generous."

"What about the Heart of Huánghūn?"

Gerba frowned. She did not like Cant Naysayer. He always saw things too clearly. Her eyes darted to the place where she kept the

Book of Kos hidden away. "This is not a conversation I would like to have over breakfast, Mister Naysayer."

Ice-blue eyes bored into her. "You were supposed to use Nepenthe as a compass to find the Heart."

"As I shall. When the time is right." Gerba settled back in her chair and studied the bounty hunter. In truth, she had already tried to use Nepenthe several times. The elven majik within the stave was too weak to dowse for the Heart of Huánghūn. Not with only three pieces. The other four were caught between spheres, trying to find their way to Keymark. Until then, the best tool she had at her disposal was patience. "All things in good time."

"And the strîgoi—"

"*Mister* Naysayer." Gerba Whipmarples stood and cleared her skirt, an orange gown the color of marmalade. "I have spent more than a decade researching this island and the things that lie beneath it. I was here before the Black Accord was broken, before the Agrat-ban-Haifa could make a single sound. I have built this place stone by stone. Do not presume to tell me my business." She stepped forward like a mother protecting her child. "You continue to make a commission from the Locke Institute. I ensure you are paid quickly, expansively, and often. That is the extent of your interest here." She tilted her long horn, sizing him up. If it came down to a contest between the two of them, Gerba could not be sure of the outcome. *Let's nip this in the bud.* "I would hate to see us at odds, Cant."

The warlock said nothing. The bounty hunter had always been clever, saying only what needed to be said, and he was smart enough to say it now. "My apologies, headmistress. Forgive me if I overstepped."

Good. Gerba sat and straightened her napkin. "I have commissioned your brothers to assist us on Bounty. Unfortunately, this means they will not be able to join you on your expedition. But I *do* expect to see you back for the trial, Mister Naysayer. You have two months."

"As you wish." The bounty hunter offered a long scarecrow bow, then he was gone.

Gerba adjusted the brooch on her collar and took a long breath. *Patience, dearie. Patience.*

She leaned in and watched the pikacheep nest, waiting for the next egg to hatch.

"All right, skags! I'm pulling a few students for a special detail." Winston addressed the assembled convicts in the yard at the dawn of a new day. Gerba had been absent during this morning's announcement, and Portia had delivered the 'work will make you free' speech.

Jack didn't hear Winston run down the list of names; he was lost in a never-ending treadmill of plans, calculations, and contingencies. The caves, the runes, the shiq, the phosphorus, the bell... It all tumbled around in Jack's head like a load of laundry in a drier that never stopped. There were too many unknowns, too many variables, and he had to account for all of them. *If I miss something, we're dead.*

Jack Swift had walked out of the pit a different man. His former self would never have been able to assume control of Hyena camp, exile Ransom, enforce the new dinner dash rules, or assemble a secret team of escape artists. The wolf was part of him now. Its voice was silent, but it had taken something from him. His innocence had perished in the pit. Now he was constantly wary, on guard against lies, hidden dangers, and betrayals. Jack suspected everyone, even his own crew, and almost never slept.

When he did doze, he collapsed into the recurring dream of Leah Archer, a woman he hadn't seen in more than two and a half years. In the strîgoi pit, Jack had gripped the dream of Leah with both hands, a bittersweet fantasy to counteract the ever-growing presence of the wolf. She told him that everything would be all right, that she would spirit him away from Huánghūn, that she loved him. His dreams were his only source of hope, a lone weapon to combat the fear that dogged his every step. But the dream of Leah was nothing but wishful thinking. His waking mind, his intelligent mind, chastised him whenever he turned to her for comfort, and little by little his dream soured like curdling milk, a silly fairy tale he'd constructed out of desperation. These days, Jack didn't want to go to sleep, didn't want to suffer that false hope every night. His only real chance came from the plan. From logic. From science. And it would only be delivered by his own two hands.

"...and Black Jack."

His head snapped up as he realized he was included in the special detail group. Looking around, he saw a few other familiar faces had been selected. Patch Picaroon, Billy Pilgrim, and all three bosses: Eightfingers, Hook, and Flynn. "You lot, come with me," barked Winston. "The rest of you, get to it." Attercops ushered the other prisoners to work. Jack saw Yenrab and Copper Dave glance at him, confused. Further back, Farah departed with the crowd and looked over her shoulder.

As they went, Jack leaned in to Patch. "What's going on?"

Patch shook her head. "Beats me. But anything different is a step up." Jack glanced at the jinx. She had gained a bit of weight in the last month, but her fur had lost its accustomed sheen. Patch Picaroon had somehow always defied the gnawing, corrosive toll of the penal colony, but these days she looked as tired as Jack felt.

Attercops shoved black canvas bags over their heads and led them into the tunnels. As always, Jack counted the steps, trying to account for the rise and fall, changes in direction, a GPS in his head. They headed down, and before long the slow stink of sulfur was replaced with something new. "Do ya smell that?" Boss Flynn's voice sounded gleeful. "The *sea*."

The bags came off, and for the first time in nearly eight months, Jack Swift stood outside the Locke Institute.

He found himself on the other side of the wall, where the land met the sea. A cool breeze curled around his body as the gentle susurrus of waves broke against the shore. Gulls cried overhead, wheeling in the sky, spying for fish. He stood at the base of the long dock, nearly half a mile of wood and stone that thrust into the bay like a giant's lance.

Grins broke out among the prisoners as they breathed free air. None was wider than Rooker Flynn's. The attercops and acolytes herded the prisoners down the pier toward a beaten-up barge christened the *Hup Two*.

Quickly, the convicts were ushered aboard and put to work manning the oars. Without fanfare, the boat cast off from the pier and raised its ancient sails, and they were upon the sea.

"Where are we going?" Jack whispered to Patch.

"How the hell should I know?" She bent to her oar, her face miserable.

Despite her years on the water, Patch took ill and vomited before they reached the end of the pier. Jack tried to comfort her; she thanked him with a string of obscenities woven between spurts of puke.

Rooker ignored the retching jinx and stood at the prow of the ship, yelling at the captain. "Yer the worst sailor I ever *saw!* Release the jib, let it fly a little. *Hey!*"

Razorsquid darted beneath the boat, feeding on Patch's leavings. Jack had never seen razorsquid before, not close up. Iridescent and nearly translucent, the squid looked like tiny underwater disco balls with legs, more jellyfish than cephalopods, glittering a rainbow of pearlescent light. Dozens swam together, glistening. A tuna moved through the squid, blossomed contrails of cloudy blood, and came to a halt as it was murdered one slow lash at a time.

Soon enough, the *Hup Two* broke past the end of the pier. All that lay before them was a collection of boats, most with golden sails.

Rooker stood upon the prow, his body straight as an arrow. *"There she is!"*

The *Venture Brigand* made berth two hundred yards past the end of the pier, levitating above the water on long outriggers. This was the first time Jack had seen the giant catamaran up close in a long time. He didn't know much about boats, but from here, she looked more majestic than any ship in the harbor, a tiger among housecats.

"Yellow sails," groused Rooker. "Damn Naysayers still have her wearing yellow."

Jack recognized his opportunity. Every escape plan he'd concocted ended with a boat, and the *Venture Brigand* was the finest ship in the bay. Wind whipped his hair as he climbed up beside Rooker and leaned in close. "How could we make it to the *Brigand* from the docks? We'd need a boat to *get* to the boat, right?"

"That's easy." Rooker snorted and jerked his chin at the selections on the dock. "Those skiffs, the pinques, and the ketch are garbage. The xebec is too big. I'd commandeer the cutter." He pointed at a medium-sized vessel, then eyed a large three-master. "I wouldn't mind taking that corvette, but she's too big for six."

Jack averted his eyes, but Rooker caught the look on his face.

He grinned. "Ya got a six-man crew, right? You, me, Patch, Yenrab, Copper Dave, and whazzername? Farah?"

A six-man crew. Sure. Jack found it comical that Rooker had injected himself into the team. The pirate continued, eager. "Four landlubbers in that crew, useless on water. The only two that know their way around a ship are me and Patch." The jinx-cat hurled the contents of her stomach into the bilge. "And she don't look so good."

"Sit down!" came a shout from the stern. Jack sat, and Rooker grudgingly dropped into the seat beside him. His dark eyes peered at the *Venture Brigand* as they approached his former ship.

Jack tried to contain his curiosity and failed. "I don't get why it's such a big deal they changed the *Brigand*'s sails from red to yellow. What does that mean?"

"Yellow sails mean it's a yellowjacket ship."

Jack scowled at him. "That doesn't help me, Rooker."

"Yellowjackets. Reeves. The long arm of the law."

"Like police?"

"Is that what you call 'em in the Tosh?" They traded a look, then Rooker shrugged. "Thugs who know how to stay on the paying side. And yellowjackets have interceptors that will outrun that corvette. No." He stared at the *Venture Brigand*. "She's the only way to get free." They passed within thirty yards of the catamaran, her supple, graceful body suspended over the waves. As they passed, Jack swore he could hear the boat sigh.

"Hello, girl." Rooker leaned on the deckrail, a moonish look in his eyes. "I'm still here."

Jack stifled a laugh. Rooker looked like a lovestruck puppy. "Come *on*, Rooker. It's pretty but... it's just another boat."

"Bite yer tongue off and spit it in the sea, *wasteka yaban hito*." Rooker pointed at the corvette. "*That* is just a boat." He pointed at the *Brigand*. "*That* is nautical perfection."

Jack enjoyed watching Rooker fume. "Perfection, huh?"

Rooker jammed his finger in Jack's face. "The *Venture Brigand* is the finest ship that ever has or ever *will* sail the Irridin. She's the fastest thing on water and can outdistance any one of these scrapheaps on her worst day. There's no storm that can break her, no wave that can capsize her, and no doldrum that can hold her."

The pirate's eyes gleamed as they never had for a treasury full of gold. "She is freedom itself."

Jack almost chuckled. "Very romantic."

Rooker turned, ignoring him. "She knows me. She hears me. She's been my home since..." Rooker paused, his eyes focusing far off into the distance. "My whole life." He turned to the *Venture Brigand*, a grin curling his lips. "She loves me."

Now Jack laughed. "The *boat* loves you."

"Like a faithful wife." Rooker didn't bother looking at him. "I could whisper her name and she'd come to me."

"Really."

"She would." Rooker smiled. "She would come."

"Okay, then do it." Jack put his hands on his hips. "Call it over."

Rooker looked at Jack like he'd grown a third asscheek. "She's anchored with iron. If I was on deck, sure, but from here? How's she supposed to do anything at the end of an iron chain?"

I know how she feels. Jack watched the *Venture Brigand* slip away. He settled into his seat and peered at Patch, who was still unloading breakfast. "Any idea where they're taking us?"

"Not to Javernis Twist for brunch." Rooker scowled. "Probably that skerry lump." He pointed at the south end of the bay. Jack had seen the little spit of land before, but it was so small it hardly seemed like a destination, not even big enough to be called an island, just a speck of nothing in a sea of nothing.

Jack peered at the little islet. "So why is she taking us there?"

"How would I know?"

Jack adopted his most cutting tone. "You're her pet, aren't you?"

Rooker scowled. "Maybe she wants to maroon us." He turned to Jack with a wicked grin. "Or maybe it's just a good spot to kill ya quietly."

The skerry lump failed to get any bigger as it drew closer. No larger than four city blocks, the spit of land was small enough to circumnavigate in fifteen minutes. The *Hup Two* rounded a bend, and Jack saw a brand-new wharf had been recently constructed, big enough for a dozen large ships. It stood deserted.

Disembarking with the others, Jack noticed sinuous carvings in the pillars of the wharf: sharks, sea-creatures, and mermaids frozen in the wood, all detailed in vibrant paint so new it glistened. The wharf met a wide road paved with polished white stone that gleamed in the sun. *Is that marble?*

Attercops stayed with the *Hup Two* as acolytes took command. They attached strands of small bells to the bottom of their veils, making them jingle as they led the prisoners down the marble road. As Jack followed, he watched the light reflect up from the white stone, making the acolytes' pale robes seem to glow.

Jack Swift came over a rise to discover a vast expanse of tree trunks severed at the base, a denuded jungle of dead stumps upon a carpet of sawdust. He heard construction: saws, hammers, and men calling to each other. He realized how long it had been since he had seen an animal other than shiq, raiptar birds, and ringslugs when he was shocked by the appearance of two dray horses hauling a load of timber. Pleasantly surprised, he spied more animals familiar to Keymark: a group of tams.

Three-foot-long geckos, the tams snuffled like dogs between the stumps, licking up fallen bugs and grubs. Jack grew excited at the sight of them and thought of his little tam, Fuji, who had once followed him across Keymark as a loving pet. The geckos craned their necks at the prisoners from a copse of palm stumps. One licked its eye as Jack passed, grinning as if it knew something.

The marble path terminated at a green timber wall three stories tall. At the base, a pair of closed doors arched halfway up the wall. In front of the doors, half a dozen acolytes waited by what looked like a big table covered with a bumpy sheet.

"Wait here," announced Gita from behind her niqab. "You will be allowed to enter when the construction crew breaks for lunch. You are permitted to explore the Isle of Bounty if you choose. In the meantime, please enjoy your banquet." She pulled back the sheet like a magician's trick, and Jack's mouth hung open in shock.

Long-forgotten scents flooded the air. The succulent humidity of roasted pork, the savory scent of pad thai noodles, the bitter tang of pecorino cheese, the sweet kiss of sliced guava... enough for a hundred men.

The prisoners fell on the smorgasbord like barbarians. Jack felt himself shoved out of the way as they nearly knocked the table over. Few had tasted anything but galt for months and fell to stuffing themselves with a vengeance. Some tried using utensils and plates, but most just shoved the feast directly into their mouths. Every prisoner ate until their belly was fit to burst, but still more deliciousness remained. The idea of leftover food seemed like a crime, so they continued gorging themselves until they couldn't move.

Jack Swift couldn't remember tasting anything so good in his life.

An hour later, he lounged against a stump, staring at nothing. He had removed his belt along with the top two buttons of his denims. He stared stupidly at the tropical sky, one hand rubbing his distended stomach. It would have been a perfect moment had it not been for the sound of Patch retching nearby. "Are you okay?"

"Shut up," Patch groaned.

"Hey." Jack felt a foot kick his backside and turned to find Flynn standing above him. He looked ridiculous, a pot belly hanging over skinny jeans. He slapped his gut. "I need to walk this off. Ya comin'?"

Jack glanced at Patch, who wasn't going anywhere soon. "Yeah." With some effort, he managed to drag himself upright and waddle after the pirate.

Rooker hollered at one of the acolytes. "Yo! Sheetface!" The acolyte turned and glared at him through the slit in his veil. "We can go anywhere on the islet? Yer not gonna shoot us or anything?"

"Stay outside and do as you like," replied the acolyte.

Making little groaning sounds, Jack and Rooker ambled down the beach. For a while, they just breathed fresh air. Eventually, Jack started to feel less like an overstuffed jelly donut and picked up the pace. The big wall continued for quite a way, masking the interior of the islet in an oblong loop. What was inside remained a mystery.

Along the shore, a few live trees still took root, but most of the land was nothing but ringslug-cut stumps. Moving toward the tip of the island, they found a series of small cabins that looked much older than the green timber wall. A few acolytes tended animal pens filled with tapir and chickens.

Beyond that was only the endless sea.

"Well." Jack rubbed his swollen belly. "That's the whole island."

Rooker let fly a resonant belch, then cocked a thumb over his shoulder. "Ya notice that?"

Jack nodded. "No yingcao palms."

Rooker eyed him. "Does that mean no shiq?"

As they looked at each other, neither man could stop his smile. The mere speculation of a night without spiders crawling all over them was cause for joy.

"Ya wanna swim?"

Jack's body was tacky with sweat and grime. He eyed the crystal-blue water. "Yes, I do."

The pirate waded into the surf and pointed to a stone outcropping fifty yards out. "C'mon, race ya to that hullbreaker."

Jack scratched his gut. "I don't know..."

"O, come on, ya puppy, I don't know wh—"

"*Onetwothreego!*" Jack ran to the water and dove in.

Shouting, Rooker sputtered curses and threw himself after Jack. It was a good race. Jack was an excellent swimmer, and his methodical freestyle was far more efficient than whatever stroke Rooker used. But the pirate had spent his entire life on the sea and was no stranger to speed. He caught up on the return trip, grabbed Jack's leg, pulled him backward, and beat him to the shoreline. "Ha!"

Both of them collapsed in the sand, panting. Jack spat water, grinning. "You cheated!"

"*You* cheated!"

"Yeah." Jack nodded. "Wanna go again?"

"Yeah."

They did.

Two hours later, the hammering and sawing behind the wall fell silent. Acolytes gathered the prisoners in front of the door. Jack stood with the convicts and stared up at the massive entryway. Rooker leaned toward him. "What the hell ya think they got in there?"

Jack snorted. "King Kong."

A long-horned figure emerged on the parapet and strode atop the wall. She was dressed in yellow and matched the sun, a wide-brimmed derby hat upon her head. Gerba Whipmarples stood directly over the doors and raised her hands. "Students! Welcome to the Isle of Bounty!" She clasped her hands and tilted her head. "I am looking forward to embarking on this journey with you. Until now, the Locke Institute has helped you develop skills that will make you useful to society. Good, honest labor, a trade, and the pride that goes with it." She raised a finger. "But at the Locke Institute, we must not forget to hone the skills that bring joy to others. Art. Sport. Entertainment."

Jack saw Billy Pilgrim perk up. Some of the prisoners looked at each other, liking the sound of that. They pressed forward, eager to hear more. "My darling students," chirped Gerba. "Today, we begin the next level of your education."

Dramatically, the doors creaked open, revealing a whole new world.

A theater in the round.

Tiered rows of viewing boxes, chairs and benches lined the inner wall, enough for an audience of several hundred, and every seat faced the center of the oval. The stage itself was the base of the theater, gleaming in the midday sun, a hundred tons of white sand delivered from the shores of Bounty.

The dozen dirty convicts moved onto the white sand and gazed up at their surroundings. Jack squinted to find twenty hammerd-warves staring down at them from the gallery, their tools in their hands, silent.

Billy Pilgrim sprinted to the middle of the sand and struck a chord on his banjo. He listened as the sound echoed back to him. He placed his feet apart, spread his arms, and sang at the top of his lungs.

Heroes and villains of every age
The world comes alive here upon the stage!
Masquerade, love, pain, bemusement, and choir
The audience beckons a great muse of fire!

"Good acoustics," said Rooker.

As the other prisoners milled about, Jack put his hands on his hips and took in the vast arena. "I don't get it. We're... what... actors now?" He turned to Billy Pilgrim. "You, I get. You can sing. I can't." He turned to Patch. "Are we supposed to do a... performance?"

Rooker chuckled and sucked his teeth. "Ya don't get it, do ya, bubba? Look."

Jack eyed the eight-foot-tall enclosure that separated the outlaws from the audience like a gigantic baseball dugout. It circled the entire stadium, dotted with latticed metal windows and portcullis doorways at regular intervals.

Jack lowered an eyebrow. "Are those... entrances to the stage?"

"It ain't a stage."

Rooker spat.

"It's a gladiator pit."

D!RTY=OZEN

*All the world's a stage,
and all the men and women merely players.
They have their exits and their entrances;
And one man in his time plays many parts.*
William Shakespeare

R OOKER TURNED AT THE sound of cranking metal and discovered a portcullis door rising, opening like a black mouth. All around him, the dozen outlaws stepped toward the cage door, curious. Fed up with not being able to see, Rooker elbowed his way to the front. Before the spiked door had fully opened, a shadow emerged, revealing a misshapen and powerful creature.

Boss Eightfingers took a step back. "Is that thing a man or a monster?"

"Both." Rooker narrowed his eyes. "That's Wont Naysayer."

Wont's lumpy head ducked under the opening and hooked his ram's horns beneath the door. He lifted the portcullis the rest of the way with rippling biceps and muscled broad shoulders through the doorway. As cloven hooves clomped on the white sand, Rooker saw the bounty hunter's horns were painted a bloody red.

Ugly sonofabitch. Rooker hated all law-dogs, but only Wont Naysayer had embarrassed him in front of the *Brigand. Big, ugly sonofabitch.*

"All right, let's get this over with." Wont scratched his chest. "Anybody wants to take a shot at me, go ahead. And just to make it interesting... Any convict who puts me on the ground gets a pardon from the Locke Institute." He gestured. "Your weapons are over there."

Another portcullis door opened, revealing a cage wall hung with an array of swords, axes, mauls, shields, nets, and tridents.

Rooker launched himself at the rack and was there before anyone else could move. His greedy hands flickered over the weapons and plucked a worn but sturdy scimitar from the rack, then snatched a short sai, a disarming bladebreaker. He checked the edge. *Sparring blades. Dammit.*

He belted them at his waist as Patch arrived and selected the basket rapier he'd known she would want. She snapped up a bullwhip and danced aside as the rest of the dirty dozen hit the rack in a scrum for steel.

Rooker watched them fight and realized Jack didn't understand what was happening. By the time the kid got to the rack, the only weapon left was a double-handed six-foot claymore with a leather pommel that looked like it had been chewed on by dogs. *Damn thing's bigger than he is.*

"Okay." Wont Naysayer spread his massive arms and grinned. "Have at it."

Boss Hook lunged at Wont with a bastard sword. Two assassins, Weasel and Leadbelly, joined him, blades flashing. Wont's apelike forearm deflected most of the blows, but he took a few hard hits from Hook. The Naysayer didn't seem to notice. He slammed Hook to the ground, headbutted Leadbelly, then kicked Weasel as Boss Eightfingers and his crew of Vultures launched a sneak attack from behind, a fusillade of blades.

Rooker threw his arm across Patch's chest to stop her entering the fray. She snarled at him. "Don't." Rooker eyed the fight. There was nothing he'd like more than to put Wont in the dirt, but that wasn't going to happen. "Save yer strength. Unless these are majiked blades, nobody's going to give him a bruise."

Sure enough, the fight ended with eight outlaws lying in the white sand, a few sporting broken noses. Unharmed, Wont glanced at Patch, Jack, and Pilgrim. "Any more takers?" He looked straight at Rooker. "Flynn?"

Rooker shrugged. "Yer ugly enough as it is."

Wont's face turned as red as his horns, but before he could re-act, Gerba Whipmarples' amplified voice erupted from the stands. "Students, I would like to introduce you to your new physical education instructor: Mister Wont Naysayer."

"Self-defense!" Wont straightened. "Right now, you're all am-ateurs! Everything you just did was wrong. Untrained, undisci-plined, and frankly embarrassing. For a bunch of killers, none of you is any good at killing. But we're here to change that. Boys!"

Wont shouted and Rooker watched a group of shadows emerge from the doorway.

Yellowjackets. Rooker recognized the painted leather splint mail that protected their chests, the yellow insignias on their scabbards signifying rank and loyalty. The men were as scarred as their armor, their faces rough enough to use as sandpaper.

Rooker had always hated the smell of yellowjackets. For whatever reason, they all used the same liniment, which smelled something worse than a dead skunk.

He folded his arms and assessed the fighters. He recognized two former pirates, Harker and Fallow, along with a pair of overweight ronin named Mingo and Bobby Puce. Most of the men were turncoats for the Inquisition, outlaws gone yellow. Rooker snorted. "Half these guys outta be in prison with us."

Jack glared at him. "They are."

Rooker squinted at Jack's claymore. "Did they not have anything bigger?"

"Heya, Rooker." A sneering yellowjacket weaved forward with a sneer on his gin-blossomed face. "Where's the *dog*?"

"Heya, Fallow." Rooker cocked his chin. "He was sleeping with your wife but found a better-looking bitch."

That got a laugh from convicts and yellowjackets alike. Growling, Fallow pointed his sword at Rooker. "You'll pay for that, Flynn."

"Listen up!" Wont Naysayer lumbered to center stage. "Pair off! One of yours versus one of mine." The two groups of hardened outlaws stared each other down. "Let's see what you're made of, one on one. Whoever's left standing wins."

A dozen battered yellowjackets drew their swords and spread out.

Rooker avoided Fallow, who was deadly with a blade, and edged toward Harker, a hulking brute with a scar across his face. The man's sword was barely out before Rooker batted it aside. Harker kept his grip and swung. Rooker caught his blade in his sai and knocked him on the temple with the scimitar's pommel. The yellowjacket dropped like a bag of dead fish.

Rooker turned to find none of the other combatants had moved yet. They just stared at him with wide eyes. "Well?"

Patch almost won her bout, but Mingo was huge, brutal, and quickly put her on her tail. None of the others came close. Rooker suppressed a laugh as Jack tried to wield his claymore and got thrashed before he got one swing in. Outlaws rolled on the ground in pain, including Boss Eightfingers and Boss Hook, while yellowjackets laughed through smug grins.

For once, Rooker agreed with Wont. "Pathetic." The hulk moved to the wall around the arena and flipped over an hourglass. "Listen up, you cheap thugs. When this runs out, you go again. We are going to practice and practice and practice. Sunup to sundown, every day. Got me?"

A round of grumbles rippled from the convicts.

"Now, now, students!" Gerba clapped her hands, the sound sharp within the arena. "Let us look for the silver lining, shall we? You have not yet heard the best part!" She cleared her throat and a proud expression crossed her horned face. "All of you are *lucky* to have been chosen, and I will tell you why! Ten days from now, you will be given an opportunity to *graduate* from the Locke Institute." That caught everyone's attention. "Ten days from now, we will have a Steel Trial."

A thrill ran through Rooker's body. Steel Trials were an old tradition within the Inquisition, a custom that hadn't been used in a hundred years. A convicted criminal could prove their innocence in trial-by-combat. Any prisoner who bested the Inquisition's representative in a Steel Trial would be absolved of one crime.

The only downside, of course, was getting murdered.

I've got eighty-three life sentences. That means eighty-three kills.

Rooker eyed the yellowjackets and grinned.

I could do that.

"You have been given a golden opportunity, students." Gerba spread her hands like a generous benefactor. "I suggest you make the most of it."

As the convicts murmured to each other, Rooker heard Jack whisper to Patch. "What's a Steel Trial?"

"Same thing ya just did." Rooker flicked the edge of his blade and grinned at Jack. "But for real."

The kid went white as a sheet.

Sunset.

All the prisoners gathered outside the colosseum and watched the sun descend toward Huánghūn with nervous eyes. Every one of the dirty dozen shifted, anxious. Rooker was no exception. He had already picked out a caged spot in the dugout to lock himself in when the shiq came. As the sun fell beneath the horizon, one convict started hyperventilating. Another made strange, worried noises in his throat. When the final ray of sunlight winked out, Rooker sucked in an involuntary breath. It had been beaten into him, just like everything else in his life. The setting sun told Rooker Flynn to *flee.*

For a few moments, he didn't breathe.

He listened, waiting for the *churr* of the shiq.

Nothing came.

Outside. Rooker licked his lips. *At night.*

Billy Pilgrim struck a chord on his banjo and everyone jumped. Jack laughed and slapped the troubadour on the back. The other outlaws did the same. Laughter turned to shouts, which became cheers.

Nothing's coming to get me. Rooker let out a breath. *Not tonight.*

He snapped his fingers and ignited his flame. In no time at all, he had a bonfire going on the beach. Pilgrim played his banjo while outlaws danced around the flames. They joked and sang, eating the roast ham they had been served for dinner, toasting each other from the ale keg that had come with it. Convicts wandered through the dark, gazing upon the moons they had not seen in months, seeing the stars they had only dreamt of on Huánghūn. The white moon rose past the orange, Gamilat waxing, Anika waning, two star-crossed lovers in the dark.

"Hey, Pilgrim." Rooker smiled. "Give us a little Gamilat and Anika."

Billy strummed his banjo and sang, his voice sweet, melodious, and loving.

Pale milky skin upon her face
She rises now to his embrace
All know that none may e'er replace
My Gamilat and Anika

Gentle kisses as they fly
Their eyes together fortify
Against the day they say goodbye
Do Gamilat and Anika

Yet pulled apart they lonely course
Between the stars weep their remorse
The softly drifting slow divorce
Of Gamilat and Anika.

The convicts stared at the moons, watching their slow dance in the sky.

As the night wore on, the party broke up. Most of the convicts went back to the colosseum to sleep, and Rooker found himself sitting with Jack and Patch, along with Billy strumming his banjo. Jack and Patch were deep in conversation, but Rooker saw the frustration in their gestures. *Heh. All those plans down the drain.* "Wishing you were back on Huánghūn?"

Patch scowled at him. "Who would want that?"

"Someone with an escape plan." Billy looked up, surprised, and twanged a questioning note on his banjo.

Patch glanced at Billy and shot a look at Rooker. "Bite your tongue. If we can make it through the Steel Trial, she'll send us back to the Institute."

"Sure. That's why she built all this. For one trial."

Patch snarled at him. "Idiot. She'll bring new fighters. You think she wants the same group every time?" She glanced at Jack, who was still bruised from his bout. "Don't worry, we'll go back to Hyena as soon as we get through this." Patch pointed across the sea to the shadow of Huánghūn's cliff wall. "Nine more days and we'll go home."

Rooker sucked his teeth and hoped Patch was wrong. The Steel Trial was the best possible thing that could have happened to him. He'd been miserable as Jackal boss, isolated and alone. This place put him back with Jack and Patch and on better footing. They had no secrets to hide from him here. *Besides, a little swordplay's a small price to pay to get rid of the shiq.*

"Ugh." Jack sagged in his hammock, sporting a black eye and cradling his arm. "I miss the Great Bell right about now."

Rooker swigged his ale. "Yer a terrible fighter, bubba."

"I'm not *that* bad."

"Without Nepenthe, yer useless as teats on a bull." Pilgrim bent another note on the banjo, a sour slide that matched Jack's face. "Personally, I'd rather stay on Bounty." Rooker leaned back, getting comfortable. "They've got ham."

He stared at the sky in silence, then closed his eyes, listening to the crickets, the waves, and the strum of Pilgrim's banjo.

Jack's voice came quiet in the dark. "We're not really going to fight to the death, are we?"

Rooker didn't bother opening his eyes. "Only half of us."

Bloody knuckles were the price of admission to the arena. Hands are the first thing to get stung in a fight, and Rooker's were raw before noon. Wont ran drills all morning long, a dozen bouts before lunch.

The yellowjackets weren't superb fighters, just Inquisition dregs low enough on the totem pole to volunteer for gladiator work, so Rooker was stunned when he fell to Fallow, then Bobby Puce. Rooker bristled at the losses, realizing his swordplay was rusty as an old door hinge. It had been months since the last time he'd handled a blade, and his shoulders lacked their old quickness. He secretly wished for his singing saber, Bessie, her familiar weight, her sharkskin grip. Rooker bested eight of twelve yellowjackets but knew it was nowhere near good enough. He should have ruined them all.

Patch matched him, eight of twelve. She used the bullwhip to her advantage, startling her opponents and getting them off guard for a strike. Rooker noticed the jinx was stiff as well, a bit slower on the rotation than he remembered. By the end of the sixth bout, her perfect, glossy fur looked ragged as an alley cat, a good-looking woman who'd been roughed over too many times. *Huánghūn's taken its toll on both of us.*

Jack was a total loss. The yellowjackets knew he was the infamous Black Jack and delighted in bashing him into the dirt. Wont Naysayer had to stop every bout, making sure the kid stayed upright long enough for the next one. By the time they broke for lunch, Jack was winless.

Only Billy Pilgrim was worse. The troubadour didn't even attempt to fight. When a yellowjacket swung at him, he collapsed and howled loudly, yelping like a beaten dog. It got a laugh out of everyone, including the yellowjackets. Between bouts, Pilgrim would strum on his banjo until the next fight began, then pull a funnier variation of the gag. It was distracting, it was amusing, and it was a sure way to wind up dead.

Rooker splashed his face from a water barrel before the afternoon session, watching his next opponent eye him warily. Rooker's fighting style was the same he used in life: big moves, half of them fake. No opponent could predict if he was going to strike, disarm, defend, or talk. The yellowjackets hated him for it. *As long as I save a few tricks for the Steel Trial, I should be okay.*

He began the next duel with a little shuck-and-jive, keeping his body light. Rooker glanced over his shoulder to find Jack standing like someone had planted him there. "Hey!" Rooker shouted. "Move yer feet! Get on yer toes!" Rooker easily defended a swipe from his opponent as he watched Jack fumble his feet, barely defending a lazy hit.

Rooker frowned. "Lord of Sea and Sky." Without looking, he stabbed his opponent in the ribs and stormed toward Jack. "Come on, bubba, yer embarassin' yerself."

Jack's yellowjacket turned, surprised someone else was entering his bout, and Rooker chopped his scimitar into the man's ribs. Rooker spun his blade, smacked Jack's falchion out of his hand, and struck Jack with every word. "Don't. Do. What. Yer. Doing." Rooker kicked Jack in the chest and sent him sprawling in the dirt.

Angry, Rooker spun on Wont Naysayer. "Ya call this *training*?"

Wont shrugged massive shoulders. "I'm just here to keep things civil. Win or lose, it means nothing to me."

Rooker spun on Jack. "Ya fight like a *child*. Get up." He extended a hand to help Jack to his feet.

The kid batted Rooker's hand away with his sword, refusing to touch him, his eyes pure hate.

"All right!" yelled Wont. "Eleven more bouts before supper! Let's go!"

Rooker hadn't realized how much he'd missed the dead of night until she opened her dark wings to him. On Huánghūn, there was no shadow unoccupied by the shiq, but here on Bounty, the night belonged to him. Darkness made it easy to slip away from his hammock after everyone had fallen asleep, easy to creep along the dugout to the hidden trapdoor he had spotted earlier, easy to pick the lock without being noticed. Once inside the secret staircase, he snapped his fingers and lit his majik flame. One hand on the scimitar on his belt, he crept upward.

"Dammit, this isn't what you promised!" Rooker recognized Eightfingers' voice behind the door at the top of the stairs.

"We had a good thing going back on the big island!" came Hook's protest. "Why do you have to ruin it now?"

Rooker wasn't surprised the other bosses hadn't invited him to their little bitch session; they hated him almost as much as he hated them.

"Gentlemen." Gerba Whipmarples' voice dripped with false charm. "If you remember, I told you what would happen if you could not control your camps." The headmistress sounded as if she were a schoolmarm addressing petulant children. "I simply made good on my word."

"But when are we going *back?*" Boss Hook whined.

"Not to worry, dearies." He heard the trol's heavy weight shift. "You will return to where you belong the moment your Steel Trial is complete."

Damn. Rooker had hoped Patch had been wrong. Going back was the last thing he wanted. Here on Bounty, he could fight his way to freedom in eighty-three trials. It might take three years, but it was better than going back to Huánghūn, where the only thing waiting for him was an escape plan that he would never be invited to join. *So. Let's change that.*

He heard a few grumbling sounds of protest from Boss Hook and Boss Eightfingers, then the two men departed. Rooker silently eased open the door to discover he stood at the rear wall of the biggest theater box in the arena. Gerba was alone with her back to him. He entertained the idea of killing her with the scimitar, but knew it was nothing but a fantasy; her hide was too thick. Instead, he slipped into a chair as if he had been there the whole time.

"I was wondering if you would show up." Gerba Whipmarples sipped her chai as she turned, her face bathed in twin moonlight.

Rooker shrugged. "Saw yer ship on the wharf. Figured ya might be workin' late."

"As, it seems, are you."

Rooker heard the soft scrape of steel at his hip. He turned to find a black feathered hand slowly removing his scimitar from its sheath. At the same moment, he felt the sai extracted from his belt, silent as a snake.

Shant Naysayer was barely more than a shadow. Rooker hadn't heard him, hadn't seen him, hadn't smelled him. His long beak curved into a raptor smile. "Wouldn't want you getting any ideas, Flynn."

Rooker forced a grin. "Sneaky bird." Shant removed himself, along with Rooker's weapons, to the corner of the box and disappeared back into shadow. Rooker turned his attention back to the headmistress. "I gotta to admit, ya had me flummoxed, Whipmarples."

She cocked her head. "Why, whatever do you mean, Mister Flynn?"

"Yer dirty dozen." He sniffed, casual. "Ya got eight hundred candidates at the Institute, but ya picked these twelve. Couldn't figure why. Then it dawned on me. Every one of them's an infamous renegade down here in the Precipice Archipelago. Patch, Leadbelly, even those two chucklenuts." He jerked his thumb at where Hook and Eightfingers had disappeared. "Names that will draw a crowd." He cocked a grin. "You need asses in seats."

"How astute of you, Mister Flynn. This arena does not pay for itself." She sipped her chai, watching him. "And the Institute has become rather too successful of late. Too many students, you see. A sporting event such as a Steel Trial provides funds for the school while eliminating superfluous pupils. What the Toshans call a win-win."

"One thing I don't get. Billy Pilgrim." Rooker tilted his head. "Nobody wants to see that guy dead."

"Any good show needs a clown."

"A good show?"

"Certainly!" Gerba spread her hands. "The thrill of battle, the hand of justice, the roar of the crowd. The audience will find it exciting."

"Ya haven't thought this through." Rooker leaned in. "Ya got a Black Jack problem."

She narrowed her eyes. "Mister Flynn. Black Jack is my greatest asset. He is our headliner! Citizens from all over the Precipice Archipelago are clamoring up for tickets to see him in the ring."

"Yer *still* not thinkin' it through." Rooker locked eyes with her, demanding her full attention. "When the crowd sees him fight, what do ya think they're gonna say?" He let that idea sink in. "They expect Black Jack. They expect a *legend*. But the kid can't fight his way out of a barn dance." He cocked his head. "They'll know he's a fraud. And they'll know *yer* a fraud, too." He watched Gerba's face pucker, her reaction much stronger than he'd expected. *Must have hit pretty close to the bone.* Pressing his advantage, Rooker drove the point home like a sword tip. "If ya put him on that stage, yer big show will close opening night."

Gerba leaned back, considering. "Why do I have the feeling you are about to propose a solution?"

"Because Wont Naysayer is useless." Rooker heard Shant shift behind him, a whisper of black feathers. "Let me train the kid." He unfurled a devilish grin. "And I'll give ya one *hell* of a show."

Chapter

11

=TO THE=
DEATH

*As iron sharpens iron,
so one man sharpens another.*
The Book of Proverbs

J ACK HAD ALWAYS HATED gym class, but he'd never had a PhysEd coach as bad as Wont Naysayer. The big hulk was lazy, sloppy, and couldn't care less about his students. He wiped a fried egg from his lips, ignoring the three that were stuck to his shirt. "Drills!" he shouted. "Change it up today. Students versus students." He belched. "Get going."

Jack glanced at Patch, hoping to spar with her. She had been sick and sullen since they'd arrived on Bounty, but the jinx had a vested interest in keeping him alive. Plus she could fight. Jack took one step toward her and found a fist around his collar.

Rooker Flynn dragged him across the sand. Jack spun in his grasp, trying to get free, but Rooker held on tight. "Gettin' some fresh air, Wont," the pirate barked as he dragged Jack through the gigantic arena doors.

Outside, Jack managed to slip free, but Rooker threw him to the ground. "I thought ya toughened *up*, bubba."

Jack scowled and got to his feet. "Leave me alone."

"No. I can't watch ya flail around anymore." He strode to a copse of bamboo and used his scimitar to hack away at a stalk. "Ya can't use a sword, ya can't swing an axe, ya can't even figure out a damned mace." He cut a seven-foot rod and threw the bamboo at Jack. "At least ya know how a *stick* is supposed to work."

Jack snatched the bamboo out of the air to find Rooker already charging. Jack brought up the stave to defend himself and deflected one shot before Rooker punched him in the gut and put him on the ground again. As Jack scrambled back to his feet, the pirate circled just out of reach. "Didn't they teach ya to fight in Chegago?"

"Fistfights," Jack spat. "Not swordfights."

"Bet ya lost every one."

Jack felt a flush beneath his skin as he remembered all the beatings he'd taken in the bottom rungs of the foster system. "I held my own."

"I doubt it." Rooker paced him. "Yer not strong. Yer not quick. The only hope ya got is to outsmart 'em." Rooker spun the scimitar, all flash. "This is the cobra eel. It hypnotizes you." As Jack watched the sword, prepared to deflect a strike, Rooker flicked the sai to his neck. "This is the stinger."

Jack flinched. "Okay, I get it."

"No. Ya don't. Never watch what I *want* ya to watch." Rooker brought around the sai. Jack raised his staff to defend against it and felt the scimitar slash across his femoral artery. "Never watch what I want ya to *watch!*"

Jack jerked away, angry. Rooker danced on the balls of his feet. *He's enjoying this.* The pirate jerked his chin at Jack's staff. "I can't know which end of that thing is comin' at me. Get it whippin'. Hit me."

Glad to. Jack struck at Rooker, then spun around from the other side. The pirate defended both strikes without even moving his feet. "Slow." Incensed, Jack sped up, trying to get a strike, but Rooker's blades fended off every blow. "Switch left to right, you're all on one side. Predictable." Jack jabbed the stave at Rooker's face and the pirate ducked out of the way. "Both ends, damn ya! Faster!" Jack felt sweat trickle down his brow. He was in the best shape of his life, but he'd always thought of his body as a second-class citizen, just a vehicle for his brain. Now he felt his prison muscles sing with the joy of strenuous exertion. He went after Rooker strike after strike, pounding at him, getting the feel of the staff. Rooker was right; Nepenthe had shown him how it should be done. All his muscles had to do was remember how it felt. The stave whirled around him, faster and faster, until Rooker was forced to take a step back.

The pirate threw the sai into the dirt and came at him with only the scimitar. "Defend!" He hit Jack in the side, in the leg, on the shoulder, on the neck, driving him back with every strike. "Get yer arm up!" Rooker hit his bicep. "Up!" Jack fended off the blows as best he could, but even with only one sword, Rooker was all over him. He took more hits in a matter of minutes than he had his entire time in the arena, each of them sharp and painful. He found himself desperately failing more and more as the beating continued. Finally, he caught a blade square on the knuckle. He yelped and dropped the stave to the dirt.

Rooker slapped him in the face with the side of the blade. "Up."

Jack stomped away, his hand throbbing from the blow, his cheeks singing with humiliation. "I *tried*!"

"That's what dead men say." Rooker plucked his sai from the sand and stuck it in his belt. "Ya got seven days before they kill ya, bubba. Do better than *try*."

Jack felt blood boil in his ears. He got to his feet and ripped the sleeve from his shirt. He wrapped it around his knuckles and wiped his bloody nose. "Again."

Life was combat.

Rooker never quit waging war against him, every day the same. The pirate rose before dawn, shook Jack awake, and drove him into the sea. They would swim to the hullbreaker rock, then race ten laps around the entire island. Into the sea again before a breakfast of fried eggs, biscuits, and orange juice, followed by Rooker screaming at him for several hours. They fought without pause, without mercy, doing their damndest to beat each other down. At lunch, they never spoke, silently chewing thick beef sandwiches and washing them down with cold milk. All afternoon, they dueled, hacking at each other until dinner. For dessert, they did ten more laps, followed by a swim to the hullbreaker. At the end of the day, Jack collapsed into his hammock, only to have Rooker shake him awake and start all over again.

Every strike, every bruise, every scrape was fuel for Jack's anger, and he couldn't have had a better target than Rooker Flynn. There was no one he wanted to hit more.

Hour after hour, Rooker outmaneuvered him, hit him, and barked insults peppered with occasional advice. Jack came again, got hit again. His fingers were wrapped in bandages from holding the staff in the wrong place at the wrong time. He took blow after blow, lost duel after duel, all with the single goal of knocking Rooker Flynn on his ass.

"Slippery! Ya gotta be slippery!" Rooker shouted as he slid away from Jack's strike. "Like a mungfish. There's always somebody stronger or bigger or quicker. But they can't win"—he ducked under Jack's swing—"if they can't hit ya."

He tapped Jack on the forehead with an arrogant finger.

Fuming, Jack spun the staff and cracked Rooker across the nose. A thrill of pride sizzled through Jack's body as the arrogant pirate staggered back.

Rooker wiped blood from his stubbled beard and grinned. "Better."

Day after day, they spent every waking moment locked in an endless battery of physical and mental conflict. They went at each other like competing lightning storms, fast and violent. By the end, they had spent so much time together, they had developed a single train of thought, an endless monologue that went on even during their fiercest combat and made it difficult to tell where one man left off and the other began.

"Go left—"

"—around the other side to get—"

"—past 'em and take the elbow out. We should go get—"

"—that pineapple, I know, it's—"

"—so sweet. Try it with the pork."

Rooker always found another insult to sling, another bruise to press, another carrot to dangle. Jack attacked him hour after hour after hour. He forgot his weaknesses, forgot his pain, focused only on trying to hit the pirate. It took a long time to realize it, but Rooker knew exactly what he was doing, providing him just enough hate to keep him vicious.

"Okay, you two," said Wont Naysayer. The sun simmered low in the sky and the white sands of the arena were turning dark. "Day's up. Go get some grub."

Jack spat. "Not until I take him."

"Yer not that lucky, bubba." Rooker flipped the sai.

Jack smiled. "Come at me, you chum-guzzling fudge smuggler."

"I said *enough!*" Wont Naysayer shoved Rooker. The pirate flew twenty feet, hit the ground, and bounced. "You're done when I *say* you're done!" He shouted to the other convicts in the arena. "Dinner!"

Jack ran to Rooker, who did not get back up. The pirate's face was a clenched rictus of pain. *He's shaken off way worse than that.* "What's the problem?"

Rooker couldn't speak, agony etched onto his face.

Jack leaned in. "Come on, y—*oh.*"

The pirate's humerus bone hung loose from the socket.

Holy hell, he dislocated his shoulder.

"Lie on your back."

Rooker fell limp without complaint. Jack manipulated his arm, bringing it behind Rooker's head as the pirate gasped in pain. "Okay, can you reach the back of your neck?" Rooker grimaced and did so, barely. "Great, now reach to your other shoulder." Rooker strained, trying to extend his arm. Jack waited for the bone to pop back in, but it refused to fall into place. *This is how they do it in the NIH manual. Why isn't it working?*

Yellowjackets and convicts alike lingered in the doorways around the ring, watching Rooker struggle, enjoying it. "Get me up," he hissed.

"You need to—"

"*Get me up.* They can't see me like this." Jack dragged Rooker to his feet. "Just pop it back in."

"I can't—"

"Do it."

Jack set his feet. A short quick strike in the right spot should do the job, although it would hurt. As he steadied his hand, Jack couldn't believe he was enjoying this.

He struck Rooker's shoulder with the flat of his palm. The pirate screamed, but the shoulder stayed where it was. A baleful eye glared at Jack.

Um... I have to... um... "Come on." Desperate, Jack led Rooker to a dugout door.

Sweat beaded on Rooker's brow. "Hurts more than a wasteka shark bite." Jack positioned Rooker's shoulder against the doorframe and placed his palm against Rooker's back. *Got to flatten him out, pop the joint back in.* "One. Two. *Three.*"

He shoved. The pirate screamed, hollering a string of curses that would melt paint, but his shoulder didn't budge. Rooker's breath came fast. "What kinda damn doktar are ya?"

"I'm sor—" Jack had to hold down a laugh. "I'm sorry." He spread his hands. "I've only read about it in books. I've never actually done it."

"*Well, actually do it!*"

Jack shoved him against the doorframe and pushed. As Rooker invented a new dictionary of curses, Jack tried to keep down the hilarity bubbling in his chest but couldn't.

Rooker screamed at him. "Will ya quit *laughing*?"

Thok!

His bone fell back into its socket with a hollow, meaty sound. Surprised, Rooker blinked. He joined Jack's hysterical laughter, nearly screaming, his eyes white and wide.

Jack got ahold of himself, catching his breath. "You okay?"

Rooker decked him in the face.

As Jack's butt hit the dirt, Rooker rolled his shoulder and winced. "Yeah, works fine."

Jack couldn't stop laughing. He raised a hand.

Rooker took it and pulled him up. "Ow." He rotated his shoulder. "Come on, let's get some chow."

Jack chuckled, wiping blood from his nose. *Worth it.*

Jack never won a bout against Rooker, but playtime was over. The Steel Trial had arrived.

The gladiators were locked inside the arena, but they watched from the colosseum's parapet as dozens of boats began to arrive at the wharf. Shortly thereafter, Wont separated the outlaws from the yellowjackets and locked them into the dugout. By noon, the stadium was half full of sailors hollering to each other and laughing, reminding Jack of a bunch of rowdy football tailgaters.

Rooker was not impressed. "Look at this crowd! Farmers and fishermen!" He made a disgusted face. "A bunch of local yokels!"

Jack had to admit, this was not the audience he had been expecting. Only one well-dressed man sat in a theater box, some local official, but the rest of the throng looked dirty, drunk, and mean. This was no coterie of posh nobility; these were soccer hooligans out for blood.

"We got *prisoners* who dress better than these skags," growled Rooker. "Not a silk shirt in the bunch."

"Ladies and Gentlemen!" Gerba Whipmarples emerged from her box, dressed in a crimson kurta with long silk scarves around the sleeves. "Welcome, one and all, to the Steel Trial!" Enthusiastic applause erupted from the audience, followed by hooting and catcalls. Gerba bowed as if they were cheering for her. "Each of these dastardly criminals has been sentenced to death for their crimes.

But here, thanks to the largesse of Lord and Lady Locke, they have been given one last chance to be redeemed before the Almighty, before Lady Justice, and before all of *you*!" Applause and boos thundered from the audience, many of whom seemed ready to jump into the ring themselves.

"For our first trial!" Gerba raised her hands. "The maritime marauder who looted twenty-seven ships right here in the Precipice Archipelago, the Pinkyless Pirate, Captain Chiba *Eightfingers*!" As the crowd went wild, Jack watched Boss Eightfingers grin and grip his new blade. This was no sparring sword; its edge was sharp as a razor. Eightfingers sauntered into the arena, raised his hands, and took in the applause from the crowd. From the other side, a yellowjacket dressed in freshly painted splint strode to meet him.

Jack and the other convicts stood at the barred doors, watching.

Eightfingers lasted thirty seconds. A duck, a feint, a blow, then blood as the yellowjacket's steel dug into his chest. Boss Eightfingers sobbed a whimper and collapsed. The crowd went berserk, yelling and thumping their seats as the yellowjacket bowed. Jack stared at the twitching body in the sand. He didn't like Eightfingers, no one did, but seeing him on the ground was a shock. As Wont dragged the bleeding boss offstage, Jack realized Eightfingers was still alive, gurgling blood.

Jack swallowed. *And my turn is coming.*

(yes it is)

The wolf prowled his thoughts, slavering at the taste of Jack's rising fear.

Wont appeared at the door and checked the list written on his forearm in grease pencil. "Hook. You're up."

Boss Hook was stabbed through the liver inside a minute. Leadbelly was killed outright. So was Weasel. Men Jack had fought with, drank with, broken bread with. Dead.

Patch was next.

She looked terrible, slow and ragged, on her way to the ring. Jack was certain she was about to die. But once the fight started, the jinx became electric, lashing her bullwhip at the yellowjacket, cracking the air, driving him back. The whip coiled around her opponent's sword and yanked it free of his hand. With the furious speed only a cat can muster, she released a flurry of blows that put him on his heels. She screamed as she drove her rapier into the yellowjacket's throat, releasing a barbaric yawp of triumph.

After so many months of imprisonment, the convicts erupted with primal joy as they witnessed one of the Locke Institute finally get their due. Banging on the cage bars, the prisoners unleased their pent-up fury like a geyser, outshouting the audience. Every wasteka outlaw screamed victory, none so loud as Jack. He hugged Patch as she returned to the dugout. She pushed him away, a hint of a smile on her face.

"Billy Pilgrim," chuckled Wont. "You're up, banjo boy."

Billy stared at Wont blankly, then snapped to his feet and walked onstage without a weapon.

O God. I can't watch.

Pilgrim marched like a toy soldier. The audience murmured, confused. Billy darted to the edge of the arena and wordlessly gestured for a woman to lend him her long lemon-colored scarf. She refused, but he dropped to one knee as if proposing, and she laughed. When she dropped it to him, he blew her a kiss and wrapped the scarf over his chest and shoulders, making a mockery of the yellowjacket's armor. He resumed his goose-step march to the center of the area. The audience laughed. His opponent scowled.

"Begin!" shouted Wont.

Billy shrieked and ran like a chicken. He waved his hands in the air, sing-screaming like he'd been stabbed, fleeing no one. More laughs from the crowd as the yellowjacket stood dumbfounded. Given no choice, he pursued Billy, who led him on a merry chase as the wordless troubadour ducked, dodged, and derped his way out of each attack. When the yellowjacket stopped, panting, Billy bent over and produced a thunderous fart with his mouth. The audience laughed, and the yellowjacket set after him again. Pilgrim ran toward the dugout and threw himself upon the wall. His gangly limbs scrabbled at the brick, and he managed to climb over the top just before the yellowjacket got him. Billy pulled the scarf over his head like a babushka and cowered against the woman who had given it to him, wailing. The crowd went nuts, laughing as the frustrated yellowjacket paced back and forth, shouting for him to come back down.

As the crowd roared, Billy joined in, pointing at the yellowjacket and laughing with the throng.

Jack couldn't help but snort a laugh. *He's Keymark's Charlie Chaplin.*

"Up!" yelled a voice from the throng. "Up!" cried another, and another. Thumbs shot into the air all around the arena. "Up the Pilgrim! Up the Pilgrim!" Billy stood, gesturing *Who, me?* The crowd roared.

Frowning, Gerba Whipmarples eyed the audience. Finally, she conceded. "Fine. Clemency for Billy Pilgrim!"

Applause thundered across the colosseum as the yellowjacket threw down his sword and stormed off, denied his kill. Billy made a series of exaggerated bows to the crowd, then cuddled up with the woman who had given him the scarf and settled in to watch the rest of the show.

The score was 1-8-1 when Rooker Flynn took the field. The sun hung low, the time filmmakers called the magic hour, when everything was touched by golden light. Jack glanced up at him. Rooker rotated his arm and winced, still half-paralyzed from the dislocated shoulder. The words escaped Jack's mouth before he could stop himself. "Good luck."

It was the right thing to say. No one in Keymark put as much stock in luck as Rooker Flynn. He nodded his thanks, his face relaxed. "See ya in a second."

As he jogged onto the sand, Jack watched a nasty face emerge from the yellowjacket pen.

"Fallow!" Rooker grinned, speaking loud enough for everyone to hear. "Did ya pick me on purpose?"

The yellowjacket grinned back. "Told you I'd make you pay, Flynn."

"Catch," said Rooker. He flipped his sai and threw it at Fallow's face. The yellowjacket ducked aside and watched the thing spin past him. He smiled and turned to find Rooker's scimitar in his chest. "I said *catch*."

Blood spilt to the sand and Fallow hit the ground. As Rooker leaned in, Jack barely heard his words. "That'll teach ya to make fun of my *dog*."

The crowd roared their approval as Rooker rose and flicked the brim of an imaginary hat at them. "Lousy wasteka skags."

He strode back into the pen as if he'd just finished a stroll in the park. As he passed, he slapped Jack on his backside. "Stay loose, bubba. Can't be slippery with a broomstick up yer ass."

Gerba's voice echoed from the colosseum walls. "And now, ladies and gentlemen, the grand finale of the Steel Trial, the reason you are all here. The most nefarious outlaw in history, adored by lawbreakers, despised by the nobles, the Man Who Stole a Billion Marks, the legendary *Black Jack*!"

The crowd hit their feet and roared applause.

Jack felt pandemonium flood over him as he stepped out onto the sand. It was wonderful, terrifying, marvelous, and cruel, the sensation of hundreds of men and women cheering just for him and for all the wrong reasons.

(they're cheering for the man who's going to kill you)

Jack shuddered as his shadow circled him, feeding on his fear. The wolf brushed under his hand, and he felt its silky fur against his fingertips.

(here he comes now)

From the far door tromped the biggest, meanest yellowjacket of the bunch.

Mingo.

(yes)

No. Jack straightened, forcing the wolf back where it had come from. Somewhere deep inside him, Jack felt Leah Archer smile. *I'm not dying today.*

Rooker had forced Jack to observe every yellowjacket fight during the bouts, analyzing their styles, their patterns, their faults. Jack rifled through his memories. *Mingo. Step-step-swing, always from the right.*

Without preamble, Mingo darted at him. Jack dodged away and watched the longsword slice past his nose. As the yellowjacket turned, Jack spun behind him and rapped him smartly on the tailbone. The crowd laughed.

This is funny to them?

Mingo growled and charged, blade weaving like a cobra. Jack's stave knocked aside each blow in a thundering barrage of wood against steel. His hands slid deftly along the joints of the wood, keeping his fingers clear. His feet never stopped moving. *Stay two steps ahead.*

It was unnervingly easy. After sparring with Rooker Flynn, fighting Mingo was like dueling a sloppy drunk. Jack struck the yellowjacket's face, rang his ear, and caught him with an uppercut on the return. He darted sideways, brought the stave around in a full arc, and belted the yellowjacket between the eyes.

Mingo stared at him blankly. His knees jiggled. Then he collapsed to the dirt.

I... won?

Applause thundered from the audience, all of them on their feet. Jack turned to see the masses in the stands applauding and hollering. He couldn't help but smile, just relieved to be alive.

Wont ushered Rooker, Patch, and Pilgrim onto the sand, presenting the four victors.

They raised their fists to cheers.

Bathing in the admiration of the crowd, Jack Swift savored his win right up until the moment he caught a glimpse of Mingo's sword in the sand. The yellowjacket's blade was blunted, nothing but a sparring weapon.

His eyes shot to Gerba Whipmarples. As the crowd roared around her, she grinned at him and nodded.

She'd never intended to let him be harmed. It was all for show. *All for nothing.*

"Wonderful, wonderful, wonderful!" Her amplified voice resounded through the colosseum. "I do hope that you have enjoyed yourselves, ladies and gentlemen! That concludes the Steel Trial!" Half the crowd had already stopped cheering and were headed for the exits, back to their boats. "Be sure to tell your lords and ladies about the magnificent spectacle you saw here today! Do sail safely! And thank you from all of us here at the Locke Institute! Good night!"

"Not bad, bubba." Rooker slapped Jack on the back.

"She rigged it."

"Rigged what?"

Jack picked up Mingo's sword and showed it to him. "The whole thing."

Rooker scowled at the dull blade. "Dirty wasteka *harridan.*"

As the crowd disappeared, Wont tried to usher the remaining gladiators back to the dugout, but Jack saw the hulk had deposited the fallen outlaws near the big door. He broke free from the bounty hunter's thick arm and ran to them.

Of the dozen gladiators who had entered the arena, six were dead. Only two, Hook and Eightfingers, still drew breath, waiting to bleed out, go septic, or drown in their own blood.

Jack stripped off his shirt and bent to Boss Hook, utilizing the cloth as a makeshift tourniquet. The bleeding bandit groaned. "Open the door. Let's go!" Jack shouted.

Wont didn't move. No one did.

"Hey!" Jack's voice was sharp and frantic. Helpless, he glanced up and saw the big trol standing on the parapet over the door, her shadow at the zenith of the colosseum.

"Open the door, Gerba!" Jack yelled, angry. "We've got to get them to the *Hup Two*."

Gerba tilted her horn. "Whatever for, my pet?"

Why is she playing dumb? "So they can get back to the Great Bell!" Jack shouted the obvious. "So they can be healed!"

"You said..." Boss Hook sputtered blood, one half-lidded eye pleading with the trol. "You said... when it was over... we would go *back*."

"Ah yes. I see." Gerba nodded. "A teensy misunderstanding. I promised you will return to where you belong. And so you shall." The headmistress turned. "Mister Naysayer, will you see to the injured?"

Wont lumbered toward Hook, lifted a thick iron maul, and crushed the man's skull like a Halloween pumpkin.

"*No!*" Jack screamed.

He lunged for Wont Naysayer, but Rooker grabbed him and pulled him away. The hulking bounty hunter raised his maul once more and settled Eightfingers.

"Four victors!" Gerba clapped her meaty hands. "And a good show, too! Well done! In celebration, you will have a special dessert tonight! Crème brûlée!" She tittered and made a nummy sound. "After all that effort, you should get your rest! A new batch of contenders arrives tomorrow morning. You will want to show them the ropes." She spread her hands, smiling like a circus ringleader. "After all, it is only a tenday until your next Steel Trial."

Jack felt the blood drain from his face. *We're never getting out.*

"I thought..." Patch panted, desperate. "I thought we were going back!"

"O, you cannot be expected to put on a show worthy of the nobles with just one rehearsal, dearie. These are only the previews!" Gerba grinned beneath her long horn. "We have *months* of work before opening night!"

AÑEJO

*Friendship is unnecessary,
like philosophy, like art....
It has no survival value;
rather it is one of those things
which give value to survival.*

C.S. Lewis

S UMMER MARCHED STEADILY ONWARD and the sun lingered longer every day as the heat on the Isle of Bounty grew unbearable. Convicts and yellowjackets alike found themselves caked in sweat when they woke each morning. Both teams took to stripping down during gladiator drills as heatstroke became a bigger danger than sparring blades. Every tenday saw another Steel Trial, another audience, another show. More outlaws died, and more prisoners were brought in to fill the space they left behind. Covered in the spilled blood of a hundred kills, the white sand of the colosseum had turned a crusty brown.

Rooker Flynn found he was almost enjoying himself.

He finished his duel and paraded shirtless before the cheering crowd, muscles flexed, bladed fists victorious in the air. *Eight fights, eight wins. Only seventy-five to go.*

As the audience roared, he watched Gerba Whipmarples scribble more notes. The headmistress was addicted to fiddling with the show's lineup in pursuit of the perfect performance. Black Jack always went last, the grand finale, and Rooker usually occupied the featured spot right before intermission, when the acolytes would sell overpriced drinks and take bets at profitable odds from the increasingly large throng of spectators. Today, Rooker had been bumped back one slot to make room for a notorious Precipice Archipelago villain named Cassian.

He wouldn't last.

"Have fun, pal." Rooker nodded at Cassian as the big bandit rose for his duel. Rooker knew the man would be dead in a few minutes. Some new gladiators made it through a trial or two, but all of them went down sooner or later. None had Rooker's skill, Patch's speed, or Pilgrim's... whatever it was that Pilgrim had.

In a most unlikely fashion, Billy Pilgrim thrived as a gladiator. He wore his role of clown like a king's robe and was a showman to the bone. Through pantomime alone, the mute minstrel had somehow convinced Gerba to bring in a group of musicians. The group, called the Rainjons, played music between bouts, which proved to be the biggest single improvement to the show. Pilgrim spent more time with the band than on the sand. He played to the audience from the time they walked in the door, strumming his banjo and singing songs to the prettiest girls. By the time his bout arrived, he had the congregation eating out of the palm of his hand. He couldn't talk and he couldn't fight, but Rooker had never seen him in danger of a blade as 'Up the Pilgrim' became a familiar cheer.

Patch Picaroon had no fans, not in the audience nor the dugout. The jinx had always been acidic, but as summer had dragged on she had become staggeringly irritable. She snapped at anyone who dared speak to her, including Jack. Rooker had tried to ask Patch what was eating at her but had wound up with a bloody lip for his trouble. After that, he'd given up trying to get on Patch's good side. The jinx slept most of the day, hidden inside the brick dugout, emerging only to fight her next battle to the death.

Jack Swift, of course, was in no danger. He was protected from on high. Not that he appreciated it much.

The kid had never accepted the fact that Gerba let the wounded die. After every Steel Trial, Jack tried to save the gladiators with his fishbone needle and thread, but Gerba never let losers linger long before she put them out of their misery. The Isle of Bounty had no walking wounded. Robbed of his opportunity to save the dying, Jack was relegated to treating minor cuts and lancing the occasional boil with his ridiculous little bamboo scalpel, but the doktar only delayed the inevitable. Rooker knew Jack would never embrace the truth: No one wanted a Steel Trial without a little death.

The fights won't kill me. Rooker scratched his chin. *But the loneliness might.*

Patch was impossible to talk to. Pilgrim couldn't speak at all. And Jack... well.

There had been moments when Rooker had thought they might go back to the way things had been. Just moments. A smile, a laugh. But it had never lasted. Jack remained distant, refusing to let him get too close. Whatever friendship they'd once had was dead. These days they were nothing more than business partners, dedicated to a career of survival.

Jack would never trust him again.

Forgive me if you can.

Jack's words echoed in his head, day after unrepentant day.

Rooker Flynn would never ask for forgiveness. It was impossible. As impossible as climbing to the moons. 'Thank you' and 'I'm sorry' and 'Forgive me' had been beaten out of him by his father, by Jasper, by Roper Jon, by a lifetime of bad men. Asking for forgiveness was weak, and there was no weakness left in him.

Not a drop.

Pursuing Jack Swift was pointless. He knew it. There was no angle, nothing to be gained, no bargain to be made. Nothing.

I just want my friend back.

Rooker heard the crowd erupt and knew Cassian had met a lonely death.

He leaned his head back against the wall and wondered how to avoid the same end.

The stars were bright in the warm night sky when he found Jack at the back of the island, out past the little cabins. The kid was alone, as always, sitting on a stump near the fire. Nearby, one of the tams, the big geckos that littered Bounty, stood on its haunches, looking confused. Jack made a series of gestures with his hands as if he were trying to communicate with it. Rooker scowled, feeling almost jealous of the animal. "Make a new friend?"

Jack turned, surprised to see him there. "You remember that tam I had? Way back when?"

"Fiji?" He hadn't thought about Jack's little blue and gold gecko in more than a year. In general, Rooker didn't like tams. They were always underfoot and annoying as hell, but Jack had loved the little thing like a family dog.

"Fuji," Jack corrected him. "I taught him to do sign language, remember? I thought this one might learn it too."

"Uh-huh." Taking advantage of Jack's distraction, the tam snatched the biscuit from the kid's fingers. Escaping, it crawled up a tree into the palms. "How's that going?"

"So, *so* well." Jack sighed. He grabbed his whetstone and went back to sharpening his scalpel.

"Hey?" Rooker edged closer, making a show of checking to see no one else was nearby. "Check this out." Unable to help himself, Jack looked, curious. "I made a deal with one of the acolytes down on the wharf. Something special." Rooker held up the bottle. It had taken him nearly a month to get it, the only peace offering he'd ever known to work. "Roi-Tan añejo. Liquid gold."

"Tequila?" Jack frowned. "No thanks."

Rooker masked his disappointment. "C'mon, ya gotta taste it, bubba. Drinking Roi-Tan is like... kissing an angel."

Jack snorted. "I don't think alcohol is going to fix anything."

"Tell me ya don't want to forget this place for an hour." He saw the look in Jack's eyes, and Rooker knew he had him.

Rooker edged in closer. "We got nine days until the next trial." He raised the bottle and jiggled it. "What could it hurt?"

They were drunk inside an hour.

Roi-Tan was Rooker's favorite booze for a reason; it kicked like a rented mule. The savage agave burned his lips and his throat, fluid fire, and Rooker found himself off-balance before he knew what hit him. Jack was slow on the uptake and talked his ear off, complaining how terrible Gerba was to kill the wounded, babbling on about *skience* and *fiziks* and other made-up words, and kept repeating his complicated plan to "Bring the Bell to Bounty."

It was all boring as hell.

Fed up with the repetition, Rooker made up a drinking game where they had to take a shot every time they said the word "should." That did the trick. Jack took three shots in a minute.

"I'm jush saying, instead of bringing *us* to the *bell*, we should bring the *bell* to *ush*. *Us*."

"Should." Rooker poured him another shot. "Drink."

"But if we bring the bell…"

"I heard ya. Drink." Jack did a shot and gasped for air. His eyes took on a goggly look. When he opened his mouth again, Rooker cut him off. "Just shut up and drink with me, Jack."

They stared at the ocean and felt the warm wind arrive from mysterious lands far away. Rooker imagined the rum runners out of Javernis Twist cutting through the dark sea for ports unknown. Above, the palms danced in the breeze, clattering together in a way that almost sounded like rain. Below, the fire crackled, low and quiet. A faint rumble of an earthquake trembled the world around him, but Rooker felt none of it, floating above the world.

He turned to find Jack staring at the fire, his eyes glazed over. Rooker nodded. The kid almost looked content. "Seems like ya got yer wolf under control."

A long pause. Nothing but the sound of the sea filled the empty space between them. Finally, Jack's voice came. "What wolf?"

"The one that comes cruising 'round every time ya get spooked." Rooker didn't know much about Jack's lupine shadow, but he knew the thing was real as a rock. He knew the wolf was somehow tied to Jack's fear. Beyond that, it was all guesses.

Jack was too loaded to argue with him and simply nodded, half a confession.

Rooker pushed a little harder. "I haven't seen it since yer first fight."

"Shadow." Jack said. "He only comes around every once in a while now. Just at night. You saw him?"

"Once or twice." Rooker shrugged. "How'd you get control of it?"

Jack let out a long breath. "Every time I feel Shadow closing in, I just... think of Leah."

Rooker chuckled. "A pretty face is all it takes, eh?"

"It's more than that." A peaceful expression came over Jack's face. "She protects me. My guardian angel." He took a drink. "She's coming for me."

So that's it. Rooker knew convicts who pulled this trick. A way to hold on to their sanity in prison, they would raise a wife or a mother or some fantasy figure on a pedestal. Copper Dave did the same with his daughter and that stupid macaroni shell necklace. Something to hope for. A savior. A talisman against the dark.

Rooker looked out to sea and imagined the far-off silhouette of the *Venture Brigand*. "Still dreaming about her, eh?"

"Every night."

There are worse dreams. Rooker toasted him with the Roi-Tan. "Whatever keeps the hound at bay."

"Where's the dog?"

Rooker flinched. He turned to see Jack's hazy eyes staring at him. "What?"

"Where's the dog?" Jack repeated. "I've heard three people say that when they met you. 'Where's the dog?' What's that mean? Is that like... pirate code?"

Rooker stared blankly at the fire and saw the akita pup watching him from the other side of the flames, just like it had all those years ago on the icy shores of the North Waste. The only true friend he'd ever had. Rooker closed his eyes and forced the pup out of his mind. "It doesn't mean anything. Just a thing people say."

"It hadda start somehow." Jack leaned on one elbow. "Where *is* the dog?"

"Where d'ya think he is?!" Rooker barked, furious. *"He died."* Rooker opened his eyes and the pup was gone. He took another shot of Roi-Tan to steady himself. "It died. Same as every other damned dog. Long time ago. When I was a kid."

Jack snorted a drunken laugh. Rooker's eyes snapped to him, angry. "What?"

"I can't imagine you as a kid. Were you always... *this*?" Jack spread his hands at him and laughed again. "What was little Rooker Flynn like?"

"Shorter." Rooker took another drink and, only because of the añejo, let slip one more word. "Gullible."

"Tell me." Jack leaned in.

"Nothin' to tell." Rooker tossed back another swig and felt alcohol fuel his blood. "Da was a drunk. Never knew my ma."

"Brothers? Sisters?"

Rooker frowned and found Jasper's face staring at him from beyond the fire. "Not really."

"I never had either." Jack took a swallow, then laughed, his face boozy and red. "I gotta be honest with you, Rooker, you were the closest thing to a brother I ever had."

Rooker stared at the sea. Jasper stood beyond the fire, thirteen years old, dressed in his new coat, real as a rock. "Brothers aren't all they're cracked up to be."

Lightning struck somewhere out over the Irridin. The wind from the sea picked up, blowing Jack's corn silk hair. "What did he do? Hit you? Steal from you?"

"Sold me." Rooker tossed back another swig.

Jack straightened. "What do you mean, sold you?"

Rooker had never talked about Jasper out loud, not once in ten years. *Nobody ever asked.* The words came easier than he'd expected. "Pirate slaver out of Cull Laverlock. The *Seagle*. Jasper—that was my brother—sold me to Captain Roper Jon for four sacks of grain and a new coat." Rooker swallowed another gulp of añejo. "That's what I was worth."

Wind filled the space between them. "I'm sorry."

Don't be, Jack. I did the same to you.

Rooker eyed Jasper, mesmerized by the añejo and the boy's coat flapping in the wind. "I searched for him, ya know. For years after I got free. Finally found a spice merchant who knew him. Turns out Jasper sold my sister, too. Jammy. A few months after he sold me. She got bought by a pleasure barge, caught the pox, died. Then he sold Ferd. He drowned somewhere off Corsugal. The other two died of exposure. I don't even remember their names." Rooker nodded, staring into the dark. "Took me five years to find Jasper. Under a gravestone in Tilport. Knifed in the eye for a pair of candlesticks."

Jasper winked at him.

Rooker remembered Jasper's gravestone. Remembered how angry he'd felt at being denied the opportunity to kill him. Remembered trying to dig his brother up so he could get some semblance of revenge, one final word. It had taken three gravediggers to stop him. Rooker took another drink and chuckled. "Turns out Jasper did me a favor. I'm the only Winegrad brat left alive."

"Winegrad?" Jack straightened, a ridiculous smile on his face. "You... your name is *Winegrad*?"

Rooker hadn't said that name in years. *Winegrad.* It felt like a foreign word, something unfamiliar in his brain. He nodded and stared into the dark, remembering that long-ago name. The one he kept hidden way down in the dark.

He'd never shared his true name with anyone since he was ten. Never once. "They called me Pip." He chuckled and felt relief at letting it go. "Pippin."

Jack broke up laughing, braying like a donkey. "Pippin! Of all the people who don't look like a 'Pippin,' you're the top!" Jack cackled, taking another drink, half-singing off-key. "Pippin Wine-graaad. I know your true naame. I have power over *youu.*"

Rooker couldn't help but laugh. "Okay, don't get too excited."

"Heh... wh... why do they call you Rooker Flynn?"

Little Rooker the akita pup re-emerged from behind the fire, wagging his little tail and watching him with mismatched eyes. *I'm not sharing that story with you or anybody else, bubba.*

"Yer turn. What was Black Jack like when he was a little pup? Back in Chegago?"

"I'll tell you a secret." Jack leaned in, barely able to hold himself up. "Jack izznt even my real name."

Rooker scowled. "What?"

Jack locked eyes with him. "I'm *Johnathan.*"

"Hah?" That was the dumbest thing Rooker had ever heard. "Short for 'Johnathan' is 'Jon.' How do Toshans turn 'Johnathan' into *Jack*?

"Blame the Germans." Jack laughed and raised his glass. "I go by many names! Black Jack! Johnathan Andrew Swift! And *Chicken Legs!*"

Rooker chuckled and raised the bottle of añejo. "Well... here's to Johnathan Swift."

"And here's to Pippin Winegrad."

They toasted each other and drank.

Jack scooted in. "Here, here, come here." Rooker could smell the booze on the kid's breath. *He's never been able to hold his liquor. At least he's cheering up.*

Rooker leaned against the log. "What?"

Jack whipped out his scalpel and held it up, the blade's edge bright.

"Hey." Rooker scowled. "Watchit."

He looked at Jack's face and found his eyes earnest in a way usually reserved for children. "I nev-never had a brother. And your brother was... *really* bad." Jack put his hand on Rooker's shoulder. It took everything he had not to flinch. "So maybe we make our own brothers. We're brothers, Rooker. We fight all the time, and you're a complete wasteka, but you're still the closest thing I got. And we're gwan-going to make it official."

Jack slit the scalpel down his palm.

"Hey!" Rooker winced. "Are ya outta yer *head*?"

"Blood brothers." Jack nodded with the absolute conviction only God and alcohol can provide. "We should be blood brothers. Do you have those in Keymark?"

Rooker eyed Jack's bloody hand. "Yeah. We have 'em."

"Then that's what we are." Jack straightened. Or attempted to. "Blood brothers. Here." Jack handed him the scalpel.

Rooker scowled. "I don't—"

"Rooker. I don't have anybody else." Jack's eyes were warm and wet. "Nobody. And neither do you." Rooker felt something tug in his throat. "But we're not alone. Because when we're together, when we're brothers, we are *great*."

He felt something in his chest roll sideways, and it hurt. He watched Jack's face, open, innocent, true.

Don't do this to me.

He swallowed, looking into Jack's eyes.

Rooker sliced his palm. He raised his hand and Jack clasped it in his own, knuckles up. Rooker felt the warmth of his blood, of Jack's blood.

He felt it going under his skin, becoming part of him.

"Brothers." Jack nodded.

Rooker looked him in the eyes and, for a moment, let himself believe it.

He woke to a terrible idea. It hit him all at once, a thunderbolt that appeared, complete and whole like a revelation. Rooker felt a smile spill across his face as he stood beside the cooling fire.

He kicked Jack and the kid snorted awake, drunk, half his face caked in sand. "Wha?" Rooker wrapped a bandage around his palm and stuck the añejo in his pocket. "Wait here. And try to remember ya hate me."

Jack groaned and planted his face in the sand. "I *do* hate you."

This is such a bad idea.

Rooker stumbled into the darkened arena, through the dugout, and made his way to the secret door. He stumbled up the stairs and bumped into the wall, making plenty of noise. Normally, the smell of green wood was overpowering in the tight staircase, but he couldn't smell a thing through the reek of the añejo fumes. Sprinkling the last of the Roi-Tan on his neck, he patted it into his skin. At the top of the stairs, he paused at the door, took a breath, wondering why he was doing this, and stumbled through the door.

Gerba's booth was dark. "Mister Flynn," came her voice. "You are going to wake the entire island."

"Nah, they're all sawin' logs," slurred Rooker. "It's jest us."

A moon emerged from behind a cloud, illuminating the headmistress of the Locke Institute. Her horn was drawn up in a sneer. "Mister Flynn. Are you *intoxicated*?"

"Not a little." Rooker put a finger to his nose and blew a snot-wad clear across the box.

Gerba wrinkled her nose, disgusted. "Go back to your cell."

"I forgotta tell ya somethin' to report. Summa the new prisoners are talkin' about poisoning the yellajackets." He let his voice rise to a drunken shout. "So watch the soup!"

Her eyes narrowed to slits. "The soup?"

"And the boats. They're gonna tryda steal a boat."

"They always try to steal a boat. They have not succeeded yet and they will not succeed tomorrow." She took a step and towered over him, angry. "Is there anything else before you leave?"

"Nope!" He turned away, making sure to slur. "Jest some stupid junk Jack was spoutin', but iss nothin'." He turned and took hold of the door handle.

"One moment, please."

"Hah?"

"What junk?"

Rooker belched loudly. "I dunno. Some way to fix the gladiators without movin' 'em. Bring the bell to Bounty!"

"Way to fix..." She blinked, confused. "What *way*?"

Rooker shrugged. "Don't ask me. I din't understand a word of it." He snorted another hocker. "Maybe ya can translate Toshan. I can't. Anyway." He turned to the door. "G'night."

"Wait." Rooker halted and crossed his fingers. "Mister Naysayer, will you be so kind as to fetch our young doktar?"

Shant Naysayer detached himself from the shadows of her theater box. Rooker hadn't even noticed the creepy bird at all and jumped, knocking over a table. Smiling, the bounty hunter silently disappeared out the door.

Rooker shifted. "Maybe I should go, yeah?"

"Nonsense." Gerba flicked her fingers. "He knows what you are."

"*Pfft*. Right." Rooker nodded. "Ya got anything to drink?"

Before long, Shant Naysayer was back with Jack. As the bounty hunter forced him into the room, Jack's eyes went wide at the sight of Rooker. For a second, Rooker felt worried the kid was too drunk to play his part, but he broke free from Shant and punched Rooker in the jaw.

Rooker put a hand to his face, covering his smile. *Nice touch.*

Jack thrust an accusing finger at him. "Damn you, Rooker! I knew I shoulda kept my mouth shut!" Rooker had to hand it to the kid. Maybe it was the Roi-Tan, but the kid played his role to the hilt.

"Mister Flynn only mentioned you persist in your efforts to heal the wounded." The headmistress folded her hands. "I share your compassion for our students, doktar. But if there were a way to bring the healing majik of the Great Bell here, I would have done it already. And believe me, we have tried. Even on a windless day, the toll of the Agrat-ban-Haifa will not carry this far."

Jack scowled at her, drunk. "That'z because you're *stoopid.*"

Gerba frowned. "I beg your pardon?"

A sneer crossed Jack's face. "Even as backward as you Keymark cavemen are, you *have* noticed sound carries farther at *night*, right, dum-dum?"

She clasped her bosom, affronted. "Well, I—"

"Why does everyone put a bell in a tower?" yelled Jack. "Because the sound travels *farther*, moron." Rooker had to bite back a laugh. "Given the distance, air density, and the cooler temperature, all you have to do"—Rooker watched Jack grab a quill and make little chicken scratches on the page—"is raise the bell about ten yards above the top of the wall." He finished his drawing and shoved it at Gerba. "Then you ring it... at *night*... and the sound will carry all the way here."

She picked up the sheet and stared at the calculations. "That cannot be."

"It's physics!" Jack hollered at her. "I did the math a hundred times! Not that you'd understand it, ya ugly harridan."

Gerba's face broke into an angry scowl. "That is quite enough, *doktar.*"

"It doesn't matter." Jack's face was a maddening grin. "You're too stoopid to make it work anyway!"

"Remove him!" She gestured, angry, and Shant muscled Jack through the doorway. The kid gave Rooker a dark look as the door closed between them.

Rooker scratched at his face, falling back into a drunken slump. "Like I said." He eyed Gerba through his hanging hair. "Nonsense. Babble."

Gerba stared at the paper. "I don't think so."

Okay, play out that fishing line just a bit further. "What?" He snorted. "Don't tell me ya understood what he was sayin'?"

"Quite well." She settled into her seat. "It would solve more than one problem."

Rooker managed to summon a belch that perfumed the room with Roi-Tan. "I doubt it."

Gerba frowned. "I will make my own decisions regarding the Locke Institute, thank you very much."

"Hey!" Rooker set his feet. *Best not to leave too easy.* "How's about a little something? Ya know, for the information?"

She eyed him like a troublesome mosquito. "Perhaps I will allow you to live another day. Would that suit you, Mister Flynn?" She waved her hand at him. "Return to your cell."

Rooker descended the steps, humming. He strolled outside the arena and was making his way down the path when he heard someone step behind him in the dark.

"Did she go for it?"

"Hook, line, and sinker." Rooker pulled the new bottle of añejo he had lifted from Gerba's office and tossed it over his shoulder. He heard Jack catch it. "All we had to do was make it her idea."

Jack thumped Rooker on the shoulder. "I gotta admit it, you're pretty sneaky when you're drunk."

"Here's to bein' sneaky. And drunk." He raised his glass.

As they toasted, Rooker felt the sting in the cut on his palm. His bandage, identical to Jack's, swelled a single drop of red.

Blood brothers. Heh.

Never had losing a little blood felt so good.

Chapter

13

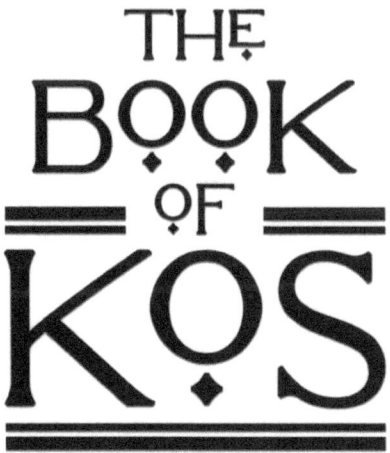

THE
BOOK
OF
KOS

To be great is to be misunderstood.
Ralph Waldo Emerson

TROLS CANNOT SWIM. THEIR body mass is too great, their hide too heavy, their bones too dense. Even with such powerful arms and legs, there is nothing they can do to stay afloat. It is said the easiest way to kill a trol is to drop them in the sea, but there is nothing easy about getting one there.

Gerba Whipmarples went voluntarily.

Waves lashed the side of the *Hup Two* as she departed the Bounty wharf, setting sail over the black deep once again. Gerba had navigated this stretch of water thousands of times; the narrow strait between the two islands no longer held any dread for her.

Ten years this month, she thought as she pulled the sail tight. *Ten years since I tricked the old wizard into showing me the Book of Kos. Ten years since I arranged his death. Ten years since I first came to Huánghūn.* She felt the sea spray splash her face and smiled.

Back then, the Agrat-ban-Haifa had been silent, as had all the Great Bells of Keymark. Its healing majik had been dead for nearly a century. Just another hunk of bronze from the Old World sitting useless on a tropical island overrun with giant spiders.

Buried somewhere beneath the bell lay the Heart of Huánghūn, her one true purpose, her only desire, her destiny.

Ten years.

In those days, no sane man would set foot on Huánghūn for fear of the deadly shiq. Gerba Whipmarples solved the problem by establishing a beachhead the only place she could: the Isle of Bounty. The little speck of land was rife with water buffalo and hogs whose ancestors had fled the shiq. She bred them and sold them, earning just enough coin to pay for a sturdy boat, a crate of mining equipment, and a dozen slaves.

In the first month, she lost her crew to the shiq. They failed to reach the boat by sunset, and she herself had barely escaped with her life. She had only survived by fleeing into the sea, holding onto the capsized boat until dawn as the razorsquid lashed at her legs, trying to bleed her out. Undaunted, she bred more livestock, purchased new slaves, and began again. Gerba Whipmarples was nothing if not persistent.

She turned the rudder and tacked into the wind, keeping the nose of the *Hup Two* centered on her destination. *What is the Toshan expression? Slow and steady wins the race.*

In the third year, her livestock were plundered by raiders. In the eighth year, the original *Hup* sank during a typhoon, drowning another twenty slaves. That had been the darkest time of all; the incident had left her bankrupt. There were no more livestock. No more slaves. Undaunted, Gerba sailed between the islands alone, digging until dusk, eating lonely meals under silent stars.

Then, a miracle.

With the death of the Fell Prince, the curse had been broken, and for the first time in a hundred years, the Great Bells rang out loud. The Agrat-ban-Haifa came to life on that miraculous day, and Gerba Whipmarples found herself in possession of one of the great majiks of Keymark.

She always had a talent for manipulation; bending the bell to her will was no great feat. All it took was a simple Caged Eight with a funnel of blood majik to rule every shiq on the island. The only hitch was the Caged Eight faded within half a month without a death to feed it. Animal sacrifices simply did not work, and slaves were too expensive. It was then Gerba realized there was an exceptionally reliable source of cheap death.

In this way, the Locke Institute was born.

Now she had more slaves than she could put to work, more blood than she would need in twenty years. Now, her tunnels grew every day, bringing her closer and closer to her destiny. For ten years, Gerba Whipmarples persisted through spiders, storms, and strîgoi, marching patiently toward her goal one step at a time. Day after day, she chipped away at the rock, searching for the Heart of Huánghūn.

Ten years.

As her boat pulled into the dock, the headmistress of the Locke Institute looked up at the cliff silhouetted above her and thought the same thing she did every time she set foot ashore.

Perhaps today is the day.

Hammerdwarves hate surprises. They are methodical, precise, and harbor a deep need for order. Most make their homes inside tall pillars of rock carved over the course of decades, hideaways that offer a long view of the world from high up in the sky. These structures give them the ability to see threats and opportunities from a distance, so they have time to decide what course of action is best.

"This is not what we talked about," growled Niko, her hammerdwarf foreman. "You want me to take one of the greatest artifacts in Keymark and raise it into the sky?"

"Think how splendid it would look! I am certain you will agree." Gerba smiled, focusing her subtle manipulation majik. Playing to a hammerdwarf's pride was always a good beginning. "And you, Niko, shall be its architect."

Even as a child, Gerba Whipmarples had excelled at getting her way. By the age of five she could get her father to agree to anything she wanted, no matter how ludicrous. From there, it had been a short step to dominating her mother, and after that, she simply got everything she wanted. She liked horses, as most girls did, and learned how to command them. As she grew to adulthood and wanted more than her gypsy parents could provide, she manipulated the rich. Flattery worked wonders on the wealthy, and she learned to use their whims to line her pockets. Finally, she graduated to manipulating wizards.

And their secrets were delicious.

She touched Niko on the shoulder, her eyes locked on him. "Every bell in Keymark is the same, mounted on two pillars under a crossbeam. How dull." She spread her fingers at the bell, presenting it anew. "But the Agrat-ban-Haifa could be your masterwork, Niko."

She heard him inhale. *Pride. So simple to inflame.* Atop the butte, wind whispered around Niko's grey hair. The sun was half-lidded by clouds, a series of God-rays over the sea, the smell of rain still fresh in the air. "Imagine it," Gerba whispered, letting his mind do the work for her. "Gleaming above the sea like a star. People would come from all over Keymark just to see it. A true wonder of the world."

"Yes." The hammerdwarf stared at the bell. "That would be something worth signing my name to."

Gerba smiled and let Niko run with the idea. Raising the bell might heal the wounded on Bounty, as the doktar intended, but that hardly mattered. The nobles would arrive soon, and combining the safety of Bounty with the pleasure of the bell would play nicely as a grand finale to the Steel Trial. The show was built to be her coming out party, her revelation, and it had to be perfect.

The Caged Eight had given Gerba her first taste of true control. Persuasion, negotiation, coercion, all these were useful tools, but they had never given her true dominance. That power always lay with someone else, the decision ultimately theirs. She had never ruled them. Not completely. Even a well-trained animal could bite. And Niko could still tell her no.

But the Caged Eight had given her what she'd always wanted. The shiq could not refuse her. She had sovereignty over them and it was glorious.

Raising the bell would extend her influence over the shiq, the razorsquid, the attercops she had brought here from Pell Isle, the dragon that came from who knows where, drawn by her power. All of them her willing slaves.

"I can see it," said Niko, spreading his hands toward the Agrat-ban-Haifa. "Two pillars supporting the bell, arched on the outside like fans, a latticework of natural wood. Intricate. Delicate. Half-circles flowing to a single point, the bell a crown in the sky." His eyes shone. "It would be magnificent."

"Excellent." Gerba clapped him on the back. "You have five days to build it."

"What?"

Gerba flashed her best smile. "You can do it, Niko. Put it on top of two exceptionally large tree trunks if you have to. Just complete the job in the next five days. That is, if your men want to be paid." Niko stammered, trying to pick which argument he wanted to address first. Gerba didn't give him the opportunity. "Thank you!"

She descended from the rooftop of the Locke Institute, ignoring Niko's pleas. Sometimes the simple ways were best. Gerba Whipmarples had long since learned that she who controls the purse strings controls the world. *Money works as well as manacles.*

As she swept down the staircase toward her solarium, she wondered if her package from Highyon Garde had finally arrived. She had commissioned the item two months ago, and it was long overdue.

Perhaps today is the day.

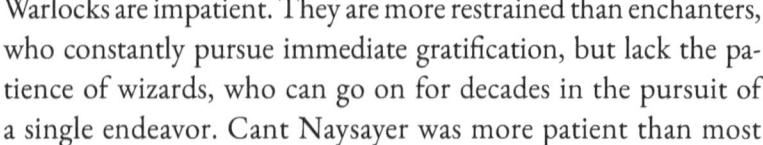

Warlocks are impatient. They are more restrained than enchanters, who constantly pursue immediate gratification, but lack the patience of wizards, who can go on for decades in the pursuit of a single endeavor. Cant Naysayer was more patient than most warlocks, but even he had his limits.

"Nine months." He paced, bootheels clocking on the solarium floor. "It's been nine months, Whipmarples. You told me you could break him."

"That is no way to begin a conversation, Mister Naysayer." Gerba descended the final stair. "Welcome back." She settled into her chair, removed her heels, and rubbed at her calves. As anticipated, a package tied with blue ribbon was waiting on her desk. She was eager to open it but would not do so in Cant's presence. "I am merely your employer, Mister Naysayer. If you feel I am wasting your time, you are free to pursue another."

"When I brought you Rooker Flynn, you promised you would deliver me control of the *Venture Brigand*." His voice took a sharp edge.

"If you recall correctly, I promised I would try." *And I am certain you remember my exact words.*

"I'm sick of waiting."

Good. Gerba felt like a chef whose roast was almost cooked. Negotiating with Cant Naysayer was always like walking a tightrope, and she never quite knew which way it would go unless she offered a little push. "Mister Flynn has proven more intractable than I imagined. He is pliant in all ethical matters, but when it comes to your ship, he will not listen to reason."

"I *told* you."

O, he is perturbed. How wonderful. She poured a chai and twisted the knife. "I expected him to beg for his life before his first combat in the Steel Trials. However, he has proven himself a more accomplished swordsman than I gave him credit for. He's a cantankerous fellow."

"And I'm done waiting for him," Cant hissed. Gerba held her breath, awaiting the inevitable. "You requested to be given the first opportunity to buy the boat."

Gerba spread a bit of butter on her biscuit. "I did."

"It's yours for ten million marks."

Outrageous. She could purchase half a fleet for that. However, Gerba couldn't help but smile. *Another game ended well. It seems all my ships are coming in today.* "You know, it just so happens I received an offer... Ah, here it is." She plucked the scroll from the table. "A written offer from Baronet Ket. He will be attending the next Steel Trial, along with several dozen other nobles. He is *extremely* interested in witnessing the death of Black Jack." She tilted her horn. "In fact, he is willing to pay handsomely to guarantee the outcome."

Cant shifted his weight to one hip. "Let me guess. Ten million marks."

Gerba giggled, shaking her head. "He *was* embarrassed about being thrown from his horse." Gerba tossed the offer on the table. "I will have the money for you in five days. Will you and your brothers be able to vacate the *Venture Brigand* by then?"

"I'm not sailing that bucket ever again," Cant growled. "After the Steel Trial, we're departing on the *Hydra*."

"Then I believe we have an accord." She offered her hand. Cant took it, and the deal was done. *One more feather in my cap.* "Now, if you will excuse me, Mister Naysayer." Gerba glanced at the blue-ribboned package on her desk. "I must be about my day."

Cant turned to go but paused in the solarium door, his dark shadow framed by trellised vines. His rattlesnake voice was quiet, thoughtful. "You are good at this, Whipmarples." Gerba straightened, not sure if he was offering an actual compliment. "In the beginning, I thought you were nothing more than a jumped-up warden, but I am beginning to think you may get what you came here for." He paused, then turned. "When all this is over, I presume you will return home to the Juttlands."

She narrowed an eyebrow. *Careful.* "You may presume whatever you like, Mister Naysayer."

"I will." He straightened. "If an enterprising woman were to present the *Venture Brigand* to the King of Trol, she would be lauded as a heroine of the kingdom." Cant stepped forward. "And if she were to deliver the Heart of Huánghūn... Well. She would earn a seat within the Ring of Fire and whisper in the ear of the king himself." Cant tilted his head. "An enterprising woman, even one of lowly birth, could become a queen."

Well, he is a clever one, isn't he? She settled back in her chair and eyed him with a half-hidden smile. "She would have to be an enterprising woman, indeed."

"I concur." There was respect in his voice now. She was certain of it. "When that day comes, and I suspect it may be soon, I look forward to continuing our business relationship in a more... advanced capacity. It would be an honor to serve one of the Sacrum Cabal." He removed his hat and bent at the waist, his long duster dipping against the floor. "I wish you the best of good fortune in your endeavor, milady."

She couldn't help but be charmed by the honorific. "And you in yours, Mister Naysayer. Good day." She watched him return the wide-brimmed gambler's hat to its rightful place upon his skull and descend the stairs.

The Sacrum Cabal. Gerba Whipmarples had never breathed a word of her secret hope to anyone, but somehow Cant Naysayer had sniffed her out. *Within my grasp.*

Gerba plucked up the blue-ribboned box and opened it. The single glove inside had been custom-made for her large hand, tatted lace in cornflower blue. She pulled it on, appreciating the symbol inscribed in the palm, contained within a circlet of gold. The rune was a tenasi, a minor spell sometimes used in the gauntlets of ancient generals or older swordsmen with palsied hands who wished to avoid embarrassing themselves in a tourney. The tenasi made it impossible to drop their swords, a grip of iron that could not be broken.

She discarded the box and walked to her office, flexing her fingers inside the glove.

Now I have you.

She pulled aside the red curtain and revealed Nepenthe.

Six joints of bamboo, pinned to the wall in iron clamps. It had taken months for the third and fourth joints to arrive from the Tosh, but the fifth and sixth had come more quickly. She had trapped them all in iron. Each piece of bamboo coursed in waves of blue majik that danced within the carvings, each piece seeming to crave the next. The air hummed with *wikk*. Gerba Whipmarples ran her hands over the wood, her face illuminated in blue light.

One more piece to go. But still. Let us see.

She took the key from a chain around her neck, unlocked an iron clamp, and gripped one of the rods with her new glove. She released the next piece of Nepenthe and watched it fly to its twin in her hand like a magnet, connecting with a sharp *tak*. With each piece she unbound, the power in her fist grew stronger. It pulled against her, straining toward Bounty, wanting to return to its master, to Black Jack.

But the tenasi held it fast.

No no, dearie. You belong to me now. Gerba chuckled, pleased. *And I need you to find something.*

Her eyes were lit with fiery blue embers, the power delicious and exciting.

Perhaps today is the day.

Strîgoi do not die. The vampiric dæmons can be stabbed, burned, drowned, flayed, and torn asunder, but they will not succumb to death. Unless they are destroyed by silver or dragonfire, strîgoi will rise again to pursue the blood their dark master craves.

Gerba arrived in the lava pits just in time to witness her pale pets feast. She did not remember the student's name, but the Vulture boy put up a brave struggle before he fell. As the strîgoi crowded the cage wall to slake their thirst with his blood, Gerba covered her nose with a handkerchief. She had never gotten used to the stink of the pit and did not enjoy descending this far into the labyrinth.

This was the only place on the island where she felt like a captive.

In its way, Huánghūn had always been a prison. According to the Book of Kos, it was here, at the end of the Old World, that the mighty Kos had summoned a mountain of fire to consume the strîgoi and trap them forever beneath the earth. The dæmons were the island's first prisoners, bound within cooling magma that eventually formed the island.

Gerba watched the largest strîgoi, the alpha, pace the cage wall. She remembered the thrill of discovery, so many years ago, when she had first unearthed the beast. The lone strîgoi had been trapped in the stone like a baby dragon inside its egg, fetal and helpless in the bowels of the earth. It had been weak then, and she had caged it with iron and salt before it woke from its centuries-long slumber. Only then had she begun her long study of the beast and its behavior.

"Headmistress!" A dark acolyte tossed the last of the blood vials through the cage wall and bowed. "I was not expecting you. How may I serve?"

"How many do we have in the coven today, Lucien?"

"Six, praise RākŞhasa." Lucien eyed the fresh corpse and the dæmons lapping up the broken blood vials. "Still only six."

"Very good." Feeding the strîgoi was a constant balancing act. If their victim was too weak, the strîgoi would not touch it. If the victim was too strong, the dæmons would drain the body and reanimate the corpse to create another strîgoi. To make matters worse, the bloodthirsty dæmons would periodically eviscerate each other in a violent frenzy. Inevitably, the alpha would bury some of their corpses under rocks in the lava pits so they could not rise again. Gerba had solved the problem by arming her living sacrifices with weapons. Fighting prey seemed to satisfy the dæmons' lust for blood without increasing their number. The last thing she needed was more strîgoi.

Not yet.

She eyed the alpha. *Even you will learn to obey your betters, dearie. Soon enough.*

Gerba Whipmarples gripped Nepenthe and focused on the *wikk* within the staff. She summoned the dæmonic hieroglyph in her mind, the secret name hidden in the Book of Kos.

Nepenthe responded and pulled against her hand. It had caught the scent.

At last. Gerba smiled. For a decade, she had tunneled blindly in the dark, patiently searching for her treasure. Now she had a compass, a dowsing rod to lead the way. The Elven Fremest had created Nepenthe to hunt dæmons; it would find what she could not.

Concentrating, Gerba focused on the staff.

East.

Gerba left the lava pit and followed Nepenthe into the dark. Led by the pull of the staff, Gerba found herself exploring a dusty excavation site she had long since abandoned.

Nepenthe's pull was more urgent now.

Closer.

Black stone walls reflected Nepenthe's cerulean glow as she descended into the cobwebbed depths.

Closer.

Nepenthe jerked in her hands, pulled Gerba to a halt, and struck the wall with a single *tak*.

There.

Gerba gazed at the rough stone wall, just one of the hundreds of tunnels she had excavated beneath the Institute over a decade.

But this place was special.

This was the x in her treasure map.

She spotted an old pickaxe on the cave floor and picked it up.

The shiq were nothing, the students were nothing, the Locke Institute was nothing. All of them were simply a means to an end. The Book of Kos had told her what the island was, Nepenthe had shown her the way, and now, after a decade of questing in the dark, Gerba Whipmarples had finally found her path to the Heart of Huánghūn.

She hefted the pickaxe and prepared to strike.

Perhaps today is the day.

Chapter

14

COMES THE DRUM

Fear is pain arising from the anticipation of evil.

Aristotle

B LAMELESS BLUE SKY HUNG over the Isle of Bounty, a sapphire morning dotted with a scattering of pink clouds that refused to confess dawn was gone. A perfect day for a Steel Trial.

Rooker walked with Jack through the sunrise, meandering toward the wharf. The air was filled with the scent of spices. Jack carried a short stick, a kabob of delicious little round cakes he had deep-fried in oil just after sunrise. Sprinkled heavily with sugar and cinnamon, the cakes were sweet and spicy all at once, and Rooker had fallen in love with them at first bite. He licked his fingers, still feeling sugar on his tongue. "What d'ya call these things?"

"Donuts," Jack said through a mouthful of cake.

Rooker plucked another off the stick, stuffed it in his mouth, and signed with his hands, *Good.* Sign language lessons with the tams of Bounty had gone badly; they were just as stupid as Rooker remembered. Jack hadn't been able to teach the little lizards, but Rooker was quick on the uptake. *I. Was. Hungry.*

Jack snorted laughter, spewing a bit of donut. Rooker frowned. "What?"

"You just said 'I was horny.'"

Rooker laughed and made a gesture with the donut. "Been too long since I saw a healthy woman."

Jack laughed and threw one at him. Rooker snatched it out of the air. "Okay, I believe you about donuts. Tell me something else. Something about cars."

Jack sighed. Rooker knew the kid was getting tired of the truth-lie game. "Okay. Um... cars run on gasoline, which is made from million-year-old dead plants that get pumped out of the ground. And giant lizards."

Most of the time, Rooker couldn't tell which stories about Jack's bizarre sphere were true and which were made up, but this one was easy. "Lie!"

"Errt!" Jack smiled. "True! A lot of people think it's made from dead dinosaurs, but most of it is algae and marine plankton. Interestingly—"

Rooker rounded the corner and came to a sudden stop, dumbfounded.

The wharf was full of ships. Nearly a dozen were tied to the cleats, another twenty moored further out.

And such ships.

All dressed in silk, every one of them. Rich purple, shimmering gold, opalescent white. Their mainsails and jibs were resplendent in bold colors, prominent sigils and crests thundering their significance upon the water, each ship more a peacock than the last. Every hull was made of teak, acacia, and paulownia, hand-crafted by masters, lacquered thick, each with a carved figurehead at the bow. Rams, lions, and dragons surrounded the wharf.

Rooker scowled. "The nobles are back."

"What?" Jack said through his donut, then stopped when he saw the armada of riches.

Rooker recognized several sigils, including the green-trimmed sail with the trident crest. "That's the Sheikh of Baaza." He scanned the other ships. "Thakur Kroll. Viceroy Chen. And Baronet Ket." Rooker whistled. "Half the noble houses in the Deep Blue South are here."

Jack peered at the two dozen armed guards who protected the wharf and rubbed his side where he'd once caught an arrow. "So this is what we've been rehearsing for."

Rooker nodded, remembering his last encounter with the nobles. The killing fields must have gone over like hotcakes to draw this kind of crowd for a second event. The rich and powerful of the Deep Blue South had thrilled at the taste of blood, and now they gathered like flies for more.

"Yep." He spat. "The main event."

"Tonight's Steel Trials will begin after sunset!" shouted Wont, addressing the collected gladiators inside the arena. "Yellowjackets and convicts stay separate from here on out. When your name is called, report to the main cage below." He snorted. "You have new costumes for the show."

Billy Pilgrim's head snaped up, smiling. The other prisoners glanced at each other. *Costumes?* Rooker squinted at Gerba's theater box. *She's going all out for this, isn't she?*

"Until then, you're all confined to quarters." Wont gestured to the acolytes as they closed the colosseum doors and barred them from the outside. The gladiators were penned in, kept separate from the nobles like animals at a zoo. "To make sure you all stay good little girls and boys."

An hour later, Rooker stood atop the wall, planning a dozen escape routes using the nobles' ships. The sea surrounding Bounty was colorful as a carnival, rippling brightly colored sails. He leaned his chin against the rail and daydreamed about stealing all of them. *That corsair wouldn't be half-bad if I had five sailors to man it.* In the distance, off the tip of Huánghūn, he could see the *Venture Brigand* waiting for him. *And I'd drive it straight to ya, girl.*

He went back to identifying noble houses. "There's three vessels for Viscount Preis. Three. And here comes another one. Lord Lund." Rooker turned to Billy Pilgrim. "Lund. They threw ya in here, right?"

Pilgrim bent a banjo string that said *yes*.

Maybe we should teach him Jack's hand-talk. The silent troubadour still didn't speak; music remained his only voice. It made Billy Pilgrim a difficult man to know. All Rooker remembered about the story was that Pilgrim had performed a song at some gala that had gotten him arrested, a hilarious ballad about a jackass named Lund. The next morning he was on his way to Huánghūn. "I don't get it." He cocked his head at Pilgrim. "You *know* the Lunds. You *know* they're vindictive as hell. So why sing the damned song where they could hear it?"

Billy smiled, staring far away over the sea. He plucked his banjo and sang a wistful tune.

> *Sister spinning dark prevail*
> *Emerges softly nightingale.*
> *He sings to her his waking lullabye*
> *Silence crouches on her chest*
> *Forever drifting dispossessed*
> *Heart beating out the blood so mystified*
> *Forever dry dry dry dry dry.*

Rooker blinked. The tune was unfamiliar and the lyrics didn't make any sense, so it gave him no insight. He harrumphed. "Okay. Gotcha. Yer still crazy."

Pilgrim patted his arm, refusing to let go of Rooker's attention. The balladeer removed a little paring knife from his pocket, scratched at the wood of the amphitheater wall for a moment, then gestured to the mark he made, the same in every language.

"Love." Rooker stared at the heart. "Yeah." He glanced across the sea to the *Venture Brigand*. "That'll get you in trouble every time."

Their names were called early for their costume fitting; Rooker and Pilgrim were the two biggest divas in the show. Deep in the dugout cage, a trio of seamstresses descended upon Billy Pilgrim, cooing like a nest of partridges. In moments, they had the troubadour dressed in a fabulous purple topcoat with brass buttons down both sides of his chest. They went to work on the singer's orange hair, teasing it until it stuck off the top of his head like a brush fire. The balladeer held up a sheet of gold silk and pulled his topcoat back, conveying without words that he wanted a gold lining inside the coat. The ladies agreed.

Rooker felt himself growing jealous and struck a pose. "Darlins. Don't forget the good-lookin' one."

One of the seamstresses scowled and pointed at Rooker. "Strip."

"Cover yer eyes, ladies." He grinned. "Yer passions may overwhelm ya."

Half an hour later, Rooker felt like a man. His hair was trimmed and washed, his beard was trimmed, and he wore a new red shirt made of soft pima with leather accents and ties at the wrists. The chestnut suede pants were tight as a second skin. He checked himself in the mirror and admired the way they clung to his backside. "No, sweetheart, look." He gestured at the crimson leather stripe that ran from his hip to his ankle. "The line should be *straight*, like an arrow. Straight, see?"

"You're done." The seamstress slapped new leather boots into his arms.

"Now listen, honey—"

"Next!" She waved in the next outlaw.

Excommunicated, Rooker moved into the tunnel that circled the arena. He sat, dusted the sand off his feet, and slipped on his new boots. *Not bad. I don't—*

A shadow moved. Something on the ceiling, something bestial and quick.

Rooker stopped, watching. The creature was small, the size of a dog, and crawled upside-down on four legs, a long tail behind it. Rooker balled his fist as the thing picked up speed, crawling through the shadows at a run.

Is that a tam?

In a burst of speed, it leapt from the ceiling and hit him in the chest.

Rooker staggered backward. The thing wrapped itself around his arm and pawed at him with tree-frog fingers.

"Geddoff!" Rooker tried to shove it away, but the tam held on. As he gripped its body, he saw familiar blue and gold markings on the thing's pebbled hide. *Wait. Is that—*"Fiji?"

The blue and gold gecko licked his face like a joyful dog, making little happy sounds. It wiggled excitedly and crawled all over him, wrapping him in an ever-moving hug.

Rooker stared at the thing, trying to figure out how Jack's old tam had gotten on Bounty. *No. It's not Fiji. It's—*"Fuji. What the hell are you doing here?"

Fuji blinked and licked its eyeball.

Frowning, Rooker tried to remember the correct gestures in Jack's hand-language. His fingers fumbled, searching for the words. *How. You. Here?*

Fuji cocked its head and watched Rooker's fingers move. It blinked big yellow eyes and signed back. *Apple?*

Rooker scowled. *No, I don't have an apple!*

Fuji crawled into Rooker's shirt and walked around his chest. Its head came out and sniffed his pocket, looking for food. *Apple.*

Rooker frowned. "Dammit, say something other than apple!"

The tam's fingers were a blur of motion. Rooker tried to follow the hand-talk, but he didn't know most of the signs the tam used. "Wait, wait, slow down." The tam tried again, signing more deliberately, as if Rooker was a small child. Even then, Rooker only caught "ship" and "moons." *Stupid hand-talk.*

He realized Fuji wore a thin chain around its neck, an identical color to its blue pebbled skin. At the bottom of the chain hung a small brass sphere inscribed with a tiny silver symbol.

Rooker tilted his head as he read the word aloud. "United."

United? United with what? The nobles? Some viscount or daimyo? "Who are ya with, dummy? How did ya get here?"

Fuji blinked. **Apple.**

He glared at the tam. *Stupid animal.* "Let's find Jack. Maybe he can—"

"Hey!" came a voice.

The tam's head shot up, yellow eyes wide. Wont Naysayer stomped down the hallway toward them. "Flynn! I holler and holler and you don't—"

Fuji shot down the tunnel and fled past the mammoth bounty hunter. Wont laughed and tried to stomp on the tam. It darted around his foot and headed up the wall, attempting to get away. "Stupid tams." Wont reared back his fist to squash Fuji.

Rooker lunged forward to grab Wont's arm, but he was too late. Stone smashed and debris flew as Fuji disappeared under the Naysayer's fist. Wont grinned. "Like a bug."

Chirrup? came a sound from down the hall. Rooker found Fuji upside down on the ceiling, fifty feet down the corridor. It tilted its head and coughed. *Hak!*

"Damn tam." Wont picked up a rock and threw it, but the blue gecko was long gone. Rooker watched it escape through the bars and disappear into the arena. The goliath scowled at Rooker. "Report to the armory, now. There are new blades for the show." Wont lumbered down the hallway. "I'd wish you luck, Flynn, but I've got good money against you tonight, so I hope to see you dead."

"You first." Wont laughed and trundled down the tunnel. Rooker dusted off his new shirt. *This is shaping up to be an interesting day.*

Finding the kid was more trouble than Rooker imagined. Jack wasn't in the main cage or in the arena, but the stands were coming to life in preparation for the show. The acolytes administered the final touches on the banners and bunting and lit tall braziers in preparation for nightfall. The Rainjons, the band out of Javernis Twist, arrived to set up their bigger drums. But Jack was nowhere to be found.

As Rooker looked through the little cell-sized rooms that circled the arena, he heard the telltale sound of someone violently emptying their stomach. He pulled aside a half-drawn curtain to reveal Patch Picaroon vomiting into a chamber pot.

Rooker wrinkled his nose. "Damn, Patch."

"Get out of here, Rooker!"

Patch had been nasty since they arrived on Bounty, but no one saw much of her these days. She'd become a ghost. A mean one. "Ya smell like bile." He watched Patch retch and discovered he felt something almost like pity for her. They'd been friends once. Well, not friends, but... partners, anyway. Frowning, he handed her a waterskin. "Rinse yer mouth."

She did, spat on the floor, and sagged against the wall. "Just go."

"What the hell's wrong with ya?"

She shot him a hairy eyeball. "You think I want to talk to *you* about it?"

"I don't see anybody else."

She sighed, wiped her mouth, then leaned against the wall. Rooker saw her body slump, surrendering. "Have I ever told you about my knack?"

Rooker blinked. A knack was minor majik, garden-variety majik, like how he could snap his little flame into existence or the way Copper Dave's nails were always sharp. "Let me guess. Ya got a knack for puking."

She shot a glare at him. "Glamour."

So that's her secret. Glamour was illusion majik, usually reserved for fancy ladies, a bit of deception that improved their appearance. A longer neck, a slimmer waist, a bosom with just the right amount of plump. *That's how she always stayed clean.* On Huánghūn, Patch's fur had always been glossy and bright, never a dot of mud on her, her tail always curled just so. Rooker had chalked it up to the jinx's natural fastidiousness, but he realized Patch Picaroon had always looked a little too good.

Used to, anyway. He eyed her matted fur. "I'd say it ain't workin' for ya."

Patch scowled at him and leaned against the wall. "I'm using too much of it. All the time." She closed her eyes, exhausted. "Even in my sleep."

Rooker opened his mouth but didn't know what to say. The longest he'd ever kept his little flame going was an hour. After that, it started to get painful. He couldn't even imagine keeping it up for months. "And I thought I was the vain one."

She laughed, just a short burst, but at least it was something. "I feel like a lemon with all the juice squeezed out." Patch checked the curved hallway behind him to see if it was empty. "Rooker, if you see me... as I am... you can't breathe a word." Her eyes went hard as diamonds. "You can't *fink* on me, Rooker. Swear it."

"Okay, fine, I promise. Here." Rooker pulled the curtain shut, sealing them off from the rest of the tunnel. "Now we've got some privac—"

He turned around to find a ragged alley cat where Patch had been. Hunks were missing from her fur. Her teeth were yellow, her eyes bloodshot, her coat was stiff and stained. She sat hunched, cupping one arm under a distended belly the size of a melon.

Rooker stared. When his voice finally came, it came soft. "Oh, Patch."

She raised a tattered paw and pointed a claw at him. "Not a word."

Rooker eyed her over. *Now it makes sense. The nasty looks, the pissy comments, the bad balance, the vomiting.* "When are ya due?"

Patch breathed a long sigh. "Half a month, maybe less."

Quick math that told him the deed had been done on Huánghūn. "So the father—"

"Doesn't need to worry about it." Patch shot him a look, daring him to press any further.

Rooker put two and two together. "Boss West."

She raised her chin, her eyes fierce. "*Major* West."

"Did he—"

"No. We were..." She shrugged. "Not in love, exactly. But close enough for prison."

That explains why she spent so much time in Hyena back when West was alive. And why she wanted to take Ransom's head off. Rooker took Patch's hand and pulled her up, settling her onto a rickety stool. "So the glamour..."

"Hides the belly. Keeps me looking like I'm... you know... normal." She looped her paw under her stomach. "But it's getting too big to cover. I'm stretched too thin."

"Does the Institute know?"

"*Nobody* knows." Patch scowled. "Nobody *can* know. I'm trying to keep it together, but if anyone finds out..." She shook her head. "A baby? In the Locke Institute?" Her eyes lifted to his. "You know what would happen."

Rooker set his jaw. At best, Gerba would sell it off as a slave. More than likely someone would just dash its head against a rock and be done with it.

Patch let her head drop, defeated. "I thought I could cover it up, figure out something, but..." She sank in the chair, ragged and exhausted. "I'm played out, Rooker."

"Yeah." Patch would be lucky to make it through tonight, much less half a month. "That's tough."

He watched Patch give in to despair. She dropped her head and stifled a sob; her breath hitched on the way out. "I can't figure out how to keep it alive." She stiffened and stared at him with hard eyes. "But I'd rather die than let her have my moggie."

Rooker just stood there. He had no idea what to say, no idea what he could do about it. Patch was done for. And so was her baby.

The curtain clattered; Rooker spun to find a figure in the doorway. On instinct, he gripped the outlaw's coat and slammed him against the wall. Rooker realized he held Billy Pilgrim half a foot in the air. The troubadour's eyes went wide. Rooker looked over his shoulder and realized Patch was back to her normal shape, fit and trim, as if nothing had happened. "What?" She arched an eyebrow.

"What?" growled Rooker.

Looking at them both with wide eyes, the mute balladeer spread his hands. *What?*

Rooker unbunched his fists and let Pilgrim go. As the balladeer fixed his jacket, Rooker glanced at Patch.

There's nothing I can do.

So he did the only thing he knew how to do well. He walked away.

Escaping down the tunnel, Rooker felt forced to say something. Anything. His voice sounded tight and strange to his own ears. "Good luck tonight."

"Yeah," came Patch's quiet voice as he left her behind. "See you on the other side."

Nobles entered the stands and moved to their seats as servants laid down plush cushions to protect their delicate backsides. The big audience box was occupied by the sheikh, along with several lords and ladies from Javernis Twist. The Rainjons played an overture from the time of King David, adding to the pageantry of anticipation as the nobles mingled and gossiped, complimenting each other on their finery, all of them looking forward to the show.

Rooker snuck up the secret staircase for the final time. As he picked the lock to Gerba's box, he knew he was grasping at straws. His plan was thin as tissue paper, but he had to do something to keep Patch off the sand, and there was no more time. He opened the door to find Gerba studying her script, pacing behind the drawn curtains, preparing to open the show. She was dressed in an ankle-length gown of sparkling emerald sequins that made her look like a walrus made of glitter.

As Rooker stepped forward, he found Shant Naysayer's knife at his throat. The bounty hunter's voice whispered in his ear. "It's locked for a reason, convict."

The headmistress turned, surprised. "Mister Flynn! This will not do! You are supposed to be waiting in the wings!"

Rooker edged away from Shant and flashed his best smile. "I jest saved yer show, Gerba."

She tilted her horn, eyeing him. "I beg your pardon?"

Rooker tried to keep the panic out of his voice but felt it coming off him like the stink of a dead animal. *Smile, dammit.* "Ya want to put on yer best show tonight, right? Well, the crowd loves me. I'm the most popular fighter ya got."

Gerba blew air through her nostrils. "That is why you close the first act, Mister Flynn. Now if you will excuse me..."

He stepped in. "What if I open the second act as well? Like a whatdayacallit... a reprise?"

She lowered an eyebrow. "The cold open of the second act is Miss Picaroon's role."

"But ya got a better option." Rooker cocked his leg up on a chair and set one fist to his hip, putting his new outfit on full display. "Think how much the nobles would love a second helping of *me*."

Gerba sighed, frustrated. "Mister Flynn. I am not changing the run-of-show half an hour before we open."

Keep pressing. "Patch isn't feeling tip top." Rooker dropped his voice, bringing her into his confidence. "Case of the runs. No one wants to see *that*."

"How unfortunate for her." Gerba managed to keep her tone civil. "Let us hope she rallies before her trial."

Rooker set his jaw, desperate. "Gerba. I'm tellin' ya, if ya want a good show, we need to chan—"

"We? *We?*" The headmistress straightened to her full height and towered above him. "You forget your place. There is no 'we.'" She stepped toward him. "You are nothing but a common criminal and a two-faced snitch. This is my event, not *ours*. Mine."

Rooker scowled. *Fine. Time for threats.* "If ya want me to keep feedin' ya information about Black Jack—"

Gerba laughed. A high, bright titter that burbled straight from her belly. "Mister Flynn, you are a caution!" She wiped a tear from her eye. "I suppose this is my fault. I made you feel valuable, giving you little baubles in exchange for your assistance. If you think you have any leverage here, let me be clear." She leaned in, almost touching her horn to his nose. "After tonight, Black Jack will no longer be the Institute's concern."

Rooker saw the cold glitter in her eyes. He felt gooseflesh run over his skin. Patch wasn't the only one he was saying goodbye to tonight.

She's going to kill him.

Shant grabbed his arms. Rooker didn't struggle as the bounty hunter forced him through the door and down the stairs. "You should be grateful, Mister Flynn," scolded the headmistress. "Tonight, your victory is once again assured. You are, as you say, extremely popular with the crowd." Gerba Whipmarples waved him away. "I expect you to have a role in the Steel Trials for a long, long time to come."

Shant muscled him downstairs into the dugout and deposited him in the big cage where the other outlaws huddled. They reeked of sweat and fear. Patch slumped against a wall, her eyes closed, her body limp. Wont shoved new weapons into Rooker's hands and forced him to the gate. He slammed against the portcullis and found himself next to Jack Swift.

"Hey." The kid smiled. "Like my outfit?"

Jack spread his arms, displaying the ridiculous costume he'd been given. His too-loose pants were studded with dangling conchos up the side, topped with a silver belt buckle the size of a saucer. Silver embellishments studded his shirt, the arms hung with silver fringe. The tricorn hat was two sizes too small and pointed like a dunce cap. Tiny silver bells hung from all three corners. "I look like an entire mariachi band."

He's gonna die tonight and he's worried about his outfit.

Horns blared from the arena, announcing the beginning of the Steel Trials.

"Here we go." Jack slapped Rooker on the back and offered a smile. "Good luck."

He's all out of luck. Rooker glanced at Jack, but no words came. The kid's smile was easy, relaxed, completely unaware of what was coming. *She's going to kill him.*

And there's not a damn thing I can do about it.

Jack caught the expression on his face. "What?"

Rooker eyed the scar on his palm, then the one on Jack's.

Forgive me if you can.

"Luck to you too." He swallowed. "Have a good show."

Chapter

15

BLOOD
&
SAND

As for life,
it is a battle and a sojourning in a strange land;
but the fame that comes after is oblivion.

Marcus Aurelius

F ANFARE SPLIT THE AIR as the last rays of sun sunk below Huánghūn's horizon. Torchlight revealed a riot of color, a colosseum filled with silk gowns, stylish bonnets, and expensive jewelry. Green was fashionable this summer, and the ladies competed to display the most lavish viridescent dresses, emerald embellishments, and lime accessories. The gentlemen wore glittering summer vests, their mustachios curled and waxed. Elegant peacock feathers, the new fad out of Javernis Twist, crowned half the female heads, whether jaelin, jinx, or llystra. Music lilted from harps, pipes, oud, and timpani. The Rainjons were dressed in black and white motley and played upbeat marches that promised glorious, bloody deaths. The nobles cheered, their faces red with drunken anticipation.

Rooker wished every one of them dead.

Gerba Whipmarples emerged to trumpet fanfare, twin moons shining behind her. Rooker had heard her opening speech half a dozen times, but now she spent forever calling out the nobles in the crowd, the Sheikh of Baaza, the Baronet Ket, and Lady Locke herself, founding patron of the Institute, thanking them all for their attendance and contributions to tonight's event. The remainder was rote: Bet heavily and enjoy the show. "And now, ladies and gentlemen..." Gerba raised her hands, pausing for effect. "The Steel Trials!"

Music leapt from the Rainjons as the audience burst into thunderous applause and cheers.

Yeah. Rooker glanced at Jack. *Let the games begin.*

Osmann Throt had the opening act. The barbarian was exactly the kind of criminal every noble wanted to see dead: ugly, huge, and primitive. Throt was a *haka* warrior, a savage out of Chult, and danced around his opponent, baring his teeth and howling obscenities. It made for good theater and the audience loved it. By the end, they were all hollering and hooting, mimicking Throt with every lunge and feint. When the contest concluded with

Throt's head five yards away from his body, they cheered louder than the band.

The nobles would not stand for Billy Pilgrim talking to them, much less touching them, and so his scarf-swapping schtick would not fly here. But the troubadour knew his audience and spent the overture pretending he was a clumsy bumpkin looking for his seat. His buffoonery made increasingly large sections of the audience laugh aloud as he tumbled down the stairs with ever-greater pratfalls. Pilgrim had every eye in the audience on him by the time his name was called. He appeared so surprised that he nearly fell off the top of the colosseum. As the audience laughed, he marched down the steps to the colosseum singing at the top of his lungs. The tune was a favorite with the nobles, the exploits of the Keymark Kings. By the time he hit the sand, Pilgrim had the entire crowd singing the words. As the match began, Pilgrim conducted the Rainjons, keeping the song going while his opponent chased him around the ring. On the fifth chorus, he leapt into the audience and disappeared into the grandstands, only to emerge an instant later with the band, dressed in Rainjon motley as he belted out the final lyrics of the song.

His applause was thunderous, peppered with cries of "Up! *Up!*" Only Lordling Lund protested the bard's pardon, but the crowd outshouted him as Billy Pilgrim bowed deep.

As Rooker awaited the inevitable, he found himself overwhelmed by an emotion he hadn't felt since he was a child, not since the days of the North Waste. The emotion was so unfamiliar that he had difficulty recognizing it. He had nothing to fear tonight, he was the one protected from on high, and yet still he was overwhelmed with dread. After tonight, Jack would be dead. Patch would be dead. Just as sure as the little akita was dead.

Unable to deal with the surge of feeling, Rooker shoved it down deep as he always had and clamped it under lock and key, where the strange emotion slowly boiled into toxic rage. *All that's left will be me and her, fighting for the* Brigand. *Gerba Whipmarples, my last friend in the world.*

By the time Wont called him to the arena, Rooker Flynn was as angry as a nest of hornets.

Ignoring his opponent, Rooker stomped toward the edge of the ring, climbed up the brick wall, and stood at the top. There was a thick line of salt circling the top of the dugout, and Rooker dusted it off his hands as acolytes came running with spears, ready to force him back into the arena. "Hey, Sheikh!" The corpulent potentate rested upon several cushions in his theater box, wrapped in silk robes and attended to by his several mistresses. "Bet ya a thousand marks I win this one, ya fat bastard!"

Sheikh Baaza's coterie made affronted noises, fluttering silk fans in front of their faces, appalled. Rooker enjoyed their shock. "I'll give ya two to one odds!" The crowd reacted with approval, excited to see a three-man duel. "Bring me another one out here!"

Acolytes forced Rooker off the dugout wall as he glanced at Gerba. She frowned, whispering to Shant, trying to figure out how to rig a fight in a few seconds. Rooker felt dark joy bubble up within him while the rational part of his mind shouted at him. *Yer willing to get killed just to piss her off?*

He was. Absolutely.

Wont Naysayer shoved a second yellowjacket onto the sand and the Rainjons struck the gong to start the fight. The two men separated, flanking Rooker on either side. They both came at him at the same time, but he spun, too quick, too canny, too angry. He sliced their hands with his blade and disarmed them. "Try again, ya wasteka skags." He flicked a yellowjacket's sword back to him, daring the man to finish the job.

They came again. He skewered one through the chest, then slashed the throat of the other with the backswing. Just like that, it was over. It did nothing to slake Rooker's rage. His fury roiled beneath his skin, a snake filled with too much poison.

Boos rained down from the crowd. Rooker eyed Gerba, then held his palm out to the sheikh. "That's a thousand marks ya owe me, Tubby Wumpkins! Pay up!" More boos rained down on him. Rooker opened his arms, cherishing every one of them. In the end, Wont was forced to remove him from the stage, and Rooker Flynn ended the first act of the Steel Trial on a deliciously uncomfortable intermission.

"What the hell was that?" asked Jack as Rooker came through the cage doors. "Are you *crazy*?"

Rooker threw himself into a seat and said nothing, his face stitched into a frown.

He watched Patch. She paced the hall, her tail flicking back and forth. Her glamour was under control, her belly hidden, but her fur looked ragged, her eyes bloodshot. Too soon, the Rainjons started the fanfare announcing the second act, and Wont called Patch to the gate.

He knew there was nothing he could do. All he could offer her were a few lousy words, and none of them were good enough. He set his jaw and felt grief in his veins. "Give 'em hell, tiger."

Patch gave no indication she heard him and stumbled into the arena holding her belly. The drunken audience did not approve of her inauspicious entrance and started booing. Patch ignored them and dragged herself to the center of the ring, head down. Her shoulders sagged as her yellowjacket strode confidently into the ring, eager for an easy win. The Rainjons hit the gong and the gladiator lunged at her.

He got Patch's rapier through his mouth.

She left the sand before he hit the ground. Boos flooded the arena as the yellowjacket kicked his last, trying to draw breath and failing.

As the band struck up and the next gladiator entered the stage, Patch stumbled inside the door and collapsed against the wall. She held her belly, her breath shallow. She barely looked at Rooker. "One. More. Day."

Rooker jerked his chin at her. She jerked hers back. *One more day. It's not gonna matter in the end, Patch.*

All that remained was the grand finale.

Jack bounced from foot to foot, overconfident. Rooker watched each move like it was a stab to the heart. Fury rose inside him again, and he was on his feet.

If Patch pulled it off, maybe so can you.

"Yer too slow!" He grabbed Jack's shirt and yanked him close. "*Move*, damn ya!" Rooker knew the truth: If Gerba wanted Jack dead, he was dead. *But I'll be damned if I'll let ya go out looking a fool.* "Don't let him get one hit in, Jack! Not *one*, ya hear me? Show these chum-guzzling fudge jugglers they can't beat you."

Jack snorted and laughed, radiating confidence. Rooker nodded. *If ya gotta go, do it with yer chin up.*

Horns flooded the colosseum in a wave of sound as Gerba's voice rang out. "And now, ladies and gentlemen, the moment you have all been waiting for, the most nefarious outlaw in the history of Keymark, the legendary *Black Jack!*" The nobles hit their feet, a wall of sound screaming for blood.

Rooker held Jack's eye, knowing this would be the last moment they would have. Rooker rubbed at the scar on his palm and felt an empty void suck the air out of his soul, a hole Jack had, for a moment, filled. "Thanks for..." He masked the tremble in his throat. "For sticking with me. Even when I didn't deserve it."

Jack's eyes narrowed. "Rooker—"

Wont slapped Jack on the back and led him toward the arena door. Rooker winked. "Go on, outlaw. Give 'em hell."

As the cage door shut, he closed his eyes, his voice a whisper. "And forgive me if ya can."

Jack Swift entered the ring as boos flooded the colosseum. Shouts of 'Black Jahk!', that weird way the nobles had of pronouncing the dead outlaw's name, thundered against his body. His boots strode across the sand and he felt like a TV villain, a professional wrestling heel, the man everyone loved to hate. Black Jahk. Drums pounded, fueling the audience's rage, creating a cacophony so loud it was heard on Huánghūn itself.

Jack ignored it, his mind locked on Rooker. The pirate's face, the unfamiliar expression, the strange melancholy. *Why does he look like that?*

(because he knows the truth)

A cold voice shivered through his spine. Shadow loped alongside him, nearly invisible, merely a shimmer. The wolf matched his steps, prowling.

(she doesn't need you anymore)

Jack glanced up at Gerba's theater box. A smug smile curled her lips, a cobra staring down a mouse.

(and they're far more important than you ever were)

All around Jack, lords and ladies roared, their faces rage-red atop emerald costumes so expensive they could feed the Locke Institute for a year. These were the powerful elite, the dominant class, the idle rich, and the only people in Keymark who mattered.

Opposite Jack, seven feet of hulking razorback stepped through the doorway. Muscles curled his shoulders and arms like racks of cordwood, his neck as thick as Jack's thigh. His movements were measured, controlled, meticulous. This was no bottom-of-the-barrel yellowjacket; this was a trained killer.

(the pirate knows... this time...)

In the razorback's hand was a longsword sharp as a razor.

(...you die)

Jack was surprised by his reaction. He wasn't afraid. The wolf could prowl all it wanted, but Jack had taken the antidote to fear.

At his core, Jack knew Leah wasn't real. She was only an emotional wall, a psychic shield he'd constructed little by little, night after night, to keep the wolf at bay. She was nothing but a figment of his imagination. But if Leah was only a figment, so was the wolf. She was his bulwark, his talisman against the dark, and she would not let him fall. He imagined he saw her green eyes in the audience, her face half-hidden. Those eyes gave him faith, and Jack Swift would not waste her gift.

He took his position within the ring and readied his blackened stave.

For her.

(we shall see)

The Rainjons thundered a thrilling crescendo that brought the crowd to a frenzied roar; every man and woman in the stadium leapt to their feet, shouting for the death they'd traveled so far to see.

The gong sounded; steel came at Jack's face.

Blockblockblock. Jack retreated, spinning the stave as fast as he could. He deflected a series of sword strikes, but the razorback's merciless barrage never stopped. Jack fell back and heard the roar of the crowd far in the background. Rooker Flynn yelled something.

Blockbloc—

He missed a stroke and steel caught his hand. Blood sprayed the air. Jack stifled a scream. Part of his mind watched his pinky finger hit the ground.

It bounced, waggling at him.

The razorback came faster and smashed him blow after blow.

Hand sticky with blood, Jack parried again and again, forced to retreat against the arena wall. The crowd clamored, thrilled as Black Jahk ran out of room.

Three, two, o—

He thrust his leg back, planted it on the wall, and kicked himself toward the razorback. Jack ducked under his swing and broke the yellowjacket's nose with his forehead. The man stumbled back, and Jack hammered him half a dozen times in the face.

Shouting fury, the razorback sliced his blade at Jack's stomach. He ducked, cracked the man's hand, and almost knocked his sword loose. Jack struck him in the eye with the bamboo stave, then brought the other end into his crotch. A huff of air went out of him. Jack hit him in the throat and took out his knees from behind. The razorback hit the ground. Jack hammered at his face, smashing his eye, his ear, his lip, his chin, battering the man to—

(yes)

Jack stopped. He held his breath, heart triphammering in his chest. The razorback was finished, unconscious, his face a sticky red mass. Another touch would kill him.

No.

Surging heat flooded Jack's body. He thrust the staff skyward and screamed victory, unleashing his pent-up fury upon the air.

Stunned silence fell over the colosseum.

Their judgement started as a hiss, the sound of a tremendous snake. Green fans beat against the seats, the opposite of applause. The hiss grew to hoots, jeers, and curses. Jack was left panting in front of a thousand people who still wanted him dead.

Come on, you bastards. I've got nine fingers left.

As the crowd booed, furious, the Rainjons struck up and Wont Naysayer paraded the surviving Steel Trial victors to the center of the ring for their traditional closing bow.

Wont left Rooker behind and locked the cage door on him.

Wait, why would—

Through a haze of ebbing adrenaline, he heard Gerba Whip-marples' chirping voice thunder through the colosseum. "Ladies and gentlemen! Ladies and gentlemen!" Some of the audience quieted, turning to their hostess. "That concludes the Steel Trials for this evening!" The crowd continued booing, hollering their fury. Their appetite had been whetted and left unsatisfied, and they had no intention of leaving until they got exactly what they came for.

"Wait!" said Gerba, holding up her hands as if she were surprised. "You want *more*?"

The crowd shouted agreement.

"You came here to watch these criminals face *justice*?"

Yes, they roared.

Gerba smiled and spread her hands. "Then that is no way to end our show, is it?"

No, they screamed.

Jack heard Patch murmur under her breath. "What the hell is she doing?"

(what she came here to do)

The wolf's head crept over Jack's shoulder, a hungry slaver upon its white teeth.

(can you smell it?)

The headmistress of the Locke Institute's sea-green eyes flashed cruel victory. "Then it is time for an encore!"

The audience burst into a standing ovation, ravenous for more.

"My lords and ladies!" Gerba's majik intensified, raising the volume of her voice. "The Locke Institute would like to present you with something unique! Something marvelous! Something no living noble has seen!"

Jack saw a cage door at the far side of the arena open like a mouth. The darkness masked what waited within, but Jack felt ice claw up his stomach.

Jack swallowed. *What has she got in there?*

(your death)

Wont Naysayer emerged from the dark, wheeling a silk-covered cage into the arena. As the bounty hunter passed through the door, two acolytes mounted the wall behind him and poured a bag of salt over the entrance. An inhuman shriek pierced the air, and Jack's blood ran cold. *I know that sound.*

"Returned from legend, risen from the pits of hell, ladies and gentlemen, I give to you..." Gerba Whipmarples spread her hands. *"The savage strîgoi!"*

Wont threw off the silk covering and the dæmon threw itself at the cage bars, snarling and gnashing teeth. Pale body, long arms, clawed hands. Glowing crimson eyes glared hatred at the world as black smoke issued from its throat. It tried to lunge through the cage and found the gap too narrow, its flesh blistering against the iron. Jack felt a shudder of fear grip him as the hideous thing from the lava pits shrieked.

Nobles gasped at the horror before them. Some cried out and stepped into the aisles, ready to flee. "Never fear, never fear," admonished Gerba. "You are in no danger. Our stage is lined with salt, poured just this morning. The dæmon cannot escape." Some nobles began to settle down at the announcement; others were so bold as to approach the stage to get a better look at the deadly curiosity. "Only you lucky few, the elite, will bear witness to a creature that has not walked the earth since the Highway of the Nomads and your great forefather, King Esau!"

Wont retreated into the pen and locked the iron gate behind him. All around the arena, Jack heard the stage doors lock one by one, trapping the gladiators inside the ring with the caged dæmon.

Jack glanced at Patch and the other survivors. "Weapons," he hissed. "Now!" They ran for the arena wall and seized swords from the rack, terrified.

Jack stood in the center of the ring, feeling his Shadow grow larger, nearly as tall as he was, the wolf's low growl in his ear. As terror turned his blood to ice, Jack tried to summon Leah's face, but he could not. She was gone. He was alone. All he could see were the snarling fangs of the dæmon.

(are you ready to die?)

"Ladies and gentlemen, bear witness!" The headmistress of the Locke Institute raised her hands. "To *true* justice!"

She gestured with one finger and the clamp holding the strîgoi cage sprung loose and clattered to the sand. The door creaked slowly open on rusty hinges.

"O God," whispered Patch, backing away.

The dæmon hissed and lowered into a predatory crouch.

Jack yelled, "Don't let it t—"

The strîgoi leapt from the cart, landed on all fours, and shrieked a howl of savage damnation. Jaguar speed bounded across the arena and the white body hurled itself at one of the survivors. The gladiator got his sword up and drove it into the thing's shoulder, but it simply did not matter. It tackled him to the ground and savaged his throat like a dog with a dishrag. The man screamed. Blood fountained from his neck as the strîgoi bit down and severed his trachea.

O God.

The nobles watched with thirsty eyes, entranced.

Fangs dripping blood, the dæmon seized a second outlaw and flung him to the ground screaming. Its claws shredded the man's flesh in a spray of red.

"It's gonna rip us to pieces!" Patch shouted.

Jack summoned the only thing he knew about strîgoi. *Iron. An iron cage.* "We need to get behind bars!" Jack grabbed Patch. "Come on!"

He fled for the nearest door as he watched the strîgoi eviscerate a third convict and thrust its head into the dead man's belly to guzzle his blood. Jack arrived at the portcullis and found Rooker on the other side of the bars, furiously trying to force the door open. "Help me!" Jack yelled. Patch came alongside and lent her strength. Billy Pilgrim joined them, pushing, but it wasn't enough.

The strîgoi hurled aside the man's head and its coal-red eyes came to rest on Jack. The crowd roared as the beast charged straight for him.

Jack gave up on the door and gripped his stave in bloody hands. "Well, if we're going, let's go."

He stood his ground. Patch straightened at his side. Billy stood with him, his hands empty, his eyes white.

(you will not survive)

The strîgoi plunged into them, a mass of claws and fangs. Jack tried to fend off its attack and felt the staff shudder in his hands and shatter to pieces. Billy hit the dirt and scrambled away. Patch stood to Jack's side, blades whirling. Screaming, she struck furious blows at the strîgoi. It spun and lashed its claws. Jack heard a low grunt escape Patch's lips.

Blood sprayed Jack's face in a fine mist as she fell. *"Patch!"*

Her eyes wide, she grasped at her blood-soaked shirt. She fell backward into the sand, one leg twitching.

The strîgoi turned on Jack with a feral snarl.

Time slowed.

Jack watched black fumes escape the dæmon's fanged mouth.

Billy Pilgrim lay on the ground screaming.

Patch writhed on blood-soaked sand, her body contorted in agony.

Above, the crowd bellowed with savage delight.

The wolf's yellow eyes burned, its mouth a bristle of fangs.

(give in)

Time snapped together as Jack scrabbled up the wall like a frightened animal. He jerked his leg up just before the strîgoi tried to take it off at the knee. Jack gripped the top of the wall to find his hands caked in salt and an acolyte armed with a pike ready to run him through.

(surrender)

Jack Swift hanged helpless as the strîgoi climbed the wall toward him.

(surrender)

He saw the wolf in the leering faces of the noble throng, demanding he die, demanding more blood, demanding more sacrifice. In his last moment on earth, Jack Swift wanted nothing more than to take something vital from these vicious animals. To make them pay for this savage world they had so successfully constructed in their favor.

Now.

The words left his lips before he knew what he was saying. *"Is this what you want?"* His voice thundered throughout the colosseum. Every noble eye was locked on him. *"You want blood?!"* Jack pulled himself atop the wall. "You *got* it."

He slashed his arm across the top of the arena wall and broke the line of salt.

Chapter

They sow the wind and reap the whirlwind.

The Book of Hosea

C HEERS COLLAPSED TO BLOOD-CHILLING screams.

Rooker watched from behind the bars as the dæmon leapt for the break in the salt ring. It launched itself past Jack and tackled the acolyte with the pike. Rooker couldn't see what it did to the man, but the faces of the nobles went pale. Panic erupted inside the stadium. The strîgoi leapt into the stands, grabbed a viscount by the cloak, and dragged him off his feet. His mistress looked on, shrieking, until the strîgoi removed the scream along with her throat.

Rooker frantically worked the lock on his door. Sweat rolled down his face as he felt the hasp lift and click free. *What am I doing?* He was safe behind iron bars and cursed himself a fool for unlocking them. But he couldn't stand here and watch.

Above, panicked nobles fled into the stands, knocking over food, drinks, and each other in their mad dash to escape. One buffoon stumbled backward into a burning brazier and caught himself on fire. Ignoring the flames, the strîgoi ripped the face off a lordling and roared like a rabid wolverine.

Rooker felt perverse satisfaction watching the nobles run like chickens, reaping the slaughter they had so purposefully sowed. He hesitated before lifting the portcullis, unwilling to leave the safety of cold iron. *Damn it, move!*

Rooker jammed the cell door open and ran for Patch. She lay on the sand, her body contorted and bloody. Skidding to her side, Rooker glanced at her belly and felt a moment of relief as he realized her gut was whole. Her chest, however, was ruined with three bloody stripes that cut to the bone. Her glamour was gone. All that remained was a distended bloody mess. Rooker hooked under her armpits and dragged her toward the cage. The weight grew lighter as Pilgrim helped haul her over the sand, the troubadour's eyes wide and frightened. Rooker glimpsed Gerba disappear into the passage at the back of her theater box to flee the scene. Rooker felt a bitter grin cross his lips. *I hope it tears ya apart, ya lousy harridan.*

He dragged Patch through the door and leaned her against a wall. Her eyes were wide and panicked, not seeing him, staring at the air. Her breath came in rapid, shallow gasps like a dying fish. Both hands clutched her belly, repeating over and over, "Not my moggie. Not my moggie."

"Stay with her!" Rooker yelled at Pilgrim. He thrust a finger at the iron bars. "And get that door shut!" The troubadour nodded once and Rooker hit the sand, sprinting for Jack.

The kid lay crumpled at the base of the wall, covered in blood, unmoving. Rooker felt a moment of terror and thought he was dead. *No, no, come on.* He slid to Jack's side and realized most of the blood was from his severed finger. Jack's eyes were open, his face pale, his mouth locked somewhere between a smile and a scream. "Did it work?"

Rooker let out a breath. "If yer plan was to take a few of 'em with ya, yeah." He looked up into the stands where the strîgoi severed one noble bloodline after another. "It worked." Rooker grabbed Jack's hand. "Get off yer ass. We gotta move."

Jack came to his feet and drew a shuddering breath. "Where's Patch?"

"Safe."

"Is she okay?"

"We got bigger fish." The cold truth was that Patch wasn't going anywhere, and Rooker Flynn knew an opportunity when he saw it. He'd never get a better shot at a prison break than right now. A dozen ships were tied up at the wharf, and Rooker could only imagine the chaos headed that way. "Come on, help me get this door open."

As Rooker picked up a sword, he saw the strîgoi's feeding frenzy was now lit by several fires blazing within the stadium. One noble escaped burning to death only by throwing himself screaming over the top of the arena. "Let's get the hell out of here." He forced the blade between the big double doors and caught it under the cross-beam outside. Rooker had never picked a lock with a broadsword, but now was the time to learn. He sliced his palm on the blade and ripped off part of his shirt to protect his hand. Trying to get some leverage, he angled his body close to the door. Jack helped him push, straining against the heavy weight. Together they combined their might against the lock. Rooker felt the beam lift off its hooks and clatter to the ground outside.

He slammed his shoulder against the doors and shoved them open.

The night was spectacular chaos. Nobles escaped from every staircase in the colosseum, screaming and running for their lives. The Sheikh of Baaza and his perfumed coterie fled down the path toward the wharf, followed by jade-clad sycophants. Gerba's acolytes stood dumbstruck, unsure what to do, their headmistress nowhere to be found. Panicked shouts echoed in the night air as black smoke billowed from the arena. Inside, Rooker heard the ungodly shriek of the strîgoi and the terrified screams of its victims.

"We can get to the ships!" Rooker grabbed Jack. "Come on!"

Jack stopped him. "What about Patch and Billy?"

"Do ya not see what's going on?" Rooker shouted at Jack. "We get a boat, we get to the *Brigand*, and we're gone!" The kid paused, glancing back at the arena. *Damn doktar.* "There's nothing ya can do for them! Jack, we got a chanc—"

Something slammed into Rooker's gut. It felt like the kick of a pony, small but powerful. He looked down to see something sticking out of his abdomen. Rooker blinked, trying to figure out why there was a piece of wood in his stomach.

An arrow.

He looked to see an acolyte holding a longbow in shaking fingers. He recognized her eyes. *Portia.*

His knees buckled and he staggered. Jack leapt at Portia, snatched the bow out of her hands, and smashed her across the face with it. He kicked her into a gulley, her arrows clattering loose down the hill. In an instant, Jack was at Rooker's side. "It's okay. You're okay."

Rooker was not. Blood soaked his shirt. The fletching of the arrow pulsed to the rhythm of his heartbeat. He felt cold, his head dizzy. He tried to make words, but all that came out was *'hrugh.'*

He saw the look on Jack's face and knew it was bad. The kid swallowed and reached for the arrow. "I'll pull it out."

"*Nuh—*" Rooker shook his head, trying to clear the fog. He gritted his teeth. "Too deep. Gotta... gotta push it... through."

The effort cost Rooker his consciousness. His head dropped and he felt the world go black, then spring back to sharp focus as he felt the arrowhead pierce through his back from inside. Screaming, he grabbed at Jack's shoulder. The kid reached around Rooker's back and pulled the bloody arrow through.

"Don't move, don't move." Jack's voice was somewhere far away. Rooker collapsed on the marble pathway. His head fell to one side and he watched his blood trickle over the white stone.

Ignoring his missing pinky finger, Jack produced his needle and thread from his costume and set to work sewing him shut. Rooker didn't even feel the needle go in. *"Ah."*

"Stay with me, Rooker." Jack's nine fingers worked fast.

Stay with me.

Rooker felt his blood pool around his back.

Don't leave me.

"Hey! Don't pass out. We're going to escape on a boat, okay? We're going to get you to the *Brigand*, you hear me?"

"Hrng."

"Okay, almost there. Almost there." Rooker's head lolled and he saw a silhouette atop the wall above the main entrance. The strîgoi. It feasted upon a woman it held like a broken lover.

257

"We're getting up," Jack said. "Put your arm around me."

"*Ngah.*" Rooker hooked an arm over Jack's shoulder. Blood came up his throat and leaked from his mouth. He forced himself to take a step. Another.

"Almost there." Jack dragged Rooker, sweat beading his brow. "Almost there."

Rooker's head lolled forward as his hand gripped his bloody belly. "*Dun...*" His burbling voice came thick with blood. "Dun leave me."

"Come on, we just have to get—"

A scream came from the sky. It ended as the noblewoman's body landed at the base of the doors with a bloody *thwak*. Rooker saw the strîgoi launch itself into the air and hurtle through the night to land on its bloody victim teeth first. It devoured blood from her shattered corpse, drinking its fill.

"Faster." Jack dragged Rooker toward the wharf. "Move."

Rooker could barely hear his own voice. "I ca... can't—"

A shriek erupted behind him. The dæmon had spotted them. Rooker heard a low animal growl that sounded like it came from the thing's chest.

"Hafta... go,"murmured Rooker, unable to keep his head up.

Slick with blood, Jack's feet tangled with his, and they fell. They hit the ground together in a tangled heap. Rooker grunted and rolled over in a pool of his own gore to see the strîgoi charging him.

"Dun..." Rooker staggered to his feet and dragged his scimitar free. The sword dangled in one nerveless hand; he could barely close his fist, much less keep his eyes open. "Dun leave me, Jasper."

The strîgoi galloped at him, its face slathered in crimson. Rooker gritted his teeth and summoned his last remaining strength. "Well, if we're going, let's go!"

It leapt.

Rooker exhaled his final breath.

Black fire ignited the world.

Flame flooded the marble path, a dark inferno that stretched to the sky. Rooker felt his skin draw tight from the blazing heat, his eyes and mouth baked dry. In the center of the pillar of flame, the black fire turned indigo, then jade, then black again as the flames consumed everything in their path. Rooker watched the silhouette of the strîgoi gibber and twitch, a living inferno as the dæmon burned to slagged ash.

Rooker fell backward, unable to do anything but blink. His boots were on fire, but he couldn't feel a thing.

As quickly as it had come, the firestorm was gone, replaced by the head of Gerba's dragon. The long, serpentine neck of Xeusia ul-Styx twisted, its spider face pocked with eight soulless eyes. Liquid fire dripped from its mandibles. The dragon beat massive eight-legged wings, and the blast of air disintegrated the cindered remains of the strîgoi.

Rooker felt pieces of its corpse catch in his hair, still burning.

Xeusia withdrew its long neck, revealing Gerba Whipmarples in its saddle. The dragon's membranous spider legs reached for the colosseum wall and it ascended to the peak where the strîgoi had stood a moment ago. It bellowed a roar of triumph atop the burning arena that deafened everyone on the island.

Rooker couldn't hear the roar of the dragon, couldn't feel his burning feet. All he knew was that he was dying. Blackness closed in around the edges of his mind, threatening to overwhelm him. He reached out, seeking Jack, but couldn't find him. He was gone. Rooker struggled to keep his head up, searching for the kid.

Don't leave me.

Then he, too, was gone.

GONG.

He felt the Great Bell more than heard it. The sound was distant, almost a whisper, but the sound didn't truly matter; its majik reached him, even from so far away. As Rooker's body responded to the healing majik, heat flowed through him like a warm bath and his flesh came alive with a rippling tickle. The hum vibrated throughout his skin, a tremulous shudder that healed the wounds on his hands, his arms, his feet. The *wikk* of the Agrat-ban-Haifa plunged inside the hole in his gut and shimmered to his core, radiating vitality from the inside out. The gigantic slash to his abdomen slowly puckered together and closed like a mouth; it spit out a few splinters of wood as his guts twisted back into place.

Rooker threw up.

Alive.

His little con game with Jack had paid off. *Gerba raised the Great Bell.* It was the only thing that made any sense. Rooker should be a corpse right now. But his heart kept beating thanks to Jack's Toshan science. *Still alive.*

His eyes opened and he realized he was no longer outside. *Where is this? The gladiator pit?* He tried sitting up and found he was lying on a table in a small wooden room, his wrists and ankles bound. Confused and disoriented, he struggled against the ropes but only succeeded in making his bonds tighter. His head felt fuzzy, like his brain was stuffed with cotton, and his guts still moved inside him like a nest of snakes.

Rooker checked the wound in his belly. The cut was just a pink line across his stomach that grew healthier by the moment.

Jack's stiches remained in his gut, a zig-zaggy mess of black xs that crisscrossed his otherwise healthy flesh.

Bubba used a lotta twine. Musta been a bigger hole in me than I thought.

He discovered his torn shirt was a ruin, crusty and matted. His leather pants were stained with red smears and his boots were charred through. He looked over the side of the table and saw the floor was covered in a staggering amount of his blood. It was surreal, staring down at that much of himself wasted on the floor.

Even with stitches, I'm lucky I made it.

Rooker blinked and wondered how long he had been here.

Long enough for blood to dry. So where's Jack?

The door opened and Rooker saw an acolyte's feet move fast. A clinking sound, and the ropes around his wrists were replaced with manacles. Rooker cleared his throat. "Hey, what are—"

"Shut up!" He felt the tip of a knife prick him in the back as he was forced through the doorway. Rooker came outside to discover he had occupied one of the little cabins at the back end of Bounty, where acolytes penned the animals. *So where's Jack?*

"Run!" The angry acolyte forced him to sprint. As Rooker obeyed, he smelled the colosseum burning. Acolytes and hammerdwarves darted to and fro, trying to control the damage. The open double doors were ablaze and inside the stadium he saw half a dozen nobles littered the burning stands, their corpses sprawled in ignoble positions. He glimpsed two gladiators, hale and hearty thanks to the bell, but didn't see Patch or Pilgrim. Forced onto the marble walkway, he found the stone path still held the heat of dragonfire; it seared Rooker's feet through his charred boots as he passed the lump of ash that had once been the strîgoi. Forced to the wharf, Rooker discovered it empty. Every single ship was gone. Out to sea, he could make out their outlines, a dotted string of silk sails that stretched into the moonlit Irridin, abandoning the smoking remains of the carnage they had purchased. Bounty had been abandoned by all but the Locke Institute.

The Steel Trials were finished.

Gerba Whipmarples stood at the end of the dock, shouting at the acolytes. Her fancy gown was torn at one shoulder, smeared with stains and burn marks. Her makeup was smeared across one side of her face, furrowed with angry creases. Gone was the mask of the schoolmarm. Gone was her composure. Gone was her sanity.

"*Dead!* Six nobles *dead!* They were supposed to enjoy a *show!* They were supposed to witness *justice!* I had them eating from the palm of my hand like trained *dogs!*" Her voice rose to a shrill scream. "But *now* all they are going to remember is that Baronetess Ket is dead!" She hurled a wine bottle to the ground, shattering it. "*Dead!*"

Rooker couldn't help but smile. *Nice to watch her bleed for a change.*

Gerba's blazing eyes found Rooker. She thundered toward him. "Where is he?"

He couldn't help but laugh at the sight of her. The headmistress looked crazier than Billy Pilgrim ever had. She was broken, and Rooker loved it. "Rough night?"

She slapped him hard enough to see stars. *"Where is he?"*

Rooker spat. "Where is *who?*"

Gerba Whipmarples seized him. Rooker was overwhelmed by the sheer strength of her. The power in her muscles made him feel as small as a two-year-old. Her trol horn loomed dangerously close to his neck. "Don't play games with me, Flynn. Where. Is. Jack?"

Rooker blinked. "He's here."

Gerba growled between her teeth. "Tell me where and this will go easier for you. What was the plan? Where is he hiding?"

Jack isn't gone. "What the hell are ya talkin' about? He was *right beside me.*"

Gerba snorted. "He was bound in a cabin! Just like you! And he vanished! He *couldn't* have gotten out on his own!" She stuck a finger at Rooker and snarled. "You *helped* him escape!" She gripped his shirt and thrust her horn against his nose. "He told you about the bell. Was *that* part of the plan? Did he use majik? How did he do it?!"

He gaped at her, dumbfounded. Jack had said nothing. *He escaped? How?*

Rooker Flynn glanced down at his palm. His body had healed, his gut, the cuts in his skin, his burned feet. And his scar, the one he and Jack had shared, the mark of his blood brother, that was gone too. Disappeared from his flesh as if it had never been.

Somewhere in a dark corner of his mind, Jasper Winegrad laughed.

He left me.

Gerba searched Rooker's face. When she saw nothing useful coming out of his mouth, she hurled him to the wharf deck like a discarded toy. "You're not much use as a spy, are you?"

"Headmistress!" One of the acolytes arrived, the bells of her niqab jingling. "We've searched everywhere. In the tunnels, in the huts, in the passageways. He's not here."

Rooker barely heard her.

He left me.

"Search again!" erupted Gerba. "There are only so many places he can—"

"He's not on the island." Cant Naysayer's boots thundered down the dock. "Use your dragon. Fly out there and catch the boats." He jammed a finger at the flotilla of silk sails fleeing toward the stars. "Get after him!"

"And just which vessel is he on, *Mister Naysayer*?" Gerba shouted at the bounty hunter. "Or do you want me to fly out there and just start landing on nobles' ships and interrogate them? Perhaps I should burn a yacht or two!"

"It wouldn't be the worst idea you had today." Cant's duster flickered in the wind, his voice sharp as daggers. "This is *your* fault, Whipmarples. You didn't have to show off the strîgoi, not now. But you just *had* to put on your big goddamned show." Gerba stiffened but before she could speak, Cant showed her what real anger looked like. "I want my money for the *Venture Brigand*. *Now*."

Rooker's head snapped to Gerba. *Wait, what?*

"What do you expect me to do, Mister Naysayer?" shrilled Gerba. "Request ten million marks from Baronet Ket for *killing his wife*?!"

Cant Naysayer's steely eyes snapped to Rooker. "*You.*" He pointed a finger. "You know where he went."

Rooker spat. "I got no clue, wasteka."

"Lies. You two are thick as thieves. You *know*. And you're going to tell me. Now."

"I don't know—" Rooker felt scorpions crawl up his legs, under his shirt, in his hair. He ignored them, knowing it was just another one of Cant's illusions. "Yer guess is as good as mine, ya ugly beanpole!"

Cant smashed him to the ground and rapped Rooker's head against the wharf. The Naysayer crouched on him like a tiger. A silver stiletto slid from its sheath and came to rest against Rooker's cheek.

"Last chance." Cant leaned in. "Where did he go?"

He abandoned me.

"Go to hell." Rooker spat the words for Cant and Jack alike.

Cant hissed, furious. "Why can't you ever just do as you're told?"

The bounty hunter's hand lashed at Rooker's face.

There was a sting of pain, and one eye went dark.

Fire shot through Rooker's skull. He blinked and saw the blade in Cant's hand was red with blood... and something else.

Rooker blinked again. He couldn't feel anything against one eyelid. It was deflated, empty.

As the pain in his head swelled into a yowling banshee, Rooker finally realized what was on the end of the bounty hunter's knife.

Cant Naysayer flicked Rooker's eye into the Irridin, and the screaming started.

PART 3

TOMB

Chapter

17

HALF A MAN

They say that abandonment is a wound that never heals.
I say only that an abandoned child never forgets.

Mario Balotelli

H UÁNGHŪN SWALLOWED HIM ONCE more, as inescapable as sunset. The dawn was robin's egg blue and smeared with grey clouds as the *Hup Two* crossed the narrow strait. The air that blew their sails was perfumed by the acrid stench of the coliseum smoldering behind them. Above, the blue vault of heaven met with the white-capped water below and formed the perfect marriage of sea and sky, a sphere divided only by a thin horizon too indistinct to see in the mist, the kind of day that calls sailors home to the wind.

Rooker Fynn did not notice any of it.

He kept his head down, staring blankly at the deck, and did not move, one palm cupped against his face, protecting the empty socket where his eye had been. His face and stomach ached from the blows Cant had rained down on him until the acolytes had finally pulled the bounty hunter off, but Rooker didn't feel the wounds. His injuries were deeper than that. All he could feel was the nothingness inside his body, the hole carved out of the center of him.

He did not remember arriving at the dock gate of the Locke Institute or ascending through the tunnels or being deposited without ceremony in the assembly yard. All he knew was when he started walking toward Jackal camp, someone grabbed him, Patch or Pilgrim, he wasn't sure, and led him in another direction. One of them stripped off a bit of cloth from their tattered costume and tied it around his head to cover the hole where his eye had been. "Hey." Patch's face came into view and she adjusted the covering. "Got to keep up appearances, right?"

Rooker stared at nothing.

Their entrance into Hyena was surreal. With one eye, Rooker watched the camp stare at him like he was a ghost. He did not recognize most of the faces. There were too many new prisoners, too many new frosh. Even had he known them, he wouldn't have cared to. He heard the questions, heard Patch's responses, but it all faded together into a slurry of meaningless words. The gladiators had been missing for two months; everyone on the island had naturally presumed they were dead. Rooker felt the hollow sensation of attending his own funeral.

Copper Dave could barely contain his excitement at their sudden appearance. The big croc was loud and joyful as he tried to hug the survivors, but only Billy Pilgrim returned his embrace. Rooker felt the llystra thump him on the back, but he did not respond, his insides cold as ice.

Pilgrim disappeared at some point and Rooker became aware that Patch was walking him up the steps to the strange out-of-the-way clique where he'd once tried to make peace with Jack. Yenrab Bialik sat on the front porch, filthy, shirtless, and smoking a pipe. The Red Dwarf made a big show of welcoming them all inside, but Rooker got the impression the old drunk didn't want him there. Inside was a dark, mousy girl Rooker knew he had met before, but he couldn't remember her name.

He was shown to a bunk and simply curled up facing the wall. His hand protected the emptiness where his eye had once been.

He heard the questions, heard the whispers, heard Patch tell the stories of the Steel Trials, the strîgoi, the dragon, and Black Jack's mysterious escape. He heard about the new prisoners, the new hierarchy in each camp, and the new bosses' names, including his replacement in Jackal, a tyrant named Boss Manx.

Rooker stared at the wall without blinking.

After some time, he got the feeling the others were talking around him, finding subtle ways to discuss the outsider in their clique without using his name or revealing whatever they were trying to hide from him. He didn't care. They could talk about him like he wasn't in the room. He wasn't.

None of it mattered.

Nothing ever changed. The rest of his life would be the same; more blood, more failure, more betrayal. Expecting anything different was madness. Life was a losing game, no one got out alive, and Rooker Flynn was tired of fighting the tide. If Huánghūn wanted to kill him, that was fine. He'd let the island win and count himself lucky that he wouldn't have to play the game anymore.

After some time, the conversation ground to a halt, and the clique descended into a long and awkward silence. Feet shuffled in and out of the door. The mousy girl whose name Rooker couldn't remember brought him some water, which he did not drink.

He kept his hand to his eye, attempting to come to terms with the empty socket. He'd accepted the pain of it, but the hollow feeling simply would not go away. He opened his hand and stared at his empty palm. The slash he had made to share his blood with Jack Swift was gone. There was nothing there, not the barest mark, just the filthy creases of an empty pirate's hand.

He stared at the nothing for a long time.

Several hours later, Copper Dave brought him two slices of galt. After so many months of real food, Rooker had forgotten about the tasteless taters. The mere thought of trying to choke down galt was simply unimaginable, and only made the pit in his stomach yawn wider.

There was one other cruelty he had almost forgotten during his time on Bounty.

As the sun set, he felt a long-forgotten panic creep inside his chest.

A shudder worked through him. Rooker gripped the edge of his bunk with white knuckles. He dreaded what was coming, but, more than that, he hated the inevitability of it, the unstoppable wheel, and the knowledge that no matter how much he struggled, it would always end the same way.

At dusk, the shiq came.

He stayed in bed for two days before he was forced to assembly to relearn the rules of the Institute. Gather at sunrise. Be inside by sunset. Obey your betters. The only thing that was different was the Great Bell was higher and Gerba Whipmarples did not make an appearance. In her place, Portia made the morning announcements as if nothing had ever happened while the pale smoke from Bounty rose behind her. Attercops paced the wall, on edge. Work assignments were handed out, and a thousand prisoners were set to the day's labor.

All day, Rooker stood knee-deep in muck and cut rice stalks with a blunted blade. Some of the prisoners sung work songs, but he did not join in. He felt his scythe move, mowing down one life after another, mindless as a golem.

"You seem... not like self."

Rooker turned to find Copper Dave. The croc seemed perfectly at home in the humid heat, his denims rolled to the knees. If Rooker didn't know better, he would have guessed the legbreaker was enjoying himself. He grinned a saurian smile.

"Rooker Flynn loud!" He gestured. "Big noise. Big laugh. Also angry. All of time, angry!" Dave dropped his hands and his smile fell. "Now... too quiet."

Rooker said nothing.

"Sometimes..." Copper Dave shrugged. "Sometimes is best not think. Sometimes best forget." He gestured around them. "Forget island. Forget shiq. Forget..." He trailed off, looking at the smoking speck of Bounty on the horizon. "Forget bad things." He turned back to Rooker. "Is too much."

The big lizard reached down and gently touched his ridiculous little macaroni heart necklace. He held it up for Rooker to see.

"Think good thing." He looked at the necklace, his eyes warm. "Even if gone. Even if far away." He put a hand on Rooker's shoulder. "Forget bad. Remember good."

Rage geysered inside Rooker and he shouted his first words in days. *"Get yer damned claws off me!"*

Copper Dave jerked his hand away as if stung and stared at Rooker like he was a rabid animal. After a moment, the big croc walked away. Rooker's burst of emotion disappeared into a hollow echo of itself, and he went back to work in silence.

The way back to the Institute was muddy and slick from hundreds of dripping feet. Rooker slipped on a wet patch and grabbed for a handrail. He thought he knew where it was, his mind told him it was there, but when he tried to take hold of it, his one eye simply lied to him. He missed and fell into the mud, humiliated.

Rough hands grabbed him. He turned to find Yenrab hauling him up. The Red Dwarf shoved Rooker to his feet and clicked his tongue. "Busted headlamp. It'll get ya every time."

Rooker ignored him and wiped the mud off his chest.

Yenrab gestured at his own missing eye. "Put us together and we got one good set, eh?"

Rooker grunted and walked away.

"Hey!" Yenrab's gruff voice came. "You want some advice?"

"No."

The redneck snorted. "I been a cyclops longer'n you been alive, ijit." He grinned crooked teeth. "You might learn a thang or two."

Rooker managed a scowl.

"First off, here." The dwarf handed him a bowed flap of leather. It was threaded with a strap, smooth from use. "Eyepatch. One of mine. I got extra." The dwarf jabbed a finger at the filthy strip of cloth over Rooker's eye. "Get rid of that thing. You look like a hick."

Rooker turned away, strapped the leather around his head, and adjusted the new patch. He could feel it over his empty socket, cool and textured, bowed away from his face to keep it from rubbing. It reminded him a bit of his days at sea when his mates had cupped one eye before going belowdecks to prepare their vision for the dark.

"Finally!" Yenrab nodded. "*Now* you look like a pirate!"

Rooker almost smiled but didn't.

Yenrab folded his arms. "Distance is tricky with one eye, feller. When you need to reach for something..." He outstretched his arm in a wide arc. "Sweep your hand. You're probably gonna miss what you're aimin' at, but if your whole arm's looking for it, you'll find it. Plus you keep your dignity."

Rooker didn't care about dignity. He gave a *hmph* but offered nothing further.

A long pause followed. When the Red Dwarf's voice came, it came soft. "It's tough to lose a piece of yourself. An important piece."

Rooker said nothing.

"My brother." Yenrab cleared his throat. "Barney. We was twins, together from the beginnin', you know? When he died..." Yenrab didn't say anything for a few moments. He cleared his throat again. "It was like a piece o' me went with him. Like I'm not the same any more. Not without him." Yenrab sighed. "I'd tell you it gets better, but I don't know. Sometimes I think you jest... get used to 'em bein' gone."

Rooker flinched. He needed to say something, so he just said whatever came first. "Doesn't matter," he growled. "My eye will grow back with the next hanging. Everything will be just like it was."

Yenrab's wizened face grew angry. "Everything will be—" He cut himself off. The dwarf's red face went through a kaleidoscope of emotions, but in the end, he simply shook his head and walked away. "I feel sorry for you."

"Feel sorry for yerself, shrimp!" Rooker hollered after him. "Yer the one who ain't gettin' his eye back!"

He felt the anger sizzle behind his empty socket. It felt good. It almost made him feel alive.

Almost.

The next day Rooker slapped ringslugs around tree trunks, cutting timber for Hyenas to trim and haul away. He performed his task mechanically in mindless lethargy as the sun rose into the sky.

When they broke for lunch, Rooker disappeared into the jungle. He walked alone through the palms, travelling toward the sea. He finally found the spot he'd been looking for, a raised promontory of rock on the edge of the island that overlooked the bay. He had sat here with Jack once, a long time ago. He felt the sea wind riffle his hair and cool the sweat on his body.

He settled on the rock and stared at the three-masted outline of the *Venture Brigand*.

Hey, girl.

He could barely see her from here, just a spot on the ocean a mile away. He could just make out her furled sails, her three masts, her long legs. He considered using his spyglass rings to look more closely, but he knew it would just hurt him more. He could hear her in his mind, the soft creak of her wood, the ripple of her sails, the soft clink of the fore-bell. He tried to imagine standing on her deck, to conjure the feel of her boards beneath his feet... but he couldn't.

It had been too long.

Ten years he had spent beneath her masts, travelling from one side of the world to the other, free upon the sea.

Now he couldn't even hear her voice.

Talk to me, girl.

"I thought I might find you here."

Rooker turned to find Patch standing near the edge of the promontory, wind riffling glamourized fur. She narrowed yellow eyes. "What are you doing?"

He turned away. "Nothing."

She sat next to him and dropped the glamour. Her belly stretched to full size, her fur went ragged, and she let out a relieved sigh. "Ah. Just staring at the *Brigand*?"

Rooker shrugged, wishing she would leave.

She didn't pick up on the idea. "It's a good boat."

"A good..." Rooker frowned. "She's the most perfect thing in the world."

"She's fast, I'll give you that."

"Fast, beautiful, loyal." The words tumbled out of Rooker's mouth before he could stop them, but he found he didn't want to. "She's out there, waitin' for me to come home."

"It's not a person, Rooker."

"No. She's better." He straightened his jaw. "That's the problem with people, Patch. They're no damn good. They all leave. Sooner or later, everyone walks out on you. Parents, brothers, sisters, lovers, mates. All gone. No one stays." He stared at the *Brigand* with his one remaining eye. "But she'll be there. She'll never leave me."

Patch scowled. "Rooker—"

"Tell me I'm wrong, Patch. Ya were chummy with yer crew in the old days. Needles, Meeks, that gal ya palled around with, Mariska. Where are they now?" He gave her a hard look. "It wasn't prison that made them leave. They were all long gone before ya got caught. Even in here it's the same. Major West." He watched her squirm at the mention of the old Hyena boss. "The two of ya were cozy as lice. Lovers. I bet he whispered sweet nothings in yer ear.

Ya bedded down with him, held him tight, maybe even loved him. And where is he now? Gone."

She scowled, staring at the ground. "That's not—"

Rooker pointed at her belly. "That lump ya got. Pretend ya get lucky. Pretend it lives. Hell, pretend ya get a pardon from the Institute and yer set free with yer little moggie, go to some backwater town, get to nurse it, feed it, watch it grow up, watch it become a woman. And then what?" He snorted. "She'll leave ya. Off with some man or off on some ship or killed in some squabble. One way or another, she'll leave ya. Yer own flesh and blood, she'll abandon ya." He felt Patch shrink away from him. "We're all of us alone. That's just how the world rolls along. Sooner or later, everyone gets left behind."

The susurrus of the waves on the rock was the only sound for a moment. Then came Patch's quiet voice, "I would never leave my moggie."

"Give it time. You'll figure out a reason." He settled back on his hands. "It's easy to remember the truth, Patch. Everyone leaves in the end."

"Rooker." Her voice was quiet. "I'm here. Right now."

"Yeah. Now." Rooker stared out at the sea. "Where ya gonna be tomorrow?"

"I only have so many tomorrows left." Patch rubbed her belly.

Rooker refused to look at her. Her moggie was as good as dead. Even if it survived childbirth, it wouldn't survive Huánghūn. Patch knew it. Rooker knew it. What he didn't know was why she tried to pretend. More than likely, her baby would be the death of her.

"She'll be here in a few days. I can feel it."

Rooker said nothing. It didn't matter. It was all the same in the end.

Patch shook her head. "I have to protect her. I have somebody who needs me."

Rooker sighed. "All ya got is a fetus that would be better off born dead."

She slapped him hard.

It stung, but the surprise was worse than the pain. Rooker put his hand to his cheek and saw the look on Patch's face was pure contempt.

"You're a son of a bitch, Rooker. You always have been. You hated everybody you ever met. And now I get why. You're so terrified of getting left behind, you kick anyone who gets close enough to hurt you. Stab 'em in the back before they stab you, right? Everyone you meet is out to get you, so they're all expendable and it's all a big joke!" She got to her feet and jammed her finger in his face. "Well not everybody sees the world like you do, Rooker! You've got people all around you, people willing to *help* you, and you don't even see it! Did you ever think that maybe the reason everyone *leaves* you is because you've always got a knife in your hand?! And for what? So you can sit around with that sour look on your puss and bitch about being alone. Well you got what you wanted, Rooker, and all you're left with is a damn boat!" Patch walked away, then wheeled on him, her eyes angry slits. "I respected you, do you know that? But now I see you for what you are. You're just a scared little boy afraid he's going to get left behind. You pathetic wasteka *child*. And I used to think you were tough."

Rooker heard the sound of Addie Winegrad's voice yelling at him to toughen up. He remembered the sound of his own throat yelling the same to Jack.

"If you're going to give up, then give up!" Patch shouted. "Just go to the green! Get it over with and put the rest of us out of our misery! No one will miss you. Just the way you want it!"

Rooker's cheek stung.

"I can't *afford* to give up." Patch's voice went cold. "Either I get off this island in the next few days or my baby dies. That's a fact.

And I can't make it out of here by myself. I need help. I need other people. And I was an idiot for thinking you'd be one of them."

She stormed away, done with him.

Rooker tried to keep the question in his throat, tried to wait until she was gone, but he couldn't hold it in long enough. "What people?"

Patch stopped, her back to him. "Yenrab thinks you won't rat us out. He doesn't like you, but he almost trusts you. Copper Dave trusts everybody. And Farah thinks if you see the problem, you might be sneaky enough to solve it."

Problem? What problem? And who the hell is Farah? "So yer talking behind my back."

She kept her back to him. "Me? I *know* I can't trust you. At all. You'll sell us all out to the Institute for half a mark. But she took your *eye*, Rooker." Patch finally turned to face him. "The man I knew was tough enough to make her pay for it."

Rooker felt a fire ignite somewhere in his gut. *Go to hell.*

Patch Picaroon lingered on the path; the Huánghūn palms swayed behind her. "If you want to break out of this shithole, stop feeling sorry for yourself and get in the game. But if you're coming, bring your balls with you." Patch walked. "If not, you can just keep sitting here, mooning over your goddamn *boat*."

She disappeared into the jungle.

Rooker turned back to the *Venture Brigand*.

She bobbed in the water, waiting for him.

After a long time, Rooker finally got to his feet and followed Patch into the trees.

Chapter

18

TOM, DICK & HARRY

The opportunity of defeating the enemy
is provided by the enemy himself.

Sun Tzu

B ENEATH THE FLOOR OF the isolated clique, five criminals gathered in darkness.

Rooker hadn't ferreted out the purpose of the two-story clique or the reason it occupied such an out-of-the-way spot and felt stupid for missing the ruse. Admittedly, the escape crew had done a fantastic job of hiding their secret under a false floor, camouflaged beneath a bamboo table and a set of stools. When Yenrab threw the trapdoor open and revealed an entrance to the caves below, Rooker tried to act unimpressed.

"The pycorastic vemps, yeah I know."

"Pyroclastic *vents*, jackass." Yenrab scowled at him.

Rooker resolved not to look stupid again. "We tried this before," Rooker shot at the dwarf. "Or don't ya remember the *good* twin gettin' killed?"

Yenrab's red face went redder, but Patch stepped in before he could speak. "The difference is... now we have these."

Copper Dave produced a white gourd in his clawed hand. The croc flicked the thing through the open trapdoor. Curious, Rooker watched it fall, strike the cave floor, and ignite in a flash. All he saw was a white pulse so bright it hurt; he was instantly struck blind. *"Ah!"* Robbed of his sight, Rooker stumbled away from the opening and rubbed at his eye. Cloudy vision returned just in time to see Copper Dave descend a rope ladder into the cave, followed closely by the others.

Patch looked up at him before she disappeared. "Are you coming or not?"

Cautiously, Rooker peered down at the pale fire below. He descended the rope ladder. In the caves around him, he saw no movement. No shiq in the blackness beyond. Whatever this white majik was, it kept the spiders at bay. Rooker dropped to the cave floor and pointed at the blaze. "Okay, what the hell is that thing?"

"Whitefire," came a disembodied voice behind him. Rooker jumped, startled, and turned to see Farah's face near his shoulder.

"Lord and Lady!" Rooker let out a breath. "I forgot you were there."

"Be nice." Copper Dave glowered. "Farah is good."

"She's forgettable." Rooker glared at the dark girl. "And creepy."

"She's the reason we're not getting eaten alive right now," said Patch. Rooker glanced at Farah, unable to fathom how this waifish girl was able to conjure such majik.

"Let me show you the problem." Yenrab gestured and Rooker found one wall of the cave covered in markings, symbols, and lines drawn in chalk and grease pencil, an intricate network laid out in immaculate detail. Every angle was precisely accounted for with numbered distances and degrees of topographic incline marked along each path.

Rooker whistled under his breath. "You're mapping the *caves*."

"Hundred thirty-seven tunnels," said Yenrab. "All but three are dead ends."

Rooker eyed the dwarf. "And whitefire is keepin' the shiq off ya the whole time?"

"That's right, bucko."

"Yer braver than ya look." Rooker pointed at the map. "Ya covered over twenty leagues here."

Yenrab's one eye squinted at him. "How'd you know that?"

Rooker squinted back. "I can read a map. You got all this done in two *months*?"

"I ain't been fartin' around, young buck." Yenrab stabbed a finger at the drawing. "The three main tunnels are Tom, Dick, and Harry. And Tom's headed in the right direction."

Rooker saw most of Tom tunnel headed west. "Toward the Institute."

"Black Jack said there was door into tunnel." Copper Dave gestured into the dark. "Round copper door. Inside Institute. We break in—"

"—to break out," finished Patch. "Once we're inside the Institute, we hit the docks. From there, we steal a boat and we're gone."

Rooker lowered an eyebrow. "So why not do it already?"

"Because we're running out of whitefire."

Rooker eyed a giant pyramid of gourds against the wall. He grabbed one and flipped it in his hand. "So make more. It can't be—"

He turned to find every face on the crew terrified, their eyes wide, hands outstretched to stop him. Rooker froze. He eyed the gourd in his hand.

"Gently," said Patch. *"Gently."*

His nimble fingers placed the gourd delicately back down on the pyramid, realizing the entire stack could ignite at once and burn them all to ash. He stepped away.

"Don't expose them to air." Rooker was startled once again by how close Farah was. *Creepy damn girl.* He could barely see her in the dark, but her voice was steady, factual. "As for making more, I'm going as fast as I can, but we're using more than I can replace."

"Plus, we don't know where the door *is*," grunted Yenrab. "So it's all peck-and-scratch. Double plus, every time I go farther down Tom, it takes more whitefire to git there and back. At this rate, we'll burn through it all before we find the door."

Rooker frowned. "How much time do ya need to make enough whitefire?"

"Eighty-one days." Farah's voice had a ring of precision.

She's done the math. He eyed Patch. *And that will be too late for you.*

Rooker realized that Patch had dropped her glamour when she'd descended. She allowed her clique to see her as she truly was; there was no pretense left. Every one of the crew, Yenrab, Copper Dave, Farah, they all knew what she was facing. And all of them were trying their best to get Patch off Huánghūn before it happened. *Damn them all.*

He scowled at the whitefire gourds. "What's this stuff made out of?"

They all spoke at once. "Piss."

"Fine, *don't* tell me." Rooker scowled at the map. "This is never gonna work."

The whole plan was a boondoggle. Fumbling around in the dark, looking for a doorknob, that's all this was. They'd be lucky if the tunnels connected at all. Plus, if Yenrab was chipping his way through the pycorastic vemps, he might punch a hole into the Irridin and they'd all drown. Rooker paused, almost liking the idea. *Maybe we could flood the caves. Give the shiq nowhere to go during the day, burn 'em off.* As much vengeful joy as the thought gave him, Rooker dismissed it. There was no way to kill a million shiq.

He rubbed at his empty eye socket and searched for any hope on their faces. He found none.

We could get more people to make whitefire, but the more people know about the breakout, the more likely someone's gonna rat us out to the Institute. If Jack was here, he would—

Rooker straightened as realization hit him like a lightning bolt. "Patch." He climbed the rope ladder, ascending to the light. "Come with me."

His calloused hands hooked the next branch in the yingcao tree. As he climbed, Rooker began to see the advantages of Yenrab's arm-sweep method. It was a good way to find his next handhold. *At least I don't look like an imbecile grasping at limbs that aren't there.*

Jinx-cats are excellent at climbing trees. Even knocked up, Patch led him the entire way. She made it to the treehouse before him, although not by much, and by the time she made it, she was spent.

She lay down in a sling, panting. Her belly hung out, resting against her leg, her fur patchy and grimy. "Okay," she said. "This better be worth it."

Rooker pulled his rings off and scanned the wall. "Ya ever heard of a Caged Eight?"

"No, I—" Patch panted. "Wait. I think I heard Farah talk about it maybe? Months ago."

"It's a rune." Rooker cocked a grin. "A warding glyph. Works on spiders. Gerba's got 'em all along the wall."

"Like... what... a majik fence?"

"Right." *Spider stoplights.* He handed her the rings. "Take a look."

She gawked at the jewelry, impressed. "How did the Locke Institute let you keep these? They're gorgeous." She studied them, appreciating the intricate designs. "How did *I* let you keep these?"

Rooker explained the rings with his standard rigmarole. Patch got the hang of the spyglass quickly. She was a pirate, after all. Rooker called out the position. "One fathom above the doorway, four fathoms starboard. Next to the little scrub of grass." Rooker waited. "Ya see it?"

"It *is* a glyph." Patch nodded. "Hammered metal."

"She's got maybe twenty scattered along the wall."

Patch peered closer. "What is that thing made of? Steel?"

"The Caged Eight feeds off the great bell so I'm guessing bronze." He tapped her shoulder. "See the one far starboard? Out by Buzzard, real low on the wall?"

"Yeah. What of it?"

"That's the one we're gonna steal."

Patch turned and looked at him like he'd just suggested they jump into a shark's mouth. "So... *not* worth it."

Rooker held up a hand. "If we have a Caged Eight, the shiq will stay off us. At least for a while. Maybe we can stretch out our whitefire, get a little farther down Tom, maybe find the door." He cricked his neck. "Ya see the problem, right?"

"All I see are problems!" Patch shouted at him. "We would be exposed the whole time! Attercops are posted on the wall. Always! They'll spot us before you climb halfway to the rune. And once they do, they can move a hell of a lot faster than you can."

"Details."

"Add a couple of acolytes up top that might look down at any moment, plus the fact that it's a sheer cliff face that's almost impossible to climb." Patch looked at him, exasperated. "Other than that, it's a cakewalk!"

Rooker gestured 'gimmie the rings back.' She did, and Rooker counted down until the forgetting spell kicked in. *Wait for it, I'll jest hafta repeat myself.* After a moment, Patch sneezed, which was a sure sign the charm had cleared her head. She wiped her nose. "Sorry, what did you say?"

"I said I'll take care of the attercops." Rooker leaned in. "*You* steal the rune."

"Me?" Patch's eyes went wide. "I can't climb that."

Rooker almost laughed. Patch was a born second-story cat burglar and an artist on a rope. Her agility was legendary, even for a jinx. "Don't play humble, Patch. Yer the best."

She grinned at him. "I'm a fat load of dough who needs to pee every five minutes."

Rooker leered back. "True, but yer also a glamour-knacker who can make yerself the same color as the wall." *Now that I know how you're so good at sneaking around.* "Yer a chameleon."

"Do I *look* like I can hold a glamour while trying to climb that thing?" Patch snarled at him. "I could barely climb up *here,* or didn't you notice?"

"Yeah," Rooker growled. "Yer ass was in my face the whole time."

Patch pursed her lips at him. "Think of it as a mirror."

Rooker snorted. *Dammit. I was counting on her.* "Well, what about—"

"Yenrab? Could you imagine?" Patch chuckled. "He'd take three days."

Dammit again. "What's that mousy gal's name? Farah?"

Patch looked at him like he'd been struck stupid. "Farah's an indoor girl, Rooker. Weak, slow, soft. She'd probably fall off the wall and break her pert little nose." She raised a clawed finger. "And before you say Copper Dave, there's not a stealthy bone in his body. He's a legbreaker, not a grease man."

Triple dammit.

Patch grinned at his frustration. "You're the only man for the job."

"I can't think how I would pull it off."

"Try it at night."

Rooker laughed. It was the first good laugh he'd had since the Steel Trial, and it felt like fresh air. Patch snorted. "It's a moot point anyway." She jerked her chin at the wall. "You're never going to get past the 'cops."

"Not without one hell of a distraction." And just like that, Rooker's idea was born of necessity. It popped into his head like whitefire. Blinded by his own brilliance, he laughed. "Ha! Ya know what the Locke Institute *really* needs?"

"What's that?"

A vicious smile split his lips. "A good old-fashioned prison riot."

Patch chuckled, then realized he was serious. "Come on, Rooker. The prisoners won't riot against attercops. They're half-starved."

"That's why they'll get behind it." Rooker chewed on one lip, thinking. "Can ya still get in touch with yer two-face on the docks? The one that smuggled in yer contraband?"

She tilted her head, curious. "Yeah."

"There's a package on the *Hup Two*." Rooker stared at the Institute. "Yellow markings. Port locker, canvas wrap tucked up under the deckrail, about a yard long."

"Okay..." Patch leaned forward. "What's in it?"

Rooker shrugged. "I might have tucked a few weapons in there."

Patch's eyes lit up like kindling. "Are you serious?"

"I was hoping to escape on the *Hup Two*. Figured I'd stock it right." Rooker cricked his neck. The wharf security on Bounty had been designed to stop prisoners from *taking* a boat, not from boarding one. "There might be half a dozen blades tucked in there."

Patch's eyes twinkled. "You light-fingered bastard."

Rooker allowed himself a smile. "I figure we put those swords in the right hands, we've got half a riot already."

"You've certainly got your pick of troublemakers." Patch snorted. "But even with a dozen swords, you're not going to be able to fight your way up the wall."

"Who said anything about fighting?" Rooker smiled. "The swords are just a diversion. Camouflage while we snatch the rune."

Patch let out a breath. "You're talking about clearing the wall of twenty or thirty attercops." She shook her head. "Six people isn't enough."

He grinned at her. "So we'll get more."

Rooker Flynn climbed the ladder to the top of the water tower and looked down to find himself surrounded by outlaws.

Thanks to Thunderbuck moonshine, Hyena camp had become a central location for barter and trade, a kind of penal colony town square. It had only taken a few hours for the network of runners to spread the word that Yenrab Bialik was offering Thunderbuck moonshine at half price, and convicts arrived by the score.

As he took his place atop the water tower, Rooker saw how much the prisoners had changed since he'd left for Bounty. They had been thin before, but now they were nearly emaciated, just skeletons covered in a layer of skin. The galt supply simply couldn't sustain them all. They were starving, abused, worn out, the fading remains of former renegades who now only existed to survive another day.

He took a deep breath and nodded to Pilgrim. "Okay."

The troubadour hammered the big water tank with a pair of ersatz drumsticks in a fast, complicated rhythm. The sound, amplified by the water in the tank, caught the attention of every ear in camp. Standing atop it, Rooker felt the tank vibrate like a bell beneath his feet. Every convict stared at him, wondering what kind of stunt he was pulling.

Come on, boys, ain't ya ever seen a man pick a fight?

"Lord of Sea and Sky, it's like a carpet of ugly down there!" Scowls crossed a hundred faces as necks craned up to peer at him. "Wince!" Rooker pointed out a crater-faced highwayman. "Yer face is so foul the 'cops could punish ya with a mirror!" One of the convicts brayed like a donkey. "Laugh it up, Razor, ya get any skinnier and yer gonna be able to hide behind a broomstick."

"Shut up and get down, idiot!" barked a teenaged Shaver.

"Check yer diaper, crib lizard, yer never gonna be half the man yer mother is."

Laughs erupted from the men. The Shaver turned red-faced. "Yeah, yeah! Tough guy! All talk!"

"Come up here and try me!" Rooker broadened his attention to the entire crowd. "I'm tougher than the whole lot of you wasteka skags put together!"

Now he had their attention. The crowd pressed toward the water tower, turning hostile and angry.

"I've been on Huánghūn nine *months* and I'm still not dead!" Rooker raised his voice, making sure they heard him in the back. "I spent two months killing yellowjackets! Had a hundred bouts and won every last one of 'em! Had the nobles screamin' and hollerin' for my blood until their faces were red as cherry tomatoes and they *still* couldn't kill me!"

A few cheers sounded from the audience. *Everyone loves a dead yellowjacket.*

"What the hell have *you* lot done?" Rooker shouted. "I thought this place had the nastiest outlaws in Keymark! True villains! But now yer nothin' but a bunch of milksops and bootlickers! Is that all you are now? *Sheep?*"

The desperados looked at each other. "No!" came a few shouts from the crowd.

Get mad, damn you all. Rooker raised his voice. "I look out and I see pirates who used to skin yellowjacket dreadnaughts before dawn!" A few of the pirate crews glanced at each other. "I see burglars who would rob any noble house on the mainland! Bandits who wouldn't think twice about swiping a whole damn caravan, guards and all!" Rooker increased his rhythm like one of Pilgrim's songs. "Ya were renegades! Ya were dangerous! And ya *earned* those marks on your arms!"

Six hundred hands fingered Institute brands, the one thing they all shared in common, the metal that had been burned into their flesh on their first day.

"But now she *owns* you!" Rooker thrust a finger at the Institute. "She sits up there in her fancy tower like some damn brownbelly wasteka harridan *queen*! She won't even give us enough to eat and ya just sit there and take it like a bunch of peasants!! Ya *whine* about it, ya *bitch* about it, but what do ya do? *Nothing!*" Rooker grinned. "Real outlaws would throw her from the top of the wasteka *wall*!"

The crowd erupted into cheers. Their anger burned with a hot and feral glee at the thought of Gerba Whipmarples dead.

Now I got you.

"She gets rich and fat! What do *you* get?" He hollered at the top of his lungs. "For all yer blood and sweat, what do *you* get? Nothing! *Worse* than nothing! Ya get to starve to death on bloody damn *galt*!"

That put them over the edge. The prisoners hated yellowjackets, the 'cops, and Gerba, but more than anything, they hated galt.

If you want to make a man angry, remind him of his empty belly.

The throng screamed at the top of their lungs, mad as hell. Their shouts echoed off the water drum and Rooker felt the tower vibrate with their hate.

He rode the wave of sound. "I say it's time we set things right!" Cheers. "I say we remind Gerba Whipmarples she's playin' with fire!" More cheers. "I say she can't beat a horde of Keymark's greatest *rebels*!"

The loudest roar yet thundered across the camp.

"I'm not gonna choke down her galt anymore! Are you?"

"No!" came the voices in the front row.

"Ya gonna drag her lumber?"

"No!"

"Dig her mines?"

"No!" The entire assembly boiled with rage and glee at the same time, their faces locked in the fierce grin Rooker had worn his whole life.

"We may be criminals, but we're not *slaves*!"

The throng went insane. Rabid howls split the air, six hundred convicts unified in hatred against the Locke Institute.

He had his mob.

"We're outlaws, aren't we?" Thunderous voices bellowed agreement. *"Then let's start breakin' some rules!"*

Chapter

19

QUIET RIOT

When dictatorship is a fact,
revolution becomes a right.

Victor Hugo

G ERBA WHIPMARPLES HAD NOT slept since the Steel Trial. Juttlander trols have a remarkable constitution, and she had spent nearly a hundred and fifty hours smashing a pickaxe against the wall of the cave beneath the Institute. Relentless, unyielding, she struck again and again until the pickaxe broke. Without missing a beat, she picked up another and resumed her tireless rampage against the mountain.

Impudent! She struck again, furious at the young doktar for ruining her event. *Cowards!* She struck for the nobles and the way they had fled, even after she'd burned the strîgoi to ash. *Witless!* She struck for Rooker for refusing to tell her where Jack had gone or for being so stupid that he didn't know. *Despicable!* That was for Nepenthe and the wild goose chase the staff had led her down.

Fool! That was for herself.

Cant Naysayer had been right. She should never have introduced the strîgoi to the nobles until she had the Heart of Huánghūn in the palm of her hand. She had been patient for so many years, but her desire to impress the nobles, to show her place among them, had threatened her life's work. *Fool!*

Her pickaxe fell again, repeating the cycle of blame. Nepenthe illuminated the walls with crisp blue light that whickered from the symbols carved in its wood. The elven weapon had led her to this dismal hole, and every worker she could fit in the tunnel had been dedicated to mining this hole, but day after day the result was the same. Nothing. There was no sign of the Heart, and she was beginning to lose hope. *All these years, and for what?*

Cant Naysayer had abandoned her after the futile torture of Rooker Flynn. The Naysayer Brothers had departed on the *Hydra* to pursue the nobles and left the *Venture Brigand* behind, despite the fact that Cant had not yet been paid. And the only reason he would do that is that the Naysayer Brothers intended to return, this time with a bounty on her head.

Her only hope was to find the Heart of Huánghūn before the Naysayers returned.

Fool!

"Headmistress," came a voice.

Gerba turned to find Winston standing at the cave entrance. *He never comes down here.* "Winston?" She rose to her feet. It had taken a long time to learn the body language of the attercops, but Gerba prided herself on understanding every beast in her charge. *Why are you so agitated, Winston?* "I will not be attending morning announcements. You may tell Portia to proceed."

"Well, um... headmistress..." The big spider rubbed his palps together. "It's more than that."

Gerba hooked an eyebrow. "What *is* it, Winston?"

"Um... maybe you'd better come upstairs and see for yourself."

Three hundred steps later, Gerba stripped off the smock she used in the caves to keep her dresses clean. It was a long climb to the rooftop of the Institute, and she was out of breath from the effort. *Perhaps I am tired after all.* She took the final step to the top and felt the wind on her face and saw the light of the rising sun. Several acolytes gathered with the attercops at the edge of the rooftop. Usually, the two groups kept their distance. *Even curiouser.*

Hearing nothing is nearly impossible if you're not listening for it. There had been no hush of boots, no murmur of men, no early-morning grumbling, just the solitary cry of a raiptar bird and the wind in the palms.

Not one student waited below for morning announcements.

Gerba eyed the hourglass as the last grain clicked to the bottom.

For the first time in Locke Institute history, the students did not gather at dawn.

Gerba's eyes narrowed. *I do not have the time for this.* "Where are they?"

"I don't know, headmistress."

"That is not helpful, Portia." Gerba jammed meaty fists to her hips, crinkling the chiffon beneath her dress. "We have heard nothing from our spies?"

Winston shrugged eight shoulders. "We don't have many left." Gerba's mouth turned to a threatening frown, encouraging the chief attercop to think harder. "There was some talk yesterday. Kinda, you know, grumbling. About not working. But I figured, you know, it was all talk… just convict talk."

"I beg your pardon, Winston." Gerba Whipmarples' eyes flared. "Are you saying our students are… on *strike*?"

"One more time."

Rooker Flynn hid at the edge of Hyena with Patch, Copper Dave, Yenrab, and Farah. All of them looked eager to execute the plan, and he knew he had used up their patience.

"We've been through this," grumbled Patch.

"Do it."

"Nobody moves," said Yenrab. "We do the… whaddayacallit…"

"Passive resistance," Farah chimed in.

"That. No fightin'." Yenrab's one eye glared at Rooker. "Not until high noon."

"Noon come, I get attercop alone." Copper Dave ran a finger along the edge of his new sword, a sharp falchion. "No witnesses."

"And get the hell out of there," said Patch. "The goons in the other camps will start making trouble, but until you're clear, you're going to have a swarm of 'cops on you."

Copper Dave grinned sharp teeth. "I am like wind." He slung the bag of weapons over his shoulder and strode into the jungle.

"Good luck." Yenrab jerked his chin at Rooker and Patch, then walked toward his place in camp. "Don't screw this up."

Luck to us all. Rooker stood to follow but felt a hand on his shoulder.

"What about me?" Farah looked up at him.

"Keep workin'," snapped Rooker. "We need ya makin' that whitefire, darlin'."

Farah leaned in, her dark eyes earnest. "I want to help."

Rooker felt frustration boil inside him. He'd cobbled together this rickety plan in a few hours, and they were past the point of no return. *I don't need more headaches, mouse-face.* "Yer small, yer weak, and the only knack ya got is followin' recipes." Rooker watched Farah curl away from him, retreating into herself. "All ya can do is screw this up for the rest of us. Just stay outta the way."

Patch slapped him on the back. "Let's disappear."

They moved to a rise in the jungle where they could observe Hyena from afar. Yenrab walked into camp to join the three hundred prisoners who sat in a circle around the water tower.

Peaceful protest was a foreign concept to the criminals on Huánghūn, but it didn't take long for them to warm to it. As it happens, most of them were experts at doing nothing.

Rooker watched Winston and the attercops thunder into camp, shouting curses at the prisoners. They yelled and hollered, demanding Hyena report to assembly, but the convicts refused to move.

A series of beatings followed, but the outlaws were no strangers to that. Still they went nowhere. When Winston bit a pirate, the man screamed, and several of his fellow Shavers leapt to their feet with clubs, ready to fight. A high voice sounded from the water tower.

I ain't never done me nothin' wrong
I think that you'd agree
But the old longhorn done locked me up
Then threw away the key

Now longlegs make me work all day
Won't let me go to bed
So I got right up the boss-man's nose
And this is what I said:
I'm tired, gotta sit down, sit down!
You know I'm gonna sit down, sit down!
I'm just plain beat, worked off my feet
Ain't never gonna stand me up
'til I get somethin' good to eat!

The crowd laughed as Billy Pilgrim concluded the verse. The pirates glared at the attercops, but the crowd urged them to 'sit down, sit down' and they obeyed. Smiling, Pilgrim tickled a burring tremolo from the strings.

She breaks our backs but she won't pay
No, not one silver mark
No ma'm I will not dig today
It's cold and damp and dark!
Ol' longhorn shakes her finger
Sez 'Don't you give me no sass'
We'll tell her, too, what she can do
Go stick it up her ass!

The prisoners broke into cheers and howled laughter at the top of their lungs. Winston fumed and stomped and hollered, but everyone just laughed at the 'cops. Pilgrim smiled as every voice in camp joined him for the chorus.

I'm tired, gotta sit down, sit down!
You know I'm gonna sit down, sit down!
I'm just plain beat, worked off my feet

Ain't never gonna stand me up
'til I get somethin' good to eat!

Enraged, Winston webbed up one of the prisoners and started dragging him away, then surrendered as he realized he couldn't haul every outlaw to assembly. His humiliation reached an apex as Hyena camp laughed the 'cops out of camp.

Rooker couldn't help but smile. "This might work. Come on."

He and Patch serpentined through the jungle, avoiding the attercops on their way to the wall. They sheltered in a hiding place near the wall, which was crawling with agitated 'cops. They killed time until noon with a game of cards. Rooker felt for the dirk in his belt about a hundred times, pacing back and forth to keep his legs limber, hoping he could pull off this job with one eye.

Just after the sun reached its apex, one of the attercops stumbled into the assembly yard.

"Help! Help me!" Rooker and Patch watched a giant, hairy spider limp out of the jungle, dragging one leg. Another leg had been severed at the joint. It leaked a wet trail of greenish ichor. "Help me!"

Rooker took unrepentant satisfaction watching the wounded attercop struggle in pain. *So that's what it looks like when they bleed.*

Several 'cops descended on weblines toward their wounded comrade. More guards from the big stone door rushed to the thing's aid. More attercops emerged from the jungle, and a pack of giant tarantulas converged on their wounded mate.

Patch swallowed hard. "That's a lot of 'cops."

More than forty. Rooker had never been able to count the attercops. They all looked the same to him, but he'd never imagined there were so many. "Whaddaya want me to do about it?"

With a great deal of shouting, the attercops pointed and bickered amongst themselves. Finally, Winston's voice thundered, "Fetch the whips! I'll flay the soles off their feet! Hump it!" The cluster broke up, fetching weapons from inside. Soon enough, the mob of attercops plunged into the jungle en masse, bristling with whips and spears. "Let's remind these apes who's boss!"

"Go," Rooker hissed. As the 'cops disappeared into the jungle, he darted across the open assembly yard, followed closely by Patch. They hit the Institute wall and glanced at the top to see if anyone had seen their mad dash. No shout rang out. Rooker let out a breath.

There was no cover against the wall here, but it was the most direct climb to the Caged Eight embedded in the rock thirty feet above them. Rooker slapped Patch on the shoulder. "Giddup."

She hooked her paws together and gave him a boost. Rooker snatched a fistful of stone and hauled himself up the wall. He couldn't see the rune from here. It was hidden in the rock, but he knew it was there.

I hope.

Rooker had spent a year manning the *Venture Brigand*'s crow's nest, so climbing came as second nature. But in those days, he'd had two eyes and handholds had been easier to find. The cliff offered no regular footing, and he quickly found himself caught on a face of wall that was simply too flat to climb.

Damn jinx, she should be doing this.

He scrabbled sideways around the flat, got a boot in a crack, and pushed up. Straining, he grabbed an outcrop, dragged himself over it, and looked down. Patch was flattened against the wall below, but she seemed too small, too far away. He realized if he lost his grip at this height, the rocks would break him.

Keep going.

He heaved himself over another rock and caught sight of the rune. The Caged Eight was a bronze disc embedded in the wall, half-hidden behind an outcropping of grass. Rooker slung his leg up, seized a handhold, and closed the distance.

Rungs on a ladder, just rungs on a ladder.

"*Rooker!*" came Patch's whisper-yell. He looked down and saw her pointing past him. He glanced up and saw an acolyte on a balcony, her robes flickering in the breeze. Panting, Rooker wedged himself under a gap and slung his homemade hood over his head, hoping the grey fabric matched the rock.

I'd rather have majik camouflage.

The acolyte moved on. Rooker scrabbled sideways just below the rune. It wasn't big, not much larger than a dinner plate, and mortared to the rock. He thrust one boot into the wall and jammed his back against an opposing rock, hanging in midair. He pulled the prybar from his belt and hooked it under the Caged Eight. Metal was a rare commodity on Huánghūn so Rooker had fashioned the prybar out of a length of iron-hard jatoba wood. The rune was affixed with metal clamps and it took all his effort, but he felt it move a fraction of an inch. *Ha!*

Out of the corner of his eye he saw an attercop emerge from the jungle not fifty yards away.

It moved for Patch, a spear in one claw.

Where the hell did he come from?

"You, there!" shouted the 'cop. "What are you doing?"

"Um..." Patch angled backward, trapped.

Dammit. Rooker was stuck between dislodging the rune and watching the 'cop, not sure what to do. *All this will be for nothing if I walk away empty-handed.* He bent to his work.

He heard Patch say something that sounded like a question, then the attercop cried out in distress. Rooker glanced down to see Patch had maneuvered the spider so it was facing away from the wall, toward her. And something was horribly, horribly wrong with her face.

O, she's brilliant.

Patch's body was covered in boils, ugly as sin. Her shoulders were slick with oozing sores; pus slowly leaked down her neck. One eye was swollen shut, dripping some kind of jelly. She approached the attercop, reaching out with one diseased hand. "Help me…"

The big spider backed away, repulsed. "Hey! Hey! Get back!"

I guess attercops can catch leprosy.

Rooker jammed his boots into the wall and pulled with all his might. Silently straining, his muscles grew tight with quivering tension and the tendons in his neck stood out like harp strings.

Krak!

Stone shattered. The rune came free. Rooker grabbed at the thing as it slipped its moorings.

He missed.

For one instant, Rooker watched the Caged Eight, his only hope of escape, tumble through the air like a spinning coin as it dropped straight for the attercop.

By the time it hit the giant spider, Rooker had thrown himself off the cliff.

"*Akh!*" shouted the attercop as the bronze rune nailed it on one leg. The 'cop looked up to find a silhouette of a man falling from the sky. It had one half-second to scream before Rooker smashed into it. He hit like thunder and knocked the 'cop to the ground with a sharp cry of pain from both.

Rooker drove his dirk into the thing's neck. Spraying green ooze, it screamed and threw him to the ground.

Rooker snatched the rune and sprinted for the jungle.

He darted into the palms, Patch close on his heels. A shout rose behind him, the attercop in angry pursuit. "Go!" he yelled at Patch. "*Go!*"

Sweating, Rooker heard the attercop close behind. The thing was faster than either of them. He heard the *thwick* as the 'cop released a jet of webbing. He ducked sideways just in time to watch a wad of white goo slap into the tree next to him, slathering it in sticky silk.

Why isn't this thing working? Rooker glanced at the Caged Eight to find part of the rune had broken off in the fall. *Dammit!*

He snatched a dead branch from a tree and smacked the rune like a cymbal.

Work, damn you!

A dull *clonk* was all he got, but he felt a little burst of majik emanate from the Caged Eight. The hair on his arms stood up. The attercop paused, stunned by the warding *wikk*.

Patch sprinted past Rooker. All artifice was gone. She was just a pregnant, filthy jinx running for her life. "Go!" Rooker snaked through the trees behind her, but she was too far ahead. "Come on, Rook—"

A burst of webbing caught her leg and she went down.

Her chin cracked against a rock.

Turning, Rooker watched the 'cop burst through the trees, a behemoth of legs and fangs. Skidding to a halt, Rooker faced the attercop as it came with its spear. He batted away the spear tip with the Caged Eight. Metal struck metal and this time the chime resonated loud and long.

The attercop froze like a statue. Its legs flexed, its fangs opened, but the thing was simply unable to get any closer to the Caged Eight. Rooker thrust the rune toward the spider and it backed away, hypnotized.

Move, move, move.

Rooker dragged Patch to her feet. Together, they raced through the jungle, pounding through the mud. He had a moment to think he'd made it when a wad of webbing lashed his back. It tangled with his legs and he went down, taking Patch with him. The Caged Eight bounced loose into a gulley and splatted into the mud, too far to reach.

He spun to witness the giant tarantula drop from the trees above him. *Kek-kek-kek* came from its mouth as it lunged for him, fangs dripping venom.

Rooker held up his hand, knowing he was done for. He jammed his eyes shut.

Ksssh! Whumph!

Shattering shards of glass splintered the air, followed by a rush of air and a blast of heat.

Rooker opened his eyes to see the attercop was on fire.

Burning, the giant spider screamed. The hairs on its back flamed bright and spread across its body like a raging brushfire. Howling in pain, the attercop spasmed, trying to smash out the flames, but only succeeded in setting its other limbs alight. Rooker grabbed Patch and hauled her away from the flailing, burning madness.

He stopped short to find Farah, the mouse-faced girl, holding a jug of Thunderbuck moonshine with a burning rag hanging out the neck, her teeth bared like a tiger, her face lit with red flame. She hurled the jug at the attercop. It shattered and liquid fire roiled over the spider's body.

Gibbering and twitching, the thing burned black, releasing a *squee* as its back split open from the heat and boiling green gunk cascaded to the ground in gooey green lumps. Its legs curled up, twitching in the flames.

Farah's face was a rictus of furious hatred. "Die, you wasteka bastard!" She snatched another jug to throw more fuel on the fire.

Rooker grabbed her and she twisted like a mad cat. "It's okay, it's okay, Farah. It's dead."

The mouse's fury went out like a snuffed candle. She blinked and her brown eyes grew wide, reverting to her customary passive nothing-face. But Rooker knew there was a tiger hiding underneath. Finally, her mouth moved. "I... wanted to help."

"Ya did that and then some." Rooker nodded. "Patch?"

The jinx got to her feet and untangled webbing from her fur. "I'm fine thanks to you."

Farah ducked her head, her wide eyes staring at the burning attercop corpse.

Rooker snatched the rune from the gulley, stuffed it in his shirt, and ran for Hyena.

By the time they snuck back into camp, sunset loomed over the horizon and the day's damage was done. Hyena had been torn apart. The attercops were gone but left behind broken chairs, pots, and detritus littered everywhere. Trails of black smoke drifted above the camp. Most of the outlaws had fled to their cliques, but some still gathered around the water tower, all of them bruised and bloody.

Copper Dave appeared, his falchion bare in his hand. A fresh cut split one side of his face as he smiled. "You get Cage Eight?"

"Yeah." Rooker held up the bronze disc. "Farah burned an attercop to get it."

Impressed, the big croc turned to the mouse-girl. "You kill spider?"

Farah ducked her head, uncomfortable with the attention. Copper Dave smiled. "Is good. *Very* good. Better than me."

Rooker took in the wrecked camp. "What happened?"

"Just like plan. Stick and move. Make confuse." The croc took a breath. "Then, big one come. Winston. Burns clique." He pointed at a pillar of smoke and Rooker realized it wasn't from some campfire. It was the smoking remains of the women's clique. "Tell us, if not work tomorrow, they burn another." His face was dark. "Every day."

They burned a clique? Gerba must be desperate. Rooker gripped the Caged Eight. "Come on, let's get this thing to Yenrab."

Descending the ladder into the secret chamber beneath the escape crew's clique, Rooker smelled the acrid odor of whitefire gourds. As his eye adjusted, Rooker saw Yenrab's red face staring up at him.

"One Caged Eight." He tossed the glyph onto the table, where the bronze rang like a bell. A gentle pulse of *wikk* radiated, then went still. "Ya gotta hit it with metal, and we might want to hang it from a strap so it rings better, but it works." Rooker landed on the dirt at the bottom of the ladder. "Now. Let's find that door."

The dwarf's eye gleamed, a crooked grin on his gap-toothed face. "I think we just found it."

"We?"

Rooker's eye finally adjusted to the dark to discover another figure standing in the shadows.

Covered in a black cloak, the stranger wore an ebony scarf wrapped around his mouth and head. Midnight-black pants clung to his lean legs as his dark boots walked into the light. Sticking out from beneath the black wrap hung a shock of blond hair.

A familiar voice came from under the scarf. "Hey."

The pirate blinked his one eye, trying to understand what he was seeing.

Jack Swift pulled down his mask.

You.

Rooker stared at his blue eyes.

You came back.

A stunned smile overtook Rooker's face.

You came back for me.

Rooker Flynn grabbed his brother and held him like he'd never let him go.

THE WRECK =OF THE= CÍRDAN

*He may be a son of a bitch,
but he's our son of a bitch.*

Franklin D. Roosevet

X EUSIA VOMITED A SEA of blackfire, drowning the strîgoi in flames, immolating it to drifting embers.

Jack Swift felt his skin pull tight against his face from the heat of dragonflame. He grabbed Rooker under the arms and dragged the pirate's limp body away from the blaze as screaming nobles fled past him toward the wharf. He only made it a few steps before his lungs gave up, scorched by heat and dragonsmoke. Coughing, Jack watched Xeusia crush the burning corpse of the dæmon under its claws. Saddled on the dragon's back, Gerba Whipmarples' face was lit in dragonfire.

"Stop!" Jack watched her scream at the fleeing nobles. "Stop!" She turned on the acolyte who had shot Rooker in the gut. "Portia! Why isn't the bell ringing? There are nobles dying in my arena!"

"The flares, headmistress!" Portia yelled over the sound of the blaze. "They didn't work! They may have gotten wet on th—"

"Damn those hammerdwarves!" Gerba spat. "I shall ring it myself! Xeusia!" Jack was blasted backward as the dragon beat its wings and took to the air. "Take those two to the pens and chain them up! I will deal with them when I return!" Another buffeting gust hit him and Jack watched Xeusia streak for Huánghūn.

Portia shouldered her bow. "On your feet!" Jack tried to resist, but the toxic smoke in his lungs made the world an impossible smear of color. The acolyte bound his hands. Jack tried to take a step toward Rooker, but the colors shifted and he smacked his head into something.

Trying to expel the smoke from his lungs, Jack realized he was in the horse pens behind the arena, chained to a hitching post. *I think I just blacked out.* He coughed in emphysematic seizures, the alveoli in his lungs clogged with dragon's breath. His head spun and he forced himself to focus on his hand. *When did I lose a finger?* He stared stupidly at the stump. *How am I going to do surgery with nine fingers?*

He wasn't sure if he blacked out again, but he heard the door creak open. Tiny bells jingled in harmony with a set of keys on an acolyte's belt. The scrape of metal inserted into a lock. A click. One manacle fell free. The other followed.

"Where ar—"

"Don't talk." The acolyte's voice was raspy and hard. "Hands behind your back. Move."

Jack tried for a deep breath and got a thimbleful of air. His stump bled freely, dripping on the dirt floor as she shoved him outside. He staggered, nearly passed out, then a bright sear of pain shot through him when the acolyte yanked his arms up behind his back. Shocked back to consciousness, he was forced to run.

Ahead, he saw the colosseum smoking. Confused spectators stumbled through the doors. He heard screaming down by the dock. Forced along at a merciless speed, Jack stumbled around a corner to find the wharf overrun with bejeweled nobles scrambling onto their ships. Some had already cast off, others were fighting to get a seat on whichever boat was closest. Some were already overrun. One of the incoming ferry boats had capsized, flooded by panicked nobles.

"What the hell are we supposed to do?" yelled the acolyte who stood at the entrance to the wharf. "This is madness!"

"She wants him." Jack's captor pointed at a ship at the far end of dock. "There."

"Headmistress didn't say anything to me about—"

"I'm following orders!" She pointed at the end of the wharf. In the darkness, the silhouette of a hulking trol in a dress gestured impatiently to hurry. "You want to argue with her? Go ahead!"

"Forget that!" came the reply, and Jack felt himself shoved onto the wharf. His captor forced his head down as they approached the yacht. The world smeared color again, then Jack's mind came briefly back into focus as he watched Gerba's orange heels lead him up the gangplank.

The acolyte kicked the yacht away from the docks. "Sails up," she hissed. *"Now!"*

"Hang on." Jack felt the world lurch sideways and the smear of color went black. His eyes fluttered shut as his mind spat out: *There's something wrong with Gerba.* Her voice sounded wrong, like it came in slow motion. Too deep, a voice that opera singers called a *basso profundo.* "These heels are killing me."

Jack collapsed onto the deck and gasped for air like a dying fish. He heard the acolyte's voice, close to his ear, soft and gentle, like something out of a dream.

"Don't worry, Jahk." She brushed her fingers against his cheek. "I've got you."

He woke up in another world.

It tilted slowly side to side, back and forth, rocking him like a mother's arms. He blinked, slowly comprehending he was at sea. Daylight streamed through a porthole, the sun long since up. He lay on a bunk with white sheets stained with greenish-black streaks near his mouth. Raising his head, he tried to get his bearings. He squinted. Lying on the floor was a discarded acolyte robe that still smelled of smoke next to a pair of gigantic orange heels and a sequined dress big as a tent.

Confused, he turned to find someone watched over him. Her face was only a silhouette against the sun. Jack blinked and recognized her red hair, her green eyes, her slightly crooked, aquiline nose. *The best nose.*

"Are..." He coughed, and when his voice finally came, it came weak. "Are you a dream?"

Leah Archer smiled. "Not anymore."

Jack didn't know what to do but seize her to make sure she was real. He wrapped his arms around her, felt her shirt in his fingers, the warmth of her body as he hugged her tight. *She's real. She's real.*

He squeezed her tight. Too tight. Like a drowning man. He felt his chest hitch a breath as nine months of horror shivered through him like a lightning strike. His breath shuddered as if something was trying to break free, a silent sob of loneliness and despair trapped somewhere so deep it could never escape. He clutched at her with grasping fingers, terrified she would disappear, unable to let go. "Leah—"

"It's okay, it's okay. You're okay—" Her words cut off, her body rigid.

Jack opened his eyes to see his tattered and bloody shirt sleeve had fallen away from his forearm and revealed the metal brand burned into his skin. His marked flesh shone dully in the light.

He glanced at Leah and saw crippling pity in her eyes. "O, Jahk."

"Sorry, I..." Jack covered the mark with his hand. "It's fine." He turned away, fixing his sleeve back into position. "I'm sorry, you shouldn't see me like th—" Leah hugged him close. He resisted, caught between wanting to let himself be comforted and his shame at her seeing him like this. Seeing what he had become. He jammed his eyes shut. He tried to stop the sob from escaping but failed. His voice whispered a plaintive "Not like this."

"It's okay. It's okay. They're not going to find us." Her voice was steady, calm. "We've got food and some medicine. We need to keep the bandages on your hand, but everything's going to be all right."

Everything's going to be all right. Jack stiffened at the sound of her voice, the softness of it, the familiarity of it. The voice he'd heard when he'd fallen asleep every night. His dream made flesh. He looked into her eyes, still unsure if she was real. "Was that you? Talking in my dreams?"

"Not very well, apparently." A sad smile crossed her face. "You could hear me? You could understand me?"

"I don't know," Jack stammered. "Not words. Just thoughts. Just... feelings."

"What kind of feelings?"

Jack thought of all the nights Leah's voice had kept the wolf at bay. "Hope." He felt half a smile touch his lips. "You gave me hope."

Leah held him tight.

"Hey." Jack felt a deep voice rattle his chest. "Don't hog him."

Jack turned to find a giant rhinoceros head sticking through the cabin door. He threw himself at it and hugged the trol's horn. *"Memphis."*

Giant leathery hands gripped him gently and Jack felt himself pulled into the air, out of the cabin into the sunlight. Acorn brown eyes looked back at him. "Hello, boyo." Memphis Kubiak's deep, reassuring voice washed over him. "You got taller."

Jack tried to wrap himself around the trol's massive chest; it was impossible, like trying to hug a Chevrolet.

Memphis chuckled. "Good to see you, too, boyo. We tried to tell you we were here to break you out. Did you get our message?"

Jack blinked at him. "What message?"

Something crawled over Memphis's huge leathery shoulder and wrapped itself around Jack's face.

He recognized the blue and gold pebbled skin, the webbed feet, the smiling gecko face. *Fuji.* The tam licked his face like an excited dog. "Hi, Fuji. Hi. Okay, okay. Hi."

It licked his cheek one more time and signed with tree-frog fingers. *Apple Jack.*

"I don't... I don't have an apple but..." He signed: *I love you.* Fuji chirruped and slid its face around him like a cat, rubbing between Jack and Memphis in a three-way hug. As he patted Fuji,

Jack spotted a pendant around the tam's neck.

Leah jerked her chin. "*That* message."

Jack found he couldn't stop giggling as Fuji licked his face. "You sent Fuji onto Bounty to find me? That was smart."

"But it didn't work." Leah detached the pendant and unscrewed it, revealing a small parchment hidden inside. "Instructions for your escape. If Fuji had found you."

"You planned all th--"

"Okay, hold your horses." Memphis set Jack on his own two feet. "I'm glad to see you, boyo, but I can't hug you anymore. You stink." The trol turned his head and coughed. *"Wow."*

Jack looked down at the bloody Black Jack costume and realized he reeked of death, sweat, and dragonfire. "Sorry."

"You *are* pretty ripe." Leah chuckled. "Here. Let me give you a hand." She placed her fingers on his chest and shoved him overboard.

Jack hit the water with a splash. A cloud of grime billowed up around him as flakes of dried blood and gunk drifted from his skin. He sputtered to the surface and drew a breath. Fuji jumped in and paddled around him, trying to lick his face.

"Lather up." Leah tossed a sponge at him. "And get that stupid costume off."

Treading water, he tore off his concho-laden Black Jack costume and let it drift away. The dark fabric flared out in the blue Irridin Sea like a manta ray set free. As it descended to the depths, Jack found the worst part of the last few months escaping with it.

"How the hell did you find me?" Jack scrubbed his hair dry with a towel, beginning to feel more like himself. His body was scoured clean. His new clothes, a belted pair of leggings and a loose linen shirt, were dry and soft. "How did you even know I was in Keymark?"

Memphis crouched over a little table, assembling a dainty supper of apples, cheeses, and dried meats. Fuji kept stealing his apples. "Have you ever heard of Viscountess Jimenez?"

Jack nodded; he remembered the name all too well. The only female noble at the killing fields. "Yeah. She's a lousy shot."

"She's also a blabbermouth gossip." Leah threw Jack an apple. "Four months ago, I attended an event with her, and she couldn't stop talking about some remote island out on the edge of the world. Very mysterious, very exciting. And on that island, for fun, she had the opportunity to hunt the famous outlaw known as Black Jahk." Leah took a bite. "At first, I didn't believe her. Noble families haven't done thrill kills in ages. But her story was full of details, like how there were big yellow spiders and the music was dull, but she liked the snacks." She took another bite. "So then I thought maybe they dressed someone up as Black Jahk. But she described you perfectly." Leah eyed him. "Blue eyes, blond hair, slim little nose." She gestured with the apple. "That's when I first reached out to you."

"In my dreams."

Leah snorted. "A sending is supposed to be stronger than just a *dream*. I'm not very good at it yet. I'm only learning."

"Don't let her fool you. She's good," said Memphis. "I can't perform a sending at all."

Leah shrugged. "I couldn't tell if you could hear me, but I could *feel* you. Which meant you had to be in Keymark. So I came looking."

"*We* came looking," corrected Memphis, annoyed at being left out.

Leah scowled. "You didn't even believe me!"

"No, I did not. But I came anyway." Memphis folded his arms. "I wasn't going to let you go off on some wild goose chase to the edge of the world to track down a penal colony on an island full of giant spiders."

Jack blinked. "You've been looking for me for four *months*?"

"Asking questions for four months. Put to sea thirty days ago." Leah unsheathed her belt knife and severed a hunk of cheese. "Took us a while to find Huánghūn. It's not on any maps. And once we found it, knocking on the front door didn't seem like a good idea, and it's impossible to sneak ashore and get back alive. Those razorsquid are nasty." She flicked a hunk to Fuji. "We tried signaling at night but didn't have any luck. I kept reaching out to you with the sending, but no dice there. Then we found out you weren't even on Huánghūn. We didn't know about the Steel Trials until those posh yachts started arriving on Bounty."

Jack fed an apple to Fuji. "That wasn't part of your plan?"

"Plan?" Leah glanced at Memphis and both of them laughed. "None of this has been a *plan*, Jahk. We got lucky. I recognized this yacht." She gestured at the ship they occupied. "The *Kestrel*. Belongs to Kumari Bana, duchess of the Pipen Gulf. We flagged her down off Bounty. I put on the lady-in-distress act. Told her I had been invited to whatever was going on and my baggage had gone overboard in a storm."

"You know some fancy people."

"More than I'd like." Leah flicked another hunk of cheese to Fuji. "Once we docked, they didn't let anyone on the island, so we sent Fuji in to look for you, but *that* didn't work. By the time the Trial started, we were between a rock and a hard place. So I strapped on a ball gown and went to the show."

Jack glanced at her. "You saw me in the arena?"

"I saw everything." Leah's eyes were locked on him, proud. "I thought you were dead, but I didn't know how to save you. That stunt with the salt was genius." Jack didn't know whether to duck his head or stick out his chest. He did neither. "After everything went to hell, I followed the guard. Knocked her out, took her keys, put on that ridiculous uniform, and brought you..." She glanced at Memphis. "Here."

Something passed between Leah and Memphis. Jack didn't understand the look, but the tone of the conversation had changed. He lowered an eyebrow. "Where is here?"

Memphis stood and put a hand on his shoulder. "Here is where you go *home*, boyo."

Jack held his breath. "What?"

"Take another look."

Memphis gestured over the side. Jack stepped to the edge of the *Kestrel* and looked down. Beneath the waves, a hundred feet below, he saw the *Venture Brigand*, sunk at the bottom of the sea.

Impossible.

Jack blinked, unable to believe his eyes. *Wait.* Underwater, he saw a current of fireflies circling the masts like a school of minnows. *Pixies.* As their light spiraled around the ship, he saw the figurehead was different, the masts slightly closer, the forecastle in the wrong place. The hull was littered with too many barnacles for a vessel that had been afloat yesterday; this ship had been sunk a century or more. *It's the Brigand's twin sister.*

Her outriggers lay on the ocean floor, her body tilted sideways, one leg broken, a wreck. Scraps of tattered sail hung limp from her yardarms. Her pale mast stretched for the sky above, unable to reach, a drowned maiden. Atop her sunken mast hung a black banner; Jack recognized it as his discarded Black Jack costume, waving under the sea like a ghost pirate flag.

"What is that?"

"The *Círdan.*" Memphis's voice was low, almost reverential. "One of the three aräs windjammers, the *Arania*, the *Flin,* and the *Círdan.* The elves made them. Woven from majik, centuries ago, built to ferry their gifts across Keymark." Memphis pointed at the circling pixies. "There is enough *wikk* down there for me to create a jaunt gate." He eyed Jack. "To Chicago."

Jack stared at the ghost of the *Círdan.* He watched the ocean ripple over her broken hull, giving her the appearance of a phantasm. The ship was isolated, broken, alone, drowned. To Jack, the *Círdan* seemed a cruel omen, a glimpse into the future. In it, he could see the fate of the *Venture Brigand* and her captain.

"I'm not going until Rooker's safe." The words were out of his mouth before the thought was complete.

Leah shared a worried look with Memphis. She spread her hands. "Jahk, I tried. I'm sorry. I didn't even know Rooker was *there* until the Trial. And I barely got out alive with you." She touched his shoulder. "Listen to me. We can't go back."

Jack stared at the wreck below. "We'll figure something out."

"Jack." Memphis leaned in. "Look at yourself." Jack peered at his reflection in the water and found a half-emaciated captive, scarred and burned, with only four fingers on one hand. The stranger stared back at him. "You can't go back there. You'll die."

"I don't care. I'm getting him out."

"Jack—"

"I'm getting him out!" Jack shouted, his voice like a whip. He registered the shock on their faces, as if he had just slapped them

317

both, but he didn't care. He would *swim* back to Huánghūn if he had to. He stared at the scar on his palm, the mark that shared Rooker's blood. *I'm getting him out.*

Memphis raised a thick finger and started to argue.

"Stop." Leah held up her hands. "Memphis. Stop. He's too weak to go back. He's too weak to survive the jaunt gate. Nobody's going anywhere." She straightened. "Not right now. So." She pushed something into Jack's hands and he glanced down to find it was a plate. "What we're going to do is eat dinner." She looked Jack in the eye. "While you tell us everything that happened in that prison."

The story took until the moons were up. Jack remembered telling the tale, but what he most remembered of that night was the strange similarity of the sea and sky, a blur of light and dark. As the blues darkened and stars arrived above, they were mirrored by pixies below, tiny green trails of light swimming in a luminescent spiral around the mast of the *Círdan* just below the sea. A shooting star zipped across the sky while a pixie echoed its trajectory beneath the waves. Jack didn't remember nodding off, but when he woke in his bunk, Fuji was curled atop his chest, warm and dry. He shifted and the big gecko cuddled against him, purring like a contented cat.

"You want chai?"

Jack opened his eyes and saw Leah sitting in the opposite bunk, holding a delicate porcelain cup of steaming tea.

He got to his elbows, knowing he had slept too long. It was afternoon already. "Got any coffee?"

She chuckled. "It amazes me. You know everything in the universe, *doktar*. And still you think coffee is better than chai." She blew on the cup and sipped it, enjoying the taste. "You don't know what you're missing."

Jack watched her eyes sparkle. Her half-smile crinkled her mouth on one side. That spectacular nose. The way her lips kissed the porcelain.

He readjusted the covers, realizing he had not seen a healthy woman in months. *Stop staring.*

"Come here." She put the cup down. "I need to change your bandages."

Jack scooted over and presented his hand. Leah unwrapped the bloody linen. The missing stump of a finger still stung, but the real pain came from the dragonfire burns. Xeusia's black flames had never touched him but still his skin had burned. His flesh was riddled with blisters, although they had stopped suppurating. As she checked him, he looked into her eyes. "You saved my life, Leah." He shook his head. "I don't know how to thank you for that."

"Don't be so willing to throw it away." She unstoppered a small jar that smelled like eucalyptus and rubbed ointment on his burns. It tingled like menthol. "Memphis doesn't want to take you back to Húanghūn."

"I don't want to argue about this right now, Leah. I'm tired."

Leah *hmphed*. "You're missing a finger and your skin is burned to blisters. You fought a dæmon three days ago. You spent nine months in a penal colony. You've been starved, beaten, tortured, branded, and forced to fight for your life. Any man would be tired." Her green eyes found him. "So why not rest?"

"Because you're not the only one who saved my life." Jack took the bandages and re-wrapped his hands. "Rooker rescued me out of my first camp, gave me a place to live, protected me, helped me."

"He also stabbed you in the back." Leah's voice was hard. "More than once."

"Leah--"

319

"Listen to me." She placed her hand gently on his arm. "You're *tired*, Jahk. I don't know if you were listening to the story you told last night, but I was." She leaned in. "Do you think Rooker Flynn would go back for *you*?"

Jack didn't say anything for a moment. He remembered all the times Rooker had bolted, all the times he'd turned his back, all the times he'd looked out only for himself. All his life, Rooker Flynn had lived like a distorted mirror of everything his father and his brother had been. He was only a reflection of the world around him. If Jack left Rooker behind, the pirate would know, once and for all, that no one could be trusted. If he abandoned Rooker now, Jack would be no better than Jasper Winegrad.

He looked at the scar on his palm. Without him, Rooker's fate would be the same as the *Círdan*'s, eternally reaching out for a hand that would never come.

"It doesn't matter what he would do." Jack thumbed his scarred palm. "I made a promise."

Leah stared at him. The silence seemed to go on forever, Jack unable to read her eyes. Finally, she let out a long breath. "Then I suppose it doesn't matter how tired you are."

She got to her feet and headed for the deck. "Oh." She reached into her pocket. "You dropped this when we escaped." She tossed something small and he caught it. In his hand was his scalpel, the little homemade blade he'd made during the Steel Trials. "A doktar should have his tools."

"Leah—" Jack looked up to find her watching him intently. "What?"

Leah Archer appreciated him as if she saw him with new eyes. "He's right. You *are* taller."

She disappeared through the doorway.

Two days later, the *Kestrel* floated a quarter mile off the southern coast of Huánghūn, just outside the breakers.

Jack stood on the deckrail, stripped to the waist, an oilskin pouch strapped to his back. It contained his clothes, his boots, and his tools, none of which would matter unless he made it to shore. The sun descended toward the sea, threatening his first night of shiq in a long, long time. *Now or never.*

"If anything goes wrong, we can't come get you." Memphis was nervous. "Please, Jack. There's got to be another way. Let me go with you."

We've been over this. He's just stalling. He checked his equipment, making sure his air bladder was full. "As soon as we reach the docks, I'll signal you."

Memphis scowled. "With what? What's the signal?"

Jack frowned back. "I don't know. I'll try to come up with something you can't miss."

Leah eyed the shoreline. "You sure about this, Jahk?"

Jack laughed under his breath. "Not a bit."

"Well then, there's only one thing to say." She smiled. "Good luck."

Jack Swift dove into the sea. He skimmed just under the surface, bobbed on the water, took one last look at the *Kestrel*, and swam.

The air bladder acted like a life vest and kept him on top of the waves, but it was awkward. He felt the first razorsquid lash the moment he crossed over the breakers, a stripe of pain across his feet. He kicked harder, making for the shore. Another twenty lashes stung him, one at a lime, like long, slow paper cuts. The pain was agony, but he kept swimming. He took another twenty lashes before he made it to shore and dragged himself up the beach, finally beyond the reach of the razorsquid.

He ran for the trees, hunkered down, and unfolded the oilcloth, revealing the black clothes and his tools. For the next hour, he sprinted through the jungle to reach Hyena before sunset. Once there, he discovered some kind of protest had broken out in the camp. Forced to avoid prisoners and attercops alike, he wound up crawling on his belly into his old outsider clique at the edge of Hyena camp, still bleeding from the razorsquid.

Every cut was worth it just to see the look on Rooker's face.

Chapter

21

CANDLELIGHT

Long is the way and hard,
that out of Hell leads up to light.

John Milton

R OOKER HELD JACK LIKE a vice and wouldn't let go. He thumped the kid on the back, unable to keep the ridiculous grin off his face.

He came back for me.

Rooker Flynn hadn't hugged a man in his adult life and realized Yenrab was watching. Rooker broke the embrace and stepped away, not sure what to do with his hands. He hooked his thumbs in his belt and regarded Jack through one smiling eye.

"Hey."

"Hey."

Nothing more needed to be said.

Any further awkwardness was broken as Patch, Copper Dave, and Farah descended the ladder to discover Jack. A cry of surprise and elation filled the secret room. As they riddled Jack with a million excited questions, Rooker just stood and watched. *He came back.*

The kid raised his hands. "Okay, okay. Listen. I've got two pieces of good news. One: We've got help on the outside."

Patch cocked her head. "From who?"

Jack turned to face Rooker. "Leah Archer and Memphis Kubiak are waiting for us." Rooker stared at him, dumbfounded. *Leah? How did—*Jack's smile widened. "On the *Venture Brigand*."

Rooker's heart nearly leapt out of his chest. "The *Ven—*" Rooker found he was too shocked to speak. *How did he—*

"Two: We're getting out of here tonight." Jack grinned. "Right now."

The room burst into chatter. Only Rooker kept his mouth shut. He doubted he could form a sentence if he had to. He had a million questions about the *Brigand* and Leah and Memphis and Jack's escape, but the only thing he could hear in his head was *he came back, he came back, he came back.*

"Me 'n Black Jack went over the map while y'all were out makin' trouble." Yenrab grinned crooked teeth. "He knows right where the copper door is, left at the y in Tom tunnel. Just two hundred more feet." With a triumphant grin, Yenrab grabbed a grease pencil and marked the spot with a red x. "Right there."

Copper Dave stared at the mark, then at Jack. Clawed fingers fidgeted with his macaroni necklace. "You are sure?"

"He's sure." Rooker eyed Jack. "He's always sure."

Yenrab chewed his lip. "But we don't have enough whitefire to get there." He glanced at Rooker. "Unless—"

Rooker held up the bronze rune in one fist.

Now it was Jack's turn to be astonished. "You *stole* a Caged Eight?"

"Me and Patch. And Farah." Rooker enjoyed the look on the kid's face. "Don't look so surprised. It was yer plan."

Jack eyed the piece of the rune that had broken off. "Does it work?"

Rooker grinned. "Stopped a 'cop."

"The shiq leave the caves at sundown." Yenrab slapped his hands and rubbed them together. "Let's grab our stuff. We're leavin'. Now."

Patch nodded. "I need to get Pilgrim."

"Cops got him." Dave shook his head. "Did not like song."

Jack jerked his head up. "Can we—"

"No time." Yenrab frowned. "It's now or never. Let's move." The dwarf hustled up the ladder, followed by the others, leaving Rooker and Jack alone once again. They stared at each other in silence for a moment, both grinning like idiots, not sure what to say.

Jack cleared his throat. "What happened to your eye?"

"Wanted to look tougher."

The kid chuckled. "What's wrong with Patch? She looks terrible."

That's right, he doesn't know. Bad time to bring it up. "Constipated." He jerked his chin. "How did Leah look?"

Jack broke into a smile. "Good." He nodded. "So, so good."

Rooker couldn't help but laugh at the look on Jack's face. "I bet."

An awkward silence passed between them. Rooker had no idea what to say. There was so much emotion running through him he didn't know what to do with it. He'd spent a lifetime crushing his feelings before they had a chance to take root; this was unexplored territory. He settled for a single word, one he had not used in a decade. "Thanks."

"I'm with you, Rooker." Jack slapped his shoulder. "To the end of the line."

Rooker Flynn couldn't contain his smile.

He descended the rope into the inky blackness of the cave, knowing one way or the other, this was the last time he would ever see the inside of a clique.

Rooker snapped a torch alight and peered at the cave around him. Amethyst crystals caught the firelight, casting it back in a thousand purpled facets. Dripping moisture fell in quiet plips that echoed like a haunting birdsong. He smelled the cold, dry air beneath the ground, the earthy scent of lichen, and the ammonia-like odor of the shiq.

Far down the cavern, Rooker saw a flicker of white cloth tied to a stake in the ground.

"The white ones are Tom tunnel markers," announced Yenrab. "We stay on those lines." He put his fists on his hips. "Them yeller bastards have learned to avoid this place, but we'll run into some further down the trail. When you hear 'em git close, smash a whitefire gourd. That'll give y'all about a hundred heartbeats of light, so we gotta hustle." Yenrab pointed his finger at each of them. "If y'all stop running, y'all are dead, git me? Our job is to make it to the end of Tom as fast as we can afore we run out of whitefire."

"What about the Caged Eight?" Rooker growled. "I didn't rip this thing off for nothing."

"Save it for the end," Yenrab growled back. "We'll want the light to run. Don't fall behind." The dwarf snatched the torch out of Rooker's hand and took off down the tunnel.

Rooker raced to keep up. The dwarf was remarkably quick and knew the path well. Jack fell in right behind him, followed by Copper Dave, Patch, and Farah at the rear. They followed Yenrab's torch through the dark.

As he sprinted through the caves, all Rooker heard were the thud of his feet, the breath in his lungs, and the rhythm of his heart. Soon enough, another sound joined them: chitinous legs skittering on the walls. It sounded like a rain stick, a cascading ripple of tiny flickers joining together to make something greater than itself. After a few minutes, the ammonia odor of the shiq surrounded him like a noxious cloud.

Then Rooker heard the sound that made his gut twist.

Churr.

"Light it!" Farah's voice was anxious. "Light it, please!"

"Not yet." Yenrab's voice came from far ahead.

Rooker turned to find Patch lagging behind; her breath came in hard gasps. He grabbed the jinx's arm and encouraged her to move faster. "Light it, damn ya!"

Brilliant white light blossomed in the cave. Rooker's eye stung as his pupil dilated from wide open to a painful pinprick in his head. As he threw his arm over his eye, Rooker glimpsed yellow legs retreating into the darkness.

"*Ah!* Is too bright!" yelled Copper Dave.

"Good thing, too!" Yenrab waited for them by the burning gourd, his face a pale mask lit in whitefire. "We ain't close to done.

Git humpin'." He raced down the cave as fast as his stocky legs could carry him.

Rooker ran with Patch. He saw the next marker go by. Far ahead, Yenrab chucked another gourd and the tunnel lit up, revealing a long path of purple amethyst heading west. This time Rooker saw a dozen shiq. They shrieked in pain, retreating into their cracks and hidey-holes.

Rooker slowed to Patch's pace. She breathed heavily, cupping her stomach with her arm. "Ya okay?"

Patch gave him a glare that would melt paint. "Move, idiot."

A third burst of light flared too far ahead. *Dammit, he's going too fast.* Rooker nearly dragged Patch to keep up with him. By the time they got to the flaming marker, the others were gathered around it, their faces confused and angry.

Yenrab was nowhere to be seen.

He left us. He left us.

"Where did he go?" whispered Farah, her eyes wide and white in the flames.

"Yenrab!" whispered Copper Dave. *"Yenrab!"*

Rooker scowled. "I'll murder that little hillbilly—" A rope hit him in the face.

He looked up to find the Red Dwarf squinting at him from a crack in the ceiling, his dark eye glinting in the burning phosphorus. "Up here. It's tricky at the top, just pitch yourself over. Come on."

Rooker pointed down the flat tunnel they'd been using. "What's wrong with *that* way?"

"Y'all don't want to go thataway, *believe* me." Yenrab disappeared into the hole. White light flared where he had gone.

"Wait." Farah's face was bathed in the harsh firelight and looked hauntingly like a skull. "That's half our whitefire gone."

"Then climb faster." Rooker flung himself at the rope. One by one they scrambled up after him. Patch was last. She struggled, grunting as her back paws clawed at the hemp. By the time she reached the top, only Rooker and Jack waited for her. The others had moved on.

Patch's breathing was too ragged, too fast. Rooker saw the desperation in her face. He glanced at Jack. The kid had eyes. He knew the truth. And the look on his face said he didn't know if she was going to make it.

"Patch." Rooker looked her in the eyes. "Move yer ass." He yanked her to her feet.

Jack followed Yenrab's light. He crawled through caves that bent and twisted and branched out in every direction around him like spiderwebs. The tunnel led to a maze of narrow lava tubes with footing so bad Jack had to half-crawl on his hands to keep moving. As the cave got bigger, Jack was forced to take a breather. Sweat poured down his neck. *Leah was right. I'm not ready for this.* Rooker came up beside him, half-carrying Patch. "Yenrab went"—Jack panted—"through *all* these tunnels?"

"And I always thought he was"—Rooker gulped air—"so *lazy*."

They arrived at a wide three-way y in the cave where all six escapees surrounded Tom's last white flag.

This was the edge of the map.

All eyes fell on Jack.

Okay. I better be right. "Left. Two hundred feet."

Yenrab's wary eye glared at Jack. "You sure, Freckle?" He pointed down the other tunnel. "*That* way's the Institute."

Jack swallowed and forced himself to run the calculations one more time. He knew the distance, he knew the angles, the only thing he wasn't positive about was the elevation. *We might be forty feet below the door. Or above it, for that matter.* He glanced at Rooker. *Better to pretend you know than let 'em wonder.* "I'm sure."

"Ya heard him, stubby," barked Rooker. "Move."

They climbed the remnants of some long-ago lavafall. The ammonia tang of the shiq was thick as soup now, and Jack could hear the *churrs* growing louder. As he hauled himself up the rock, he could sense the vastness of the caves around him, the weight of the earth above him, the restlessness of the shiq swarm. The pressure built in his shoulders as fearsome reality sunk in: He was trapped in a giant arachnid hive, just waiting for the light to go out.

The gourd sputtered and died, leaving them all in darkness for a terrifying half-second. Yenrab lit another, leading the way into the black.

"We should be close." Jack counted footsteps in his head, trying to keep from screaming. "Keep your eyes open."

It was the worst thing he could have said.

Now every corner was tinged with hope. When nothing revealed itself, their hearts pounded in despair. Each new disappointment cut deeper than the last, and soon their movements became too frantic, too desperate.

They came to another bend and the tunnel split off in five directions.

"Where in tarnation *is* it?!" yelled Yenrab.

"Keep yer voice down!" hollered Rooker.

"What th'hell does it matter?" shouted the dwarf. "They're all over us!"

Jack swallowed and pointed. "That way."

Please, God, let it be that way.

Yenrab hurled himself into the narrow tunnel like a mongoose into a cobra den. Jack wriggled through after him and his heart stopped cold when they hit a wall.

"Dammit!" shouted Yenrab.

I led them to a dead end.

A wolf's growl sounded in his ear.

(you killed them all)

No. Think. Sweat on his brow trickled into his eye. He blinked it away and felt his breath come faster. He tried to ignore the swarms of shiq behind him. *Think.* "We have to go back."

"Back?" Yenrab screamed. "Back *where*?!"

Rooker snapped at him. "Shut up and move."

They entered the five-way cave again. Patch let out a low moan that didn't stop. She flailed at Rooker. "Stop. Stop. Put me down." He laid her on the floor. The jinx's face was wrenched in pain. *"Ahh!"*

"It's that way." Jack's voice trembled as he pulled at his lower lip. "I know it."

"Spread out," hollered Rooker. "Find a hole!"

Jack poked his head into one of the caves and found another dead end. "Nothing!" came Copper Dave's voice in the dark. "Is nothing here!"

"We're trapped!" Farah's voice cracked.

The sound of crashing metal split the air and Yenrab began screaming. His pickaxe pounded the wall with the berserker rage of a man fighting for his life. Copper Dave put out a hand to stop him, but Yenrab threw the croc off, hammering at the wall in a mindless frenzy, desperate to get out.

Patch wailed as the smell of ammonia grew thick as a blanket. Jack saw yellow legs move in the shadows all around them. "Hang on!" he yelled, not sure who he was yelling at. "Just hang on!"

"They're coming!" Farah screamed. "Light another one!"

Yenrab hammered at the cave like it had murdered his twin. Enraged, he screamed and drove the pick through the wall. With a sudden rumble, stone fell away and sluiced into the tunnel. The Red Dwarf hurled a gourd into the hole and white phosphorus illuminated the vacant space beyond. Another tunnel.

"Come on!" yelled Yenrab.

"I can't. I can't. I can't." Patch's face was twisted in pain.

Rooker hooked his arms under her. "I'll carry you."

"No." Patch grunted. "She's coming. She's coming *now*."

Jack held his breath. "Patch, did your water break?"

"Ten minutes ago," she grunted through gritted teeth.

Jack let out a long breath. He turned to Yenrab. "Get up there and find the damn door!" he yelled. "All of you!" The dwarf was already gone, the others hot on his heels. Only Rooker Flynn remained.

"Rooker." Jack panted. "It's up there. Believe me."

"I do." Rooker pulled the Caged Eight from his belt. "But if you're not goin', I'm not goin'."

"*Uugh!*" Patch screamed and bore down.

Jack eyed the burning phosphorus as it started to sputter. *Okay. Pretend this is a human delivery and pray it's the same thing.* He steeled himself and moved into position. "Deep breath, Patch. Now push."

She did. Jack watched her eyes clench shut, giving what little strength she had left. But she was too worn out. On the sixth attempt, she went limp, panting. Jack patted her leg. "Come on, Patch. On three. One—"

The phosphorus went out and left them in darkness.

The sound of a hundred legs skittered toward them.

Crimson majik blossomed all around Jack. Whickering the air with the chime of the Caged Eight, a red radiance blossomed a protective circle around them in devilish light. Rooker stood illuminated in scarlet, the dirk in one hand, the rune hung from a strap in the other.

Shiq ringed them. Hundreds of legs glowed fiery orange in the light of Gerba's perverted majik. They did not stop moving, crawling over each other. They came no closer, nor did they flee. They paced the shadows beyond the Caged Eight.

Jack swallowed hard and watched the circle of spiders surround him. He turned to Patch and kept his voice steady. "Again."

It seemed to go on forever. Patch strained, Jack talked, and Rooker protected them both. Jack did not know how long he encouraged Patch, but he began to notice that each time Rooker rang the Caged Eight, it lost a bit of its strength. The chime dulled with every toll, and the circle grew tighter.

Rooker scowled at the broken section of the rune, but he didn't have to say it. Jack knew it was only a matter of time until the majik ran out.

"I can't…" Patch panted, her wasted body exhausted. "I can't…" *She's not going to make it.*

Part of Jack wanted to run. Just take the rune and flee, leave Patch behind, disappear into the caves, away from the shiq, away from the dark.

(yes)

He felt the scalpel Leah had given him press against his leg. He fumbled it from his pocket with shaking hands. *We're out of time.*

He glanced at Rooker. "Keep them off her." The pirate nodded and gripped the dirk tighter. Jack looked Patch in the eye and spoke in the calmest voice he could manage. "Patch, I have to cut your belly open to get the baby out. You understand?"

She nodded, her face a mask of pain in the crimson glow. "Please."

Jack eyed her belly and felt his gorge rise. *Don't think. Do it.*

He cut.

Patch screamed as he made the incision. Jack's fingers tried to shake, but he kept them steady. *Not too deep, not too—*

Her taut skin split open, forming a long, narrow opening. *Laparotomy. Done. Now the hysterotomy.* "Don't pass out, please don't pass out," Jack whispered, not sure if he spoke to Patch or to himself. He could see the uterine wall, pale pink and glistening wet with blood.

It wasn't moving.

"Rooker, I need light." The dirk struck the Caged Eight and Jack saw shiq a yardstick away, pacing the edges of the ring.

Don't think. Jack repositioned his scalpel at the top of the uterine wall, took a breath, and cut. He felt the organ spasm under his blade, angling his scalpel in the wrong direction. Jack gritted his teeth and finished his cut. He dropped the scalpel and gently reached inside Patch's body. His fingers found something inside and pulled it out.

The fetus, a tiny lump of matted fur in his hands, did not move. Dead.

"*Nhh!*" Patch screamed, seeing the limp head. "*Nyhh!*"

"*No.*" Rooker's voice was a ragged whisper.

Jack's shoulders went slack. He looked at the little body, the delicate infant they had tried so hard to save. He felt a chill wash his blood like ice and a desperate, hollow sensation overwhelmed him. *No.*

Something moved in the wet mess of Patch's belly.

Jack's head snapped up.

He placed his hands into her uterus and felt a slick wad inside. As he pulled it out, the twin jerked and kicked one dewy leg.

Jack felt a smile split his lips.

In the palm of his hand it mewled, tiny eyes squinted shut, mouth open wide, miniscule paws grasping the air. He presented the infant kitten to Patch. She hugged it and curled protectively around the baby, looking in its eyes. Her breath was thready, her body exhausted, and the smile on her face was edged with tears. "Hello, little moggie."

Jack Swift fished for his needle and thread and there, in the dark, surrounded by giant spiders, closed the caesarian section, making sure to get the stitches tight. He glanced at Patch. "I'm sorry it hurts."

"I can't feel a thing," Patch Picaroon murmured as she held her baby close.

Jack tied off the sutures and looked at his work. It was an ugly job, rudimentary meatball surgery, and she would have one hell of a scar if they lived. *Plus whatever infection I've given her with these filthy hands.*

But she's alive.

Rooker struck the Caged Eight again, but the chime barely traveled at all; the light was fading fast. His one remaining eye fell on Jack. "We have to move."

Jack got Patch under one side, Rooker under the other. She cried out with a broken voice and clutched her baby as they lifted her off the ground. Together, Rooker and Jack made for the opening Yenrab had made. The ground between was covered in shiq, their bodies swaying, waiting.

Rooker gave the dirk to Patch. "Let's get the hell out of here." Rooker kicked a shiq out of the way. It squealed, hissing in the dark. He held up the brass rune and Patch struck it with the dirk. As majik flared, Rooker and Jack stepped forward, carrying her.

Together, they cleared a path. As Patch continued to ring the Caged Eight, the *wikk* that came was dull and weak, darkening to a bloody crimson. *Keep working.* Jack and Rooker carried Patch into the dark, looking for anything but blackness and spiders.

Churr.

In the fading light of the Caged Eight, shiq swarmed over themselves in a wall of legs four feet high, almost close enough to touch, fangs clicking. The whole world moved with arachnid hunger.

"Please." Jack heard Patch's voice, a plea to something larger than any of them. "Please."

Her baby made a tiny mewling noise.

Please.

She struck the Caged Eight again, but nothing came. It was finished.

Dead.

"I'm sorry, little girl," Patch whispered as the light faded.

Rooker snarled. "I'll keep them off as long as I can."

The majik extinguished and the world went black.

Jack swung his staff in the darkness and felt it collide with a rigid body. Rooker hollered at the top of his lungs, battering the spiders away with the bronze disc. Jack felt something crawl up his leg. He smashed at it with the staff, then something attached to his arm.

He felt Patch dragged away from him. She screamed, clutching her baby, then she was gone.

Jack went after her, but something jumped on his back. A spider leg brushed across his face. Something took out his knee. He fell forward, one hand grabbing for the ground, blindly trying to stop his fall, and landed on his face.

Alone in the dark, Jack felt the shiq crawl over him, their claws brushing over his body. He shouted, lashing out with his fists, kicking at them, but they swarmed over him.

Jack screamed and felt the wolf open its jaws to devour him at last.

(mine)

Blazing light lit the cavern. Shadows fell before it, dark washed away in white. For an instant, Jack saw shiq all over him, then they were gone, fled from the radiance. He glanced up to see Patch a few feet away, her eyes wide, the newborn infant still in her arms.

"Move!" Rooker grabbed Patch and carried her toward the light.

Jack ran after them. As he passed the burning phosphorus, he saw a faint crescent of light ahead. A round copper door rolled half-open. In it, Yenrab, Copper Dave, and Farah's silhouettes urged them onward. "Run, damn you!" Yenrab shouted. "That's the last one!"

They ran. Stinking ammonia gagged Jack as he watched Rooker disappear into the doorway with Patch. Spider legs grappled Jack's boots and he threw himself through the opening.

He skidded past Patch and bashed against the iron bars inside the Locke Institute. Rooker grabbed the big door and put his shoulder into it, but the thing wouldn't budge.

Beyond the door, the world was made of shiq, thousands of them crawling over each other, a wall of twitching legs. Copper Dave and Yenrab hurled their weight against the door and it rolled. Yellow legs reached through and grabbed Rooker's hands.

"Yeagh!" The copper door rolled shut and crushed shiq legs, slicing them in half. Milky ichor splattered as exoskeletons popped, staining the walls white.

Thunnk. The door closed, walling off the horror.

Jack panted, his heart racing. Patch was slumped against the corner of the cage, staring at him. Smiling, she moved her arm and revealed her baby, sleeping peacefully.

Jack let out a breath and glanced at Rooker. The pirate snorted and sagged against the bars.

"That went great!" Copper Dave shouted, delighted.

Everyone turned to him, their faces a mix of shock and disbelief. The big croc spread his hands. "What? Is good! We go in with six." He gestured at the baby. "Come out with seven!"

Chapter

22

NO GOOD DEED

Not for ourselves alone are we born.

Cicero

R ooker's quick fingers worked the lock while everyone else caught their breath. Using the picks he had crafted from jatoba wood, he tickled the tumbler inside the lock until he felt the click. The cage door swung open with a creak.

Heat sizzled the air, combined with the reek of sulfur and the low rumble of shifting rock. Scowling at the stench, Rooker snuck from the cage and peeked around the downhill corner. Below, he saw a floor-to-ceiling iron lattice wall that marked the end of the caverns and the beginning of a lake of molten magma. Rooker stared at it, unable to believe his eyes. Beyond, in the shimmering scarlet heat, he glimpsed crouched silhouettes knee-deep in lava: shadows of strîgoi.

This is where Jack was.

Where I put him.

A shudder shifted the world around him. A low earthquake, just enough to shake his bones. "Rooker," Jack whispered behind him. "We're going the other way. Dave, you got her?"

Rooker turned to find the big croc carrying Patch. The baby pawed at his pink macaroni necklace. "I have her."

Farah stared at the caged strîgoi. "What's the plan?"

"Ninety-seven paces uphill. Left forty-five degrees. Big wooden door." Jack closed his eyes, thinking. "That should get us to the overlook above the dock gate. From there"—a smile cracked his lips—"home."

Home. Rooker's heartbeat quickened at the sound of the word. The *Venture Brigand.*

After so many months, after so many broken dreams, after so many nights of wondering if he would ever be free again, Rooker Flynn finally allowed himself to feel hope. All that stood between him and home was one more door.

Jack led the way up the incline. As Rooker followed, he thought he heard a sound behind him. He glanced over his shoulder at the lava-dwelling dæmons, still caged behind bars, and hurried to leave them behind.

Mercifully, he soon escaped the heat of the pits. Rough-hewn rock gave way to hammerdwarf design as the floor became even and smooth. Rooker heard another sound, impossible to place with the rumble of shifting stone all around him. He motioned for the others to halt and silently scouted ahead. He discovered an alcove with dark cloaks hung on pegs, along with a few other items the acolytes used for work. "Get these on," Rooker hissed and handed a black cloak to Jack. Without niqabs, they couldn't pass for acolytes, but the soot-smeared cloaks would help hide them in the dark.

As Rooker slung a cloak over his shoulder, Jack used a red grease pencil to draw on the cave wall. "We come around this way," he whispered, drawing a curved path to the left. "Don't take any of the branches. The dock gate overlook is down here." He circled the end of the line. "Got it?"

"Less talk, more move." Eager, Rooker took the lead around the bend and nearly stumbled into an acolyte putting on his boots.

Startled, both men stared at each other for half a heartbeat. Rooker hooked his hands around the man's head and drove his knee into his nose. The robed figure grunted and stumbled back. Rooker raised his dirk to strike.

Don't! came Jack's silent plea.

Rooker flipped the dirk and slammed it butt-first into the man's temple with a *krok!* Boneless, the acolyte collapsed to the ground. Rooker spun on Jack. "Good enough, Jimmy Cricket?"

The kid almost laughed but managed to keep his mouth shut. Rooker snatched the acolyte's ring of keys and darted to scout the path ahead. Despite his feigned confidence, Rooker felt a fearful dread growing in his stomach. He couldn't shake the idea that something was coming for him, pursuing him. Maybe the strîgoi, maybe just a monster of his own design, but every step closer to the *Venture Brigand* sharpened his unease. The further he went, the more he had to lose.

Several tunnels splintered off from the main path, but Rooker followed Jack's plan and ignored them.

Then he got a whiff of fresh air.

Sea air.

It was faint, muffled, but there. Rooker followed his nose and ran ahead to find a closed door at the end of the tunnel, thick wood with iron corners. He inserted the key into the lock, turned it quietly, and opened the door a crack. He peeked inside to find the dock gate overlook.

Twenty feet above the dock gate, the large room was dominated by a gigantic oval-shaped window carved into the seaward side of the Locke Institute, a panoramic harbormaster's view of the entire bay. Curved hallways exited either side of the room like a bull's horns and descended through the rock to the dock gate itself. But Rooker only had eyes for the view.

Black sea. Black sky. Pinpricks of stars glistening over the waves. Gamilat and Anika bright in the sky, half-masked by thunderclouds in the distance, heat lightning skipping between them. And leading the way to it all like a bridge to another world was the dock itself, the long pier that stretched far into the Irridin, pointing like a giant's finger at his one true love.

Moored a quarter mile out to sea, the *Venture Brigand* floated proudly above the waves. Her sails were unfurled, ready to run. Rooker took a deep breath and watched her sway, as if beckoning him to hurry.

I'm comin', girl.

Jack clapped him on the back. "Well, if we're going, let's go."

Rooker hustled toward one of the curved hallways that descended to the dock and felt the sweet pain of hope surge in his heart.

Then he heard the sound.

Footsteps. They ascended toward him, joined by the sound of voices. He gestured to the crew to stop and darted to the other curved hall. It was no better here. They were coming up this way too. He saw robed shadows on the wall, four acolytes carrying pickaxes, ascending toward him. He retreated quickly into the overlook as hope turned sour in his chest. *Did we just walk into the middle of a shift change? Of all the lousy damned luck.*

There was nowhere left to go.

He spun to find Jack's face was pale. Copper Dave gripped Patch and her moggie in muscular arms while Yenrab and Farah stared at him, wide-eyed and desperate. Rooker didn't know what they hoped for. There wasn't another exit and it was too late to spring an ambush.

"Back," Rooker hissed and gestured frantically at the others. "Go *back*!"

They were slow to react and Rooker was first to reach the big wooden doorway. *We can hide in the cav—*

The door crashed open and knocked Rooker aside like he'd been kicked by a horse.

He felt his teeth click together as the back of his head smashed into the wall. He crumpled to the ground. Dazed, he tried to get to his feet as he realized a monster had followed him from the hellish pits below.

Gerba Whipmarples filled the doorway. Her schoolmarm appearance was gone; she was nothing but a beast. Her fanciful dress had been replaced by a gigantic workman's smock that reeked of sulfur. Caked in soot, her hide and horns were black as pitch. Black diamond dust embedded in her skin reflected the blue light of Nepenthe in her fist.

The staff was almost complete; six pieces radiated elven majik powerful enough that Rooker felt it tremble in his flesh.

"Someone is in the pits!" she shouted as she thundered through the door. "They knocked out Yannik! Seal the—" She stopped,

realizing the black-cloaked group did not belong to her. Gerba Whipmarples blinked and stared at Jack Swift. Her face twisted into a feral snarl. *"You."*

Rooker staggered to his feet as acolytes ascended from the exits and froze, not understanding what was happening. The room was locked in a tableau, the escapees trapped on all three sides.

He knew he stood no chance against the monster in the doorway. His only way out was through the acolytes. *I'm comin', girl.*

Rooker charged straight into them. He bashed one in the face and shouted at the top of his lungs, "Get to the dock!"

Jack was right behind him. His staff broke an acolyte's nose as Yenrab barreled into them like an animal.

Rooker checked over his shoulder to see Copper Dave hand Patch and her moggie over to Farah. "You go." The big croc unsheathed his falchion and turned to the monster in the doorway. "I stay."

Copper Dave made his stand between the trol and the prisoners. Gerba's blackened face twisted into a snarl of rage. Simmering heat warped the air around her in a haze of *wikk* as Nepenthe glowed bright.

Copper Dave struck first. His falchion buried itself in her chest. Gerba Whipmarples screamed.

Rooker Flynn had a fraction of a second to take joy in her pain before the trol's fist thundered down and snapped the falchion's blade in half. Her other hand whickered a blue sizzling arc that shattered every bone in the croc's face.

Copper Dave, the Hammer of Bego, toppled and fell, broken.

Clutching Patch and her moggie, Farah screamed.

The trol swept Dave's limp body out of the way and stormed toward Rooker.

One of the acolytes swung her pickaxe and drove the sharp end into Yenrab's side. The Red Dwarf cried out and collapsed to one knee.

Furious, out of control, Gerba swung Nepenthe at Rooker. Rooker danced out of the way and jammed his dirk into a soft spot between her armored plates. The trol shrieked, then gripped him around the chest like he was a child's toy. She picked him up with one hand and smashed him into the ceiling. Rooker felt his head bash into the rock. As stars danced before his eyes, Gerba Whipmarples hurled him to the floor and shattered his ribs.

Everything turned slowly, like the world was moving through molasses, the colors too bright, the sounds too loud. Rooker gasped pain, unable to catch his breath. He saw Farah slumped against the wall, screaming, crying. Patch was unconscious, the baby clutched in her limp arms yowling. Yenrab bled on the floor, twitching. Copper Dave lay where he fell.

Jack Swift was the last man standing.

Trapped between Gerba and the acolytes, he shot out his hand and commanded, *"Nepenthe."*

The staff *bent* in Gerba's fist.

It arched like a longbow, almost to a C, reaching toward him, quivering, straining to answer the call of its master.

But Gerba did not let go.

Majik pulsed from her fist. Nepenthe labored to reach Jack's hand but could not escape Gerba's lace glove. Individual rods of blazing bamboo tried to flee her clutches, but the glove's rune majik ensnared them together, refusing to let them fly. The *wikk* of the staff strained against her grip and rose to a banshee shriek of longing and pain.

As the sound rose to a fever pitch, the very air itself jerked sideways and distorted, rending a tear in the fabric of the universe. Something whickered through the sizzling hole. A thunderbolt collided with Nepenthe with a blast of majik that blistered the air blue.

The seventh piece had answered Jack's call.

It collided with the stave in Gerba Whipmarple's hand. A *snap* split the air, and the struggle was over.

Nepenthe was finally whole, and it belonged to the headmistress.

No.

Rooker watched Jack's face fall, his eyes wide with disbelief.

Gerba laughed. Covered in soot and reeking of sulfur, the headmistress laughed loud and long. "Now, my good doktar, you have *finally* served your purpose." She towered over him, her face a cruel mask of horns and ash. "At long last, I am finished with you."

She crushed the awesome might of Nepenthe into Jack's head.

The staff was under her control, but Nepenthe refused to kill its old master. An instant before it connected, its azure light went out like a snuffed candle. The bamboo smashed Jack's ear bloody but left his skull unbroken. Gerba frowned at the stave in her fist and struck him again. This blow knocked him to the floor. Furious, she cracked him again.

Again.

Again.

"Stop." Rooker wheezed, unable to draw a full breath. He tried to crawl to Jack but could only watch as the beating continued.

Jack attempted to defend himself, but the trol was relentless, her intensity only building, smashing him like a hammer to a nail. "You ruined everything!" Blood sprayed. "Everything!" Flecks landed on Gerba's face, her eyes burning hatred. Again. Again.

Rooker tried to get to his feet and failed.

No.

Nepenthe shattered Jack's jaw. Blood sprayed from his mouth; Rooker heard teeth clatter across the floor.

Jack lay bleeding, his blue eyes wide and helpless. He had devastated her precious Steel Trial, and Gerba Whipmarples meant to kill him for it.

Stop!

Rooker saw it then. The wolf.

It was only a shadow, but Rooker saw its outline loom behind Jack, its hunched shoulders, its long claws. He watched the wolf's slavering jaws open. A cruel fanged grin split its face, a hunger eager to feed.

Rooker felt a desperate, clawing fear in his own chest.

Jack raised one bloody hand to Gerba. His mouth barely worked. "*Plse...*"

She raised Nepenthe for the killing blow.

Only one way out.

I can't.

Rooker knew there was no other choice. Even so, he could not bring himself to say the words. He couldn't allow his only friend to die. Nor could he do what needed to be done to save him. The words would kill him, they would leave him empty and barren and cold. Of all the trials he had faced on Huánghūn, the shiq, the arena, the captivity, this was the cruelest of all.

He came back for me.

"*STOP!*" Rooker commanded, his voice so loud it felt like it came from someone else, someone stronger than he had ever been.

Gerba's head snapped to him, her eyes blazing.

Rooker Flynn staggered to his feet. "Spare him." He straightened and stared her in the eye. "And I'll give you the *Venture Brigand.*"

He felt the immediate *NO* in his chest, the voice of the *Venture Brigand* screaming out to him, horrified. It was the first time he'd heard her voice in months, not since that night Gerba had invited him aboard and convinced him to betray Jack. Rooker stared at his ship through the overlook window. He saw her sails, her elegant silhouette against the orange moon, a thunderstorm at her back. *NO.*

I love ya, girl. Since the moment I laid eyes on ya.

He could see the little akita pup running on the *Venture Brigand*'s deck, barking at the pixies in the cave where he'd first found her, nothing but a little boy named Pip, who was alone in the world with nothing but a dog and a ship to love.

But yer only timbers and silk and canvas.

Rooker turned to stare at Jack with his one remaining eye.

He's blood.

Gerba paused her final blow. She considered him, suspicious. "The *Venture Brigand*." She eyed the half-dead boy at her feet. "For *this*?"

Rooker watched Jack's bloody face. His half-lidded eyes fluttered, barely conscious, trying to speak through broken teeth and failing.

NO, came her cry. *NO*.

Rooker nodded. "Under oath."

A slow grin spilled over Gerba's broad lips. "All this time... and *this* is all it took." The trol raised her hand and majik shimmered the air around her. Rooker felt her dark *wikk* gather, ghosts and shadows come to bear witness to the geas curse. Nepenthe glowed brighter. Rooker saw the wolf watch him with narrow eyes, angry witness to his oath.

"Under geas curse and with the will of the *wikk*, I swear by my life." Gerba straightened, staring down her horn at Rooker. "If this depraved *fraction* of a man standing before me gives me absolute and total control of the aräs windjammer called the *Venture Brigand* in the next ten heartbeats"—she breathed deep—"I will never harm this stubborn and broken Toshan at my feet." She straightened. "And if this crooked, lying pirate *fails* to deliver on his word, the geas curse shall strike him dead." She thrust her palm toward Rooker. "This I swear."

Pact majik charged between her thick fingers. Lightning struck the sea, far out in the distance. It lit a stripe behind the *Venture Brigand*, burning the ship's silhouette into Rooker's eye.

He swallowed.

I love ya, girl.

He spat into his hand and took Gerba's, shuddering at her touch. "This I swear."

A sharp stab of majik snapped his palm as the thunderclap roiled its finale, sealing the bond between him and the monster.

Rooker felt his soul crack.

"You have ten heartbeats." Gerba Whipmarples tilted her head. "Before the geas eats you alive."

Rooker gritted his teeth. "Open yer hand."

The trol opened leathery fingers to reveal two brass spyglass rings lying in Gerba Whipmarples' palm.

"This?" She stared down at the tiny rings. "This is all?"

"They're part of her." Rooker hung his head. "She listens to anyone who holds them."

"Anyone?"

Rooker lowered his head. "Anyone."

Gerba paused, waiting until the ten heartbeats were complete, waiting for the geas to destroy him for his lies, the trick she knew he was trying to play. On the eleventh heartbeat, Rooker Flynn was still alive, if only on the outside.

Gerba held the rings up between her fingers, her eyes twinkling. "Fascinating. I had presumed *you* were the key. I thought you shared some deep, special bond with the ship." She laughed a harsh bark. "But the only thing that made you special was... *this*."

Rooker knew it was true. There was nothing special about him. There never had been. He was just a boy who had gotten lucky once, a long, long time ago.

He let his hair fall in front of his eyes, hiding him from the *Venture Brigand*. He longed for her voice, for her gentle *yes*, even her panicked *NO*, but the only whisper Rooker heard was the wind.

For the first time since he'd found her, he could not feel her in his heart at all.

It was as if she were dead.

As if they both were.

Forgive me if you can.

Gerba tucked the rings into the pocket of her smock. "Marguerite." She flicked her fingers at the prisoners. "Remove these students, please."

Acolytes dragged Copper Dave and Yenrab from the room. Farah tried to protect Patch and her baby, but the acolytes grabbed her and bound her wrists. "Make sure the infant is not harmed," Gerba commanded. "We would not want to damage perfectly good merchandise, would we?"

Rooker limped to Jack, his chest wheezing. He grabbed the kid under the arms. "Hey." Jack's body leaned against him, dead weight. His head sagged like a broken marionette. "Hey, Jack. Hey."

The kid opened his eyes. Blood flowed from Jack's mouth, bits of teeth on his bloody lip. He tried to speak and failed.

Rooker forced a smile. "It's okay. I'm here."

Gerba frowned. "Take the doktar to the holding cell." She rolled the rings in her fingers. "Handle him... gently."

Acolytes pulled Jack away. Rooker tried to keep hold of his brother, but his broken ribs hurt too much to keep him. "Wait." Rooker held out a hand, but the acolytes paid no attention. They dragged Jack from the overlook, and just like that, Rooker was alone with the headmistress and her one remaining acolyte.

"*Mister* Flynn." Gerba's voice was giddy. "I always knew you were half-clever. The geas spell prevents me from harming him." She turned. "It does not, however, protect *you*."

Rooker felt his empty heart freeze.

He hadn't thought of himself. All he had cared about was keeping Jack alive. But in doing so, he had failed to devise any defense for himself.

And without the *Venture Brigand*, Gerba Whipmarples had no more reason to keep him alive.

Rooker watched a wicked smile curve over Gerba's lips like a cruel serpent.

"Marguerite, we must see to the young doktar's health. After all, we are *sworn* to keep him well. For that, I believe we will require an execution this morning."

Gerba Whipmarples' sea-green eyes landed on Rooker Flynn. "And I have just the man for the job."

END BOOK TWO

THE LOCKE INSTITUTE TRILOGY
CONCLUDES WITH
THE EXECUTION OF ROOKER FLYNN

THANK YOU! PLEASE READ!

THANK YOU SO MUCH for reading Rooker's story. Before you go, please leave a rating!

Amazon ratings are critical for indie stories like this one, which need help to stand out among millions of other books. If you want me to keep writing, tapping those stars is the most powerful thing you can do to help. If you know someone who would enjoy this story, pass it on!

Thank you for sharing my passion. I promise that I will keep telling you stories as long as you keep asking for them.

Your #1 Fan,
-Andy

Scan to Rate the Book

A. R. WITHAM is a three-time Emmy-winning writer-producer and a great lover of adventure. He is the world's foremost expert on the history of Keymark. He loves to talk with young people and adults who remember what young people know. He has written for film and television, canoed to the Arctic Circle, hiked the Appalachian Trail and been inside his house while it burned down. He lives in Indianapolis, home of the greatest spectacle in racing.

If you would like a free novella, a free short story and sneak peeks at his upcoming work or events, please sign up for his newsletter:

Linktree: linktr.ee/arwitham
Website: arwitham.com

ACKNOWLEDGEMENTS

If you want to go fast, go alone.
If you want to go far, go together.

I want to thank my editor, the indomitable Sarah Chorn, for wrestling with me through the early stages of the trilogy and helping pull all the strings of this story together into a single rope. Esmay Rosalyne Borst, Thiago Abdalla, and the Red Fury, Joshua Thompson, are heroes of Keymark. Their time, enthusiasm, and invaluable assistance made this story better than I could possibly manage without them. All of you are awesome and deserve more than I can ever give. I would also like to thank Isabelle Wagner for her spectacular proofreading skills and her astounding good humor. In addition, I would like to praise Andrew Mattocks and Kayla Yetman for their steadfast encouragement and friendship. I want to thank every reviewer, reader and indie fan who has taken the time to discuss and promote my work; there would be no more stories without you. As always, I want to thank my mom and dad for encouraging me to follow my own path.

William, my dear son, you are a miracle.

And yes, I love you most of all, Glo.

ALSO BY A. R. WITHAM

Novels

The Legend of Black Jack

The Crimes of Rooker Flynn

Novella

The Tale of the Border Knight

www.ingramcontent.com/pod-product-compliance
Lightning Source LLC
Chambersburg PA
CBHW060224030726
47499CB00004B/1179